SWITCHER

PAYBACK FOR BULLIES

VOLUME 1

RAND E OERTLE

OAK TREE LANE PUBLISHING
Printed in the United States of America

ISBN# 978-1-7341030-0-7

First Printing December 1, 2019

Dedication

Novel writing is said to require a cast iron butt, especially a first novel. But having the help to correct my mistakes by people who are willing, is a major blessing. For example, it only took my wife, Carol and I, six or seven cage fights to get the first several full-book edits done. My daughters helped with editing suggestions that left me only slightly bloodied. Then there was Milt Jones, a university English teacher, who dismantled me and my writing cell by cell and in the process improved my writing three fold and believe it or not, we've become good friends, although our foils remain sharpened and still loom while he prepares to publish his own latest creations.

My mother dreamed of publishing the stories she had written. I visited her regularly and frequently, when I went in her door, I'd find her reading her own writings and laughing her head off. I have a book of poetry **TREES IN SKELETON** ready to be published and I'm including a few of her poems. I hope she would be thrilled to see her work in print. I thank her for giving me the desire. My brother, V. Lee Oertle, was a writer in the recreational vehicle industry and he once told me he had 30 articles in print in one month under his own name and a host of pen names.

It may sound nuts, but during the challenge-of-writing this book process I was diagnosed with Sporadic Inclusion Body Myositis and complications left me in bed full-time. The setback has given me a resolute focus and I have Volume II of **Switcher: The Return** outlined and well on its way.

Thanks to all who helped with ideas and suggestions and support.

Introduction

On my second day in the ninth grade, I was walking to the front school gate with a friend. Without warning, five gang bangers brutally attacked and beat my friend unmercifully. He was targeted because he was the biggest boy in our class. This memory causes me great regret because I didn't muster the courage to go to his aid. I remember those bullies to this day because they were sending a message to my friend and the rest of the junior high freshman students: "Don't mess with us or we'll take you out."

Today bullies have expanded and intensified their attacks to injure and do as much harm as they can, whether it's physical injury or psychological anguish through social media. Hateful words, false accusations, and attacks on reputation . . . are launched like grenades that can bring ultimate tragedy to the bullied—suicide—a cost too high.

Switcher was written, not just for my own failure but as recognition of society's limited success in the fight against bullies. This book also illustrates how bullies come in all ages, who can be male or female, found in every imaginable setting but seldom get the comeuppance they so richly deserve. The main character is a hero for the bullied and I have named him after my beautiful grandson, Nathan, whom we lost fifteen days after his birth due to impossible circumstances.

Bullies trade on the perceived disparity of others by taking advantage of the weaker, slower, and less popular or attractive merely for their perverse pleasure of causing grief. But, this book also shows how bullies can pay an enormous price no matter their age or station. Switcher suffers the pain of bullying while young, but in this story had to face one of the most powerful bullies on earth with only his unique capabilities to defend himself.

**This is just an observation about the shift
from elementary to junior high school.**

The first day of junior high can be glorious or notorious. First, you're out of elementary school and thinking you're hot stuff and not in the confines of the "little kid's" school anymore. Next you think you are gaining some respect for being with the "older" kids. That being said, it's also a time that you've become the low man on the totem pole in relation to everyone else. You've graduated from being among the oldest in elementary school to being the youngest in junior high where pecking orders are essentially the next item of business. Being bullied can be a painful time of that reality and bullies should pay a price.

1

Bullies Pay a Price

A flock of new junior high school students including sixth, seventh and eighth graders headed across the street anticipating their first day. The sixth graders had both anxiety and excitement in equal proportions. One of the new students was Buddy Bass. His first name was Thomas, but everybody knew him as Buddy. Among other things, Buddy was the tallest and biggest of the sixth graders, not fat but just big for his age, in a class of newly enrolled former elementary students. He was as friendly as they come, played trumpet in band and was an all around good kid.

As the light changed and the kids started walking, a man in a brand new Duel Scorpion Corvette waited for the kids to cross, "Geeze, these kids are squirrels," he thought, as he watched the menagerie running and bumping their way between the crosswalk lines. Most of the faces of the kids were glued to their device screens oblivious, it seemed, to everything outside their hand-held worlds. They texted each other even though they were walking side by side. So engrossed were the kids that only a few noticed his dazzling car. After they'd passed he turned into a convenience store parking lot opposite the school and put the striking vehicle between a pair of painted lines.

The man climbed out of his low-slung ride, closed the door, and gently leaned against it pulling out his vibrating cell phone, at the same time absently watching the kids walk down the sidewalk across the street heading toward their school gate. His conversation had barely begun when he saw a gang of five teens with blue bandanas tied to their heads, jump Buddy, who was walking at the edge of the group.

The gang of five immediately began pounding him unmercifully. It was not a fair fight by any means and the blood flowed almost immediately. All Buddy could do was try to get into a fetal position and protect himself as best he could, but with five guys punching and kicking him, it was all he could do.

The man with the fancy car was startled, not to mention shocked. It dawned on him that a first day of school message was being sent. Buddy was being singled out because he was the biggest sixth grader. "Don't mess with us," was the message. He tried yelling at the kids from his parking slot, but his message still went unheard over the din of traffic and screaming kids. The throng separated into a circle yelling, fight! fight! Then, just as suddenly, the gang acted as though each of the five had been hit with a sucker punch of mortal fear. They ended their attack as quickly as it had begun and ran. It appeared the five were running for what they must have thought was safety or, at least a safer place. "Strange," he thought, as he listened to their screams of fear. But what do they fear? It was five against one!

In trying to intellectually determine what had happened the observer made an instant assessment. It wasn't as if the bullying gang bangers wanted to stop. It appeared to him that they had suddenly felt an all consuming fear. He'd watched intently from the curb and could see the gang's eyes and body language and their instinctual flight response kick in with the penetration of an ice pick.

He continued to stare. To his additional shock at the very same time, he had noticed a young man under a shade tree with his hand pointed at the fight and what appeared to be emanating waves. They were like sound waves, unheard, but the man could somehow see them flowing from the tips of his fingers shooting out from the darkness of the tree shade to the bright light of the sun and at the bangers. Apparently, the light differences between the darkness of the shade tree and the brightness of the sun revealed the waves but just for an instant. They had become barely visible when he saw them. The waves were somewhat like the heat waves coming off the surface of a Death Valley highway. It appeared to him that the gang saw nothing but they obviously felt something. What did they feel? Why did their fear appear so deep?

The man's transfixed stare blinked and he began an immediate unintentional narration of the blow by blow to his friend who had just called his phone. It was clear that something amazing had just happened but he couldn't figure out exactly what.

What also happened, a split second later, was the young man who had been pointing his fingers at the melee of flailing bodies turned his bright lavender eyes directly on the man across the street. The boy somehow noticed the man's intensity and his scrutinizing stare. But the man's focus shifted from the fight and was now directed intently at the young man under the tree.

What happened in one more instant was beyond the man's rational explanation. He received the full attention of the boy and the full intensity of his penetrating eyes that---that did what? What or who was this boy with the hand-direction bit doing? The boy's eyes penetrated into the core of the man's being. They hit his emotional and intellectual centers and wreaked havoc although, as he thought about it, the boy wasn't just looking into his mind; it was more like rummaging around with a meat cleaver. The impact to his senses caused him to drop his cell phone onto his shoe. Fortunately it didn't fracture. Next he saw the boy return his sun glasses to cover his eyes.

There would be unexpected consequences that would reveal themselves later as the man stood mystified by this experience.

Shaking, he bent and retrieved his phone and continued his real-life TV narration to his compatriot, but with a voice that had abruptly and obviously been affected.

The man listening on the other end of the phone asked: "What the hell is going on. Are you OK? Why does your voice sound like you've just seen an albino Bigfoot?"

His mind raced trying to make sense of what he'd just seen and especially felt. He realized he had provided a blow by blow description of the event and he knew his conversations, including this one, were routinely recorded for business purposes, it would need an explanation. The nature of the penetration into his mind and soul was a whole different matter. He simply couldn't explain it and the more he tried, the more he failed to comprehend the complexity of the incident.

He gave a lame excuse and ended his conversation telling his friend that he'd talk to him at length in their afternoon meeting. He picked up a cup of coffee at the store, the familiar aroma briefly bringing him back to a new reality. He returned to his car with his own set of antennae on amplified alert.

As was his businessman's nature, he began to organize his thoughts. Three things had happened. The first thing was the fight! Second, was the flash of waves aimed at the gang bangers. Third was the flash of "something" into his mind from the eyes of the boy in the shade. He was startled at just how fast everything had happened and just how deeply it penetrated him.

He had no clue where the young man or the gang's target had gone. They'd just seemed to blend into the mob of kids turning into the school gate. With the invasion into his emotions and of somebody trampling around in his mind, he had become distracted and unfocused.

Surprisingly after the incident, he noticed an intensified visual stimulated response to things and particularly the colors around him. Maybe "re-noticed" would be a better description. The pearl essence stripes on his car that ran from the center tip of the hood, split and continued to the front side window post and dropped along both doors. They came together on the trunk deck and flowed over the back with a faint etched line on the back window glass and terminated on the car top. The scorpion tail split into two stingers going in opposite directions and ended with a drop of candy apple red venom hanging from the scorpion's needle sharp tails. The translucent pearl, purple and blood red drops seemed to dance with color. Never had he seen them so vibrant. The power of the boy had enhanced his color perception in a way he'd never thought possible.

Other visual and emotional stimuli were enhanced to levels unknown to him before. He immediately thought of the descriptions of LSD trips old friends had described from the 60s and 70s.

The depth of the pearl seemed to be ten times more intense than when he'd first seen it. Was it the impact on the "emotional" part of his brain? The same was true of the black purple on the rest of the vehicle. What at first might appear just black was actually a deep purple that seemed to fight its way to the surface of the paint and explode visually. That color explosion usually only happened when the sun caught the surface just right. Now the purple color was obvious on the entire vehicle as he seemed to absorb the color with his enhanced visual sensitivity.

His question "why or what" was all he could think of now. His only answer was that his normal feelings had been brought to the very essence of his emotional mind by the boy's cutting glance. His life had been totally changed in a flash and he had to know why. What was the power in this young man—really just a boy . . . that this non-descript kid (except for the unusual color of his eyes) had used on him and how. His sudden new passion was all consuming! His mind leaped with unfettered possibilities. As a multi-billionaire broadcasting mogul, specializing in the latest in communications techniques, his brain was filled with a flood of questions.

Again, he thought who or what was this kid? He'd worn a pair of moderately used blue jeans, a faded camo-colored jacket and a pair of army-green sneakers. It was as though the boy didn't want to even be seen or wanted to just blend in with the other kids. But the power of those two eyes flashing into the man's stare, apparently had felt like the power of two high level blue lasers.

This episode was over in seconds, but, the long term significance was just beginning to be revealed.

2

Switcher Revealed

Shaken but excited, Maxwell Cabe slipped into his car and drove from the mini mart and, for the umpteenth time, turned left onto Huntington Drive. He headed to Old Mill Road turned north just blocks from his San Marino estate. For some reason his mind picked up on Huntington and he thought of his buddy, John Huntington, the great, great, great grandson of the man for whom the street was named, along with Huntington Beach and Huntington Library. Huntington Drive was a four-lane street with a fifty-foot wide median strip of grass, flowers, bushes and trees that were all kept in pristine condition. It was mowed weekly, never a leaf left lying on the lawn for more than a minute or two, even as fall approached.

John had died of cancer not too many years ago and it was strange, he thought, that this memory of John would come up now. Again he felt that his senses were still somewhat heightened and alerted. He kept saying to himself, "this is weird!" Rarely did he notice the amazingly opulent homes on both sides of the road all manicured to the enth degree with nothing out of place. Today, many of the homes looked like the cover of Architectural Digest's retro editions remembering the evolution of large homes through generations and decades. He noticed the leaves on some trees in the median were already starting to turn.

"It's weird, just weird," Cabe continued to muse out loud.

Although Cabe's San Marino home was one of four he maintained around the world, it was also his favorite--and was patterned after a southern plantation house. It had long wide porches, mammoth Southern Oaks which were mixed with the ubiquitous Southern

California palm trees that seemed to touch the sky. It was immaculately landscaped and with only one thing missing---southern moss that hung like permanent antebellum Christmas decorations on the stately branches of Southern Oaks. He always felt it was such an inviting vision of hospitality. A circular drive started with huge iron gates designed after the pattern of the iron works from the New Orleans French Quarter. He realized he may have mixed a few stylistic metaphors during the reconstruction and remodeling, but for the most part he stuck with the concept of a genteel home.

The gates were set back from the street a discrete thirty feet. In his opinion some wealthy communities like Bel Aire looked as if home owners wanted to just flaunt their wealth. San Marino, while obviously wealthy, had more old money and traditional homes and he liked the relatively low key feeling of the community, mostly because it wasn't Bel Aire or Beverly Hills even though both were much closer to his office. Although he was extremely wealthy, money was the by product of his vision and work ethic rather than major focus of his daily life.

His home's sophisticated security systems made three readings as he pulled into his driveway. First, it photographed and identified the vehicle; second it weighed the whole vehicle and determined that the driver was exactly the right weight, and that there was no other person in the car. Next the system took a recognition laser scan of the driver to determine if there were any signs of obvious nervous tension. If any of the elements did not record as planned, it would request a voice confirmation. After a few seconds the gate opened and Cabe drove into the just opened garage stall designated only for the Scorpion. If all elements of the system hadn't been cleared, it would have remained closed with six-inch spikes popping up all across the drive a yard behind the rear wheels.

The house staff had already been notified by the gate scanner that he'd arrived and they were scurrying to get the last details ready for his return.

Controlling all of Cabe's enduring and constant traits of

promptness, preparedness and timeliness was the all-consuming attention to the most minute detail. They knew his routine: shower, shave, dress and prepare for the day. Important messages were laid out on his desk.

His home office probably wouldn't have fit the accepted decor and style of an antebellum mansion. The rug was opulently plush, a deep forest green color and there was brass trim that accented the rug and walnut grain's powerful colors and patterns. Bookshelves and wood trim were old growth walnut that he'd obtained from stumps taken out of an orchard between Chico and Red Bluff years before. The stumps had been saved and dried for just this type of wood work.

Some of the trees were at least a hundred and twenty-five years old. Crotch wood, which is taken from the trunk where main tree branches divide create grain patterns twisted into bizarre lines and colors of deep brown, black and waves of lighter brown. The wilder the grain patterns the more highly prized the wood, especially for molding, panels and cabinet doors. The wood was nothing short of unbelievable. The most extraordinary grain patterns of all were saved for Cabe's massive desk and looked like they'd been created by a frenetic lunatic.

The farmer, who had saved the special wood, culled it from stumps at the end of their productive life in a walnut orchard. The old tree trunks and root clumps were then extracted whole with newly grafted young trees replanted in their place. Orchardists had learned early that English walnut limbs grafted onto black walnut trunks and roots provided the best of both worlds: high quality English Walnuts and the tree life (about a hundred years) of the Black Walnut root system. The other big plus was insane patterns of the root balls were even wilder than the trunk lumber and harder to get. Cabe had first learned of the walnut grain story when he selected his personal stock from a gun stock maker in Northern, California. Joseph Harris had removed hundreds of stumps from walnut orchards and had five acres of them drying on property not far from Whiskeytown Reservoir.

Obviously, Cabe's home office and especially the desk were creations that screamed of his attention to detail. As he sat down to a breakfast of a Denver omelet, toast and a virgin blood bull, his first call was to Mike Drobick, the voice on the other end of the line to whom he had narrated his life-altering event. "Mike, I'd like you to get some general information about the Rocky Creek School before we meet. I'll be there at one and we can meet at two-forty," Cabe said.

"Anything you want specifically?" Drobick asked.

"Not until we meet," Cabe said and hung up abruptly.

As a highly successful entrepreneur, Cabe was acutely aware of the growing potential of inadvertently revealing information through phones, computer correspondence, and especially since he was a targeted subject, as most of the wealthy are.

His butler, Jeeves met him at the door and queried: "How was the flight from Shanghai, Siiiirrrr?"

Jeeves was much more than a butler since he possessed other useful traits and skills including a black belt in Brazilian Jiu Jitzu, Tae Kwon Do and Golden Gloves, Light Heavy Weight Champion at the height of his run.

"A little bumpy approaching Hawaii," Cabe said looking out of the corner of his eye.

"Yeah, those bumps over Hawaii can be brutal," Jeeves said, rolling his own eyes a bit.

Cabe didn't return the jibe which Jeeves noticed with concern. Maybe things were worse than he thought, and maybe something much more ominous was brewing.

With Cabe's mostly personal requirements met, he set about dealing with the issues on his desk involving his various homes and some personal investments. With those taken care of, he began considering what he'd do when he reached his Century City office where his corporate VP would be first in line.

For the moment, his mind turned to some other tasks. "Hey Jeeves," he yelled, knowing Jeeves would be within hearing distance.

Jeeves' real name was McClain Bills. When Cabe hit it big, Bills had been by his side and Cabe asked him to run the San Marino house, oversee the other houses and work with him on special assignments. As old pals, he found it amusing to give his buddy the name Jeeves from the book "My Man Jeeves" which were the comedic stories of a highly competent English butler. They'd been best friends since the third grade. His trust in Bills was implicit. Bills was naturally and almost aggressively the quiet type. He was everything Cabe wasn't and it became a handy trait that both used to maximum potential.

"Whatcha 'need boss?" Jeeves said as he walked in.

"I saw a very odd incident when I stopped at the "Quick-n-Go" store by Rocky Creek Middle School. I'm still trying to figure out what it was that I experienced. Do you know anybody over there?" Cabe asked.

"Believe it or not," Jeeves said. "I do. It just so happens I met the principal at a fund raising event a couple of months ago. His name is Fred Reese. Nice guy! Good principal! No nonsense!"

Cabe paused, thinking about the new information. "I need a little recon at the school. I can't even tell you exactly what I want, just some of your general feeling on a student I saw and a feel for the place. Did we give anything to their charity event? Yeah, we donated one of those antique English, pristine condition, steel rolling horses we had stored. It even had the original wooden wheels. He auctioned it off for a couple thousand bucks and was very happy."

Again, Cabe paused. "McClain, I just kind of need to….." Cabe's mind drifted back to the emotional impact of the morning's incident. Jeeves registered the reticence, an uncommon state for Cabe, but he also knew Cabe just didn't use his real name unless it was serious.

Cabe continued, "Look. Why don't we suggest to Reese that the kids of the school partner up with another school in an area of lesser means? They can also raise some money for computers and accessories? Rocky Creek is well-heeled so this will let our kids learn about personal sharing."

"I'll give $45,000; the Rocky kids could work to match some of that and choose how to divide it up based on what they determine the other school may need for their future. I'll also match any other contributions raised by the kids themselves dollar for dollar."

"Seems like overkill if you ask me," Jeeves said. "We could give the principal another thousand, take him out to coffee and he'd be happy as a clam."

"No, it's not about him or the school directly." Cabe said. "There's a particularly unique kid there who I'm hoping will participate. I want to get some intel on him but I don't want to single him out or make him feel threatened in any way. Actually, I don't want him to even know I'm interested. I'm thinking that you might sit in on the kids recommendations for the sister school and take notes specifically on him. I want to know how he thinks so let's make sure the sixth graders are part of the project and I'm fairly positive he'll be part of the choice committee. If not, see what you can do to make sure he is. How you do that, I'll leave to you."

"Unique?" Jeeves asked. "Sounds a little fishy to me! How can you possibly know that this kid is going to show up for the committee selection? You going bonkers?"

Cabe did not respond immediately and again Jeeves realized this was not a normal situation. Finally, Cabe turned in his chair, looked out the window and said, "I'm not really sure, but with what I think I felt, I assume the kid is very empathic and compassionate and would participate just because of his natural mental makeup. Can't prove any of that, just hunches."

Non-plussed would be an understatement for Jeeves. He hadn't heard the narrated conversation from the Quick-n-Go parking lot that morning. Of all the assignments he'd undertaken for Cabe, this seemed the oddest, bar none.

His question was how to do it. Jeeves immediately called Reese and told him that his boss wanted to do a little more in a different way. He told the principal the general outline of the proposal. Reese's response was "great, let's get together Thursday? A week and three days from today" Reese suggested, writing a note on his calendar for the following Monday to remind himself of the meeting.

"Sounds good," Jeeves said. "I'll call you or you can call me if there's a change."

Reese took a second thinking about the idea. "Wow, what a great way to start the school year. Can't wait to see what the kids come up with."

Among the things Cabe told Jeeves, was what the boy was wearing. "Thanks," he thought to himself. Half the kids in the school probably wore the same things. But when Cabe described the eyes of the young man he had seen, he realized that he probably wouldn't have much trouble identifying the boy he wanted to learn about.

When Cabe told Jeeves that he believed the kid would for sure be one of the kids in the sixth grade group who'd be selected for the meeting. Jeeves thought, "Yeah, right!" "What'd Cabe get in Shanghai, the crystal ball flu?"

3

A Magnate's Choice

Cabe finished his work and thanked the staff for their help and walked to a new Jeep Wrangler. To any Jeep lover, it appeared to be a normal top of the line Jeep. Under the paint, however, was an armored vehicle with so many gismos, nerds could be kept dreaming for months just thinking about the possibilities.

It was equipped with the finest GPS, armor out the wazoo and zero air tires. Bullet proof glass and electronic response were both defensive and offensive. Cabe's favorite was the electronic skin that looked like a deep maroon paint job. In reality, it was a short inducer that would ground anyone who touched the car without permission… kind of like tasering yourself. The electronic skin engage button was operational.

By the time he turned onto Constellation Boulevard he still hadn't reached a conclusion about his next course of action. You can't just kidnap a kid and then demand: "What did you do?" And, perhaps the more important question: "why did you do what you did?" Most important to Cabe was "how" the boy did it. That was the real question.

He drove into the West Century Plaza Tower parking lot. The two towers were triangle shaped and housed his corporate offices and cable station on the 39th, 40th and 41st floors.

The most intriguing question to Cabe was what had happened to him personally. He really didn't want to face that question head on, or admit how the real power of the boy had impacted a man of stature and the depth to which it had changed his life. No kid could possibly have that kind of power over him and Cabe wouldn't stop until well, he didn't really know when the "until" might be.

Deep down were more lingering and much darker questions. Given the impact on Cabe, he wanted to know how he could get that power! How could he use the power and what would it take for the boy to reveal how he got it and how it could be replicated?

It was apparent he needed much more information to even get to where he wanted to start. He was being haunted by his innate self-demanding nature that was clanging up against his growing demand to know. He paused and reached the unsettling realization of his own insecurities. He wondered if he could ever make a life altering plan about the power of a junior high school aged kid. His answer was yes because of an unadulterated fear!

There it was. It was a power he couldn't understand or control. Even a multi-billionaire was not all powerful. This boy had made that more clear in his mind than any mogul who had ever challenged him on anything.

He parked his Jeep, "Tank" as he referred to it, entered the elevator and went to the 41st floor. The instant he walked in the door, the demands of a CEO hit. Decisions needed to be made and now that he was back, it seemed everybody wanted his attention. The idiot "Schultz" was demanding the six o'clock time slot again and a hefty raise. That guy can be really tedious, he thought, not to mention beyond greedy, with an ego far beyond his less than modest talent. Normally, this type of constant barrage would be handled by Cabe with staccato style orders:

1. Tell Mr. Harry Shultz to eat a vomit sandwich, or be relegated to midnight on every other holiday.

2. Tell Mark Cuban he looked like he had his fins cut off in the "Tank" last night.

3. And, "no, I won't be attending the Vogue party after the 'Occupy' premier. In fact I won't be at the premier either. One of my employee's daughters was raped in the New York encampment and got head lice to boot. I'm beginning to think they're just a bunch of free loading filthy parasites."

Today, he answered the most important questions asked of him and simply ignored everything else. Another example of the impact of that boy! He greeted everyone with grace and ease, but everyone also caught the malevolent undertones of his voice. Back off, and back off now.

Once he reached his office he continued issuing orders. The first was "No!" into his cell phone. "Hi, Vickie how are you today?" Another phone order, "No nothing---just orders." Vickie Manwaring was his executive assistant although that was an understatement too. She could give orders just as effectively as Cabe and frequently did. Seldom did Cabe change anything she decided even without his permission.

Out came the agenda: "Get me Drobick." "Contact Palumbo for tomorrow at 8!" "Coffee," which Vickie knew he took black.

He walked through his inch-thick glass door portal and stood on the front side of his other massive walnut table desk. It was a modern version of his home desk with the same insane walnut grain patterns. No papers were visible and he looked at nothing particular in his office. He briefly glanced at the "car ants" inching along below on Constellation. He turned his back to the door and stared out his windows into the distance. His office was essentially a parallelogram. One of the acute angles was the angle of the tower and the other acute angle formed the inside walls at the other end of the space. Two walls were formed by the building . All the walls were glass. Glass doors hung on one side of the two interior walls. On the opposite glass wall hung an eight-foot by sixteen-foot glass creation.

It was slump glass and by itself was spectacular. The artist, Virgil Tyler, had infused the glass with thousands of flecks of colored green and turquoise glass to form the exterior of the God's Eye nebula and wandering pearl white intermittent stars surrounding the form of the nebula. Where the green/blue ended, a field of transparent black glass flecks formed the iris which gradually turned to a transparent candy apple red. Its red flecks became the pupil of the eye to perfectly match the nebula. Because it was both transparent and opaque in some places, the effect created a depth that gave the viewer a glimpse into what could be described as eternity.

In the afternoon, with the sun coming in from the West the iris was iridescent red. It was an ever changing glass painting, every angle and every time of day and even time of year offered something new in the "Eye of God."

It took two years to create and nearly a half million to execute, not counting installation.

The glass creation which he loved was one of his favorite possessions. What it depicted and its beauty inspired him, especially in reaching any decision he needed to make. It was as though the Eye of God was looking on. Today, he came to a surprising conclusion as he peered into the glass sculpture. For him it was that he had seen someone he could easily fear. It was an experience he'd never really had, even as a child. It was mind numbing to him.

Vickie came into his office. "Black coffee," she said. "Mike's on the phone," pointing at the blinking light.

Cabe immediately pivoted, stared right into Vickie's eyes and with a voice soft as velvet, said "Sorry Vic, my mind is on other things. Didn't mean to be short."

"No problem boss. Got it covered." She said.

With that, she returned to her desk and Cabe picked up the phone for the waiting Drobick.

Mike Drobick was Cabe's anchor. Like Jeeves, they'd been working together for years. What Drobick offered was that steadying influence for the sometimes mercurial Cabe. Drobick was a former Navy Seal, as smart as they come, fiercely loyal and up for any challenge. There was something else about Drobick that Cabe both admired and used. He was bluntly honest. It could be irritating when Cabe wanted a yes man. Drobick was a lot of things, "yes man" was not one of them.

Cabe could be intimidating. Drobick would have none of that. It would have been like trying to talk an oak out of its bark.

"Mike, I've got about three hours of crap to get through. Could you please clear your time for our 2:30, no calls, no interruptions and I'll do the same. We'll meet in the Dome. No cells either," his comments were short and to the point, nothing Drobick hadn't heard many times before, but nothing like the tinge to the voice now, a tinge Drobick had never heard before.

4

A Secret Disclosed

Cabe spent the next four and a half hours in a foul mood. He haggled over a piece of property he wanted in Canada and did other sundry chores, the no choice decisions and all. None of them seemed to stoke his juices as in past operations and negotiations.

At about 1:30 p.m. he asked Vickie to take messages for all calls except for the must-takes and she knew which ones they would be. He turned his chair to the window and blocked out anything coursing through his mind and concentrated on just what he wanted to think about.

As was his habit from college, he grabbed a two-and-half hard pencil and a legal sized lined yellow pad. He let his mind wander and made notes with the flow of his thinking. There was no rhyme or particular reason to it but all thoughts seemed to drift back to this morning---was it only this morning---wasn't it a life time ago? He also had a hard time mentally determining a framework to follow.

In the middle of his mental wanderings the intercom beeped. It was Vickie, "Dick's on line three, Sir--wants to know if he needs to bring or prepare anything."

He picked up line three. "Hi, Dick. No. Don't need anything else, unless you have anything you want to share. Can you be here at eight tomorrow morning?"

"No problem," Palumbo answered, "Whazz up." Palumbo immediately knew it was a question he shouldn't have asked.

"No big deal, but it's a just-you and me situation. One thing I would suggest is a wide-open mind." Cabe said. Palumbo recognized this was not "no big deal." It also meant, keep your mouth, even about this call, clamped shut.

Palumbo was a kind of do-it-all guy, but specializing in security and jobs that required some international expertise. In his bag of tricks, he carried a variety of surveillance equipment and experiences. They were remnants of his cloak and dagger work in tracking down copyright and trademark pirates as an attorney for another firm. Like Drobick and Jeeves, Palumbo recognized, this demeanor was not typical Cabe.

Cabe was usually very decisive and generally pretty dictatorial but with a sense of humor. He pondered that Cabe, at least in Palumbo's memory, had never, ever asked him to keep an open mind. That was a kind of invitation for Palumbo's input that was definitely unusual.

5

An Impossible Decision

At 2:30 p.m., Drobick walked into Cabe's office usually anticipating a big media purchase or something of equal importance. Keeping decisions and projects under wraps was paramount when it came to major acquisitions. But, in this case, he had no inkling of what was to come.

Cabe was on the phone with Jamal Davenport, president of his Cable News Network empire. The media mogul listened to Davenport outline the normal stuff: ratings and thus the networks income, more pressure to get to the middle of the country's economic agenda, instead of keeping the network pushing Al Gore's crap, and suggesting a gun control story supporting Bloomberg's organization.

"Yeah, yeah!" Cabe said, "Bloomberg's already hit me up for a chunk of change from the Network side. Just tell em' no. Box cutters didn't kill anybody either. Right?"

The first few comments were the usual everyday stuff, Drobick thought, as he listened to the exchange.

"Hey Jae, would you please get on Schultz's case with a hammer! Tell him to put his brain back into his head! I think it fell out through his mouth," Cabe said. "And tell him if I hear one more 'F-word' on air that has to be 'bleeped,' he's going to get that midnight holiday slot we've been talking about. Or better yet, tell him I'll turn him into the reporter covering the Wasilla City Council beat indefinitely."

Drobick let out a stifled snicker. Cabe turned with a smug smile on his face and told Davenport he'd get back in a couple of days to iron out a few things on Shultz. As detail oriented as Cabe was, he seldom got involved with the everyday on-air operations of CNM, with the exception of Schultz. Even if Cabe agreed with the loud-mouth occasionally, the idiot was a personal and perpetual irritant.

It was the first smile Drobick had seen on Cabe since he'd come back. Even his voice eased too as if the Schultz thing gave him the comic relief he needed. It was short-lived though. Cabe's voice abruptly intensified just as the two began a conversation that would change their lives and the lives, maybe, of everyone on earth. That thought, which hung in the air and seemed ridiculous at the time, would prove prophetic in days to come.

6

A Machiavellian Option

Cabe asked. "Do you have the recording of our call?" looking at Drobick.

"Got it," Drobick said, "thinking this is getting curiouser and curiouser."

The dome was a unit erected to keep all electronic devices from operating within, or trying to penetrate from without, or anything else that could eavesdrop on conversations. It was about twenty feet in diameter, fifteen feet tall and included a coffee machine, small refrigerator and other accoutrements inside. Cell phone recording devices would only work in the dome if allowed with the tightly controlled security codes that had been installed. Any discussions that started in the Dome, Drobick knew, were high security conversations.

"Why the dome?" Drobick asked.

"I don't want anybody to hear this. They would think I've completely gone off to Beserkerville!" Cabe said.

It sounded to Drobick more like a plea than anything else. Given the mysterious phone conversation he'd had earlier in the day, this was indeed perplexing.

As they walked down the hall from his office, Cabe's head was down and apparently his mind struggling. Drobick took it to mean this whole thing was as big as he'd ever been a part of. They walked through the conference room into an anteroom that had a glass dome with a mesh of copper and silver wires imbedded between two glass plates. The dome illustrated more than a tinge of paranoia in their world of business. Including the NSA, there was electronic snooping by corporate competition and especially foreign governments.

Although the floor of the dome was covered in a plush carpet, the bottom of the dome also included the mesh sandwiched into a glass floor. Sound deadening pads hung from the ceiling. The exterior room where the dome sat was also lined with sound proofing and a separate heating and cooling system that kept the interior at whatever temperature the occupants wanted. The finest air filtering system available kept the air gently flowing inside and perfectly clean.

They entered, closed and sealed the door and sat down on plush goat skin upholstered chairs. The hides were muted beige with some natural discolorations and the rug was the same color green found in Cabe's San Marino home office, an obvious leftover. It was so plush it was almost like walking on grass.

Drobick sat down even before Cabe, and thought, here it comes. Vickie had ordered the cafeteria staff to have coffee brewing, cold drinks in the fridge which included a bottle of Hugel Riesling Jubilee 1998, Alsace wine and four glasses hanging on a nearby rack. It always amused Drobick that the coffee brewing in the dome was the same as what he got at the convenience store where this whole "thing" started. A memory from Cabe's past, he thought. In fact, Cabe bought the whole "Quick-n-Go" chain when he'd stopped for a cup of coffee. Drobick frequently kidded Cabe, saying "Now that was an expensive cup of coffee."

The purchase of the convenience store chain was a kind of window into Cabe's investing philosophy: Buy what you know, like or serves your purposes.

The dome was absolutely silent except for the slight sound of air circulating and the dripping coffee brewer while Cabe paced and Drobick waited.

It was several minutes of pacing and soundlessness. In the meantime, Drobick cued up the recorder setting it to start at the beginning and continued to wait.

Cabe rubbed the back of his head, turned and faced his friend and obviously began while stressing to get the words out, but start he did.

"Mike, how long have we been friends?" Cabe asked.

"I don't know exactly Max," Drobick said, "but I think it was shortly after the Mayflower dropped anchor."

Cabe smirked and blurted out "speak for yourself old timer. You heard our call. Have you listened to it again?" Cabe quizzed.

"I have," Drobick said. "First impression? You're brain is floating out there somewhere between Hollywood, Halloween and Japanese jokes."

"I know you heard the phone narrative, but what you didn't hear were the feelings that flooded my head when that boy penetrated my mind as his eyes literally flashed at me. It was kind of a suspension of disbelief, things you couldn't believe happened. I want you to remember, I'm hoping I'm not crazy, but I've been totally consumed by the incident because it was a total invasion of my mind," Cabe said.

Another of the things Cabe particularly appreciated about Drobick was his steadiness and ability to wait for all the information while withholding comment. He didn't draw any conclusions before the time was right.

"Again, Mike, I may sound crazy as a loon but trust me. I'm deadly serious. I'm going to try to add to the narration in our call while you forward to the hand thing?"

Drobick, prepared as always, ran the recording forward and said: "OK." and pressed the button.

Cabe was immediately taken back to that morning's incident. He heard the amazement in his own voice describing the boy pointing his hand at the fighting kids. It was almost an out of body experience it was so vivid in his memory.

The recording played back the voice that Cabe had used to narrate, intonations and all. As Drobick was aware, it didn't even sound like Cabe. He kind of sounded like he was giving a rote description that was coming into his head but with a tenor of complete awe. And even though it was only a matter of maybe twenty or thirty seconds, it was unmistakable.

Cabe started again. "First, what I described just streamed out of my mouth. You already know that. It appeared that the waves flowing from the boy's fingertips were directed right at the boys in the gang members heads. They slammed into them like hammers. No, that's not quite right. It was more like the boys had all been affected at exactly the same time. But it wasn't the hitting as much as it turned their faces into a look of sudden absolute terror. My first thought was that he was hurting them. But rather, their eyes looked like somebody just put a machete at their throats and it all seemed to be happening in their minds. It wasn't obviously physical"

Cabe stopped, looked directly into Drobick's eyes, and paused. There was no hint of judgment or disbelief. Instead, Drobick looked transfixed while trying to accommodate the meaning of Cabe's words. There was no question that he knew getting the whole story was primary, but then they had to evaluate and calculate what to do about it, which was what the meeting was about.

Drobick also knew, with a little more info on this part of the incident, a plan was apparently beginning to form in Cabe's mind. Solutions to most all issues started in the dome. What that plan was, was anybody's guess, but with what had happened already and Cabe's quick response, Cabe's number one could tell it was not a plan he could possibly have anticipated. It was what made Cabe worth what he was worth. He was able to see trends, things, issues and just about anything else and then project them into the future almost instantly. Before anyone else saw the potential, Cabe already had his plan to capitalize taking shape.

"Next," Cabe said, "just as the young man had aimed, thrown or whatever he did at those gang bangers, he somehow could feel my stare and that I had somehow seen, or maybe experienced is a better word, what no one had ever seen before. He seemed to know or feel my mind. That's when he turned to me, just as the fighters were getting hit. That all this happened in a split second just amazes me.

"The boy's stare that hit me was like he marched into my brain and simply owned me! He was in complete emotional control for those seconds. I have never felt in less control of my emotions and intellect as when he was searching my feelings. I could not proceed logically, but you heard me talking so I guess I was coherent enough, but definitely under duress."

"Yeah, you could say that," Drobick mused.

"And here is the weirdest part of all." Cabe continued. "It didn't really feel like fear to me or anything like that. As best as I can describe it, it was a kind of the ultimate emotional submission. As I recall, I felt a kind of compassion from him but I was still totally at his mercy.

"If this is what the gang bangers felt, but with the kid's total domination of their emotions, it must have been a kind of ultimate acquiescence they'd never experienced, like he had switched aggression for fear or one set of emotions for another."

Cabe stopped, let out what was a huge sigh and collapsed into a chair. Drobick said nothing, suggested nothing and continued to wait letting Cabe regain his composure. Drobick allowed the time to tick by not breaking a silence he felt was helping Cabe cope.

After this short break, Cabe took a sip of coffee that had been ready on the brewer. It was as though he'd run a marathon and had hit the wall, glad that the ordeal was finally out of his head and the recording that had been playing over and over again in his mind had finally stopped. He didn't have to hear it again and that was a major relief.

The scent of the coffee and first drink seemed to lower Cabe's tension by just getting the story out of his mind so he could focus on what should happen next.

Without looking at anything, even Drobick, he asked, "OK, am I crazy or what?" He leaned his head into the headrest and waited to hear the verdict.

This was probably the most vulnerable Drobick had ever seen Cabe. His boss was spent and really not sure what to do, even though he also knew elements were falling into place from the dusty corners of Cabe's mind. That realization put Drobick into a deep funk. He'd seen Cabe financially and mentally eviscerate opponents with a kind of primal pleasure. Drobick was now on full alert to bring Cabe back into reality for the first time since the "incident." And Drobick, for the first time, began to feel some serious concern for the boy. Since Cabe had discovered him, there had to be others.

It was unspoken that anything said in the dome stayed there. With this type of situation, no matter how hard they tried, it didn't seem possible or even probable at all. Cabe told Drobick that he'd like him to start by learning everything he could about the Rocky Creek School, including the principal and teachers. It was something Cabe called getting his ducks in a row. Even though much of the research Drobick had done on dozens of "projects" was never used, there always seemed to be that odd piece of information Drobick uncovered that frequently proved a key to closing a deal.

They both stood and began walking to the door. Cabe, in a sort of an absent-minded way, told Drobick he was meeting with Palumbo tomorrow and would like him to sit in. He also mentioned that Jeeves was meeting with the principal of the school where he saw the boy was enrolled. "Palumbo?" Drobick thought a little surprised. It was a signal that Cabe's mind was definitely forming a plan. Was that another red flag, well, not necessarily red but definitely yellow or pink on the way to red?

"It's at eight," Cabe said.

"I'll be there but give me a few days on the research. It may take a while because getting unauthorized info out of schools is tough, especially if you want to keep your tracks covered and identity quiet," Drobick threw a side glance at his boss that said volumes. Cabe saw every concern in the glance but said nothing.

7

The Need to Know

Back at his desk, Drobick set a meeting with a couple of "researchers" he had used in the past. Meeting in his office was not a possibility. "There was a Jewish deli in the tower next to CNM's office," he told his guys. "They've got the best pastrami sandwiches and strawberry blintzes on the planet and we can do lunch tomorrow in the East Century Plaza Tower? Yeah, one is good, see you then. Oh, I'll be at the very back table." He hung up the phone and as his boss had done, turned his chair to the window. He wondered if he had been caught in the obsession that Cabe seemed to have been caught in. That didn't last long as he let his mind anticipate the wonderful fragrances of strawberry blintzes.

He hadn't caught Cabe's "incident" obsession quite yet he surmised, but then he didn't have nearly enough information. That was his specialty and it could bring either rabid obsession or a bland boredom of hyper-objectivity. Even some of CNM's major projects could be boring--this was not boring but he still wasn't sure what "it" was.

Drobick spent the next couple of hours finishing up odds and ends spread out on his desk. By 4:30 p.m. he was ready to put together his expectations for his researchers. For example, he penciled in what he wanted and when he wanted it. The questions were pretty simple: school-size, building construction, number of students, financials on as many parents as possible without raising eyebrows, plus teachers and administrative staff including the maintenance staff. He added questions about fund raisers and also dates students first enrolled and in what grade and where they came if from out of state and pictures, if possible.

It wouldn't be easy or quick, but Cabe had mentioned Jeeves upcoming meeting with the principal set for the following Monday and wanted to make sure he had a chance to ponder their reports. It would be another weekend at the office. One of the endearing things about Cabe was that when there were weekend work situations like this, he encouraged his top staff members to invite their spouses to come to Century City for that Saturday and Sunday weekend work.

Breakfast, lunch and dinner was paid for and even prepaid tickets to a comic club a short walk from the towers. There was use of any equipment in the 24-hour a day staffed office if the spouse had his or her own projects and there was a small but plush apartment as part of the floor, so they could stay without having to drive home.

The cost of getting reliable information wasn't cheap, but the right information that might be gathered and analyzed for any project could be worth millions. Drobick called his wife and told her it would be one of those weekends.

"I'd love dinner at the North Woods Inn anyway," she said, "and I've got a bunch of stuff for work I could be doing in the quiet."

Drobick knew it was still going to be a long weekend and he still had his own work to do.

8

Collaboration and Conspiracy

On Tuesday morning Palumbo walked into the office at 7:47 a.m. with plenty of time to grab a cup of coffee. Cabe was at the office by six o'clock so he could spend most of his morning talking to New York contacts involving media interests. By now these other issues had become a good diversion and it freed his mind up to think about something else, if only for a short time.

He finished his last call about five minutes before Palumbo arrived, answered two emails, did some texting and at five to eight, waved at Palumbo to come in. Palumbo held his cup up and pointed at it to see if Cabe wanted a refill. Cabe waved his hand and shook his head. Drobick walked over to Palumbo and they shook hands.

"Thanks anyway," he said to Palumbo, "I'm fine, appreciate the offer though."

Palumbo was an attorney who passed the bar his first try, summa cum laude from Stanford Law School. He was hired out of school by a law firm in Los Angeles specializing in intellectual properties, copyright and trademark protection issues and a variety of other specialties relating to copyright and trademark pirating both in the US and overseas.

He was literally fighting pirates, and those pirates were just as cutthroat and vicious as the pirates of old. The stakes could be enormous and running the pirates down treacherous.

Cabe and Palumbo had met by coincidence at an intellectual property pirating conference. Palumbo had moved up the ranks quickly in his three years with the law firm and had been invited to sit at Cabe's table. Cabe was one of the speakers. They discussed the media's current mutual pirating problems. What caught Cabe's attention was that Palumbo seemed bored out of his gourd doing the "lawyer" stuff and was looking to do more "exciting" assignments. A year later, Palumbo got a call from Drobick who invited him to the west tower for a "blintz" at Herbies. Any excuse Mike could find would send him to Herbies'.

Shortly after, Palumbo wound up his work for his employer and went to work for Cabe. His new job fit him perfectly. It involved lots of domestic and international travel, interesting assignments, and some legal work but most of all it was far from boring.

Palumbo brought his coffee and Cabe gestured to him to sit at one of two chairs facing each other. Cabe got up and took the opposite chair.

Cabe didn't waste any time. "Look Dick, I haven't fleshed out exactly what the plan is, but this will be one of the most, I would say, questionable, maybe I should just admit 'weird' projects, we've ever undertaken, but maybe the most impactful. I have a bunch of info to collect and evaluate, but generally I want you to find a 'place' that's not tied to you, me, CNM or anything else. Don't limit yourself to any given country and we may have to 'entertain a guest' with 'special needs' including caretakers the way I see it now. I should have more within a week or two, in the meantime, keep me posted on anything you find that's promising within the given parameters."

Palumbo spoke "Cabe" as a second language, so with Cabe's oddish demeanor and comments he knew the potential gravity and risks that attach themselves to meetings like this. It's why he loved working for Cabe, never a dull moment, but the possibilities in this case had the potential of being much more intriguing than anything in his five years at Cabe's so far. Much better than pushing papers, he thought.

9

New Found Friend

Buddy staggered toward the school's main building. Before he got there, several teachers were already running out of the building to tend to his bloody nose, scrapes and bruises. Teachers and administrators had immediately heard kids screaming "fight, fight" and ran to the site of the crowd. The gang bullies, of course, had vanished into the crowd and well beyond. The question of who the perpetrators were, would most likely never be answered," not by the teachers anyway, they knew the kids would never tell, for kids this age, it was better dead than being a rat.

Danny Woodruff, the baseball coach and geography teacher, got to Buddy first. He'd grabbed a towel on the way. He planted it on Buddy's nose to staunch the bleeding then got him to the nurse's office. She'd hardly expected the entrance of a bloodied student on the first day of school. Woodruff had seen these gang "statements" before.

Fortunately, Buddy was in reasonably good shape considering his "introduction" to Rocky Creek. And fortunately the beating had been cut short by the boy in the shade than it might have otherwise been. The yelling students had not noticed the boy under the tree as had the man across the street.

School Nurse, Terri Ann Sutherland, got Buddy patched up physically, but like any kid who's been through anything like this, he feared another attack. He only got a good look at the ring leader of the group with just glances at the others in the pack. She asked him if he wanted her to call his parents or go home.

Buddy realized, with the nature of schools, kids and gangs, going home would have been a show of fear that he simply couldn't afford in the long term. It would have set him up for what, he assumed, would be a perpetual round of bullying and pestering. Buddy, toughed it out and said no, "I'll be ok." Fortunately, after the nurse's care he was fine, with a somewhat swollen nose. But Buddy also didn't say that he had also heard the name of the ring leader, Reuben Gravatos, and he would forget neither that name nor his face.

The part played by the boy in the shade was not something Buddy could have connected to his fight. But it wouldn't stay that way. It was a long first day for Buddy. Every corner seemed like a threat as though Reuben was waiting to pounce.

Worse, tomorrow's entrance to school would test his resolve because the first day's attack had indelibly changed his awareness.

At noon, Buddy grabbed his lunch sack, and sat at a table in the lunch court. Other sixth graders, who knew Buddy, kept what they thought was a safe distance from him, but not all. Nathan Farnsworth was one who did not. Buddy was not surprised at the reluctance of the other kids to get near him. Nathan, however, sat right down across from Buddy and asked if he was ok.

"Sure, if you want to have a nose that looks like a big red potato. Who are you?" he said.

Nathan smiled, "Nathan, and yeah, that's about what it looks like. Anything broke?"

"Nah," Buddy said, "sore but mostly scrapes and bumps and a plugged up schnozzola," The fact that Nathan's eyes were a little different wasn't even a thought for Buddy. He was just glad that someone would be friendly enough to even sit near him.

It was the beginning of a fast friendship. Buddy seemed to have kept his big gregarious personality despite the fight, whereas Nathan was intense and quiet and extremely perceptive, especially in judging other people. It just seemed the personalities of these two sixth graders complimented each other.

In the middle of their conversation Buddy's mother called. She was calm but was still persistent after a talk to the nurse. Nathan listened to Buddy's conversation.

Buddy glanced at Nathan. "Now she wants to send my dad."

"Absolutely not! If you send dad I'll be hamburger." Buddy blurted out to his mother.

Both Buddy and Nathan grew a lot that first day. Buddy seemed to have gained some kind of mission and Nathan had gained a friend, his first, at the new school.

Carey, Idaho, seemed an eternity away from his new surroundings in Nathan's mind. He went from an outdoor, fishing and frolicking environment to an in-your-face existence that he couldn't have anticipated.

Nathan thought briefly about his dad's new job that brought their family to San Marino. Actually the job was at Isaac Newton Institute of Technology in Pasadena, but luckily they'd found a remodelaholic's-type dream house they could afford in the small town, which was amazing since it was an upscale area not far from the Institute. It would require lots of fixing up, but that's what Nathan's dad did for fun and he had taught his son to appreciate the value of hard work and the creative process in remodeling.

Carey's charm was fences, corrals, barns and other farm buildings that got Levi and Nathan's remodeling juices flowing in the hours in between his dad's job doing genetics research. While he was engrossed in his memories of Idaho, Nathan and Buddy were interrupted by a voice over the school intercom.

"We'll have our first assembly tomorrow at 10 a.m.," Principal Reese announced. "A little warning! If any cell phones, smart phones, IPod rings or if you're texting during assembly, that device will be taken and kept in my office and not returned until the end of the day, or maybe I should say end of the month. I seriously suggest that you turn off your devices before you even think about walking through the auditorium door."

There was a muffled boo in the lunch court and some snickering. Kids have been getting under administrators' and teachers' skins since there were kids and teachers. Devices were the latest iteration and the kids could get pretty creative in their use.

When the day was over, Buddy and Nathan had a great time getting to know each other on their walk home. Buddy was excited about his first chance at being a member of the school's marching band while Nathan talked about fishing in Idaho's back country. Mostly the boys just enjoyed walking and talking, further cementing their friendship.

10

The Sister School Project

The next morning the two boys met at the corner on their way to school where they'd separated the previous afternoon. The walk to school was a continuation of yesterday's conversation getting to know each other.

The assembly came quickly and Nathan walked in and took a seat in the auditorium. Principal Reese explained the school rules to new students and reminded the continuing students that the rules were still there and in force.

Included, were a bunch of announcements, a recruitment appeal by the football coach and several short pitches from the chess club and a bunch of other school clubs, and finally a performance of the school song from last year's seventh grade choir members. As was usual for the incoming sixth graders, there was a groan when they were asked to join the last verse which they were expected to know before starting school. Policing by the seventh and eighth graders made sure the new students joined the singing.

Following the announcements the principal, with enthusiasm, presented Cabe's offer, although his name was not mentioned as per his request. Mr. Reese told the students he would like to invite volunteers from the sixth, seventh and eighth grades to participate. He explained about the opportunity to distribute money to help another school that needed teaching materials and computers.

"We hope several of you will volunteer and we'd like newcomers to the area to participate so they get to know our students." He also encouraged a few of the older students to participate to make sure there was a good cross section. "Please come to the office to sign up after school," he added.

While Buddy wasn't at all interested, Nathan was the opposite. After the assembly Nathan went up to the stage and asked a couple of questions. "You're new at Rocky Creek," Reese said. "We'd love to have you to help us," Nathan grinned slightly at Reese but didn't commit to joining the process.

"I'll check with my Mom." Nathan said.

Reese noted Nathan's amazing lavender eyes. Haven't seen those very often if ever, he thought, remembering some studies he'd read in college about the impact on eye color when hyper-oxygenation occurs during gestation.

Nathan, meanwhile, hesitated about volunteering because of experiences had at his previous school but he also knew that his mother would be pleased if he helped out.

11

Hacker's Worrisome Find

Herbie's was crowded, but the back table had been reserved. Drobick waved at Herbie and sat down at his table. Thirty seconds after 1 p.m., the guys he was waiting for walked in. He waved a second time and they came over and joined him. The three ordered immediately at Drobick's direction and spent some time in idle chatter while they focused on the pastrami and blintzes, which were fantastic as usual.

The two across the table looked like what a cartoonist would depict when drawing a couple of computer nerds. Hair hadn't seen a comb in months and their clothes looked like Goodwill rejects. But, of course, looks can be deceiving. All computer geeks think they're the best, in this case it could easily be argued that they were because Drobick hired nothing but the best.

Sanjy Kerala was from Southern India. He'd come to America to apply his natural skills to computers at Torrents & Tangents, a computer streaming concern. While he excelled at T & T, like many immigrants, he recognized that he could also work for himself and promptly struck out on his own after hours. His business partner and friend was Billy Smith who was straight from the cornfields of Nebraska.

Billy, spent what seemed like three seemingly endless semesters at Harvard, where he considered the atmosphere oppressive and depressing. The pair met at T & T and were naturally complementary in their skill levels and interests and hit it off. They at once had become legendary in "Nerdville Country" for gathering information that didn't want to be gathered. They were more than first class hackers.

"First," Drobick said, "as usual, this job and everything about it is confidential."

"Yeah, Yeah, Yeah!!" they answered simultaneously. "When it is ever not confidential?"

"This is even more so," Drobick glared. "We need to have as much information as possible on everyone at Rocky Creek School including students, teachers, administrators and staff. The school is in San Marino!"

"Italy or America?" Sanjy asked with half a smile.

"Geeks, ya gotta love em," Drobick thought, adding out loud, "they don't have a Rocky Creek School in Italy that I know of."

"What's the matter Sanjy, you get up on the wrong side of the motherboard this morning" Drobick said. "I just bought you the greatest blintz west of the Azores. You should be a big ray of sunshine. So here's the deal, we need as much as you can find with no backwash period. I want to know where everybody came from, what the parents are worth, how they earned their money, all the students' records including grades, info on the school, even the building."

"When?" Smith asked.

"Friday evening," Drobick said. "I've got to ingest it all by this weekend. No half-fast crap."

Complaints immediately flooded from the pair. "Do you think we're geniuses or somethin'?" Sanjy said. "How much?"

"Five thousand each and nothing if anything's traced." Drobick said with no emotion.

"Seven each," Smith said.

"Done!" Drobick said. "But hard copies only, hand delivered to me at the front door of the North Wood's Inn at precisely 6:59 pm. Nothing electronic. Put the info in a box with birthday wrapping. Deliver it dressed in a delivery uniform."

"See, Sanjy. I knew we should have asked for more, he would have paid it." Smith said.

Which was easily the truth, Drobick silently conceded.

"I've got some other research down the road that's more strictly informational, but I'll get back to you on that," Drobick said as they left in different directions.

12

A High Stakes Game

Tuesday wrapped up with mostly normal business. The current pressing issues had to continue apace, although with Cabe, Jeeves, Palumbo, Drobick and the two computer quad-processor twins, it felt like a whole new corporation had been created and was beginning to spin with way too much wobble.

Without a lot of planning, a plan was nevertheless being developed, a very complex plan with no real outcome defined. It was hardly a secret. The goal was Nathan Farnsworth. What that meant was the real question.

Drobick pondered the situation and its mushrooming momentum. All of this, over an eleven-year-old boy, he thought! Jeeves was getting the human end and he was getting, what could be called, the hard copy details. The two had worked together on other projects and had a mutual respect. But this was definitely a potential black hole from which there might be no escape.

Cabe was unusually quiet. Lots of things that needed attention got pushed back til now, but could wait no longer. He was doing his best to finish things for the beginning of next week when this new "project" would start in earnest.

Vickie had two secretaries of her own who helped keep the office running smoothly and efficiently. They set about working out a schedule that would free up the first three days of next week for Cabe. Meetings and conference calls were rescheduled to make time. Personal meetings became online conference calls while travel and non-priority communications were delayed.

As the more formal discussion of the situation approached, Cabe began to see some possibilities that may not have been obvious at first. His problem, though, was that the incident was a single event. It was certainly impactful but now his more meticulous and thorough self began to emerge. He realized that he just had to wait until he had more facts. But, he was still chomping at the bit to move the whole process forward.

He got Drobick on the intercom, "How did your informational search go?" he asked.

"Look, Max. You've got to quit pushing this so hard. Let it play out. We'll have the facts to see what this whole thing really is--soon. As you know this was one incident," he said. "I suggest you do some backing off, or at least, cooling off. I'll have some information Friday.

I'll absorb it this weekend and we'll really will be able to talk coherently Monday. Until then, just chill!"

No one but Drobick would dare talk to Cabe in that tone, but Drobick was just what Cabe needed. The problem was, that even if Cabe knew he was right, his unrelenting style simply didn't lend itself to following excellent advice, no matter how good or accurate it was.

"OK! OK!" Cabe said, resigning himself to a more measured approach. "Monday then."

Despite Drobick's advice, Cabe called Jeeves and confirmed the meeting with Reese and the student volunteers. "The meeting's at 3 p.m.," Jeeves said.

"I want to be there!" Cabe said.

"Do you really think that's a good idea? It could jinx the meeting," Jeeves said. "You could lose your anonymity and I know you don't want that."

"I'll come, but very low key." Cabe said. "You do all the talking and presentation. I think it would be a good idea to explain that with this opportunity there is a high degree of responsibility.

13

Switcher up Close

Reese read the sign-up list for the sister-school project. As usual, the principal thought, five percent of the kids do ninety-five per cent of the work at schools. He had three volunteers from the seventh and eighth grades but only two for the sixth.

Since Nathan expressed a passing interest after the assembly, Reese decided to call Nathan's parents to see if it would be okay with them if he invited their boy to participate since he was not only new to the school but new to the area.

"Hi Mrs. Farnsworth, Fred Reese here," he said. "I'm Nathan's principal."

Her instant response was, "Is Nathan OK? Is there anything wrong?"

"No nothing," he said. "Actually the opposite. We're having a compassionate service project for a low income area school and would like to have student representatives from each class participate. We announced it at the assembly today, and Nathan showed some interest, but seemed to be a little reluctant. His academic record is outstanding and I'm sure he'd do a great job, just a little hesitant probably because he's new. But, again, I think he'd do a great job and would get to know some of the other kids on the committee. What do you think?"

Alice Farnsworth let out a sigh. Little did Reese know the history behind that sigh. "I can talk to Nathan. What is it you want him to do?"

Ally could best be described as a compassionate spitfire. Her description may seem contradictory, but spitfire just meant that she would help anybody and everybody if they weren't obnoxious." She didn't tolerate sloth by capable people who sponged off others, as she would say. "You can't be truly happy without being engaged in good hard work or a good cause and do it to the best of your ability," was a phrase that she repeated often.

Reese briefly explained the sister school idea and what he wanted the students to do. The first meeting would be at 3 p.m. after school so he wanted to be sure it was okay if Nathan stayed after school. "I'd like to call him myself and invite him to be part of the selection and implementation committee if that would be alright," he said.

"Let me check with him," she said "I'm sure he'd love to serve on the committee. Although he has been teased in the past but I think it would be good to start participating."

Reese simply said, "Eyes?"

"Yeah," Ally said.

"I'll be especially aware," Reese said, "but our kids are pretty good about that stuff. There are lots of kids main-streamed today and I know it can be worrisome."

There seemed to have been quite a bit unsaid, specifically referring to Nathan. But Reese figured he'd get a chance to work with him and get to know him. He seemed like a nice kid. It was also a chance for Reese to fulfill the request from New Tech to help Nathan adjust to his new school.

"Would you mind if I called him back later this afternoon about four or so?"

"Sure. That'd be fine," she said.

Later that afternoon, Reese called Nathan who answered the phone and was expecting the call.

"Hi, Mr. Reese," Nathan said.

"Hello, Nathan," Reese said. "Did you get a chance to talk to your mom about being on the committee?"

"Yes, we talked about it and she said it would be fine with her," Nathan said. "I'd be happy to be on it."

"That's great," Reese said. "I appreciate your help with this. There are 6th, 7th and 8th graders. A couple are new so you'll get a chance to get to know them. If you'll stop by the office, I'll give you a calendar of the meetings. Is there anything else you think you'll need?"

"I don't think so," Nathan said. "I'll see you at the meeting.

Everything was pretty much ready for the Monday meeting for Reese and the students.

14
The Farnsworths

Nathan's arrival in San Marino was a little more complicated than just a change of jobs for his dad, Levi Farnsworth. Farnsworth was a brilliant man with a bright future. He had had full-ride academic scholarships to the best schools—a BA from Brown, MA at Harvard and a PhD from MIT.

His blood lines had some significant names in their pedigree including Philo T. Farnsworth, the inventor of television. His love and penchant for the outdoors led him to select a research project funded by the Idaho Fish and Game Department. His successes at Fish and Game had him periodically crossing paths with researchers at New Tech which prompted intermittent calls from his friends at the prestigious Pasadena school who encouraged him to come to New Tech. But it just wasn't going to happen, at least at that point in Levi's life. The academic research possibilities were enticing, but living in what he considered a big town wasn't an attraction.

New Tech's campus, despite what Levi thought, seemed more like a tree covered park than a big city campus, but that wasn't the question.

Tramping over the mountains and splashing through the rivers of Central Idaho was his idea of heaven. Although New Tech's campus was a tree-shaded sanctuary and even included a higher-academics version of a joke with one of its fountain being called the Gene Pool, it couldn't match Central Idaho's rugged natural beauty. Although he chuckled at the clever name, his enjoyment of his studies of genetics of fish and other animals in and around the Salmon River and the Bitterroot Range kept him anchored in that expansive outdoors.

Farnsworth could not have anticipated his choice of studies in genetics could possibly have become a factor in an existential conflict of his own son's life. Nathan's familial inherited genetics plus some unanticipated gestational ordeals led to his unique genetic composition and genome. Early in Levi's career he and his wife, Alice, had became the parents of Nathan, their first and only child. They hadn't planned it that way, but the circumstances of the gestation and birth made their desire for more children not physically possible.

The issues and circumstances of Nathan's birth put Farnsworth in much closer touch with the department head at New Tech, although most of the calls were about his research for Fish and Game. For eleven years they had communicated frequently until finally he and Ally, a nickname she had become known by, decided they had to make the move when Nathan's special capabilities began to negatively impose on his and their lives. Farnsworth felt he was forced to begin using his research to find answers about Nathan's genetics. Unfortunately, the wilds of Carey, Idaho, and the periodic trips to the "big city," Twin Falls, didn't allow for the answers he sought.

15

Golfing to Relieve Tension

The rush of the initial events of Monday and Tuesday slackened. Palumbo called Cabe Wednesday morning and said he'd found some possibilities for the "venue to 'accommodate' the visitor they'd talked about." Palumbo began referring to the proposed discussion and holding location as the venue but suggested to Cabe that if there were more guidelines it would help. For example: Palumbo asked if a private jet with access was necessary or other such amenities, etc? Cabe told him yes his jet was required along with take-off and landing capabilities within reasonable distance of the airport.

"Oh, one other thing," Cabe said, "We may need enough room to unload a straight box semi transport in addition to holding rooms I also mentioned. So that's about it."

The closer Cabe got to really putting his thinking into operation, the more he began to second guess himself. What happened? Was the incident really like I remember it or was I dreaming something that was much less than remembered. In either case, he determined, he had to know, so everything was still on. He took a deep breath and rubbed his chin.

Cabe decided he needed a break to take a little pressure off and let his mind act like a smooth flat rock doing a little lake skipping. His choice was to drive down to San Diego, meet with a partner in a building acquisition there and get in a round of golf.

He called Vickie, who had developed a genius at impossible managing, last minute, arrangements. "Can you see if you can get me an overnight tonight at the Coronado? I've got a meeting with Jamie Towns on the building down there. I think he's got a membership at Torre Pines and see if he can get a tee time in the morning. I'm thinking Wednesday. It'll be a little easier. Yeah, I know, good luck," he finished the call.

If there was something at which Vickie shined, it was this kind of stuff. Seemed she knew somebody in management at all of the top hotels, although with Cabe's vast holdings and constant travel, it was hard not to know lots of people at his favorite haunts. As for the golf, she called her counterpart at Towns and Ross Real Estate and checked to see what she could do.

It didn't take long until the Coronado called back and had a suite available and luckily Torre Pines had a last minute 7:30 tee time cancellation so they immediately booked the slot. When Cabe's name was dropped, it was seldom that he didn't get what he wanted. Town's executive assistant said Jamie was pleased about meeting on the course and just what he needed. So the break Cabe wanted was perfect for both. Cabe got his respite, finished the negotiations with Towns and shot a 91 complaining that the third and eighth traps were in collusion with his clubs and personally out to get him. Overall, though, it gave him some time to ponder. Thinking between shots on the bright green grass with views of the ocean was a welcome relief. The smell of the crisp, clean, blue, Pacific air seemed to refine and heighten his senses.

16

A Rocky Creek Surprise

Long before dinner, Drobick was getting antsy. He wondered if his imperatives to his two researchers were inclusive enough. It was usually the little things that really provided the clues to most deals. In this case, it was much more of a guessing game. He began his "I can't believe you're doing this" thinking but knew it was a waste of time going down that dead end.

A thought from his past crossed his mind that came from an old boss of his from New York. Ol' Al Shulman would come out to the west coast and nearly, every time, he would tell the employees, "You're asking the wrong questions." That was Drobick's predicament, "What were the right questions?"

His wife drove over from her office at Wilcox and Sunset. It wasn't that far in miles but traffic timing was a different story. She got to

Drobick's office at 6:28 p.m. that afternoon. He saw her at the door and waived her in.

"Hi sweets," he said. "How was the drive?"

"Drive was okay but as usual it was the time factor. Almost forty-five minutes. Seems to be getting more and more claustrophobic, especially on the freeway" she said.

"No problem, it's a nine minute walk to the North Wood's Inn." He said, "I'm just about done. We can take our time and just saunter for a bit. We'll be there in plenty of time."

The pair walked hand in hand enjoying their leisurely stroll. They arrived at precisely 6:58 but Drobick paused. "Got a delivery coming," he said. Within a few seconds, Sanjy arrived in his uniform as directed, and handed his package wrapped as a birthday present. He gave Sanjy a "tip" in an envelope and accepted the box.

His wife smiled and asked, "Is that for me?"

"Sorry babe, it's for Cabe, just a bunch of papers." He opened the box and took out the envelope, tossing the wrapping in an outside trash bin. I do have something much nicer for you. Let's go in and have dinner. They sat down and Drobick pulled out a small beautifully wrapped box. "Max got this for you in China, at my request of course. He went to the pearl market and found this beautiful double string of 'coin' pearls, the best they had."

The pearls included a special clasp that could be worn as a short pendant. They were stunning and a beautiful variation on plain round pearls. They were shaped like a coin, smooth but not totally flat. They had a mild texture on the surface allowing the pearl's essence to seemingly glow with even more depth than just conventional pearls.

She was thrilled, "I love them," she said.

The aromas of broiled cheese bread, cheese spread on the russets and steak dominated Drobick's attention. "Enough of this mushy stuff, I'm starved," he said as their waitress brought their first courses, bread and red cabbage salad. "Just in time," Drobick said. They enjoyed their salads, filets baked potatoe and finished by sharing a small chocolate rum sundae.

After dinner they strolled back to the office and chilled with the bottle of wine from the dome's refrigerator and went to sleep.

Drobick opened the envelope early Saturday morning. It was comprehensive, organized and precisely what he was looking for. As usual, Sanjy and Billy had done their job well.

He examined Rocky Creek Middle School's building plans and layout first. It was built in 1978 and opened for classes in September of that year. Typical construction for the time period including sprinklers and some innovative ahead-of-its-time seismic reinforcements, perhaps suggested by New Tech engineers, some whose kids might have attend the school.

The staff info was pretty standard stuff. Most had been at the school for more than five years. The newest member was in her second year. Financials for the staff were also common investment vehicles, but higher by comparison to other schools in less affluent areas.

Drobick spent much of Saturday and Sunday assimilating the entire packet. As expected, none of the research yielded much unexpected data. But in one piece of miscellaneous information, Drobick found a notation to Rocky Creek officials that a New Tech professor or assistant had called the school confirming the enrollment of a certain student by the name of Nathan Farnsworth. The request had asked to make sure that Nathan was welcomed and suggested he/she be called if the school needed any help. The name or gender of the caller had not been included.

For Drobick it was one of those pieces of information that seemed innocuous enough at first, but with the sudden interest of Cabe, this small notation could mean something else entirely. Interest by a New Tech Professor in a specific child with a request for some personal attention suggested a "special needs" student. It was more than enough to arouse suspicions. He wondered if Nathan's "special needs" would require special treatment. It was just these little pieces of info that Drobick was famous for finding.

There was also another interesting comment written that went along with what Cabe had reported. Billy had included that there was a big fight on the first day of school on the sidewalk outside the front gate. It seems some young gang members punched out a kid and they were sent screaming away seconds after it started. Nobody knows why they scattered, but many students said they seemed to be crying in fear. Don't know if this is important but thought you'd like to know, Billy wrote.

Drobick was, of course, more than aware of the fight incident, because of Cabe's narration. Nothing but those couple of notations on the fight and New Tech seemed to apply and even the New Tech thing was a little disconcerting. But maybe one of these things would be what made Sanjy and Billie's big fee worth it. He now knew someone very important was paying attention to Nathan too. The tenor of the note, however, seemed to indicate a genuine concern more than some nefarious deception.

He and his wife spent a quiet and very relaxing late Sunday afternoon and evening. "Tomorrow," Drobick thought, "I may begin a process with almost no way of determining its real meaning or value." It all seemed too insane to even think about but also so potentially intriguing. It was just too delicious not to proceed.

17

Newton Institute's Apparent Connection

Other issues consumed Cabe's time after returning from San Diego. He went straight home instead of going into the office and asked his chef to prepare dinner for Jeeves and himself in the pool's gazebo. This was common for him to have dinner with Jeeves since the "butler" managed much more than just this property.

Cabe was particularly interested in planning their visit to Rocky Creek. They sat down for a dinner of roasted chicken and rice with a garlic and lemon dip and broccoli salad. Whenever Cabe was heading into a particularly critical project and wanted his head clear as possible he avoided any alcohol, including wine. He was especially cognizant of the potential of the school meeting.

"So, whadda ya think," Cabe began looking at Jeeves out of the corner of his eye. In this relaxed setting where rank was essentially suspended, he hoped to get not only a candid response but some evaluation too.

"I know something big happened to you," Jeeves started. "What it was and what it means is anybody's guess, most of all mine. It isn't so much the incident as much as it is what you're going to do once you get a look into this kid's head. I'll be interested to see this eye-piercing mutant. I hope he doesn't fry my brain as he appears to have yours," he said, without looking at Cabe.

Cabe smiled. "Don't think he's going to do that but Monday's meeting should give us more of a chance to see what's going to happen. By the way, I'm going to dress down and go with you. I'll sit in the back and observe. "

The rest of the weekend was quiet. Monday started out a whole different story. Traffic was terrible and Cabe thought about the close proximity of Century City to Bel Aire instead of the longish ride from San Marino. He'd have time to just get in his meeting with Drobick and a couple of other things before he had to head back to Rocky Creek School.

But the ride wasn't that bad. His security/driver was all too happy to act as chauffer and get away from the house a little. They arrived at his office at 9 a.m. He went straight to Drobick's office and stuck his head in the door. Drobick was making a few notes on the points he was going to discuss.

"How's 10 in the dome sound?" he asked.

"I'll be there," Drobick looked up with a downcast scowl on his face.

Apparently, the why of all this was getting to everybody involved. Cabe made some calls, signed the San Diego deal for Towns, and had Vickie send the signed copy it back. Then at 9:15 he ended his regular work to start thinking about what may have been found in Drobick's research. Cabe tried to anticipate the expected questions. He expected he'd have a couple of hours with Drobick, because if his prognostications were anywhere near reality, a lot had to be decided.

18

What's Important? What's Critical?

Drobick was walking down the hall and Cabe came out of his office and right into step with him. They walked to the dome in silence. The coffee was on and ready.

"Before we officially start," Cabe said, "You know Jeeves and I are meeting with Reese at the school and Nathan will be in the meeting. I'm going just to observe and evaluate. I promise, if I can't or don't see any reason to pursue this I'll drop it. But my gut is telling me something else."

Drobick grabbed coffee and Cabe had a bottle of water. Drobick brought out his information that he'd gone through systematically and Cabe took it all in making mental notes as Drobick shared what he thought was most important.

After the first round of information, Drobick said, "I haven't found anything much about the school, teachers or staff that stands out."

Drobick switched focus to Nathan's parents: "Levi Farnsworth is a first class geneticist for Idaho Fish and Game. "Papa is one very bright guy but liked the outdoors and it took New Tech a while to corral him into their fold. Why he finally agreed to accept a genetics research position may be crucial in his decisions involving both Nathan and moving. Good Dad! Never made much there and his salary at the university is commensurate with other top line researchers and just enough to get him a fixer-upper in the less expensive section of town."

"Ally, is a stay-at-home mom but has a very active life in helping the less fortunate. She probably infused Nathan with a good deal of natural empathy with her desire to help others. It could explain your reading of him through your 'connection.' His experiences with his mom may have led to your conclusion that Nathan learned his compassion from his mother's nature.

"I'll check over the info again, see if anything comes up, but at this point, it doesn't look like much of anything," Drobick paused.

Cabe read him like a tweet. As hard as Drobick tried to be nonchalant about some little piece of info, Cabe knew something else was coming. "Ok Mike, let's have it." Cabe said.

Drobick reluctantly began, "I just don't know if this is anything useful or not. Before the Farnsworths got here, some top level genetics guy and high muckety-muck from Tech called the school, told the administration Nathan was coming, and to please make an effort to make sure Nathan was 'comfortable' in his new school. There are a ton of possibilities and interpretations of the cryptic notation. My first inclination was that Nathan was a special needs kid. But adding the things you've gleaned, I think it's a bunch more. I just can't tell if it's sinister or saintly. This is where adding two and two ends up why."

"OK Einstein, keep up the math." Cabe pushed.

Drobick added, "First I'm going to make several assumptions. Nathan's special nature isn't a hindrance in the sense of a mental or physical handicap. In fact, Nathan's academics could easily put him in high school if not college. He has his father's intelligence and intuitive thinking. He may have amazing capabilities no other human has ever had.

"The kicker is that Nathan's capabilities could be a combination apparently absorbed from his mother's much heightened sense of protection and his own fire in the belly relating to heightened capacity. It's also a potentially negative influence in his nature. And that's about it."

Cabe took a slow sip of water and grabbed an almond cookie from Japan. "Want one?" He asked.

"Sure" Drobick said. "I'm speculating wildly here but it seems obvious to me as a father that his parents are simply adjusting to Nathan's particular needs?"

After a swig, Cabe leaned his head on the back of his leather chair and closed his eyes. Again, because the two men had worked together so closely and for so long, Drobick knew to wait.

It was a moment of silence before Cabe started, "I think you've confirmed for me that a next step is absolutely required. My meeting this afternoon should be a further confirmation. I'll be fascinated to see what Nathan is like in person! I'll call you after our meeting. If you find anything else adding up two and two, I'd be very interested to hear. As usual, your knack for finding those critical morsels is amazing, which is why I pay you the big bucks,"

Cabe said. "Mike, we're coming to some very critical decisions. Please be wary. Don't let me go into that dark abyss."

The pair left. Drobick went to his office. Cabe asked Vickie to text his driver to have the car ready in five.

The trip back to San Marino was another tedious slog through what seemed like the entire driving population of every car, truck, RV, motorcycle, semi and SUV in Los Angeles. He arrived home just in time to change into something much more appropriate for the situation and he acted as chauffer for Jeeves.

19

First Day Flashback

Four tables were set up in the form of a square at the front of a large class room. There were name plaques on each of the tables for the three grades. Name plaques included one for Mr. Reese and for Mr. McClain Bills (or Jeeves according to Cabe). Cabe took a seat against the wall a few feet from the tables for observation, hoping that his nervously bouncing knee would go unnoticed. He didn't want even inadvertent body language to reveal his total focus on the boy.

Cabe immediately recognized Nathan when he came in and his attention went into instant hyper drive. His first thought was: Who is this kid? Then he amended his first thought and wondered: "What is this kid?" Both questions were valid.

Cabe wore a pair of light-sensitive glasses. The lenses didn't fully change to clear which helped conceal any minute or abrupt pupil changes in his eyes that he worried might attract Nathan's attention.

He was not sure of just what Nathan might remember from their first encounter.

With the glasses and a chauffeur uniform with a funky cap, Cabe, who was a known media figure, hoped Reese would focus on Jeeves, and not recognize him. Reese and Bills had worked together before and assumed the principal's attention would be focused on Jeeves. It worked.

Cabe appeared calm and collected, appearing to use his I-Phone, but his attention on Nathan was acute. He noticed Nathan's every twitch and movement so it wasn't hard for him to mentally record Nathan's gut reaction when the boy first saw and obviously recognized Miguel Nieto, a seventh grade representative, seated across from the sixth grade table. Then it dawned on Cabe that Miguel may have been one of the gang members who attacked Buddy. There seemed to be no reaction at all from Miguel but Nathan's demeanor seemed to tighten around himself as though he was ready to condense into a one boy black hole.

It was Miguel's mere presence that put Nathan on edge. Miguel came to the meeting as a representative of the seventh grade. It was not surprising that Miguel hadn't recognized Nathan or connected him in any way to the Monday morning fight. Neither he nor any of the other gang members had any clue where the attack of emotional fear had come, least of all Miguel.

It seemed like an odd kind of reaction at first, but when Cabe made the connection, he realized it would have been a predictable reaction. Cabe didn't have time to dwell on it.

Mr. Reese rose, gave the obligatory thanks to the students who accepted the opportunity to participate and introduced "Mr. Bills." Jeeves stood, thanked Mr. Reese and mentioned his "assistant" sitting at the back of the room. He turned and nodded in Cabe's direction with a sly smirk. He thanked the students, and at the critical moment pulled out a check for $45,000 from an anonymous donor and told the kids what he hoped they'd accomplish with the money and handed the mic back to Mr. Reese.

Mr. Reese also reminded the kids that any additional money they could raise for the project would be doubled by the philanthropist. "That's a generous donation and a chance for us to make a difference." he said.

Cabe listened and smiled as his name was not mentioned, as it should not have been, but noted the gottcha and plotted to get "Mr. Bills" for that one.

Jeeves had outlined the principles and concepts he wanted the kids to consider as part of the proposal but added that the important point was to spend the money efficiently. "We'd like to hear what you students think would be the best way to handle the funds to help another school."

The meeting was turned over to the kids and the eighth graders took the lead proposing some suggestions about how they should organize into groups to talk about ideas using the contribution. When the seventh graders spoke, Cabe was totally focused not on them, but directly on Nathan. The boy's tense reaction when Miguel spoke stunned Cabe again. Nathan's focus was just as intent as Cabe's, but it was directed at the seventh grader. Why? The fight was long over, why the residual anger?

Miguel seemed like a nice enough kid. He started his comments but as he noticed the piercing stare of Nathan, he became agitated. Eye diversion, in some cultures, was a sign of respect but Nathan was having none of that.

Only Cabe seemed to pick up on the increasing tension. He was surprised when he saw Nathan's hand, which was on the table directly across from Miguel, move to deliberately and directly point at the standing boy. Again, only Cabe noticed it. Everyone else was preoccupied with the discussion at hand. Even Mr. Bills, who had come to help Cabe get a close look at Nathan, didn't notice the slight movement, which had meaning to only one other person in the room.

There it was, that same fear Cabe saw on Reuben and the faces of other gang members that first day of school. It flashed cross the seventh grader's face and he sat down abruptly, shaking slightly but under control. Cabe knew. Miguel was definitely one of the kids in the gang. The other adults chalked it up to nerves, but Cabe had seen it before and realized the "incident" on the sidewalk Monday was no fluke. It was not imaginary. It was a very expensive confirmation, but to Cabe, well worth the cost.

It was all like a subliminal circus where amazing events had occurred, and no one but he, had noticed but still hadn't fully comprehended. Cabe gradually realized that even Miguel wasn't aware of the hand movement or where the fear he received had came from. Cabe was now unalterably hooked putting every potential on the table. The little display, he'd witnessed also stirred something in Cabe's gut.

This close up encounter with Nathan made him realize his first plot needed to be altered substantially. As Cabe knew, the first casualty of war is your plan, if that's what this was. An incident like what just happened, he knew, had to be somehow recorded for a final confirmation. He had to test Nathan under some kind of manufactured and yet totally controlled conditions. The events would have to be recorded in all ways possible. If that test proved his hypothesis with observations by his team, then and only then, would it be total immersion. Every detail," he thought. "Every detail!"

He would set up some kind of confrontation to which Nathan would have to respond, record the event so the outcome could be thoroughly evaluated. It was probably good Drobick wasn't here. That indefinable abyss Drobick warned him about was staring him right in the face.

20

A New Modus Operandi

Getting into Nathan's brain was not going to be easy but Cabe was willing to do whatever it took. He realized too, that it would have to be in a totally controlled setting to be valid. The unknowable prospects were near deal-killers because he was convinced that the rewards for learning Nathan's innate capabilities were enormous.

If he could adapt what he felt with Nathan's power and project or switch someone else's emotions directly into another person's mind without the person being able to control the input, his communications empire would be a mere speck in the world of communications control. That kind of emotional control was potentially limitless.

A viable plan began condensing in Cabe's mind. It would have to be copacetic from beginning to end, to have even the slightest possibility of succeeding. "Time for Palumbo," Cabe determined.

Before he called, he had a disturbing thought. It had been lurking in, but had not emerged from the back of his subconscious. He finally admitted that it just may be that Nathan had a bit of a vindictive streak and that worried him greatly. If Miguel had been 'punished' at Nathan's instigation in the meeting, then could it be a harbinger of more vicious responses in other settings? Hopefully, it was the act of someone who was just young. Unfortunately, if Nathan had this trait and it ended up in the wrong hands, that would be a massive and chilling realization.

Palumbo answered his phone. "Hi, boss. Got some ideas, as I said earlier."

"Sounds good but we'll get to that in time. I do need to meet you and plan something and you need to be fully on board. It has to be in person. Can you meet me at the office tomorrow at 7?" Cabe asked. "We can outline the plans and goals."

"At 7." Palumbo said, "Tell you what I found then."

Besides the questions boiling in Cabe's mind about Nathan's possible retaliatory thinking, another potentially disrupting thought crossed his mind and he didn't have an answer for that either. It involved the seemingly out of place New Tech calls. He would have expected it from a mom or dad, but New Tech? There could be a simple innocuous answer but it kept gnawing at him and he couldn't get the more sinister interpretations out of his mind.

He assumed it wouldn't have been possible that Nathan's parents didn't know of the boy's powers and therefore his potential. What if the move to Tech was more than just a job decision and was a way to study Nathan or possibly an escape from problems at his former school where Nathan may have been constantly taunted?

Lots of questions flooded Cabe's mind and their associated latent affects. For now, he just had to figure out how he was going to convince Palumbo that all they had to do was abduct Nathan, examine him and attempt to learn how he might be able to tap into the boy's powers. OK, there! He put it into actual thought. That was the abyss. It was potentially exceptionally dark, and maybe pathetic. "I am nuts," Cabe's thought drifted off.

How does anybody confront a situation where the outcome might affect every living soul on earth? That was Cabe's gift. He could see potential. Nathan was the essence of potential. Then there was the other side of his insight. "If I saw it, who else might have?"

Cabe ruminated on those competing and worrisome questions for the remainder of the day while doing what had become more and more mundane, but necessary chores to maintain his empire.

The Palumbo meeting, he realized, was his greatest gamble. It could be his greatest success and like no other or it could wind up with his arrest, an interminable trial, then not passing go but going directly to jail.

21

The Plan Comes into Focus

Cabe's trip to his office was early, four in the morning. It was also a very quiet trip as his reflections continued and especially now that he was actually initiating the planning to take Nathan. His doubts remained, but surprisingly, his predictable reluctance had all but vanished.

Not wanting to be interrupted, Cabe went into the dome with a yellow legal pad. He began to formalize what he hoped the results could be that would make his highly risky actions worthwhile.

The list was relatively short, mostly because the unknowables list was so long, but the one factor that he couldn't ignore was without a close examination of Nathan, he would never know how the boy's powers really worked.

At precisely 7 a.m. Palumbo walked into the dome.

Without pretense or even a hello, Cabe began. "Dick, there are a few things I need to explain and get your ok on. First, what I'm going to do is illegal." There was a slight raising of an eyebrow but Palumbo didn't even blink. "It's sort of like abducting a kid, or more accurately, forcing him to respond to a certain stimuli all the while recording it. It could be risky both to you and everybody involved."

"It will take substantial planning in a place where there are no prying eyes, ears or electronic gnomes. I believe you said you've found a place where such a discussion could be had. I'm assuming that from the very beginning you were aware of the clandestine nature of what we'll talk about."

Palumbo did not respond but listened intently.

"Before I get you into more trouble, you should know the situation. If you choose not to work with me on this, there's no problem. I fully understand. It's just too dangerous not to have you know from the beginning what the risks are," Cabe said.

"I guess you already know me well enough to know I'm in," Palumbo said. I knew from your immediate intense interest that whatever this was, it was way beyond normal projects. "But, what is the payoff? And, is it worth it. Copping a kid is a huge step, even for you. It's a Federal Offense. You could lose everything including your freedom."

"I'll be very direct but my answers won't be very satisfying," Cabe said. My honest answers are: I don't know and I don't know. But I do know there are answers I have to have.

"Sorry boss, but that isn't too reassuring if you don't know why you are doing this?" Palumbo said.

"Before I answer that Dick, let me tell you a short version of the pertinent facts as I see them. Then we'll get back to your question. A lot of this may sound somewhat crazy and like I told Drobick, I'd rather be thought of as ruthless than crazy," Cabe said.

Palumbo was now listening warily and said, "I understand that!" He turned his whole focus on their discussion.

"Here goes," Cabe began. "I inadvertently recorded the whole incident as it happened on Drobick's phone on the office system. I'm going to play it and fill in the details. Remember, I was trying to repeat precisely what I was seeing and feeling."

He started the tape. Palumbo listened while Cabe relived the whole episode in his mind's eye. He felt every nuance and emotional impact again just as if he were still feeling Nathan's power. He then related the incidents he observed at the school meeting that confirmed to him he was right.

Palumbo appeared to be waiting for the other shoe to drop for which he would have no witty response.

"So there it is," Cabe said. I believe that this eleven-year-old boy is endowed with a totally different kind of power that has never previously been known. I don't know what it is precisely and that's a kind of answer to your question about why, but the power I felt was real.

"What needs to happen now is for us to test the power and see if we can have the boy recreate it. That's where you come in. I want to set up a situation for the kid to react to the one I experienced. I should say, repeat the actions I witnessed. As in the case, of the bully beating, I want to see if he'll come to the aid of someone he doesn't know. Since this was the first day of school, I'm not too sure whether the kid knew the victim but my inclination is that he did not. They weren't walking together or anything like that.

"We know his schedule for school, but presenting the right triggering mechanism for a response from him is a guess. I believe that it has something to do with his switching emotions or in this case injecting the emotional fear from one person under attack directly into the attacker's mind. Again it's just a guess at this point, but the theory does answer a few things, like the fear on the gang members faces. That's what he appeared to do in both the fight and in our school meeting.

To say Palumbo was dumbfounded would be a little unfair, but to say he was speechless would be more accurate. It was three sips of coffee and some stewing before he said a word. Cabe let his comments hang. He knew it was a lot to take in, but finally Palumbo gathered himself and let out a big breath.

"That's a whole lot to swallow," Palumbo said. "It sounds like you're telling me you think you've discovered," searching for the right words, "some kind of super power?

"That's what everybody says," Cabe said.

"OK," Palumbo began, "Let me see if I understand this. You want a test of the kid's capabilities?"

"Yes," Cabe said, confirming Palumbo's unease, "but this time I want to record everything in as much detail as possible: sound and video, et cetera. I just have to know that my observations are not my over-hyped imagination. Obviously, I understand it's not going to be easy. The good thing is I know your capabilities and I suggest you drop everything, turn over everything you're working on now to somebody else, and begin immediately."

"Any suggestions on a scenario?" Palumbo asked. "I'm not totally sure about the nature of what we have to do."

"I'd suggest getting to know his routine and where he goes and see what place looks the best. Remember to assume that, you're going to be seen so set up several escape possibilities for yourself. The incident could be a purse snatching, something like that. But a person has to be threatened and Nathan has to see and respond. Put together a couple of ideas and let's talk," Cabe said.

"Look, Dick, again, I know this is totally off-the-wall. But this effort to record something is just to triple confirm my suppositions. I promise that once I understand the results, I'll give you a better explanation of my thinking," Cabe said. "You and everybody crazy enough to help will deserve it. If this gambit works, we'll get it recorded and with some kind of verifiable intel, we'll be able to move forward on a more direct intervention. Nothing about this is for sure. That's what we're trying to determine," Cabe said.

"OK, let me put some ideas together. I'll do some reconnaissance of the area for the recording."

"Drobick has all the addresses involved so you can get them from him," Cabe said, finishing the conversation, and then added. "If you call your boss a loony toon, I'll understand!"

With that, Palumbo went back to his office and began putting together some ideas to run by Cabe later. Video and sound would be the most difficult but with today's miniature sound and video capabilities and the potential of hacking some security cameras, it might not be quite as difficult or intrusive in setting them up as he'd first thought.

22

The Expectations Exceeded

Palumbo, focused on his target early on. He collected information on Nathan's daily activities which he found quite consistent. Apparently, Nathan's mother insisted on his return from school on time, every day, unless preplanned. For her, it was OK when he met with Reese and the compassionate service committee after school because that was pre-planned. She believed Nathan was safer running round in the Idaho wilds with black bears and wolves than the streets of a large city.

It was Wednesday which didn't conflict with activities going on at school so Ally expected Nathan would be returning home on time. Problems at his previous school were still relatively fresh in her mind and she didn't want a re-occurrence. She remembered one case when Nathan was accused of attacking one boy and the police were called in even with no evidence or even a witness.

To say, go record someone doing something doesn't sound that hard. To do it surreptitiously on a city street with both sound and video is a different story. Palumbo began by Google-Earthing the entire site area. He examined the address info from Drobick and mapped out three potential video tape sites. He examined the locations from Google Earth Ground Level and started to hone in on a spot that would potentially work given the typical routes Nathan took home. Onsite inspections would follow before the test would be implemented.

Planning an "event" that would test Nathan was a matter of more concern. He thought about a "purse snatch," but that was too much of a grab and run than a ground and pound as in this case. He determined to make the situation as similar as possible to the original incident at the school, but it would also have to be a little different.

Palumbo put up a map. He plotted locations where vehicles could be inconspicuously parked to record data. With access to the best micro cameras and mics he decided that that part was easily doable. But since there would be no direct contact with the boy, installation and location were critical.

Palumbo called his tech guy, Mark Harding, and explained that he wanted to stage a situation. He told Harding that he wanted to do an on-the-street, real time, totally obscured shoot. He said it was a test for another big job coming up that would require hidden recording video and sound.

"I've got roughly fifty feet of sidewalk to set up for the test, both sound and video," he said. "Any problem with the distances? When we do the real thing, I'll have determined the parameters. There are three options, but the site I'm thinking about is a very quiet residential area. Maybe we can catch a couple of kids walking by to test the sound and video."

"The distance is no problem," Harding said. "What's the situation with obscuring the installation locations?"

"Trees, sidewalks at a vacant lot, for the test." Palumbo said, but he didn't even hint why the tree cover was necessary.

"Shouldn't be a problem," Harding said.

Palumbo asked "How many camera/audio recorders do you think we'll need?"

"Depends on how deep you want the coverage but I'd say four on the ground, one or two in a car." Harding said.

Palumbo wasn't exactly forthcoming in his presentation to Harding, but stealth was paramount. "How about we go to the area and see what's available. You can get a better idea of potential sites and see what's works when we set up the best site." Although he had other test site possibilities, the sidewalk location that he would propose to

Harding was his first choice. He was confident it was the ideal place to record Nathan on his way home from school.

"How about I pick you up at, say 2:15 tomorrow afternoon? Since you're in Alhambra, it's not too far and we can get a good fix on the site," Palumbo said.

Palumbo's plan was designed to be as simple as possible with as few people involved as possible. Two hours before he picked up Harding, he was examining the possibilities near Rocky Creek School. It was a 1, 2, 3 option. Number one was a vacant lot with trees near the sidewalk, parking space nearby, while the other two options were less than ideal after their onsite inspection. In addition there was one more potential serendipitous situation. A house across the street from the vacant lot was for sale and empty. A car parked in the driveway would not be unexpected, particularly if it had a real estate sign on the door.

23

A Location Determined

As arranged, Palumbo picked up Harding at 2:15 and knew it would take about ten minutes or so to get there and that Nathan would most likely walk by with his new friend Buddy.

Harding evaluated the three sites and, as Palumbo expected, picked the vacant lot.

Harding brought a brief case. When they arrived at the site, Harding told Palumbo to pull into the driveway of the vacant house for sale. He then walked across the street stood by one of the trees turned as though he were taking pictures of the vacant house from different angles, leaned against a couple of other trees and returned to the car. "What was that for?" Palumbo asked.

"Just a test of a test?" Harding said.

He opened his case, turned on a monitor and voila, a prefect scene of the sidewalk complete with sound displayed the setup they could see. The cameras had been placed perfectly without Palumbo even realizing it and were virtually invisible.

"What will they think of next," Palumbo said.

Even better, as though on cue, three kids came down the sidewalk passing by, easily recognizable in the monitor and easily heard. Even better, Nathan and Buddy weren't far behind. Palumbo recognized Nathan from a photo Cabe had quietly taken at the school meeting.

"This is a good demonstration proving the effective placement and proof of the equipment. I'd just like to get a longer distance on the sidewalk. We need to have about a thirty-five second time frame for the video and sound. As slowly as the kids walk I would say that the corners of the lot would be good. There's also a tree in the parking strip that could handle a camera." Palumbo praised Harding. "Great job Mr. Real Estate photographer and I loved the way you placed those cameras, sort of a Dirty Rotten Scoundrels pose."

"The broadcasting distances are exceptionally short too, so no one else is likely to pickup any stray signals," Harding said. "They're also short directional so if we park in this driveway for the test there is little chance we'll feed into anyone's computer. The cameras are exceptionally small and nearly impossible to notice without looking very closely."

"Does that come with a flash drive? I'd like to take it back to the office to check it out but I think you've got this knocked." Palumbo said.

Harding handed him the flash drive, pleased with Palumbo's praise.

"Surveillance isn't cheap," Harding said. "Keeping my mouth shut is even more expensive."

"Two-thousand for today's time and we'll set things up for tomorrow, same time, same place," Palumbo said. "If everything works as well as the test, which I might point out, shouldn't be more than a day's time max for everything. That's the goal."

"The real test would be an additional $10,000 plus expenses with you as a very silent partner when we do the real thing." Palumbo said, "If the real event possibility gets scrubbed we'll make it an even $3,000."

"Fair enough," Harding said.

"I suggest you get things set up on the street for the full test. Doing the real estate thing is a good cover. Just remember the distances and times," Palumbo said. "Tomorrow at two."

24

Recorded in Action

Palumbo knew that timing was everything. It was important to know where and when Nathan would be today. He'd like to get everything in one take and thus the multiple camera locations. Palumbo made one more stipulation for Harding. "I'm not expecting anything, but no matter what, do not reveal yourself from the van or that you're recording. That's what will have to happen when we set up the real thing. Don't reveal yourself, period, no matter what you see!"

Harding spent the morning testing and syncing his lap tops and programming a format Palumbo could easily examine in detail. He came with a yard-cleaning van and even did some yard work while setting the cameras in the back of his vehicle. He double checked the sync for the cameras set in the sidewalk trees. He had installed the fifth camera with a wide-view, high resolution in the back of the van shooting through the rear window.

Harding's totally calm demeanor said two things. First, he was a consummate professional at this sort of thing and secondly, in his mind, this was simply a test which he could easily re-record at another time if something went wrong.

It had been a week and a half since the original incident and though Cabe's mood had seemed to fluctuate by the hour over that time, Palumbo knew everything was rolling smoothly so far and kept Cabe updated.

Palumbo selected a parking lot just a block away from the spot of the recording. He didn't plan to be there or watch it. Harding was good at his job and didn't need direction from him and besides he could hear Harding comment as he prepared on a separate phone but not on the computer recording of the boys.

At the expected time, Nathan and Buddy could be seen knocking against each other as they walked as friends occasionally do at that age. Harding put everything in record mode and waited. The wide camera had picked the pair up almost at the corner where they turned.

Harding, a hard-core tech equipment wizard, checked his devices and everything was nominal, he thought to himself, using an old traditional Jet Propulsion Laboratories term, meaning everything was operating within specs and looking good.

Just as the boys came into view of the tree mounted cameras a woman wearing some very obvious bling stepped out into the street from the other side of the road and headed to the sidewalk the boys were on. But just as she did that, a car with another woman screeched to a stop beside the bling girl. The driver immediately jumped out and took the second girl to the ground. Unfortunately, for the robber, the bling girl wouldn't give up her purse or jewelry without a fight. The car driver started pounding her to let it all go.

Harding groaned from the back of the van, "What is this?" he said. As per unalterable instructions from Palumbo, he knew he had to remain hidden no matter what occurred outside the van.

Then he noticed one of the boys appear to point at the fight, thought again about Palumbo's warning and let the scene play out. Buddy had frozen in his tracks, the same terror in his eyes as in the school fight still fresh in his mind. Nathan on the other hand was calm and totally focused on the attempted bling snatcher. It was over in a blink.

The woman got up, still with her purse, gold chain and pride mostly still intact and within half a second, both girls were screaming and laughing and both jumped into the same car that had stopped. Fortunately, each had only a few scratches as far as the boys could tell.

The car burned rubber leaving the boys staring and wondering. Buddy looked at Nathan with a slight bit of wonder saying, "That was stupid," Buddy said. He hadn't seen his friend do anything, but felt an almost palpable emotional power coming from Nathan, but said nothing about that.

Harding continued giving birth to his cow, phoning Palumbo immediately and demanding that he call the police.

Palumbo let out a laugh almost loud enough to break Harding's eardrums.

"It was all a set up," Palumbo said still laughing. Tell me something. What color was the car?

"Don't know," Harding said.

"How about the make?" Palumbo asked.

"Don't know" Harding said, "it doesn't matter. We have it all on tape including sound. I made a quick check and everything was working great.

Palumbo let out another laugh. "Hey, the woman was my secretary, the girls were a couple of friends and I got you good."

Harding's pique receded little, "This is going to cost you another $2000. I don't like surprises."

"OK, OK," Palumbo said. "Just thought I'd make the test interesting," as he continued to chuckle.

"This better not happen in the real thing," Harding said. "You're lucky that no neighbor witnessed this thing. If someone lived in this house they'd have called the cops."

"No problem," Palumbo said, "just some fun in the shade of those old oak trees with cameras rolling. By the way, can you take a look at the video and sound and tell me what you got."

"You jerk. I'm gunna get you for this one," Harding said as he double-checked the sound and video. "Looks and sounds great."

Meanwhile, Nathan and Buddy walked to the next block and headed in opposite directions on the way to their homes. Buddy wanted to call the police immediately, but Nathan was reluctant. Having experienced some less than positive exchanges with police, he convinced Buddy to be quiet about it.

"The gal was ok, so we just have to be more aware," Nathan said.

Buddy understood Nathan not wanting to get more involved because he knew it could be a problem, and he didn't want any more than he already had in the fight. When he saw the guys who beat him up at school he cringed every time. "That's enough for now," he thought, "and decided to let this incident go too.

Harding collected all the cameras in less than thirty seconds and drove to the lot where Palumbo was parked.

He jumped out of the van, yelled at Palumbo, and added a half serious punch for emphasis. "I'd better get that bonus," and handed him two flash drives. The first drive was the compilation of the tree cameras including sound. The second was the wide angle camera shot covering just about everything that might be a threat or witness. It ran on a separate system and used a longer lens for the shot and was not obviously visible to anyone walking by. Palumbo had Harding record only on the flash drive so it was the only copy of what happened. Bleach Bit that part of your drive, Palumbo insisted.

He handed Harding $500 and said, "Your having a cow was my favorite part! Just proves you can easily do the real thing--but I know it won't be anywhere near as fun as it was today. You might even like the location, although we may not have the cover we had for the test. It's in Sun Valley, Idaho. Some high muckety mucks are going to be there as will we, but if the snow hits early this year, it could be put off. I'll put a deposit in your account in a couple of days."

25

Dinner at the Tower

Palumbo called his secretary's cell. "You OK? How'd things go?" he asked. "I hope you didn't hurt yourself."

"I got a couple of scratches but I'm fine . . . the girls are a whole different story," she said. I think you're going to have to buy us dinner at the top of the Towers for this and then some. They had an emotional blowout . . . you'll have to talk to them personally."

"They're OK? Right!" Palumbo asked.

"I'll let them tell you," she said.

"Let's plan on dinner at the towers tonight." Palumbo said. "I'll check with Cabe because I'm sure he has a standing table up there. If we head back to the office we can have dinner a little early and should be available." He said, "Ask the girls."

"It's a go. I'll confirm with the Tower but we should be ok. Want to invite your husband? Palumbo asked.

"No," she said. "Every other Wednesday is penny poker night. I'd be sleeping in the garage if I took him away from that. I'll let him know we're going-- he'll be fine with it."

Traffic put them back in Century City at about six o'clock but they made it right on time. Palumbo got the table thanks to Cabe's clout and they were seated almost immediately.

Palumbo felt guilty not getting to Cabe immediately with the flash drive, but he thought, he might get more information if he had a chance to get some direct input from someone else who had felt the power of Nathan. The more he thought about it the better. He assumed there would be answers that Cabe might be able to fill in what the girls missed.

When Palumbo called to make the reservation, he suggested that they do the Chef's Gordon's Choice. Gena and the girls met him in the foyer. On the ride up the elevator he explained that this special dinner was his way of saying thank you and apologized for their discomfort during the filming.

They were seated and when the captain came to the table he was already aware the patron would receive the prefix menu. "Please let me call our Sommelier over to start and I'll be back to give you the details for tonight," the captain said.

The Sommelier recommended an aperitif and evening wine to which Palumbo agreed and suggested Gena do the tasting honors. He poured a little, and Gena carefully sampled the aroma and took a slow sip.

"Excellent in my humble opinion," Gena said. "Let's go for it boss."

Palumbo nodded and as soon as he did, the Captain returned and immediately began: "I think you're going to especially enjoy our menu tonight," the Captain said." To begin the evening we have Royal Ossetra Caviar with poached shrimp and Brokaw Avocado Puree. Our second offering is hand cut "macaroni, Ris de Veau, Parmigiano-Reggiano and Fava Beans with Black Winter Truffle.

The third course is slow poached fillet of wild king salmon topped with morel mushrooms and Sacramento Delta Asparagus and paloise mousseline. Our final course is charcoal-grilled Japanese Wagyu along with hearts of romaine lettuce, garden radishes, crispy cipollini onions and a final touch of spicy tomato condiment, picholine olives and chickpea crust."

"Sounds scrumptious to me," Palumbo said and made a mental note to tell Cabe about the meal. He so loved to kid Cabe about spending his money. He also knew that his boss would be held in rapt attention with what "his" girls would be able to tell him about the events.

The dinner came in waves. It was as good as food gets.

"Ok guys," Palumbo started in before the luxury dining was finished, "how about your story from the beginning?"

Roxanne Post spoke first. She was thirty-something and an exotic beauty in heels and gown, but in a pair of stylish jeans and a slick light weight leather jacket, was just downright cute.

She finished her last bite of the Waygu, "Dick, I hardly know how to explain it much less completely understand what happened. It was like getting hit by a tsunami of emotional fear. It was instant and all consuming. All we wanted to do was run. I can't tell you where it came from but it pierced me to my core. I have never felt that kind of fear, a sort of emotional dagger right in my heart.

Roxanne continued. "I can't really say, but it felt like it was coming from one direction or single source is maybe a better way to put it. I don't want to feel that ever again. I thought this was just a stunt for some fun, but after, no way. I didn't really feel like I was going to die, but I did feel like if it had continued, I'd have gone stark raving bananas. Oh, there was another thing.

"I felt a lessoning of the attack, like it backed off or lowered in intensity. I have no clue what that could mean. We're just fine with no serious lingering effects, but I may think about giving up my acting dreams."

Palumbo began to think that Cabe wasn't totally crazy after all. This was the first, or maybe, he thought, his real second confirmation of the power of this boy. He realized this would be invaluable to Cabe and was pleased he would have a reasonably good description of what happened. He thought of a couple of other things the girls had said but stowed them as not being pertinent.

Nancy Manwaring, a 22-year-old college senior and daughter of one of the employees at Cable News Media, Palumbo's other friend was just as graphic, but stressed the depth of intrusiveness into her emotional self. "To the very marrow, Dick and I don't want to ever talk about it again because people will think I'm a total nutter butter."

It was evident that this direct information would be vital to what Cabe would want. He texted a note to Cabe and said he'd have a report tomorrow morning at ten o'clock.

The four finished their scrumptious dinner. Palumbo became apologetic after hearing their stories. "I really didn't know that this would be so traumatic for you and I'm really sorry. I owe you guys big time. Gena, I'm going to the office tonight and study what's on the flash drive more carefully. Could you make sure these girls get home OK?"

"Sure," she said, knowing that she too would be cared for personally. All of them had been surprised at the depth of the event; it turned out to be much more than a mere camera stunt.

Once he felt comfortable about getting the two home safely, he went directly to the office and inserted the drive. Palumbo examined and dissected both what he was seeing and the timing. He was astonished at the impact on their faces when Nathan directed his hand at them. He began to seriously consider if it were possible to subdue him. What if he chose to direct his power on those attempting to take him? That was something they would have to consider and he was sure the proposal they were suggesting wouldn't be easy.

Thankfully, the sound and video were great. He focused on the close cameras shots and would show the wide angle shot in the meeting to Cabe. He assumed most of the information would be on those closer shots. They, he thought, would give the best specific information on which to make decisions.

It was a short sleepless night for Palumbo. When he got to the office the next morning he developed a timeline for all the events since the first test yesterday. He left nothing out including the planning and how everything was recorded followed by an explanation of the fact that Harding thought this was a test when the set-up "stunt" went down. Palumbo wanted to divert Harding's attention from the truth that this was in fact, the real event, not a fictitious Sun Valley mogul meeting.

26

Video Reveals Concerns

With most special projects to which he was assigned, Palumbo felt comfortable and confident about the Intel he was giving Cabe but this case was a complete guess because it was so unusual. He didn't know how Cabe would respond or if the video would even be worthwhile.

His biggest interest was in Cabe's reaction, what would he think? Even though Cabe had roughly explained the situation he'd experienced, it was very hard to relate to, and Palumbo didn't know what to expect exactly, certainly not the response and description he'd gotten from the gals.

At ten o'clock, Cabe, Drobick and Palumbo went into a screening room. There was a sixty inch screen that would play the flash drive. Palumbo had watched the recording several times and he had estimated it was under a couple minutes if you add the different camera angles together plus the practice shot. It was also a Harding trade make of his thoroughness. If the other cameras or recorders had gone down, he, at least, had something as a backup.

Palumbo prefaced the screening by explaining the nature of how the drives were gathered. He also waited to explain the young women's responses until after Cabe saw the recording. He knew well that he'd wanted every detail, no matter how small. Collecting the slightest nuance was a common practice for Cabe's assistants. His boss was a master at collating divergent information and honing in on details which tied seemingly unrelated information together.

In a bit of personal concern, Palumbo didn't exactly tell Cabe the complete story about the ruse and Harding's response. Too much information like that can tend to obfuscate or distract from the most important points so it was something he chose not to include. Harding, who was less inclined to bring up the fact that he had fallen for the ruse, would omit the charade on the street, which was just fine with Palumbo. Palumbo wanted Harding to shift his attention to a potential Sun Valley project even if that project too, was a ruse.

"By the way, I'm going to send Harding to Sun Valley to look around to continue the process and divert his attention from the Nathan situation." Palumbo said.

Cabe nodded and appreciated the effort to deflect the minutiae but wanted to move forward with the report.

With that, Palumbo inserted the only copy of the recording into the computer Cabe's paranoia of backups getting into the wrong hands demanded no more copies. The television face was divided into four screens, one from each camera. Each scene could be opened to full size by tapping on any one of the screens or by remote.

Cabe sat up riveted to the unfolding events. Palumbo played it three times and waited. He then inserted the second wide angle recording. It was a good overall view in high definition of the events and even some parked cars could be seen down the street. A closer shot of the secretary's car, and her arrival was clear and crisp.

Cabe went through each angle of the four screens examining them in excruciating detail. Once again, Palumbo noticed, it was a guttural connection he saw Cabe express.

"An amazing job, Dick." Cabe said "Can we zoom into specific areas of each scene?"

"To a degree," Palumbo said. "There is one enlargement for each camera but it does reduce the focus some.

"Let's try each one," Cabe pushed.

Cabe couldn't seem to get enough. He had Palumbo zoom onto the screen that showed Nathan's hand pointed at the girls, but no waves were visible. It was somewhat different than the school incident in that the entire area was in shadow because of the trees. The change from shadow to sun wasn't there like the first time. That disappointed Cabe but the views were not without merit..

Through the entire process, Drobick sat quiet and stoic. Finally Cabe asked, "Can we see the flash drive when you set up and tested the camera on the first day?"

Palumbo said, "Sure, but remember, it's only about 15 seconds long and nothing happens."

"Let's see it anyway," Cabe said.

Palumbo ran the tape. Besides the boys coming into view and a few muffled sounds the only thing that happened was a guy riding by on a scooter. He spent close to an hour explaining the girl's experiences all the while Cabe questioning him like a prosecuting attorney.

Did it hurt? No! Were they scared? Yes, sort of! After a bunch of these types of questions Cabe asked a rather odd question. "Did they have any residual effects?"

Palumbo paused.

Cabe knew there was something else.

"OK, what is it?" Cabe asked.

"At dinner last night, it was just a little off the wall," Palumbo answered, "Both gals said a couple of things that were just strange. Both said one of the things they felt was something like emotions had some kind of connection to colors or maybe an increased intensity in color. Didn't really make sense to me. Maybe a female thing?"

"Anything else?" Cabe said,

"Both said they didn't feel they really explained their feelings adequately especially to themselves. They did say they felt they had just seemed to feel a twinge of revenge coming from whoever was doing this. But I think that was kind of an afterthought," Palumbo said.

Palumbo and Drobick both recognized these two small pieces of information appeared to sink deeply into Cabe's mind. After ruminating for a while, Cabe said, to no one in particular, "this is like putting together a ten thousand piece puzzle without having a picture to follow."

"This is exactly what I felt after Nathan rummaged around in my mind. Just couldn't quite get it sorted out. Emotional color," he said, "that's a really apt description. I experienced it a little differently. For me the color they're talking about must have been the intensity of color of my car when I looked at it after the school incident. Then the twinge of revenge-- couldn't really put my finger on that, but that too was very faint. I didn't get the impression any negativity was necessarily directed at me since I really wasn't attacking anyone and wasn't threatening anybody. I think he saw me focused on him so he wanted to do a once over of me because he realized I was aware of his part in stopping the fight somehow."

Just as they began to wrap things up, Drobick, who again had said almost nothing, asked if he could see the wide shot and the quick test tape again.

"What's up Mike," Cabe asked.

"Don't really know, but something has been buzzing around in my brain and I'm trying to figure out what it is. Maybe nothing," he said.

Palumbo ran the quick test drive first.

Just as the scooter went by, Drobick quickly said, "Freeze it with the scooter in the frame."

Palumbo stopped the action and went frame by frame until the side of the scooter was fully visible. There on the side of the scooter was the unmistakable logo of New Tech.

"That's it," Drobick said.

'What's it," Cabe and Palumbo spoke in unison.

"Show me the wide shot and zoom as much as possible to the cars we saw parked on the street in the real event," Drobick pressed.

Since the wide shot camera was more sophisticated and with a much higher pixel count, the zoom in, easily showed the vehicles and their car doors more specifically. As clear as day, there was a car with someone in the front seat looking toward the two boys, with a recognizable New Tech logo on the door. When the ruse started, the person quickly sat up, but did nothing else except possibly pick up a cell phone. It was a little hard to tell, just a suggestion of a hand movement really. But the movement to grab your phone is seen thousands of times a day it seems.

Then, Drobick dropped his head and said, "that's not a cell phone, it's a drone controller. Think about the effort we're going through to get Nathan. This verifies that someone else is way ahead of us and is even more intent than we are. I only hope they don't know we're here."

All three men sank back into their chairs. Each of them realized that this had potentially devastating implications not only to them but to Nathan. They all immediately saw the problem. Their rivals may not have the same concerns for his personal safety. Not that they themselves were angels. Nathan's powers could be worth untold amounts of money not to mention of his sheer power if he could be controlled and potentially dangerous if he couldn't.

"I think the person's response in the car overrules that," Drobick said and Palumbo agreed. "The watcher's head was definitely turned toward Nathan."

It became very apparent to Cabe, that they were not alone in their quest to solve the mystery of Nathan. It seemed an important player was already involved based on the obvious surveillance.

"Maybe we're just over reacting to this," Drobick said. "Obviously, San Marino must have several New Tech employees who live there and it could be we just saw a couple?"

That balloon soared only for about as long as a semi full of triple-ought buck shot would float.

"Maybe they're keeping eyes on him because they know of his previous problems in Idaho and want to be sure he's safe to placate his Dad," Palumbo suggested.

"No," Cabe said. "We either have competition or somebody in the genetics department at New Tech, besides Nathan's dad, is pulling some night shifts.

With their attention shifted to the recordings, Cabe suddenly asked to have the first words replayed on the sound of the regular recording.

Again, Palumbo complied.

The conversation on the tapes didn't seem that important at the time. Nathan was telling Buddy that the Nieto guy was not such a bad guy, maybe had just gotten with the wrong crowd.

In a way, it was a relief to Cabe. He had been building a case in his head that Nathan might not be as truly compassionate as originally thought. Cabe worried that some bullying experiences he'd had as a boy might have lodged in his thinking. Cabe reasoned that more information was necessary and it had to come from where Nathan was born and spent his whole life in Carey, Idaho.

The Book of Nathan was unfolding for Cabe line by line. The more he learned the more he wanted to know and understand plus the more personal his connection to this young man became. At the same time, he was seeing Nathan now as a target, but not just his target. There was another interested party focused on the boy and it was changing Cabe and Cabe was beginning to develop a feeling of responsibility for him. Nathan wasn't just the "The Nathan Venture" anymore.

As Cabe left the screening room he said he'd be flying to New York and would be back on Tuesday.

27

A Foe Becomes a Friend

Nathan's "run in" with Miguel at the first committee meeting seemed to relieve some hostility for Nathan. He realized that Miguel was a pretty good kid. He saw him in the hallways and Miguel was always friendly. Nathan began to make a reassessment.

It became apparent that Miguel had a natural sense of handling money and made several good suggestions about how to spend the funds they would raise for their sister school. Even though Miguel was one grade ahead, he had an easy going way about him. Nathan wondered what might have possessed him to join a gang. Coming from Idaho, Nathan had little understanding that peer pressure to join gangs was enormous. For many kids, unless there was another way to go, it was difficult to resist the undercurrent of demands for young people to join. Then the lack of fathers didn't help either.

Again, Nathan reassessed. Surprisingly, one day, instead of sitting by his gang friends for lunch, Miguel stopped by to sit with Nathan and Buddy. Needless to say, Buddy was instantly nervous and even ready to fight. But within a few minutes he calmed down and they had some fun reveling in a ton of fart and potty humor jokes.

The new friendships were not approved in any way by Reuben. He came over with the other three of his friends. Again Buddy saw a fight coming. Nathan was deathly calm but intensely and totally focused on Reuben's approach. He purposefully removed his light darkening glasses and glared at Reuben.

Reuben immediately began to mock Nathan's eyes. "Where'd you get those glass eyes," he said. Nathan said nothing and he let Reuben have his fun for about 15 seconds. Then, without hesitation stormed into Reuben's emotional mind, this time without pointing his fingers, with what was the equivalent of ice climbing spikes and proceeded to stomp around.

Reuben was so startled he nearly fell down, caught only by his buddies. He made a hasty retreat and for a while made a wide birth around Nathan, Buddy and even Miguel. "Don't mess with those guys; "I think they're all loco," he screamed. They're the loco bunch," he added, trying to regain a little respect with his own gang.

Not surprisingly, the three new friends grabbed the intended slight as a badge of honor and immediately began calling themselves "The Three Locos."

Buddy and Miguel had no idea what had just happened, but Miguel seemed to let out a huge sigh at the prospect of not having to be in a gang. As it turned out, he was an excellent student and it had earned him a place on the committee. After that day, the three were essentially inseparable at school and on their phones.

Nathan's mother noticed a huge change in Nathan. For once in his life, he had a couple of friends to pal around with. The three found not only camaraderie, but a secret name and with that, quickly developed into a strong triad. They didn't worry about the color of Nathan's eyes or his sometime quirky ways. Real buddies just didn't do that.

Junior high school can be a difficult experience during the transition from kid to that prepubescent age called "squirrelhood" as Palumbo frequently referred to it, especially when you're new at a school. "It's just a weird age," he'd say.

Alice Farnsworth was thrilled to tell her husband of the transformation in Nathan's attitude. "Maybe moving here wasn't so bad after all," she told Levi, when he came home from work. "Nathan has some friends and seems to be much happier. It's great."

28

Mining Gold of a Different Kind

Palumbo didn't have to be told once, let alone twice. There was more Intel to collect so he and Drobick got together and went over all of the information they had with a whole new perspective. There wasn't anything new in the info, but with a new frame of reference, there were some new questions, which could only be answered in Idaho. Where was this revenge issue coming from? That was the question and he agreed with Drobick on that.

Before he got on the plane to Boise, Palumbo called Sanjy and Billy to give them a new task.

"This is going to be more difficult," he said. "This is medical info and could be much harder to access."

Billy asked, "What? Have you lost faith in our brilliance? Not to worry."

"Wait till I tell you what I want to know, then show me how smart you are," Palumbo said. "There were three births. I want everything, including possible records along with any personal notes or comments and problems that may have occurred at these births and again, while leaving no traces."

Sanjy complained, "Give me a 'break,' why do you always say that? We've delivered for years, with no traces, so you can assume we'll continue."

The researchers got the info from Palumbo on all three male births at a Twin Falls, Idaho, hospital eleven years earlier. Not sure which of the three births was Nathan's, he gave Sanjy and Billy the names and instructions including specific dates gleaned from the previous school research they'd done. He repeated his earlier charge to them to find out if there was anything unusual about the births and if so, which birth and what was the problem. Billy cut in, as usual, with his money and delivery questions.

"You've got a week and $3,000.00" Palumbo said. "Talk to you later." He shortened the conversation and concerned himself with how he was going to find out about Nathan's early life without causing undue suspicion.

As he thought about it, Palumbo remembered that Cabe owned a kind of obscure medical research company called "Statistical Medical Research." Cabe used the company for an independent data confirmation source for his media group. They had come in handy when Cabe thought he was getting some flaky data from some pharmaceutical companies. He suggested it to Drobick, proposing that an official ID would help with contacts including talking to the doctors and hospital administrators.

"Could you overnight something to me at the Hilton Garden in Twin Falls?" Palumbo asked. I'll need an ID card, stuff identifying my research data priorities such as the effects of gestational diabetic variables. That sort of thing."

"Will do," Drobick said.

The flight from Los Angeles left about six in the morning. It was a little bumpy over the Sierras, but the rest of the trip was smooth which allowed Palumbo to look at a list he and Drobick had developed for people and locations to check. First was the hospital. Following that was the former home in Carey where Nathan was raised and went to school. He was not sure how the details would be obtained from the Farnsworth's neighbors. But he'd cross that bridge when he got there.

He decided to drive to Twin Falls and rented a car at the Boise airport to drive the distance, which he expected to take about two and a half hours. He did a lot of thinking on the way figuring out how to ask the questions as well as which questions were critical. He turned off Highway 89, crossed the Snake River and turned west on Pole Line Road for a couple of blocks and pulled into the Hilton Garden Inn. His ID papers were expected to arrive the next morning from Drobick.

It was about 3:30 p.m. After checking in he went to his room and laid out the plans he'd made. The Twin Falls Hospital where Nathan was born was just a few blocks away. He scanned the material again and on a whim decided to see if he could get in a round of golf at the Blue Lakes Country Club. The course was divided by the Snake River and lies on its banks between black lava cliffs. "Good way to relax my mind," he thought and was as good an excuse as any to play on this highly unique course.

He found three guys sipping beers at the Club House bar looking for an extra to round out a foursome. "Love to play a round if you three are game," Palumbo said. "How about I buy each of you a double scotch to get things started."

One of the guys chided, "Trying to win before we get off our stools?"

The four went on to have a friendly game and Palumbo waved as he left, glad that for a short time the pressure was off on the Nathan situation, or maybe it should be called the Cabe situation, was forgotten. It was early sevenish and he only had about a half-hour's light left so he made a quick trip through town, starting with a drive by the hospital.

Palumbo developed an appetite and chose a half rack of ribs at the "Snake Pit" Barbeque on his way back from golf. How could he not to try a place called the Snake Pit." It was good, a kind of Texas/Louisiana mix. He drove back to his room and immediately called Sanjy and Billy.

"I know you just got started on the hospital thing," he said, "but do you have a name yet for the doctor who delivered the babies?"

"Well, yes and no," they answered. "The doctor who delivered Nathan died about four years ago but his son, Andrew Ray took over his practice. He was in his Dad's practice for the past thirteen years and should know about an unusual case."

"This could be both good and bad news," Palumbo thought.

Since medical records are held in strict confidence, it would be hard to ask for direct information. However, maybe the son would discuss general information without names that his father, as the delivering physician, may have been restricted from answering. Palumbo felt confident that the son would know Nathan's case, although probably not all the details. It was a start. Getting a short conversation with Dr. Ray might be the hardest thing. First thing in the morning he'd call the doctor to see if he could squeeze in a few minutes. He looked up Dr. Ray's phone number and address and texted it to Drobick.

Palumbo didn't need a wakeup call. It was just something about that ultra fresh crisp Idaho air that had him awake at 5:30 with his synapses firing on all cylinders. He was amazed when there was a knock on the door at six. He checked the eye hole and saw his overnighter was there. He opened the door and accepted the package. It was much thicker that he expected. Within ten minutes, Drobick was calling.

"You're up early Mike," Palumbo said. "I just got out of the shower and haven't gotten through the material yet."

"Don't worry Dick," Drobick said. "Let me give you the quick and dirty. First, you've got an ID stating you're a PhD in diabetic genetics. You've come to Twin Falls to get some information about the birth of a child who is now about eleven years ago because another child about to be delivered that you're assisting in caring for is in the same situation. Your problem is that there were three births recorded back then and you don't know which one was which. With hospital privacy laws being so restrictive; they won't connect any birth with unusual circumstances for you. But the fact that they're not really talking about a specific child should take a little pressure off with the doctor and hospital. You can talk in a more hypothetical realm."

"Your trip was last minute since the baby is expected to be delivered in a matter of days and given that Statistical Medical Research was aware of a similar birth there in Twin Falls it establishes the urgency. So you are Dr. Palumbo as it reads on your ID. I've included some business cards to hand out with Statistical Medical Research info. If they want to check, tell them to call Dr. Frank Wolfe, CEO of

SMR. He's the head honcho. I hired him several years ago at Cabe's direction and he's exceptionally good. He's from Johns Hopkins. He's also been very helpful on many occasions and I think he's particularly interested in this case and can help us find and evaluate the official medical records we get. It fits in with SMR's primary work."

"Did I ever tell you, 'you're good'?" Palumbo said. "You're good!"

"Oh, I almost forgot, I had Dr. Wolfe call both the hospital and Dr. Ray to tell them a little more about the birth situation. If you're information doesn't exactly jibe with theirs you can tell them it's very fluid right now."

Palumbo studied the material, put cards and ID in his wallet and called Dr. Ray's office immediately after he hung up with Drobick. Ray's office wasn't open yet so he explained the situation to the answering service and asked to have Dr. Ray call ASAP and left his number. At seven he started breakfast and half way through got a call from Ray.

Dr. Ray was personable in that affable small town Idaho way and without a doubt, exceptionally bright. He said, "I'm packed today, but I take a twenty minute break in the cafeteria at the hospital at ten. Why don't we get together then? I'll sit at the table by the potted tree."

Palumbo said he'd be in a light blue shirt. "Hope you don't mind if I go a little casual. I love your town and have been enjoying looking around. Even got in a round on the snake with three friendly native Twinners."

Dr. Ray was easy to spot. He was forty-fiveish, longer hair than Palumbo expected and stood six-foot-four. He rose when Palumbo came in and waved him over.

It was apparent that he'd been briefed. He was aware of Statistical Medical Research firm so it was an easy transition, especially since Dr. Wolfe had called. He took Palumbo's card, checked his ID. And without waiting Ray started telling Palumbo about the birth of Nathan Farnsworth. Like many doctors on duty, he didn't have time for small talk. He didn't mention Nathan by name but talked about the unusual circumstances of his birth and particularly about Nathan's amazing eyes.

He said that he and his father, Dr. Gordon Ray, had talked at length about the birth. He also mentioned that from the beginning Nathan had special talents, but didn't elaborate and Palumbo didn't push. He got dates and some of the circumstances of the birth.

"Ally came in about one a.m.," Dr. Ray said. "My dad had been seeing her frequently through the whole pregnancy. Gestational diabetes and potential problems that it can cause, were of great concern to him. One thing, which was not unusual for diabetic births, was that Nathan weighed in at a whopping eleven pounds two ounces when he was born." But when the baby was born, it was apparent there was much more happening.

My dad did a Chorionic villus sampling with the ambiotic fluid very early, but the only thing we could see was that something was different with the baby, but nothing specific we could quantify or identify. It was when Ally's fall onto the rocks in the creek that we began to look closer and see changes with the other tests. It was prudent to start much closer monitoring of her.

Dr. Ray then mentioned something about excess blood and hyper-oxygenation that comes with gestational diabetes and that Palumbo didn't fully understand but didn't ask more. By that time the twenty minutes were up and Palumbo thanked him.

"Before you go," Dr. Ray said, "We followed him for several years. I know he had some problems in Carey that involved the police. If the new baby you're concerned about has the same issues, I think it would be wise to let the physicians know that this was, or is in your baby's case, a long term situational possibility."

Palumbo thanked him again, briefly mentioned that the info about the blood and oxygen was particularly helpful that he appreciated the meeting on such short notice. Palumbo also was thankful that the baby story was not true. It's particularly hard, he thought, to see children with potentially serious problems. He also asked if Dr. Wolfe could call him again if necessary.

"Sure," Ray said and was immediately whisked away by an anxious nurse who'd come in search of him.

Palumbo's next stop was the hospital's administrator. He'd hoped to get critical records that would provide more specific data. He noticed the sign on his way in to see Dr. Ray, reading that administration was on the third floor. He took the elevator and stepped onto the landing and followed the arrows to administration.

He reached large twin glass doors and wondered why it was that administrative offices in hospitals always seemed to look like the accoutrements in the Taj Mahal. He stopped in front of the reception desk, announced his name and handed the young man his Statistical Medical Research business card.

"I'm here to see Dr. Nadine Taylor," he said.

Without hesitation the young man behind the counter asked if Palumbo had an appointment.

"Not really, but if you could ask if I could see her for a very short appointment," Palumbo said, "I'm not a salesman, I'd appreciate it."

"I'm not sure she's in, Mr. Palumbo," he said

Terminally annoyed, Palumbo stared at the young man. He said, looking at his name tag…. "Bobby, I know she's in, I can see her through the glass walls and even read her desk plaque. She's sitting right there."

To which "Bobby" replied. "How do you know it's her," he said with a haute pique?

"Do you get paid to do this? Or are you a candy striper volunteer," Palumbo said in a boisterous enough voice to carry into the office he was seeking to get in to. He was totally burned that this "person" didn't have the courtesy to at least announce his arrival and ask if the administer had the time to see anyone.

She stepped to her open office door poked her head out and asked, "What's going on?"

"Dr. Palumbo from SMR is here Dr. Taylor," Bobby said.

"A little aggressive are we Mr. Palumbo?" she said.

"I'm sorry doctor but we are caring for a baby who will be born any minute," He said, handing her one of his cards. "I have no time, and I realize I'm here without an appointment but I'm very concerned about getting some information that may help in the birth, and I believe that information is here in your hospital that might help."

"You're from Statistical Medical Research? I got a call from Dr. Wolfe who told me you'd be here to request help," she said. "But we're in the business of running a hospital here not catering to a bunch of researchers," she said. "You can tell Dr. Wolfe our regulations do not allow us to share anything," she said.

Palumbo's annoyance continued. Even though this baby thing was a ruse, He couldn't believe that this doctor/administrator would not do everything she could to help a baby about to be born under potentially very difficult circumstances.

"You're a doctor," Palumbo said. "We have a short time frame and I thought we could get some help to protect an about to be born baby."

"First of all, Mr. Palumbo, "my doctorate is in hospital administration, not medicine. I'm not here to make your crisis my problem. If you don't mind, you can call my assistant next year and we might be able to discuss what you can ask and decide if we wish to respond," and with that, she pulled her head back, shut the door, turned around and pulled the blinds.

As he walked out, he heard Bobby open her door and ask the administrator, "Who's Nurse Ratchet. That guy asked what's it like to work for a real Nurse Ratchet."

Palumbo had a good smiled about that one.

While he got nothing from the hospital, the information he got from Dr. Ray was very helpful. It also created a series of questions that had to be answered. Once again, it was a dicey situation asking about police matters, especially in a small town where, as they say, "everybody knows your name."

Palumbo grabbed a meatball marinara sub at a place called, "It's in the Bag," and went back to his hotel room. He texted a big thanks to Drobick, and briefly said the doctor was very helpful but the hospital was run by the Ratchet Gestapo and told Drobick he'd be headed to Carey tomorrow. Let you know if I find anything, was the message.

He chomped into his sandwich and continued processing the information Dr. Ray had provided. He realized that someone with medical training would have to take the lead when he correlated his info with Sanjy and Billy. He anticipated they'd have a lot more luck finding the records at the hospital, at least he hoped. By the time he finished, it was 4 p.m.

Lastly, he called his secretary and tried to clear up the messages and work he'd left behind when Cabe put him fulltime on the Nathan venture.

29

Idaho Sheriff Quizzes Palumbo

Carey was a little less than an hour away. He watched a USC football game on cable and just vegged for a while. Apparently the stress was a little more than he'd expected.

He left at seven without breakfast and got there just before eight. He decided to stop at the only restaurant in town--he Carey Grocery Store with a restaurant, liquor store and an auto parts department in the back. Reluctantly, he entered. On the north side wall was an old time diner counter and a soda fountain of years past. He walked over and sat down.

The waitress came over with coffee and a cup and greeted him.

"From out of town?" she asked smiling while pouring a coffee.

"How do you know I'm from out of town," he said.

"I live here, small town, never saw you before, season's over, oh and your car's 1A," she said looking at him directly.

Puzzled, Palumbo repeated "1A?"

"That's Boise, Ada County. Carey's in Blaine County which is 5B," she said. "What can I get for you? Believe me you won't be disappointed if you try our ham and eggs and a stack of pancakes. We serve 'em all day."

He thought, I guess I can't go too wrong with ham and eggs. "I can go with that," nodding to her.

"My name's Jesse. Holler if you need anything else. It'll be just a couple of minutes," She said.

She was hardly gone when Palumbo noticed that a Blaine County Sheriff's car pulled up. In walked a Wilford Brimley clone. He went back to the auto parts department and ordered some light bulbs for his vehicles. As he waited for the parts guy to get his bulbs, the sheriff turned around and looked directly at Palumbo.

Palumbo saw the sheriff give him the once over. He thought as he looked back, why is it that people get so nervous when a cop gives you a direct look? Then he determined, "It's because they don't glance at you, it's more like those red laser scans you see in movies, head to toe. You feel guilty even if you're honest Abe."

The sheriff grabbed his bag of bulbs and he headed directly toward Palumbo. "From Boise?" he quizzed.

"Does everybody around here identify people by their license plates?" He then added, "Not really, LA."

"Mind if I join you for coffee?" Close asked, sitting down without waiting for an answer. "My favorite all-time steakhouse is in LA. The North Woods Inn."

"Know it well," Palumbo said, "and I know what you mean."

Blaine County Sheriff Jim Close seemed to relax and settle in. "Don't get too many visitors here in the fall," he said. "Anything I can help you with?" It was more a question to someone who looked interesting than an interrogation.

Palumbo sized him up as a friendly and decided to approach him with the same ruse he talked to Dr. Ray about the research for the baby to be.

"I was just in Twin Falls and talked to Dr. Ray," handing his business card and ID to the Sheriff. "I've been checking into a young man who was born in Twin Falls about eleven years ago. His birth situation was very rare and we have another birth in similar circumstances and we've looking for anything that can help us.

"Dr. Ray said the boy lived here. I can't tell you his name because of the medical information restrictions. But the doctor said he had some trouble with the police here." Palumbo paused while the sheriff checked the card and added: "You're more than welcome to call Dr. Wolfe; he's our company president and can confirm my credentials."

Much to Palumbo's surprise, Sheriff Close started talking as if they were friends, "I know the boy you're talking about. It was a strange case."

Palumbo said, "I'd appreciate any info within the bounds of yours and my restrictions."

"So you'll know," Close said, "I got a call from Dr. Ray last night and he told me you might be coming so my stop here wasn't all that random. I'm not usually the one in the county buying light bulbs for the department. He asked me to assist if possible."

"You fooled me," Palumbo said.

"You're right, I can't say much, but I do want to help. Actually, the case is one of those open secrets that everybody knows and loves to talk about but always denies talking about. 'Small town!' Can you tell me a little more about the current case you're trying to understand?"

Palumbo said it wasn't so much a case we're trying to solve as preparing for unknown eventualities. He gave the sheriff the same explanation he had given to Dr. Ray. He added that when the baby we're concerned about is born, it may have the same issues, but she could be totally normal too. We simply don't know if some of these 'issues' happened at birth or are genetically programmed."

"Damn!" Palumbo said. "You didn't hear that 'she,' hopefully."

"Sorry, I didn't hear what you said," Close said without changing expression.

"The problem is that with this kind of birth every variable may or may not come into play. We try to know everything before, but there is one thing we can't know, eye color for example or even blindness and that's revealed at birth, then we can start examining other 'enhancements' of the child."

"Enhancements, that's an interesting way to put it," the sheriff said.

About that time, Jesse brought Palumbo's breakfast. She told Palumbo to start with a bite of ham…."our specialty," she said.

"Sorry to eat in front of you sheriff, but I'm hungry, hope you don't mind," Palumbo said.

"You eat, I'll talk," the Sheriff said.

"The case or cases depending on how you look at it," he started, "were unusual." "There were four incidents that were involved and since it dealt with children, the tensions ran high."

Before, he got any further, Palumbo broke in and proclaimed. "This is great ham!"

"Made right here in Carey," the sheriff said. "Apple wood smoked just down the road. A small farm. Has a great online business if you'd like to order, do it early. But I know, the smell is heavenly. We use them as gifts to reward our officers who win awards."

"Sorry, I'm sounding like an Idaho chamber of commerce salesman. Anyway, the child Dr. Ray's dad delivered was immediately recognizable with the bright lavender eyes. He was exceptionally smart, you could tell right at birth. Talking in full sentences by one year and reading with comprehension a couple of months later. He could do complicated math at two. Then there were the enhancements, as you put it.

"As he grew up he was teased unmercifully for the eye color. He retreated somewhat when he went to school not showing his intellectual school skills but just trying to fit in. By second grade he was getting harassed constantly. Then one day on the playground and out of the blue, he stared a bully down who was harassing a younger girl and somehow filled the bully with fear. That's a big guess. He had the kid crying on the ground in an instant. The monitors on the playgrounds, who only saw the kid go to the ground, naturally blamed Nathan because he was the closest to the other boy.

"Can't tell you how he did it but the best we can tell is it was to me like some sort of emotional transference. Not pain, mind you, but fear," the sheriff paused looked up a little as though thinking of the incident. "I interview the 'victim' intensively. The parents of the bully, also of course, blamed Nathan and demanded action. We were called. Ooops, 'the boy,' he winked.

"There was nothing we could do. No one could officially say what happened. We talked to the monitors on the playground but they really didn't see anything happen. It was an assumptive cause and effect thing. Obviously there were no marks. He hadn't pushed anyone or knocked the kid down. Needless to say everything got worse after that. By six year old, he had three more similar incidents, he became a pariah. No one would play with him and the Farnsworths were ostracized to a degree, despite all the good they'd done in the county. And that's about it."

By this time Palumbo had finished his breakfast and nodded at Jesse, "fantastic" he said, and left a twenty dollar spot tip.

The sheriff's radio squeaked and he responded "10-4, show me en route."

"I've got to go," the sheriff got up as did Palumbo.

They walked to their cars and the sheriff leaned against his squad car door and said, "Dick, there's one last thing that happened just before they moved. There was a fight that he wasn't involved in. A couple of kids were pounding on a smaller kid. The little boy was screaming bloody murder. Nathan saw it and the same thing happened. Both bullies crumbled to the ground writhing in fear. That was it for the rest of the town. I think the family had to move for the boy's safety. I think they moved, to somewhere in your area. Hope I've helped." He jumped in his cruiser and took off.

Palumbo waved and yelled thanks. His worries about getting some info in Carey worked just the opposite of what he'd expected and also, as he thought about it, he got questions answered and directly from the Sheriff. The down side was the vengeance question again. It was nearly ten so he headed back to Twin Falls picked up his stuff and drove back to Boise and took a hotel room and flew back to LA the next morning.

30

Birth Report Provides Answers

Drobick picked Palumbo up from the airport. For the first five minutes of the ride it was all small talk. This was the first time the two had a real chance to spend time together talking and both avoided the subject of Cabe's latest elephant in the room project until they just had to get it out. At first, both men had wanted to believe Cabe, but had a difficult time really judging whether their boss was misreading what had happened to him. Now, the evidence of something very different was stacking up and both felt they could discuss the issue without holding back.

Drobick took their conversation in a more somber direction and asked Palumbo if he was OK. The recent flier turned his head, stared out his window and began to let out some of the questions that had been lurking at every turn.

"I thought I was a pretty open-minded guy," Palumbo said, still gazing out of his window, "but this is pretty off the wall stuff. Of all the people I talked to, I think the sheriff put it together for me. He called it an emotional transfer of fear. Smart ol' guy! He said he thought it was like, Nathan taking the fear from the mind of the victim and forcing it into the mind of the attacker causing the person to become incapable of doing anything but escaping the emotional onslaught. Can you believe that?"

Drobick turned into the drive thru at Dunkin' Donuts and got them each a cup of coffee and a cheese Danish.

Palumbo said "that stuff'll give us Dunlop's disease."

"Yeah, I know, don't worry I'll eat yours if you're concerned!" Drobick said.

"The hell you will," Palumbo complained, "hand it over."

With a bit of the tension broken, the two men talked easily all the way to the office about what had happened in Idaho and even more about the comments from the girls. One of the issues Palumbo also brought up, not just Nathan's unique faculties, was the possibility that those faculties were growing more powerful and even broadening.

"The Sheriff didn't say it directly, but alluded to several incidents that he implied seemed to grow in intensity," Palumbo said. "Do you want to hear a couple of my crazier thoughts? Like it or not, here they are. Where does he get the fear, how does he transfer it, and what would it feel like?"

Drobick didn't take the bait and shifted the conversation again. "By the way, I sent flowers and a $200 gift card to each of the girls, and apologized for the crazy turn in the events," he said. "They already think you're nuttier than a Payday bar. But then it did make life exciting listening to your narration."

"I think it just proved that I wasn't really convinced that anything would really happen." Palumbo added.

Drobick grunted a yes and parked the car. They rode up the elevator in silence.

"You know what this means?" Drobick asked.

"Yeah, there is a slight chance that we're all not totally insane," Palumbo said.

"That too," Drobick said, "but it also means that there may be some real substance to this. Do you have anything in the info from the odd couple?"

"There's just a little. I'm expecting some more in a day or two. I asked for some serious confirmations on all the medical stuff because of the nature of the case. If the stuff is at all descriptive, then that goes to your question which means we have to get a lot deeper medically to get some issues answered, like a big Why!"

"Maybe we'll find that out when we look at all of Sanjy and Billy's report," Drobick said.

That afternoon, Palumbo got the call from Sanjy. They arranged a private pickup of the intel. "Ya know, Palumbo you're getting spooky," Sanjy said. "Why more secrecy? Pretty soon we'll have to have dead drop exchanges."

"You two guys are getting way too much notoriety in some circles of the ethosphere. I'd rather not be seen taking anything from you two so let's keep your developing infamy in Nerdville!" he said.

"All this medical info is getting dicier to get all the time," Billy said in a kind of random rant. "Our reputations that you're referring to, of getting stuff others can't get, is where we score big time. The systems are getting more and more complex to crack while they're giving private medical info to more government agencies all the time. Pretty soon we're going to have to go to the IRS before we can get our tonsils out. I think we're going to change our names to the National Security Agency of America."

"Funny stuff," Palumbo said. "Rant over?"

As soon as Palumbo received the info, he went back to his office. He hadn't seen Gena yet.

"Hey, Boss, when can I get another couple of scratches again for a fancy dinner and a gift card?" she said with a half smile.

"Don't rub it in, I feel bad enough already with the way that went. What's been going on?" he asked.

"A couple of reports, including your investigation of that Glass Company that Mr. Cabe asked about, are due. Some other general stuff that you should see," she said.

"OK, I'll be able to get those done since I'll be in the office for at least a week I hope."

Palumbo got his must-dos done and started examining the hospital records provided by his "researchers."

The information confirmed the details he got in Idaho. However, the medical records, while quite complete, were much more medically complicated than his training could decipher. He texted Drobick and told him they were going to need a doctor.

"Wolfe would be perfect because he's interested enough to have called me back about what you found. Says they're once in a lifetime numbers," Drobick texted back. "Wants to work on the statistics of it."

31

Small Things, Big Payoff

Cabe returned from New York with his mission accomplished. His "Nathan" venture was another matter. A lot of people were suddenly involved which was definitely not his intention.

He wanted to keep this low key but he realized that that was not going to be possible given the nature of the information he was seeking.

The report he'd been waiting for was waiting for him when he got back. Further, Drobick and Palumbo had two other issues to resolve as a result of the Idaho trip as well. The first was the problem of understanding what the birth concerns really meant regarding Nathan. The second was getting Dr. Wolfe more involved to provide medical expertise.

There were third and fourth issues that had been developing in Drobick's mind like: "How do you appropriate someone's fear," Drobick said out loud without answering his own question.

Their meeting was much more focused since more information was available. Cabe asked Palumbo to give him a synopsis of what he'd learned on his trip.

"The first thing I can tell you is Carey, Idaho, ain't Los Angeles and they've got a very unique golf course in Twin Falls," he started. "Oh, and I know what I 'm going to get you, and some other people around here for Christmas."

He then proceeded to tell Cabe about Nathan's birth and early life, including the fact that to truly understand what happened and its potential in the real world, it would have to come from someone with much more medical understanding than he had.

"I think I've have been realizing that as of late," Cabe said. "We've suddenly gone from the three of us to a bunch who are now involved to some degree. That gives me a lot of pause, especially since I'm not exactly sure what we have. I'm beginning to more fully understand the reluctance that both of you showed at the beginning. However, I also believe that getting Dr. Wolfe involved is required."

At first I was thinking we could just take the boy, examine him and see exactly what he was doing. Now I'm not as sure what to do.

Again, typical of Drobick, he was quiet through the first part of the meeting; typical too was Cabe's patience in waiting for Drobick to give him his thinking and knew it would always contain the blatant truth.

"I'm not trying to rain on anybody's parade here," Drobick said, "but now that we have more information I think we can do some analysis. I think we can assume several things from what we know. Nathan is exceptionally bright and he doesn't exercise his power until there is some kind of provocation. He was pretty young when he first used it but we don't know the exact age. He doesn't like confrontation, but acts when he feels it's necessary. He can control several people at one time. He has some 'anger' issues we don't know much about, and probably most importantly, we have no clue to his ultimate power. Oh, one other thing: if he has these powers and uses them on kidnappers, how do you take him down?"

Cabe's mouth winced. "Nothing like dropping a bomb on the party," he said, "but that's an excellent summation of what we have to decide. I haven't focused enough attention on anything in those areas, but they're critical."

"I want to go back to something the girls said in light of what the Sheriff told us about what Nathan did in the school yard. I got an impression from what you said about the fear. So, he thought the victim's fear was then transferred to the bully? Since the girls case was a put up situation, and there really wasn't any true emotion of fear, where did the fear from?" Cabe asked.

He answered his own question. "Had to be from Buddy or previous events," Cabe said. Buddy would undoubtedly have instantly remembered his recent episode and relived his terror, if what Close said is right. I'm thinking that Nathan took the fear and panic from these other experiences!"

Drobick wasn't the only one whose questions were pointing in the same direction and again said out loud, "How do you appropriate somebody's fear. It seems such a strange question?"

There was a short pause and Drobick and Palumbo said simultaneously, "What else can he switch?"

"What else, indeed," Cabe contemplated. "Can he, in some way, stock up the fear episodes like memories to use later?"

The breadth and extent of Nathan's powers were becoming a little more defined if not totally understood. That there was power wasn't the question. They knew he had power. He could direct it. He might be able to collect fear as a weapon and direct that fear on more than one person and his power was growing.

Their realization too, was that he may have many more secrets to discover. After all, he was only eleven years old and had several years just to reach mental maturity.

"So," Cabe said, "Now what?"

It was a position that was very new for him. With a little less self-assurance of what to do, like how do you collect information from a kid you don't know, and what kind of information do you collect, began to show in the direction of Cabe's planning.

The mammoth realization that there was someone else who obviously was aware of Nathan and interested in him meant that he had to move more quickly, but with everything at stake, careful and deliberate action was much more prudent. Prudence, however, was a luxury they didn't have.

Drobick finally said, "I don't think there is any choice, we have to go with Wolfe. He's a pure statistical scientist and I think with his initial understanding of the question he's a must have guy. One thing I do know is that he's dying to have a look see. This is a one of a kind kid and the chances of studying a phenomenon like this is irresistible.

32

The Boy's Powers Continue to Grow

Following the incident on the way home and his explanation to his mother, Nathan felt exhausted. His mother was very concerned that a second event had occurred and told Levi of her suspicion.

"I think we may have to do some checking at Tech," Levi said. "I'm going to have to have a heart to heart with Dr. Phipps and set up some kind of an exam."

"There seems little else we can do," Ally said.

"I'll be there and he'll have some fun too," Levi assured her.

Nathan recovered from the second event quickly. His new and growing friendships were his salvation. For one of the first times in his life, he enjoyed going to school. With his introduction on the committee, and getting to know Buddy and Miguel, he began to relax in school activities. One of those activities was his favorite, tutoring students which he did during study hall. His new friends improved his focus on school and helped his already sky-high grades but mostly his attitude.

The older kids in his bigger school reduced his obvious difference that had caused him a lot of negative pressure that he'd experienced in a small town school. His stress now relented somewhat because he became just one more kid on a long list of other kids who had their own differences.

Though his distinction was lost in that list, he also quietly began testing his capabilities in a low key way. Because of his early experiences, he shared with no one, not even to his friends and certainly not to his mom and dad.

Nathan found it exhilarating to explore his mind. The discoveries he began to make about himself did not happen fast or necessarily easy. Each small discovery about his limitations and his powers were illuminating.

His inherited genes mixed with the events at his birth, created a one of a kind subject of study. Emotional switching feeling the emotional and physical problems of another person, was something he was born with. He could, in a way, walk in another person's moccasins, but in his case, it was in another person's emotions.

Using his power against bullies was a surprise to himself too, when it first happened. His own anger triggered that response. The instinctual reaction transferred his own fear and anxiety to his tormenter. It wasn't a long leap, when he saw a similar event, to use the victim's fear and panic and visit them on the offending bully.

He began to realize, though very young, he could take what one person was feeling and put it in another person's mind. He discovered that the density and depth of that fear was intensely powerful on a person's psyche and it was the option Nathan went to first to stop attacks. His first incident was self-protection. His motivations in all the other incidents began with a desire to help someone. After all, he reasoned, that's what his mom had taught him by example all his life.

He found out quickly, that his efforts weren't always interpreted as helping. He believed he was subduing a playground bully, which in his mind, was the compassionate thing to do. Those first experiences in Carey though, were turned on him to somehow make him the perpetrator. Trying to evaluate himself and what exactly he was, was a lonely task. He didn't feel like he could just talk it over with his parents because he wasn't sure of his own place on earth. Until he was more confident of his own understanding, he would continue to silently test himself.

As he grew older with more specific experiences he could keep and stack his collected fear experiences. Mixing and compounding those experiences was just starting to come into focus in his mind. It was another issue to understand.

During one of the committee meetings on developing a plan to help their sister school, Mr. Reese suggested that the students create a mission statement, something Nathan heard about. Seemed everybody these days wrote a "Mission Statement;" a declaration of what a person or group's goal would be and what they'd do to reach it.

That, Nathan thought, would be what he'd try to do. He Googled "mission statement," found that some guy named Covey developed the concept in one of his books. With that, Nathan began to study his capabilities somewhat like he saw his dad do in his work. Once he understood himself better he became determined to put together his own mission statement. Then, he could determine what direction he wanted his life to take.

In the meantime, he decided his first test would be to switch one person's difficulties to those of another but not in a negative way. He also knew he'd have to work on a time and a place. Next it would be important, he reasoned, to make it happen in a matter of seconds and then examine the results.

Little did he know of the extent of the dark powers that were aligning to take control of him. He believed he was always trying to help when he exercised his gifts. Help, though, was not in the minds of those gathering for their devious mission to take and control his power and if that meant taking control of him, so be it.

33

Nathan Farnsworth, Guinea Pig

A few days after the sidewalk event, Levi Farnsworth went into his mentor's office. Dr. Bernard Phipps was a post doctoral scholar and chair of Biophysics and Biology at New Tech and it was he who had pursued Levi and convinced him to join his department.

The transition between Levi's field biological studies in Idaho and rigorous study in New Tech's prestigious lab was substantially more unsettling than Farnsworth had expected. It was both exciting and deeply challenging but he hadn't expected the intensity of the publish-or-perish mantra.

Many of his data collections, experiments and sequential testing were analyzed in labs somewhat like New Tech where they were dissected and evaluated. It was during one of his discussions with Dr. Phipps, talking about his data, that Farnsworth had expressed his concern about Nathan.

Dr. Phipps was immediately interested, more than a little. He didn't tell Farnsworth that Nathan's case was known to him. He had met Dr. Gordon Ray at a medical conference at which Phipps had spoken. His subject was the "Effects of hyper-oxygenated cells, excess blood and of gene competition and their regulated expression on a baby's brain."

Researchers were looking into the issue, but the genetics and condition affecting any given child, happened so rarely, that it was hard to get control comparisons. The two had a conversation that set in motion Phipps initial interest in Nathan, but when he found out how accomplished and innovative a researcher Nathan's father was, it seemed to be a perfect match to lure Levi to New Tech and thus get a look at Nathan himself.

"What's up Levi?" Phipps said. "You're looking a little haggard."

"There have been two more incidents with Nathan," Levi said. "They seemed somewhat less traumatic for him, but I was hoping he'd get beyond repeating them."

Phipps was vaguely aware of Nathan "issues" and tried to comfort Levi, "I think you have to accept the fact that Nathan isn't going to stop doing what he does instinctively. But, Phipps also realized his assessment that Nathan wouldn't change was grossly inadequate. Nathan will change massively in years to come. He's a product of his genes and the condition of his birth and he obviously has some unusual mental modifications." Phipps rethought his statement.

What Phipps hadn't really internalized was that Nathan had actual, useable power. He had been under the impression that it was an intellectual gift of some kind.

"Ally thinks there have been some changes in attitude and contentment. He's made some friends, and has done some school committee work and tutoring which seem to agree with him, but I'm just not sure the calm will last," Levi said.

"You know we can't really get to the bottom of this until we examine him officially. You knew it had to come. The best part of this situation is that it can be done over time and not condensed into a mind-numbing series. I'd suggest that you see if he wants to come to 'work with dad' and we do some introductions to the people here. Make it a chance for him to see the things you do which would fit because he's very bright. I think he'll enjoy it. Phipps, pushing slightly said, "What'd ya say? We've got the conclusions to a couple of experiments coming up that he can see up close so you can invite him for that."

"I've promised myself a million times that I wasn't going to make him a lab rat—I just have a hard time with it," Levi said, dropping his head.

"No lab rat," Phipps said. "Just a day at work with dad. Just to eliminate any potential interpretation by Nathan, suggest to him that he bring his buddies."

Phipps could hardly contain himself that he was actually going to meet and talk to Nathan beyond just introductions when he welcomed the Farnsworths to New Tech. He felt the idea to meet him in a low pressure situation with everybody's focus on something besides Nathan was a positive. Phipps' attention however, would be totally on Nathan. He just hoped that Nathan didn't' become aware and thus defensive. It wasn't just that there was so much he didn't know, it was getting to know Nathan personally, an exciting prospect.

"As I said before, there are two experimental results we could show him," Phipps told Levi." The first is delivering of medication via nano technology to a specific site in the brain that causes epileptic seizures. If that medication gets to just the right place it reduces the intensity and length of the episodes and may lead to a total cessation of the seizures. Another exciting procedure is that we've genetically modified a person's own T-cells to recognize cancer cells so the immune system can fight them."

"I just hope that Nathan isn't bored," Phipps said.

"Don't think he will be," Levi said, "and we can invite his new friends to come along with him. His eyes are gonna bug out at the stuff around here. He has always been interested in the work I was doing."

Phipps had chosen these two studies because they'd been going on for a while and looking at the results was always interesting, particularly with the computer displays and amazing microscope screens kids could look at in the lab. Both of the tests could be graphically displayed which was why he was hopeful they'd interest Nathan especially.

Developments in mathematical modeling of gene expression, Phipps realized, would give him the tools to evaluate Nathan in ways that wouldn't be intrusive, but highly revealing. Modeling Nathan's powers may not necessarily be definitive since the protein transcription factors were still not fully understood or quantified. Being able to talk to him, he thought, would be a great start in helping Levi fully understand his son.

34

A Unique Genetic Code

"Mike, can you get the hospital records to Wolfe and ask him to check 'em out? Find out how much time he needs and then I'm thinking the four of us ought to do some serious planning. Dick found an amazing cabin at Fallen Leaf Lake at the south end of Lake Tahoe we can rent. We can fly in to South Lake, enjoy a few days to work on some things, maybe even get in a little fishing." Cabe said.

"I'll have the plane pick him up in Spokane and take him there a couple of days early to give him a chance to look everything over undisturbed," Drobick said. "I'm sure Dick can arrange some transportation to the Cabin. Jimmy can fly down here and get the rest of us and we can have our meeting."

At a certain point along Highway 89 south of Emerald Bay, both Lake Tahoe and Fallen Leaf Lake can be seen by looking Northeast for Tahoe or Southwest for Fallen Leaf. Most tourists miss the smaller lake's view because of the dominance of Lake Tahoe's Emerald Bay. Though Fallen Leaf is small, it's beautiful and amazingly hidden especially in the shadow of one of the most iconic and beautiful lakes in the world.

With only five cabins on the lake and all of the shoreline owned by a closed-joint corporation, no other cabins or structures were allowed to be built on it. It was a gated, secluded jewel of a hide-a-way. One of the cabins on the lake shore was a magnificent rustic log mansion built with natural white and red cedar logs, with the bark removed. Calling the structure a "cabin," is like calling Pebble Beach a par-three.

The entrance had two huge natural cedar logs as posts at its front door. The flaring bases were cut flat on the bottom to stand straight up, leaving the impression that they'd grown right out of the ground. Each of the double front doors were a massive four feet by eight feet with natural limb handles adorning the doors. An opaque circle of glass was inset, half on one door and half on the other. An elaborate pine tree carving was superimposed over the glass and continued into the wooden frames of each door. Openings in the outline of the branches allowed glass to be seen through the tree and also under its limbs.

The inside was just as elaborate as the outside, if not more so. Another main post was a full tree mounted in the same manner that the entrance logs were placed. It was essentially the center post of the magnificent foyer of the house which towered thirty feet to the ceiling. The diameter of the center post at floor level was twelve-feet. Behind it stood a staircase that used the naturally twisted limbs of Manzanita bushes, with totally organic shapes, to form the staircase handrails.

Huge joists and trusses perfectly cut joints in a semi-Japanese tradition unfolded above the floor when you looked up. The intricacies of the structure were amazing by themselves but when combined with the surface and color of natural cedar logs was simply stunning. Dark slate for the entrance floor was the perfect compliment.

Despite its size, it had a feeling of warmth and hominess. Embedded tubing in the floors made the ambient heat particularly even but without being oppressive. Two staff members maintained the grounds and building. A butler and chef tended to the interior.

South Lake Tahoe's airport was about a twenty-minute drive to the cabin. The flight was usually about two and a half hours by plane but Jimmy Schwartzman, Cabe's personal pilot, flew them to South Lake and put them on the tarmac in less than two hours. They too, were retrieved by the butler.

"Well Jeeves, It's good to see you in the wild," Cabe said. "Nothing like an experienced butler to keep things functioning smoothly."

"Good to see you too and to get into the mountains once in a while. I've gotta tell ya' that the chef here is fantastic. He has a great dinner planned for tonight," Jeeves said. "I've been enjoying his food while I've scoured the walls. No 'bugs' anywhere, except for mosquitoes, by the way."

"Hey Jeeves, why don't you sit in with us on the Nathan conversation this afternoon?" Cabe said.

"Well, I'd be happy to, but I hate to tell you I'm working. I'll help the chef and do some reconnoitering. You do the talking," Jeeves said, "fill me in later."

When they pulled up to the cabin after the thirty minute drive, Cabe said, "Well Dick, I see you're spending my money with your usual frugality."

"You know me boss, nothing but the most expensive," he said. "The good thing is I think the seclusion is worth the price alone. As you can see there are only five houses on the entire lake and every foot tightly controlled. No prying eyes. With the surrounding mountain basin, even satellites have such a short pass over; they can get very little cover time. It's very low key and in the middle of everything we need. By the way, everybody's gone home for the season so we're virtually at the lake alone."

Dr. Wolfe came out through the majestic entrance from the bedroom area. "You sure know how to live," he said to Cabe.

"At least Palumbo knows how he thinks I should live," he said, glancing at Palumbo with a raised eyebrow.

"The Chef has a late lunch for us," Wolfe said. "Do you mind if I live here for the rest of my life? This is definitely the life style to which I wish to become accustomed."

Lunch was fresh tuna fish salad on grilled sourdough with some artichoke hearts on the side and tea. The chef topped it off with some

Ritz Cracker pie. "That's exactly right," Cabe said, "nothing that'll get us sluggish. You're right Dick, this chef is a thinker."

Cabe walked out on the deck overlooking Fallen Leaf Lake followed by the three men. "Exceptional," he said to Palumbo. "Perfect if we need to use it for our venture. I've got to make a call. How about we meet back here at three?"

"Palumbo you go first when I get back. Drobick you fill in when there's something you'd like to add and Dr. Wolfe, you go last. Keep in mind what you saw, in light of the hospital records," Cabe said and left to call Vickie.

The deck was huge, more than 2000 square feet by itself. Four comfortable deck chairs were arranged with a low table in the middle of the four men. A steaming hot pot of coffee sat in on the table in a brewer.

Cabe returned shortly and said, "Dick, you're up."

Palumbo began reciting the incredibly life altering journey he'd just been on. Wolfe sat in rapt attention. He took notes on a few comments that Palumbo had with Dr. Ray.

"Did Dr. Ray say when they started noting the differences in Nathan?" Wolfe asked.

"It actually began long before the birth," Palumbo said. "As you read in the reports, Dr. Ray, the father, that is, treated Ally when she fell into a side tributary of the Bitterroot River. He put her on oxygen for a while after she got back to the hospital. You've got the reports so most of what I would add would be mostly the impressions I got from the sons' own intense interest in the case he inherited from his father."

Wolfe began explaining what he found in the hospital records. "That is what's so fascinating. This whole thing started very early in the pregnancy. One of the comments that Dr. Ray made, although he couldn't explain it, was that the fetus apparently was affected with the extra oxygen or maybe more accurately, had faster brain development and a more complex genetic makeup. It's just so interesting to me how they started tracking so early. Judging precisely or statistically what the increase meant was more difficult to calculate.

"Eleven years doesn't seem long, but in medicine, that can be an eternity, especially considering birth technology of today.

"Ray told me the development of Nathan's brain was obvious, but hard to take in because it was so different. To top that off, Ally had gestational diabetes. When he was born, his body was stuffed with heavily oxygenated blood. He weighed, as you know, eleven pounds two ounces. A big boy! Dr. Ray and other doctors considered removing some blood which can be typical in gestational diabetes births. The doctors chose to wait for several hours and eventually chose not to make any blood extractions."

"Let me outline what I think happened in the beginning. From the first ultrasound there was an indication of extended brain function, the point in the pregnancy at which the first infusion occurred was at about three and a half months. Within seven days, there were indications of what can only be called emanations of some kind, thought to be electrical, but the waves were not really understood because they had never been seen before and there was no real way to measure them.

"It was at this point that Dr. Ray began collecting information on the waves and consulted neurologists to track the development they determined. It wasn't ultrasound echoes or other monitoring device interference but the emanations, very slight at the beginning, and a new phenomenon from Nathan.

"All other readings were normal. Everything proceeded with no problems but the waves continued to grow in power. They didn't seem to interfere with the baby's development. It was roughly determined, without being able to be precisely measured, that the brain was developing some kind of netting over the entire surface and the waves, as the child developed, seemed to be coming from that netting.

"Dr. Ray kept a close eye on Ally and worried she might be affected but she did fine," he said. She continued hyper-oxygenation infusions with no apparent problems so Dr. Ray would let them go home between checkups. Had there been obvious problems, I think the doctor would have kept her at the hospital. The baby kept assimilating the oxygen which may have amplified the network and just continued to get stronger.

"When Nathan was born, more tests confirmed the complex interlocking net over the brain. It was fully turned on under the control of the child from the beginning but it wasn't something he seemed to use or need, necessarily. What the doctor didn't expect was that the net could project waves that could be picked up by our technology, but again, not something we'd seen before. Those waves seemed to be similar to sound wave ranges but more complex," he said.

The three men sat in rapt attention, as Wolfe went on to explain that the net would continue to function as the child did and possibly expand its capability to do other things. "What those other things might be, is anyone's guess," he said.

"That sounds like a chance to take a break," Cabe said. Let's do some thinking and start putting together some ideas of what next steps we should consider.

Jeeves noticed they were starting to get up and called from the house, "Dinner at seven."

The men all made pit stops and took off walking along the lake shore. Although it was relatively small, the lake was deep and the water quite dark but absolutely clear. The fall air was crisp but comfortable. A slight breeze rustled the aspen leaves that were just starting to drop their fall color. The sweet, musky smell of fall was pure Sierra Mountain perfume.

"I have it on good authority that we have an early morning Tahoe fishing trip tomorrow," Palumbo said.

They muttered in agreement. They walked for about forty-five minutes taking in the beauty. What surprised them most was the

6,200 foot elevation. A brisk walk at that elevation, when you're not used to it, was even more taxing than anyone expected. The sun was well behind the top of the basin by the time they got back and the chilled air was turning a bit chippy.

Dinner was, as Jeeves said it would be, fantastic. Beef Wellington with small fried whole potatoes, broccoli salad, and halved and slightly burned Brussels sprouts with balsamic vinegar and a small lightly charred crème brulae.

Bedtime was early with a wakeup call at 4 am. When each man went to his room he discovered a plush warm Tahoe worthy coat embroidered with the letters TNV on the breast pocket lying on their beds. TNV It stood for the "The Nathan Venture." They were on the dock by five a.m. and in the charted boat minutes later. The heavy jackets were necessary as the High Sierra fall made its presence felt on the surface of the beautifully clear lake in the early morning dawn.

The obligatory tour of Emerald Bay started the trip in the pre-dawn light and five hours later, the boat returned with all hands catching at least a couple of lake trout with all but a few for lunch released back into the lake. It was lake trout for lunch for everybody.

After eating Cabe said, "I see no real way to understand the nature of Nathan's capabilities without a thorough personal examination," and then waited. There was no disagreement.

Wolfe was the first to voice a concern. "There are two elements we don't know, the extent of his power and if it's substantial, how do we overcome it?"

"We've been thinking about that," Cabe said. "I've heard you describe the nature of his mind waves as similar to sound wave oscillations which is what I thought when I first saw them. In my media business, controlling sound waves or any kind of waves is what we do. There are materials that counter waves and can interrupt or disperse them as needed. The problem is that most broadcasting waves start from a stationary position; in this case there is no fixed point, other than totally having Nathan covered to disrupt him. "We have no choice but to consider taking him," he concluded.

With the issue discussed, the four came to some specific methods of what they needed to do and what they had to collect from Nathan. A totally controlled environment was needed. That dictated several requirements on the taking of Nathan. One very critical factor was the place where Dr. Wolfe could reasonably conduct the tests. Palumbo again was asked to get the details of the abduction ready for Cabe.

35

A Scientific Self-Evaluation

Two things seemed to open Nathan's world: First, his growing maturity began to help him truly recognize that he had capabilities and no one else had anything them. Those capabilities also had potential that he could use more positively than just giving bullies their comeuppance. The second element, he determined, was that he felt better about himself with friends that helped ground him in a much friendlier environment rather than hostile surroundings that brought out darker responses.

With that understanding he realized his past personal complications were no longer an impediment. He no longer felt reluctant to test himself and in fact began to relish the thought of seeing just how far he could go.

He was well aware of how his father took great pains to be precise in his measurements and thorough in his genetic research. It was in his nature under the tutelage of his precise father. How many times had his father repeated the scientific method, hypothesize a theory, test the theory, and replicate. If a theory was replicatable by others, it would be considered verified. But even then, he thought, there were outliers; he himself was proof of that.

It really wasn't a question. He would follow the process laid out for him by his dad. He realized it was a little dicey to be the subject of his own experiment.

He started collecting the information. He quickly saw that there would be a bunch of theories so he selected the most obvious variation in his genetic makeup. He could propel emotions and feelings from one person to another by controlled projection with his mind. How it worked or how he did it was a different story.

As much as he wanted to use his devices to store his experiments and conclusions on, he decided it was too risky. If they were on an electronic device the info could be hacked. To thwart hacking, he chose to prepare a hand recorded code to which only he had interpretational access. If it were hacked it would be indecipherable and useless to anyone attempting to read the notes. He called it his Nectarine code.

There were a plethora of options to consider, but Nathan defined the parameters to what he began calling "switching." He would switch the emotional feelings of one person to another for no more than a couple of seconds without having his action propel fear or anger as he felt compelled to do in his earlier experiences. The best way to test this, he decided, was to take the feeling of a physically challenged person and switch it into the feelings of one of the school's best athletes. He theorized that if he could control the switch for a specific time, say a couple of seconds that would verify one of his express abilities.

He proceeded to choose his test subjects at random and people he didn't know. As much as possible, he wanted to reduce his own potential emotional influences which could distort the test. Even more, he wanted to learn how he was directing the switching technique which had been instinctual reactions to events in his life, not a controlled test.

Another element began to flow into his mind. Could there be potential or permanent damage to those he chose to test? Judging on his previous experiences, he believed that there wouldn't be lasting effects but then these were human subjects. Who could know? He put that question on the shelf to consider later.

Neither Buddy nor Miguel could know, but he saw that having them around while conducting his tests could prove another facet of his abilities, which was to maintain his own anonymity while testing. He thought of the incident during the fight when he tromped around in the emotional being of the man in the Corvette. That couldn't happen again and was something he had to prevent. "In control" became his mantra and he was determined that no one would be hurt.

Tomorrow he would begin actual testing. He would first try at lunchtime but only for a few seconds. Because he could not or chose not to only read emotions extensively, as in the case of the Corvette man, he felt a few seconds was enough to help him evaluate the amount of emotional change he would be able to detect in the subject. If the change was subtle and short, a person probably wouldn't notice which was good, Nathan decided.

36

Bully Learns Painful Lesson

Today was the day Nathan planned to do a test. He also planned to write notes trying to describe his experience and evaluate it with the lunch court providing the location and he would make it somewhat spontaneous. He finished his advanced algebra class, where most of the students were eighth graders, and then went to lunch, picking up Buddy on the way.

They spotted Miguel at a table and went and sat down with him. They each bought a carton of milk and pulled out their sandwiches and started munching. Of course, the most important lunch items were officially banned by "food Nazis" as junk food but lovingly provided by the boy's moms.

The highlight of lunch was when the strategic and critical bartering began. Buddy had a bag of Doritos, Miguel had two handmade cinnamon churros and Nathan had a small rectangle chocolate cake about the size of a large cupcake, made by Ally. A deal was quickly struck and they each shared bites of the dessert booty. It was a good food day for all.

In the remaining fifteen minutes of lunch they relaxed and watched squirrely antics going on around them. Nathan determined that this was his chance to test his theory. He selected two individuals: a young sophomore student with Cerebral Palsy and the other, one of the school's premier athletes. He focused his attention and surreptitiously aimed his hand in the direction of the athlete, switching the feeling and difficulties of the wheelchair bound palsy sufferer to the young, strong athlete.

Nathan carefully noted the athlete's responses. This was the first time that he attempted to exercise his abilities without a strong emotional motive. The results were amazing. He was able to covertly convey what the sufferer dealt with everyday of his life and briefly implanted it into the mind of the athlete.

Although the ballplayer did not outwardly show the suffering of the spontaneous writhing muscle movements affected in dyskinetic cerebral palsy that disrupted movement and caused shaking limbs and speech difficulties. He was infused with the mental and emotional onslaught of mental disruption and an exercise in real empathy.

He timed the switch, a few seconds long, using the lunch court clock.… Amazing, he thought, how long two or three seconds felt like at times.

There was a visceral reaction from the young man learning firsthand what a person with Cerebral Palsy lives with. The next reaction Nathan could never have anticipated nor predicted. The athlete went to the young man with CP and began talking with great animation, and despite the strain of difficult communication, it was as though the two had instantly bonded.

Even in those few seconds, Nathan worried that the CP victim might feel worse if he felt the strength of the football player and knew it would not be staying with him. But that didn't happen. He had tightly controlled precisely what he wanted to accomplish.

Nathan also learned that some of the athlete's brain synapses imprinted the emotional feelings. Profound emotional reactions are some of the most intense memories for most people and thus something the young football player would not soon forget.

The wheelchair bound patient was as stunned as he was pleased. He had felt nothing during the switch. He had finally, somehow, found someone, other than other Palsy victims, who seemed to understand precisely how he felt. His face glowed with satisfaction and his new friend picked up on that glow.

Nathan had overheard a few of the excited words of the athlete who was saying he had somehow received a totally consuming insight into the difficulties of his new wheelchair-bound friend. "Emotions," he thought, are powerful things, especially on the brain and even more the heart. He wondered about their ultimate power, and made some mental notes in his quest to catalogue his tests.

"Nathan, Nathan," Miguel punched him in the shoulder. "Hey where's your brain? The bell just rang and we've got to get to class." The boys headed away from the table, as Nathan's world was beginning to change.

One of the items Nathan wanted to remember of that first incident, during the first day attack, was that Miguel had been the subject of his switching and he wanted to ask him about his response. That would have to wait for another day and the trio split up for their classes. Nathan kept mental notes using his self-made code "graft made, fruit germinated, and successful fruit ripening to be determined." It was enough for him to remember the critical elements of the event.

The best way to describe Nathan's reaction was elation. "It was exhilarating," he thought, and he was both proud and anticipating the future testing variations. One of the most important notes he took was that he had used his gift without an overwhelming negative emotion from himself or the test subjects. He was pleased with that because, again, it meant that he was in control. Tomorrow might be a good day to replicate his test.

When Nathan got home, he told his mom that his buddies shared their desserts and everybody loved the chocolate cake. He finished his homework by dinner and sat down for Pan de Elote, one of his favorites. During dinner Levi said he had an idea and wondered what Nathan thought about coming to work with him to see his new research digs.

"That sounds interesting. What's it like over there Levi?" she asked.

"Well, they've got some very unique equipment and experiments going on. You know how you're very good at math, Nathan" he asked. "We are developing mathematical models to simulate the actions of genes. And," Levi continued, "I've met a couple of colleagues in the electrical engineering department who've got some really wild stuff going on.

"I don't think that his math has gone that far," Ally said, as Nathan's eyes glazed over slightly. But what they didn't realize was that Nathan was growing in ways not even comprehended by his parents at this point. His father's explanation of the test sent his son's mind into possible directions that he'd been raising on his own as he was a testing. Although he could only vaguely understand processes of the capacity of genes to compete in utilizing proteins and genetically modified T-cells, his innate senses grasped the fundamental meaning.

Nathan asked if Miguel and Buddy could go. "I think they'd like it," Nathan said.

Levi said, "I'm sure we can arrange that. Dr. Phipps already suggested you bring a couple of friends when I asked him if this was good. But remember, I've got to get Mr. Reese's and your teacher's approval, along with signed parental permission notes, but I'll bet we can do it. You'll have to talk to your buddies and have them ask their parents. We may have to go on a Saturday or an after school trip. That OK?"

"That'd be great," Nathan said. "I can't wait to tell them at lunch tomorrow."

But the morrow came with a high price. When the three sat down for lunch they looked at Miguel and gasped. It was obvious that Miguel had come to school with a lot of bruises and a black eye. He was quiet, very reserved, and extremely alert, constantly looking in every direction. It was another message from Reuben, Nathan determined in his thoughts!

Buddy instantly felt his fear return. "Reuben?" he asked.

"Yeah," Miguel said.

Nathan had not forgotten the name or the face. His old vengeance mentality, that had lapsed, returned with retaliation as the objective. Just as he was about to tell his friends of the possible trip to New Tech, that ugly gang bully mentality returned. Apparently, the lesson Reuben learned on that first day of school or the lunch court incident had not made a lasting impression, Nathan realized.

It was at that most inopportune moment, for Reuben anyway, that the gang leader arrived in the lunch court. He directly initiated taunting Miguel by pointing at him with his fingers bent into gang signs. Nathan was livid. It was the worst thing Reuben could have done.

As hard as he tried to contain his anger and frustration, Nathan could not control himself fully. But he remembered the Idaho situation and was pre-disposed to make sure that his retaliation would be swift and invisible to anyone else. He subtly, but very surely, aimed both hands at Reuben as he passed Miguel. In a split second, Nathan poured every fear, rejection and painful emotion he had ever experienced and accumulated over the years, directly at the bully gang leader. It was a massive stream of emotional agony crammed forcibly into Reuben's consciousness.

There would be no physical scars, but Nathan's message would be sent, and this time Reuben would never forget.

In an instant, Reuben was on his knees. He shuddered, sobbed and fell face down, covering his head with the back of his hands trying to stop the rush of emotional anguish. His gang pals backed off as though Reuben had caught a dozen contagious diseases at once. Nathan did not relent even as the lunch court monitors rushed to Reuben's writhing body kneeling at Miguel's feet.

For a full minute Nathan sent his pent up anger and ache of the other victims of bullying he had known in Idaho and continued to force them smashing into Reuben's psyche. Twenty or thirty kids who'd been on the receiving end of Reuben's bullying gathered to glare at the sobbing, kneeling young man. Several "Yeahs" were heard. Several laughed at Reuben's slobbering cries. There was no sympathy from Gravotos former victims.

Finally Nathan backed off. Reuben was relieved but seemed to sink deeper into the hard concrete. Monitors could do nothing but call for help. EMT's were dispatched and within a few minutes loaded the boy onto their gurney. All their attention was on Reuben. No one noticed the smug look on Nathan's face.

In the message to Reuben's psyche, Nathan implanted a stark threat. Touch Miguel again and this would be just a small sample of what he or his friends would suffer if they bothered Miguel, Nathan or Buddy or their families.

The bell had rung several minutes before, but the students were slow to head back to their classes. None could explain what had just happened. The bully got a heaping helping of major bullying himself and now knew it's pain by times ten. There was no question of that nor where the lesson came from or how it was delivered. Who knew? Reuben didn't know, but he would remember who he wouldn't get near again. Miguel and his buddies would be left alone and in the future when Reuben saw Miguel, it would be Reuben who'd turn to go the other way.

Nathan fretted about breaking the rules of his testing regimen. But he took several things away from the experience. His power was growing, his sense of focus was becoming more acute and his disciplined capacity to control his tests was coming into focus.

The negatives, as he saw them, were his reliance on injecting his emotion and personal feelings into any test, along with his inability, in this case, of keeping his friendship from influencing him. He wasn't sure what that meant exactly, but he'd make some highly detailed notes and do analysis. He realized another thing and thought, "I have to stop using my hands for direction. Too obvious," he made a mental note: "Work on that."

He missed his chance to mention the trip to New Tech during lunch, but told his friends what the possibilities were after school. Miguel was reluctant to commit but Nathan said, "Miguel, you look like crap right now. But in a week you'll look great as always," and he and Buddy laughed and gave Miguel a buddy bump with his shoulder. Miguel laughed too, relieved by the balm of their friendship, somehow sensing that neither Reuben nor his gang buddies would ever bother him again.

37

Levi Reaches New Tech Agreement

Levi was pleased with his son's response. Now his question was: "Exactly how do I determine how Nathan does what he does?" Ironically, with this simple question, Nathan became the very thing that Levi was trying so hard to avoid, turning Nathan into a lab rat. What he didn't know was that with his and Phipps efforts, there were now two on-going attempts to determine the extent of Nathan's capabilities: Levi and Phipps who were trying to help Nathan, and then Nathan's own effort at self understanding. These were the known, legitimate, positive efforts. Maxwell Cabe's attempts to extract Nathan secrets were both personal and business related. But even his motives were somewhat tame compared to an unbeknownst fourth effort yet to be revealed.

Phipps and Levi left the building to take some pressure off the decisions they had to make and took off walking kicking some ideas back and forth.

"Ya know, Levi, I think we need to examine the medical records. What do you think?" Phipps said.

"I suppose it's inevitable, speaking as a scientist, but speaking as a father, it's against everything I believe." Levi said.

As they walked back to the office they made some preliminary plans. Phipps suggested that they could ask the three boys if they wanted to see a drop of their own blood and check it out through the microscope, they might like that. "We'd have to have permission from the parents but we could ask and even invite them to participate."

There were serious implications about examining blood and Levi knew it, but said nothing. Phipps knew it too, but was hoping to do some serious research on Nathan with as little of an impact as possible.

When they walked into the lab, Phipps saw post doctoral scholar Gerald Seperman, who everybody knew as Jerry, working on his ongoing project dealing with mathematical gene modeling.

"Hi Jerry," Phipps said, "Let me introduce you to Levi Farnsworth. He's the geneticist who just came aboard."

"Hi Levi," Seperman smiled. "I've seen you around, glad to finally get a chance to meet you formally. I'm looking forward to sharing some work time, and my favorite thing, checking out your brain for any ideas I can steal," he said.

"I'm not too sure there's anything up there to steal," Levi said, returning the smile.

"I've got a little favor to asked, Jerry. Levi's son and a couple of his friends are coming to the lab, probably on a Saturday," Phipps said. "They're junior high boys." We'd like them to examine a little blood under the microscope, some things like that. Do you have some samples we could use so the boys could compare some blood samples to their own?"

Seperman turned on like a flood light. "Oh hey," he said, "I've got some fantastic comparison samples that they'll go nuts over. They're gunna love em. I've got lion and tiger samples, scorpion blood and some yak blood. You name it. I'll put together some good ones for them and other things they can go at. There's an available microscope bay setup over by the window when you come in. I'd love working with school kids."

Both Levi and Phipps said they'd appreciate it. "We're planning it for a week from Saturday, if that's alright," Phipps said.

"Great, see you then. Just holler if you need anything else. Saturday is generally kind of quiet around here so that's why I come in. It would be a welcome change of pace to show them around."

"Thanks a bunch, Jerry," Phipps said.

"He's a dogged researcher and amazingly quick, and that's not his best quality," Phipps said. "I'm not saying he's good at jumping to conclusions, but he's really good at jumping to conclusions. The amazing part is that most of the conclusions he jumps to are usually right on. His success at extrapolating based on pretty thin evidence is almost unbelievable. I've seen him make that jump from the flimsiest results to spot-on assertions, and he's right about 97% of the time and if he's wrong, it ain't by much."

"I feel lucky we've got someone that'll show the boys a thing or two and have fun doing it," Levi said.

"That he will," Phipps said, "that he will."

38

Reuben's Aftermath

The EMTs were baffled. Reuben didn't have a mark on him except where he had a nasty gash on his arm when he hit the concrete. It was a good ten minutes before they could understand much of what Reuben was saying. It simply didn't make sense.

When they asked him about what happened he recoiled at first, not wanting to relive the event. The emergency crew at first chalked it up to some kind of mental breakdown. But as he returned to a semblance of coherence, Reuben talked about being shot by a streaming beam of fear that didn't let up.

Skepticism prevailed among the EMTs about Reuben's assertions. Stream of fear--what's that? His blood pressure and heart rate returned to normal relatively quickly. The memory scars may not have been visible, but they were certainly going to remain. There was no question that he would be a changed person and his bullied victims would undoubtedly not let him forget his crying fit at their feet.

"A-27 ETA three minutes," the head technician spoke into his handset. "Blood pressure and heart rate near normal--suggest he may need a psych evaluation. I think there's something a little odd here."

They rolled him into the hospital in a wheel chair, signed him in. His bandaged arm was checked and approved after that he was pushed directly to a psychological counselor.

"You a shrink?" Reuben asked with a meekness not common to him. "What happened to me? I don't understand what happened to me."

"That's what we're going to try and find out," the counselor said. "I'm Emma Richards. I'm a psychologist and counselor. The technicians said that other than gash on your arm, you're in good physical condition which is positive. What I'm trying to find out is what caused your collapse."

The next hour was filled with confusion and tears. Every time Reuben tried describing what he really felt during the ordeal, it sent him into uncontrolled sobs. Emma gently continued her probe.

"I got told to leave Miguel alone," Reuben told the therapist. "Miguel was one of my homies and he left my crew. We had to teach him a lesson but now I wouldn't go near him in a tank," Reuben said as he stared at the floor.

"You're hearing voices? Did Miguel have anything to do with this?" she asked.

"No, Miguel didn't do nothin'. And it wasn't really voices, but I just know that if I bother Miguel or anybody he knows, I will get hit with this again harder, so I can't let that happen," Reuben said.

The counselor leaned back in her chair. The voices thing bothered her but the other elements of Reuben's comments didn't fit any psychological disorder profiles she'd ever studied or even heard of.

"So you feel like someone told you that? Let me ask you, Reuben," the therapist continued, "Do you feel like this has happened to you before?"

Reuben's head snapped around like he'd been zapped. Looking directly at the women across the desk, he said emphatically, "Yes! I hadn't thought about that until now. But it was the same kind of feeling I had when we jumped a guy to send a message my crew shouldn't be messed with.

"The difference was the power of the feeling, like night and day. The first time it was like 'cut that crap out' and this time it was like full vengeance," Reuben said. "I gotta tell ya Doc, I never want that ta happen again. I felt like I was about to cease to exist or that my life would be a constant hell. Weird, scary. I'm never scared and this scared the crap outta me! Anytime I see Miguel again, I'm heading the other way."

The two had been talking for about an hour when the doctor said, "I think you're going to be alright, but I'd like to see you next week. Can you do that?

"No way Doc," Reuben said, "you know what would happen to me if people thought I was seeing a shrink?"

"I understand," Richards said. "Please take my card and call me if you want to talk some more. Would you like me to call your parents?"

"Nah, my mom's working and doesn't want to hear about school, and I don't know where my dad is. Don't worry about it," he said.

With that, Reuben left and the therapist knew she'd never see him again. But his story was not something she'd soon forget.

39

Sanjy and Billie Incident Report

The flight back from Tahoe passed quietly. Then Drobick got a call from Billy, of all people.

"Mike, I don't know if you care, but Sanjy and I were confirming some of our facts on the school report we gave you just to be certain everything was accurate. You know we didn't have much time, but we ran across a new report that was pretty odd. And we thought you'd want to know since you like these little odd items."

Drobick's attention was piqued. "Sure" he said, "whadda ya got?"

"Well, we probably wouldn't have been rechecking or even concerned about this, but the fight thing at the beginning of school and then now there was another collapse of a kid in the lunch court at the same school. Scuttlebutt has it that this kid was the gang leader of the first fight.

"The report we found had him collapsing on his face and sobbing. No one touched him and they thought he'd had a mental collapse. He was taken to the hospital by ambulance and had a bad gash on his arm but mentally he was a basket case," they said. Many of the statements made by the other students and recorded in the office seemed to be similar to those given at the time of the first fight. It was just odd enough that Sanjy took the liberty to look at the hospital admittance info and they took the boy to a shrink there.

"So," now Sanjy's juices were flowing. "The shrink at first thought it was some kind of psychotic break with the kid hearing voices, but in her report she also included a statement that the patient had reported that this incident was similar but a much more psychologically violent episode than the original fight. Then she said that the patient also reported that he felt the attack was from outside his head as though he was 'hit,' as he described it. "Don't know if this helps but I can tell you this is gettin' to be one interesting school."

Drobick asked several other questions relating to the incident and then said, "That is strange. What did the hospital do?"

"Checked the EMT's bandages and then had a therapist talk to him for an hour and he left. Name's Reuben Gravotos," Billy said.

"That's some good follow up," Drobick said not revealing just how interested he was to tell Cabe. "Remind me to buy you some more blintzes when you're around our place again."

40

Counting the Cost

Drobick proceeded to fill Cabe in on the new attack. Whadda ya think?" he asked.

Cabe, who'd been contemplating quietly, was fascinated.

"Son of a Banana Slug, that sucker's feelin' his oats," Cabe said. "I think he's beginning to do some more experimentation. But this is also revealing about his personal feelings. Anything else?"

"Yeah, they took the kid to the hospital and he saw a shrink. Her report said the kid felt like he was hit by an emotional tsunami. Sound familiar? He said it didn't come from within but from without and he couldn't explain it. She also said she didn't expect to see the kid again but would have loved to do some more talking with him."

"Mike, I got just a small taste of the power of this kid. I wasn't a target so it didn't bother me that much, but I can see the potential harm this could do to the mind of somebody he didn't like. It might be life altering. If he's testing himself and maybe attempting to expand his capabilities, we're going to have to have a way to control him which may become harder and harder as he develops.

"I thought we had more time but now I don't think so," Cabe said. I don't think we can wait."

41
New Tech Field Trip

With the parental permissions collected, the New Tech field trip was on. Ally and Miguel's mother Lupe, decided they'd be the "control" agents for the trip, besides they rationalized, this could be really interesting.

Principal Reese suggested the boys give a report to the members of the science club about their experiences when they got back.

Ally had called Mrs. Bass who said she was working that day. Mrs. Bass said she'd feel good knowing that Ally and Lupe were with the boys. All three moms signed permission papers for the boys giving a drop of blood for testing and giving them a chance to see it through a powerful electron microscope that was light years ahead of their middle school science class microscopes.

They'll probably get pretty excited about that," Ally said. "Levi tells me that Gerald Seperman, a world class researcher, is going to talk to the kids and has some interesting animal blood slides to show them along with other genetic research. Then the engineering guys are gonna stand their hair on end with an old Van der Garrff generator. Sounds scary to me but the boys will love it."

The school week dragged for the three locos about to visit the wizards at New Tech. Lunches were a lot quieter and Reuben and his homeboys kept themselves scare. On that Friday, the trio went to Buddy's house for an overnight and some "save the universe" video games along with munchies. They searched the computer for info about New Tech and worked themselves into a lather talking about the next day.

Ally and Lupe picked the boys up just before Mrs. Bass had to leave for work and headed to Levi's office at the Institute.

Cooler Fall temperatures continued and they each wore a light jacket and were talking non-stop as they drove down Huntington Drive. The fall leaves were turning, some red, others, orange and yellow. As they fell they created a carpet of brilliant fall color. With the contrast of the green of the evergreens it was nothing if not stunning.

Like young stallions in a fall field, the three boys were bags of energy laughing and giving each other a bad time.

The group of five arrived at the school and parked as Levi had directed. Ally had called in ahead and so as they pulled into a parking slot Levi walked out to greet them. His first item on the agenda was to walk them past the "Gene Pool" which brought yuks and smiles from the boys. On the campus, trees were also dropping fall leaves as the group crunched its way into the building.

Once inside, Levi took everybody and showed them the labs and animal testing facilities and the computer gene center. He kept everything rudimentary as he talked his way to the laboratory where they were met by Dr. Seperman. Jerry was one of those who really got excited about science. His chance to talk to the boys and their moms about his passion got him going.

Levi introduced the boys to Jerry who said, "I hear you're interested in some science."

"Yeah," they responded in unison.

"Great, how'd ya like to see your own blood on an electron microscope screen?"

All three boys said sure, although Buddy was not too keen about getting the finger prick. It was no wonder since he'd been an unintentional blood donor on the school sidewalk only a few weeks before. All agreed and Seperman arranged to have an assistant take the samples and put them on slides. "It shouldn't hurt for more than a few years!" he said with a grin.

"Yeah, right," Miguel said.

"While he's doing that I've put together several samples from various animals. There are five samples," he said. "There's a lion, tiger, sea snake, scorpion and a yak. You guys think you can guess which ones are which? I"ll give you a few clues and we can make it a game."

"I doubt it," they said, again in unison. "What's the prize if we guess right?"

Seperman kept them thoroughly entertained for an hour regaling them with a ton of scary stories interspersed with splashes of pure science. The guys were enthralled as were their mothers. Toward the end of their hour, the assistant came over with the blood slides of the boys.

They each got a chance to see their own cells close up. Seperman's assistant had set up three monitors and put on the slides of each boy's blood. Even Ally and Lupe got a chance to see the slides. Of course, being mothers, they looked at their own son's blood.

The assistant gave a subtle nod at Seperman then he directed his eyes at Nathan's scope. Seperman said, "Let me take a look." He checked out the three slides and when he looked at Nathan's, he took a side glance back at his assistant, acknowledging that there was something unique there. The two scientists traded their communications without exposing their special interest.

Just before the group left, Seperman put the slides into plastic containers and gave them to the boys but reminded them that they were glass and could break. The boys took them as souvenirs to remember the day. Levi thanked Seperman for his help and teaching. He then took the boys over to the engineering department for some fun with electricity. They had an old Van de Graaff generator and got the boys hair to stand on end. Of course, pictures were taken on their cell phones and sent to other school buddies. Undoubtedly, there'd be lots of laughs when Monday rolled around.

The day was unforgettable for the three friends and Phipps, who'd kept an eye on the events, and was particularly interested in Nathan's slide. He also was interested in Nathan's demeanor, which was calm and typical of an eleven-year-old in most ways, although it was obvious that Nathan's scientific skills were way above normal. Undoubtedly it was also the influence of his parents and his extraordinary intellectually endowed mind.

Levi walked his wife and the entourage back to the car and asked the boys how it went.

"It was awesome," they agreed. And each had their favorite moments….Buddy's was the hair event. His hair went straight out in all directions and won the prize for the wildest looking locks.

On the way home, Ally and Lupe had a great conversation and formed a mutual friendship built on some of the problems both faced with their kids, physical differences and gangs. They stopped in the driveway at Buddy's place and the boys went in to retrieve their belongings from the sleep over.

During the wait, Lupe said to Ally, "I just wanted to tell you how much I appreciate Nathan befriending Miguel. I was at my wits end trying to find a way to get him out of the clutches of those bullying gangbangers."

"That's almost funny," Ally said. "I was just thinking the same thing because Nathan had some real problems in his other school. Miguel and Buddy's friendship has been a great blessing for him and especially for us since as you personally know, it seems like we moms and dads seem to be helpless sometimes. Ya just wanna scream. But even that doesn't do any good."

Buddy waved goodbye and Ally took Miguel and Lupe home.

"Whadda think?" Ally asked Nathan, after letting Lupe and Miguel off at their home.

"I really enjoyed it," he said. "But I know enough about what Dad does and he's showed me enough blood slides and counts to understand that my blood is a little bit different. I could see it in the slides."

Ally was dumbstruck. After a few minutes she ventured "what do you think it means?" she asked.

"I don't know but I'm going to have some serious questions for dad when he gets home," Nathan said, and then turned quiet and looked out the window. Moments later they were parked in their garage.

42

Blood Secrets

Levi almost regretted going back into the lab. He knew that there was a ninety-nine-point-nine per cent chance that Seperman would spot some type of anomaly on Nathan's slide. Phipps already expected it and it was one of the things the chairman wanted to examine carefully. But Levi also knew that to help Nathan, he would have to know as much about his genetic capabilities as possible and there was just no other way.

They went into a quiet conference room. It was obvious to both Phipps and Levi that Seperman was being a little coy. They knew and he knew but didn't try to hide it. It was a "what now" moment.

Phipps looked at Seperman and said, "OK…you first."

"Why do I feel like I've been set up?" Seperman said, his eyes burning into the two men sitting across the table from him. "You could have at least warned me. Maybe I could have done something more!"

Uncharacteristically, Levi responded first and with passion. Even Phipps was surprised.

"I know it seemed totally unfair Jerry, but I had to do something to examine Nathan with the least amount of 'lab rat' mentality," Levi said. "You did a fantastic job. The boys loved it and their moms did too. It gives us, Bernie and I, a chance to introduce you to the situation and the fact that you discovered what we have to evaluate, makes it that much more valid.

Nathan is different, as you obviously figured out," Levi said. It has caused him problems and anything we do to help him adjust and live a quality life is critical to his mom and me."

Phipps chimed in, "Levi's right, Jerry. We appreciate your handling it the way you have. I expected you to spot it right away and you did. Our question now is where we go from here. It's extremely important that this be kept super quiet. You and your assistant have to agree to that! If you do, we want to work with you and figure some things out."

Seperman looked down at the formica covered table. He tapped his knuckles on the hard surface and gradually looked up.

"I understand the absolute necessity in keeping this kind of information quiet to protect Nathan," he said, adding, "but from just my brief look at the slide, I can tell you I think the results are going to be monumental. You know Bernie, the gene expression modeling we're working on, is just the precise tool we need to use here. My guess is that the activating proteins are working overtime in Nathan's case."

"Seperman, you always amaze me. That you can jump that gulf and come to conclusions with as little data as we have…a quick glance at a blood work slide?" Phipps said.

"You know me Bernie, plunge in and jump the shark where angels fear to tread. To destroy a couple of old mixed metaphors" he smiled.

"By the way I returned the slides to the kids so we don't have them to replicate the DNA. We may have to do more to collect samples to work with. We got the slide plates in a computer file, but that won't be enough."

Listening to the discussion, Levi returned to his horrible vision of Nathan as a lab rat. Phipps caught the hesitation in Levi's demeanor.

"We're going to be very careful, Levi," Phipps said. "I also think we can help you and Nathan with more information rather than just guessing. Let's figure out a way to collect some good blood samples without raising Nathan's concern and go from there. "

Levi said he'd work on getting some samples. "They may come from some scrapped knees or something like that, but that's probably what we're going to get.

"We'll work with what we have," Phipps said.

Levi proceeded to fill in some of the details of Nathan's birth. He mentioned the network that covers his brain and Ally's gestational diabetes. While Seperman listened intently. Levi explained in depth the run-ins Nathan had had in his Idaho school and first day in San Marino and the theories that had developed about the nature of Nathan's gift; if the concept of switching the emotions of one person to another was even a real possibility.

"Nothing like dropping one of the most interesting things I've ever heard of right into my line of research," Seperman said.

Phipps said, "I know you're overloaded with stuff right now, Jerry, but I think we should start developing a time frame to help Nathan." Phipps turned to Levi, "I thought that Nathan was doing well, with his new friends. He seemed like he was much less wary of people than I expected."

"Yeah, the friends have made a big difference, but in some ways I think he's feeling a little protective of them, and I don't know where that could end. I got a call from his school about another unexplained incident, but they didn't really know if Nathan was involved. It was just a courtesy call. Seems a boy had an unusual mental episode of some kind who was not prone to any breakdowns," Levi said. "Nathan hasn't said anything about it so I just don't know. Since the first episodes in Idaho, he doesn't like to say anything. He thinks we get too upset."

"I'll look at the slide file and see what stands out. In the meantime, see what you can do about more samples."

Levi left and headed home. Phipps and Seperman stayed to wrap up the lab.

As they did, Phipps began talking. "This is going to be much more difficult than I thought," he said. "For all of our sophisticated science, there are questions we simply can't answer. We may come to all the right conclusions regarding the DNA, cells, synapses, cranial network and other physical evidence and even reach some supportable data, but I don't see any way of working Nathan's psyche into the equation with any certainty. The fact is, we simply don't know how to determine what equations are necessary or how to make the calculations that motivate any actions he might take.

"When, you recognize the magnitude of Nathan's powers," Seperman added, "My concern is how do we control him if he chooses to do something we don't want? Can we physically control him? I think there are some variables that might prove more challenging than we know. We will have to consider that."

Seperman said to Phipps. "You know that's a similar problem to Azimov's 'The Mule.' Even though Nathan can't subtly adjust the mind in an intellectual way, as the Mule did, he can switch the effect of deeply felt emotions possibly to several people at once. Because of the deeper connection emotions have on the brain, they've proven to be more powerful than the Mule's delicate mind manipulation, and he's a fictional character.

"I can't begin to see what the ultimate potential is." Seperman drifted off into thought. "What is the length of time that he can direct the switch? How deep does the switch go into the person and does the switch leave emotional and damaging scars? Does Nathan's ability affect his own emotional well being? Will his power expand and develop into other capabilities? And, again, how do we control him?"

Phipps didn't like the ominous nature of Seperman's thoughts but was again amazed at how the geneticist could leap across intellectual chasms with so little concrete information to find the most significant questions. The question about control, though abhorrent to his fundamental being, had to be addressed. If Nathan was dangerous, they had to be reconciled to the possibility of taking control of Nathan's power no matter how great it might become.

Where does it end? Phipps thought to himself, and is there a chance that it could not end well? A young man's life and perhaps the lives of many others dangled over that "chasm-of-peril" Seperman had just jumped. Another thought began creeping into Phipp's mind. With his pointed questions, Seperman sure sounded like he knew a lot more about Nathan than the department chair could have imagined.

43

Nathan Learns His History

Ally called Levi's cell and asked if he could stop and get some groceries on the way home. She gave him a list and said, "By the way, Nathan's in his room and wants to talk with you when you get back. Not too sure what he wants, but I bet you have an idea."

"Yes, but I'm not looking forward to it," Levi said. "See you in a few."

Nathan had seen blood slides his father had taken of the Bitterroot Mountain trout and wondered what secrets his own blood might reveal. He was aware of various markers, proteins, enzymes and elements of blood. Levi knew that if Nathan remembered those slides, which he surely would have, given his memory and understanding then he'd undoubtedly make comparisons. Maybe the New Tech trip hadn't been such a good idea after all.

Levi dreaded facing Nathan, but knew eventually this day would come. He'd have to discuss all of the issues confronted by someone with Nathan's capacity. Better now, he thought. Nathan will be focused and interested but he hoped more than that, that Nathan would develop the maturity to fully comprehend and thus control his own powers.

Levi parked and walked into the house feeling the weight of the moment. It was five and Ally was working on dinner. She yelled to Nathan, "Dad's home. Come and set the table please."

Nathan dragged himself out of his room and did as he was told. All were silent during dinner, with Ally and Levi casting glances in their son's direction but receiving none in return.

For Nathan it was a somber dinner. After the fun-high of the New Tech experience with his friends, to go into a life altering evaluation involving the people he loved most and a potential low he didn't really want to face was an utterly sobering event. At the same time, it wasn't an option he could avoid. Nathan was becoming more and more mature for his age a lot faster than Nathan, Levi or Ally wanted or perhaps expected.

When dinner was over the three Farnsworths worked together getting the kitchen table cleared and the dishes washed. Levi washed the pans, Ally loaded the dishwasher and Nathan put away leftovers and brought the dishes over to load all in total silence except for the clanging of the pans and the clinking of the dishes.

"Dad and Mom, we've got to talk!" Nathan said.

Levi and Ally had been holding their breath while tip toeing around trying to be quiet while figuratively walking on a floor covered with Captain Crunch. Sighs of resignation and capitulation were as loud as the quiet that had just been breached.

"OK!" Levi asked. "Is this going to be a formal or informal inquisition?"

"What do you mean by formal?" Nathan asked.

"If this conversation is going to be formal I think we should go into the living room," Ally said. If it is less formal we can just sit here at the kitchen table."

"Definitely formal," Nathan said.

"Living room it is then," Levi said.

Nathan did not fully comprehend that his capabilities were conceptually off the charts. But that had begun to change when he started to test himself and particularly after the Reuben incident. He now had proof he could do something his peers in school could not. It was an awakening of sorts and he felt like it was just the beginning, shifting of confusing incidents to the goal of understanding.

The three sat down in their living room. Though plenty comfortable, most of the furnishings were from their Idaho house which was, as Ally sometimes defined its decor, early Halloween. It was a mix of beloved family heirlooms, questionable yard sale treasures, and a couple of affordable new pieces.

Nathan began. "Today was really fun and I don't want to spoil that. But you know Dad, once I saw my blood slide I knew something was different. You've shown me enough blood slides that you've taken of anomalies to give me an idea of differences. There are some things that are definitely not in the blood dictionary."

"Am I weird or something?" he said. "Look, I just want to know what is going on with me."

Nathan told them about his experiments so far and that he intended to continue them to see where they led. He also said that as he was getting a little older he realized that his abilities were changing. That's where I want to start," he said.

Levi took a big breath. "Yeah, you can be as weird as a teenager and you're only eleven. I'd call that weird. Heaven forbid that we have an eleven-year-old teenager in the house."

Levi's levity removed some of the heaviness that was in the room. It even brought a smile to Nathan's face.

"I'm not that bad, Dad!" he said.

"No, you're not. But you can definitely be some sugarless lemonade at times," Levi replied. "OK, I'll be serious. When you were growing inside your mom, we were out catching some samples for some of my research and just enjoying nature. She was about three months along, and some of the rocks were a little slippery. She took a step and went down hard onto a rounded cobble stone in the creek falling on the right side of her rib cage.

"She cracked some ribs and had a hard time breathing. I very carefully carried her to the car, and we rushed to the hospital, not knowing whether it would end the pregnancy. She couldn't take deep breaths and felt like she wasn't getting enough air. They started her on oxygen immediately and that relieved the situation, but throughout the rest of 'your gestation' the painful cracked ribs and the continued shallow breathing required regular infusions of oxygen. She was monitored almost constantly.

"To complicate things, your mom developed a case of gestational diabetes and that, at times, leads to some complications at birth. You were past full term. Your brain had been fed increased levels of oxygen from the time of the accident. The diabetes added additional oxygen and as you know you were eleven-pounds two-ounces, a big lovable baby-still are as a matter of fact," he said.

"Somehow, Nathan, the increased oxygen and the other typical elements of a gestational diabetes birth is that the baby's body is crammed with excess blood. In other words, you had a lot more blood in you than you needed at birth. Doctors frequently drain off some of the blood to reduce pressure. In your case, they chose not do that, so your blood remained and it also altered your cerebral development.

The dangerous part of what happened is that hyper-oxygenization can lead to all sorts of problems, even blindness. Doctors had to be exceptionally careful in treating your Mom and caring for you as you developed.

"Here are some of my speculations of what resulted from the oxygen influx and pressurized blood on your brain. Oxygenated blood can be detrimental, but in your case it was beneficial. Remember, none of this can be proven without extensive tests, but I think it's a pretty good guess given my experience. I also believe that your genetics are part of the equation.

"You're aware of Albert Einstein and the circumstances of his birth. He didn't speak until he was around five. When he died his brain was donated, at his request, to Princeton Hospital. A series of photographs of the surface of his whole brain were taken. His brain was then taken to the University of Pennsylvania where it was cut into slices and photographed. They have an extensive slide library of his brain using those slices that have been studied for years. Some scientists believed parts of his brain developed in some unusual ways."

"The theory is that because Einstein began speaking very late, parts of his brain that complement math skills grew more than that of the average person. Today's studies indicate that great mathematical thinkers use parietal and frontal areas in both parts of the brain, and his math skills were also stimulated by his practice of the violin. It's long been known that there is a correlation of music and math skills. His brain developed with an increased capacity for mathematical calculations and particularly spatial orientation."

"The parietal lobes of his brain where the mathematical and visuospatial areas are located showed some asymmetries that are believed to be evidence that the circuitry for these parts were expanded and developed beyond the normal capacity of most people. Einstein's brain showed that regions of his right parietal area were so dense with neurons that one of the major cortical indentations was actually filled in. It gave him one of his greatest insights using spatial visualization."

Levi suddenly stopped. "I just realized that I'm sounding like I'm lecturing. Do you want me to go on or stop," he said looking at Nathan.

"I need to know this Dad," Nathan said. "Don't stop."

"Here is where you come in. Einstein's brain also had higher than normal developed fissures, sucli and gyni on the surface of his cerebral cortex, contributing to his brilliance. In your case, I believe that because your brain was pressured at birth, and even before, your cerebral cortex experienced a similar influence. I would guess that the number of fissures you have, sucli and gyni, could be as high as triple that of the average person.

"But because you were in utero, the fissures grew and the symmetry of your development, unlike Einstein, was evenly spaced across the cortex and developed somewhat differently. It's called 'Tension-based theory.' This means the surface of the brain folds in on itself because the skull actually limits how big the brain can grow. The folds can help make additional surface area in the brain so clusters of neurons can connect, reconnect and reorganize.

Self testing is a kind of intellectual or mental exercise that those folds give you. You have more brain space which, in turn, allows you to understand and use more fully your neural network.

"Apparently, the net that sits on the surface of your cortex has something to do with your ability to project emotions. The need for a projection ability like yours is still not clear to me," Levi said.

"What about my eyes that seem so different," Nathan asked. "Why would they be a color no one else seems to have?"

"I'm not sure," Levi said. "There is only one connection that I've found in my research and it is not conclusive, only suggestive. Back in the 1940s, doctors thought giving babies more oxygen was good. But later tests showed a higher risk of blindness. You're obviously not blind, but the additional oxygen could have affected the color of your eyes but that is mostly conjecture on my part. We need to conduct extensive studies to confirm anything I've said."

"Why don't I have contacts to hide my eye color so I'm not harassed?" Nathan said.

"Your eyes are potentially too sensitive so we chose not to use contacts as a defensive measure. Better safe than sorry," Levi said.

Nathan was once again silent. He'd just received a large dose of stunning information he was hoping for. Ally too, was somewhat stunned. She knew a few of the particulars but not in the way of what sounded like an academic recitation of everything that involved her son's brain.

Finally Ally asked Levi, "What you've just outlined to us sounds like you're saying Nathan has powers no one else in the world has?

"That's it in a nutshell," Levi said.

"Why!" she said.

"Please remember, this is still speculative on my part. I'm not sure if there are adequate ways to test and confirm as much as half of what I think. Your Mom and I have been hoping that you'd have a somewhat normal childhood. Lately you've seemed happier and we've been glad to see you enjoying your new friends."

Nathan finally looked up after some thought. "Was today just a test to see my blood under lab conditions?"

Levi dropped his head and voiced a quiet, "Yes." "I'm not too proud of that, Nathan, but your Mom and I have been worried sick over the problems you've had and we just have to find out if there is something we can do to help. We couldn't stay in Carey without wondering if some of the episodes there would spin out of control. By moving here and taking advantage of the facilities at New Tech, I felt like we had a fighting chance to get the best information. Dr. Phipps is a caring guy who became aware of your situation, I think, when he talked to a former student of his, who was the doctor who delivered you," Levi said.

"When he found me and considered me to be a particularly good research geneticist who'd fit and was qualified for Tech, he came calling. I can't say if it was the quality of my work or my connection to you and that was the reason I got hired. I hope it was mostly my work but maybe a little of both. But, I believe its evidence of just how special you are. Mom and I took the move here as a possibility to help you and so far we're pretty pleased. What do you think?"

Now it was Levi's turn to be silent.

"Thanks for not sugar coating anything," Nathan said. "I have a lot of mixed emotions. I'm relieved to know you're not mad at me for trying to learn about myself by testing my powers. But doesn't this mean a life time of wonder for me? I keep asking myself 'what do I do?' Do I hide it? When I use my power, it can be so good and in some cases potentially bad. I can see that if I do something for the wrong reason, even if my intentions are good it could hurt someone. This is hard to choose what I can or should do?"

Nathan realized that they were acting not only from parental love but from a position that no other parent had ever faced. Nathan's choice was the same as his parents. There clearly weren't any instruction manuals for this case.

44

Cabe Fears Disrupting Boy's Powers

Cabe recalled the last thing he'd told Palumbo when they'd left the dome. 'Remember you can't call your boss a loony toon, which was precisely what he was feeling like. The trip to Tahoe had been great, but there were still more questions than answers.

"Vickie," Cabe said, "I'm going to wander around the floor a bit and clear my head. If you need me just buzz my phone a couple of times."

As he wandered in and out of a dozen places saying hello to his employees he didn't expect to find the answers he was looking for. But sometimes answers to difficult questions come when your mind has been thinking on its own. Cabe remembered trying to tell Drobick and Palumbo about the nature of the waves emanating from Nathan. He remembered thinking they were like sound waves so he went to the dome and sat down and let his thoughts flow.

It was a "Eureka" moment if there ever was one. A few years ago he remembered reading an article in which physicists in a Low Temperature Laboratory of Aalto University had shown how a nanomechanical oscillator can be used for detection and amplification of feeble radio waves or microwaves. Being in the broadcasting business could have its uses because waves were his business, so to speak. This, he thought, could be the most critical answer of all, how do you "borrow" Nathan. If Nathan's abilities used something similar to sound waves, like he had speculated from the beginning, it might be that the design, like his dome netting, could also control both sound and associated waves. Why couldn't a net or something like it be used to disrupt Nathan's waves?

It was time for some risk taking. If the netting of the dome could be applied to halt Nathan's projections, it just might be possible to control Nathan by putting him into a sound dome of some kind although more sophisticated than this one. With a system that is fully portable, it might be possible to control Nathan. Another risk was--could he apply the technology without sufficient testing. After all, he rationalized, there was going to be no way to test it directly on Nathan. He'd just have to gamble with no field test that it would work. It was a high stakes gamble.

Cabe called his chief sound engineer, Jens McKay. "Hey, Jens-O, how are things down on the funny farm?"

"A laugh a second," Jens replied. "I've got the whip out and they're all on task, at least for the moment. To what do I owe the honor of talking to the really big boss?" he asked. "And, by the way, I can't do it by yesterday no matter what it is, but maybe the next day."

"You're in luck," Cabe said. "Since you're the one who built the dome for me, I'm interested in the concept or possibility of making one that is completely portable, some kind of blanket or sheet form I was thinking. Secondly, what kind of waves can it block? And lastly, can we add additional wave arresting properties with additional materials? Oh, and lucky for you, I don't need it before the day after tomorrow."

"Gee thanks boss. I'm sure we can get it out by tomorrow--yuk, yuk!" he said.

McKay had been primarily a sound engineer for years before taking over Cabe's research and development department at Cable News Media about eight years before. Most of his work was based around controlling noise when amplified under normal broadcasting, so he was acutely aware of nearly all aspects of cleaning up what was called broadcast fuzz.

"My question, Jens, is can you turn that laser-like mind of yours to blocking the transmission of sound waves as you did for the dome, but with the capacity to add restrictions to dampen or stop a nanomechanical resonator from broadcasting through a flexible substance, a kind of blanket. Whadda ya think?"

"You're getting nasty now Boss! You're sounding just like me. Where are you picking up that dirty sounding engineering language anyway?" he asked. "I love it."

"I read an article from Aalto University about the process in a low temperature lab," Cabe began.

"Gottcha! Read the same article. And yes, I think it's possible. I read another article out of Aalto about a superconducting cavity resonator exchanging energy with a nanometer resonator. It's much like guitar strings resonating with the echo chamber and vibrating at the same frequency. There's one problem, the temperature in the tests were at near zero Fahrenheit. Doing the same at room temperature could be another matter," he said.

"What about blocking or dissipating those waves, are we still locked into the temperature problems?" Cabe asked.

"I wouldn't think so, but let me do some calculating and get back," McKay said. "I've got this new assistant that's working with us now. She's a whiz on computer modeling these things. Name's LeAnne Allred. I will have her take a preliminary look tomorrow."

"Looking forward to what you come up with," Cabe said.

Cabe began to feel more confident in his efforts to find a way to safely seize and study Nathan. He was still sitting in the dome when he called Drobick and Palumbo and asked them to meet him there in a few minutes. His brain was telling him he was a complete idiot for even thinking about abducting Nathan, but his anticipation over the possibility of finding a way to project or switch emotions definitely overcame his rational reality.

In about ten minutes, Drobick and Palumbo entered the dome.

"This is unexpected," Drobick said. "It's only been a few days since Tahoe and you're wanting to talk? What's on the agenda?"

"I think I may have found a way to contain Nathan. If it pans out, I'm going to want to start procedures soon. I'm thinking it may take a few weeks at this point. Perhaps we can model some possibilities to see if one will work."

"What possibilities?" Palumbo asked. "What the hell are you talking about? If the kid can do what it appears he can do, I seriously wonder if it's possible to easily capture him." Palumbo had obviously been contemplating these difficulties, since he would be the one carrying out the orders.

"OK, think about it this way," Cabe said. "We use flexible netting like on this dome. The dome acts very similarly to what I want. It stops sound and visual waves from either coming in or going out. You may remember that what I saw appeared similar to sound waves to me. I'm sure it was because of a fluke situation during the fight. Its flimsy, no question, but I'm convinced that most waves of nearly every kind can be stopped, or at the very least, dissipated to inconsequentiality with the right netting. That's the task. Since we won't have to generate anything, the wave blocker can be portable and easy to use, like a blanket of carbon fiber sheets with special filter netting sandwiched in between sheet material," Cabe said. "It would work just like this dome except more sophisticated in the number, frequency and kind of waves blocked."

"So the point is," Drobick said, "you think we can go ahead? Just one concern. The other questions are: What if we do get him, and then contain his capabilities. What kind of tests or equipment are we going to need to be able to evaluate and potentially implement what we learn. An even worse question is: What do we do with Nathan once we've got what we want from him?

"Frankly, boss, I'm thinking that this is getting less and less possible," Drobick said, pausing, "Remember that looming abyss we talked about?"

"Not so," Cabe responded. "You've heard of roofies. In case you haven't experienced them, and I hope you haven't, they wipe out your memory for any given period of time also rendering you submissive with instant amnesia! They could be used to eliminate his memory for the time he's under restraint. He wouldn't even remember a face, much less where or when it was or what happened.

"Just so you know, I've experienced the drug first hand for some medical procedures and believe me, you don't remember anything that happened, like a colonospcopy, or anything else. I talked to a doctor for twenty-five minutes and couldn't tell you what color hair she had.

"So eliminating the memory is pretty easy using roofies. I know it was in my case. We can get some medical advice from Wolfe, but I think it's doable. What I'm not so sure about is how long can the drug be used without potentially hurting Nathan," Cabe said. "If we can use it for two days, maximum, I think we can get everything we need."

"Setting aside the actual taking, what kind of equipment do we need?" Palumbo asked, knowing that this would be his department."

"Not nearly as much as you might think," Cabe continued. "The list includes multiple brain scans and blood testing equipment for clinical chemistry. We'll test blood gas for the hematology and immunochemistry analyzers. Most of those can be in relatively small packages. Except for the scanner, I think we can put them on one pallet with the rest of the collection of general lab needs. Once we get the requisite blood samples and scan readings it's pretty much over and we can return Nathan to San Marino!"

Palumbo, pondering and thinking out loud at the same time said he'd have to get together with Wolfe and make sure everything necessary was available because it would all have to come from an off-market source to avoid detection.

"I'll go check with Wolfe and get some precise directions for the equipment. But I'm going to have to change my initial location concept. It's going to have to be more sterile and clinical like. Get back to you on that one," Palumbo said.

Cabe looked at Drobick. "OK, Dr. Gloom, what are we doing wrong?"

"You mean besides everything?" Drobick asked.

"That's why I keep you around, Mike, you're always so cheerful and full of optimism," Cabe said.

"Yeah and we're saving the world, I know!" Drobick said. "Well, I just believe it's one of "Rand's Rules of Life." "You get all green lights when you have all the time in the world and all red lights when you're in a rush. And one that I know you'll appreciate: "Expenses always rise to exceed income. Other than that, 'everything is beautiful in its own way,' of course."

"Life's tough," Cabe said. "I hate it when we actually have to work. Can you and Dick get a plan together and a time frame we can look at?"

"Sure, as soon as I get out of the pokey!" Drobick said. "We'll get things organized when he gets back from talking to Wolfe for the needs list."

45

Another Test

At breakfast the next morning and out of the blue Nathan announced: "I wanna go fishing."

Fishing, for the Farnsworth family, was almost on par with their religious beliefs. It was the whole reason Levi originally went to work for the Idaho Fish and Game Department. He loved the outdoors doing work he considered extremely important and testing his intellectual skills constantly, not to mention his physical side hiking along the rivers and streams.

"Boy does that sound like something I would like to do," Ally said. "I can just imagine those riffles where the big ones hide."

"Bad news folks, the season's over," Levi said. "But maybe that should be our vacation next year. R.G. and Mary have a small cabin in the Bitterroot, and they begged us to come back and stay there. But it will have to be next year."

Levi put a roast in the crock pot just before the three headed to church. He spent the rest of the afternoon relaxing on their small patio with Ally napping in a hammock. The roast, along with potatoes and carrots, was seasoned with a family seasoning salt created by Ally herself that she called Seasonettes. A few slices of his favorite tart/sweet Cameo apples with thinly sliced Munster cheese and a red cabbage salad rounded out the food. It was a colorful Sunday dinner and included one of Nathan's new favorites, fresh lemonade from their backyard tree. It was a fruit that didn't grow in Idaho's colder clime.

As they started cleaning up dinner, Nathan began to talk, not necessarily directly to anyone but just sort of letting his mind's wanderings come out through his mouth. "If I have these special things about me, would it not be good to check things out even more?" He wondered aloud.

Levi and Ally let him muse.

"Ya know, as I said, I'm doing my own tests," Nathan said.

That one got their attention and reminded them they hadn't got to the bottom of his reminder.

"We should have talked more about that." Levi said, expecting the worst.

"You've taught me about the scientific method my whole life Dad," he said, "so I'm conducting some experiments to see what I can do using that method."

"Such as?" Ally asked, not sure she wanted to know the details.

Nathan explained the situation with his first test to switch the emotional suffering from a student with Cerebral Palsy to a student who was one of the school's top football players. "What happened," he said, "was something I wasn't expecting at all. The football player went over to the kid in the chair and they had a really animated talk. It seemed like there was a whole new understanding and connection. I really felt good about that. I think it was a good thing." He paused and seemed a little reluctant to tell the next story.

"Is that all?" Levi asked, "With the look on your face, I'm not totally sure I'm ready to hear the answer."

"Not really," Nathan admitted. "I had determined to be very methodical in my tests and as scientific and controlled as I can be. Then I saw what Reuben did to Miguel. They beat him up pretty bad and I got really mad so I put Reuben on the ground. I didn't follow my test methodology. I'm really sorry about that, but when I saw Miguel I could not let that happen again."

Nathan then described the rest of the events, at least through the paramedics taking Reuben to the hospital.

The spitfire side of Ally came out in full force fury. "I would have done it too," she said. Miguel's a great kid and his Mom is really grateful that you're friends." Then she quoted: "However, 'Vengeance is mine, saith the Lord.'"

"But I've got to protect my friends. They wouldn't have left Miguel alone if they weren't stopped. They would have pulled him back into the gang and who knows what would have happened then," Nathan said.

Levi looked at Nathan with a tightly controlled calm and asked, "Nathan, can you tell me exactly what you did? We have some general idea with your previous experiences, but we haven't ever asked you what you actually do. I think it's time we try to determine how you do this."

Without hesitation, Nathan said that he took all the emotional pain he had found in others and focused it into Reuben. He said he used his hands to direct this collection of painful feelings into the emotional part of Reuben's brain. But I've also found I've become more skilled, and may not need to use my hands to direct the impulses.

"And Dad, I really need to continue my testing. I need to know what I can do," he said. "I believe there's some kind of mission that I can do good with."

"As we've talked about this, I believe you understand a lot, Nathan," Levi said. Everything we've talked about makes me more concerned about your safety. I think we need to understand the nature of your physical and mental DNA," Levi said. "Maybe you should stop all testing until we get more information. "From what you've said about Reuben and all the incidents, I feel a backlash could be coming somehow. You may remember what happened in Idaho."

"Of all the things I want to do, the most important is to keep you separated from the natural inclination of scientists to probe and poke to find out what makes you tick. I didn't and don't want you to become a lab rat, as they say and I also don't want you hurt. "

"So what we need to do is check me out first, right?" Nathan said.

"I've tried to avoid it, but I believe we do," Levi said.

"I suppose we need to do a battery of tests, detailed blood workup, CAT scans, etcetera?" Nathan said, wondering out loud.

46

Blanket Like No Other

Cabe's research engineer, McKay, and his assistant LeAnne began mapping out a spectrum of waves they felt would most closely approximate the lengths and frequencies of sound waves Cabe had suggested. They could test the various kinds alone, but felt they should also test wave lengths slightly before and after the target waves. They were quite confident their solution could either completely stop, or at the very least, disperse most of the waves. In either case, it would reduce their intensity and influence.

It was not a sure thing, of course, but brain waves of many kinds are similar and frequencies can be scoped and tested. LeAnne spent a while lining up a series of tests and materials. While the brain waves and frequencies were similar, the potential material for the blanket that they were considering to stop or disperse them, needed to be much more integrated and complex to meet contingencies.

Leanne kept an almost unlimited virtual library of high tech fabrics with specifications and graphing charts. Laboratories around the world seemed to be turning out new and amazing materials daily and she got updates listing the newest additions. She was a whiz at plugging in the variables tempered by requirements and calculating with the highest degree of viability.

At first LeAnne assumed that a layered netting of fine silver and copper could stop or disperse 97.7% of the waves. But after examining a new highly flexible polymer thread system, she realized it could be infused with copper and silver in the polymer and thus woven right into the fabric. It would be a near exact match to McKay's design for the dome. Her modeling showed that the fabric would meet all of the requirements needed and result in a flexible carbon fabric making a very thin blanket, or more accurately, a slightly metallic looking sheet that was exceptionally strong.

Her computer modeling indicated that the carbon fiber itself didn't interrupt and distort the waves as was expected, but weaving hair-fine silver and copper would disrupt and disperse the direction of the waves. Using the carbon fiber made the portability extremely adaptable, and because the material was so tough it protected the fine wires. It could be sewn into various shapes and could even be made into clothing if necessary, although she told McKay he wasn't a runway judge and wouldn't presume to know how fabric would rate on a fashionista scale.

"I don't think they're planning on modeling it on a runway," McKay said,

Their biggest concern was that the wires might break and cause failures. The new silver and copper metals embedded carbon polymer thread solved that problem by having it woven right into the fabric. Using her model, she began her program by digitally bombarding the material with a variety of sound waves and programming in extreme temperature variables. She found the new fabric not only met the specs they'd established, but exceeded them.

As with any scientific model, it had its limitations, but it was as close to right-on as one could hope for in models like these. She sent a text to McKay with her preliminary results confirming that it met the needs but she included a proviso that actual field testing was needed. "With every theory there are qualifications as you know," she told him, "So I don't believe we're going to meet a one hundred percent threshold, but its close enough."

McKay sent his first report to Cabe outlining the fantastic work LeAnne had done. He said that realistically it would be at least thirty days to put the blanket together provided they could get the new infused polymer material they wanted. He included an attachment from an article commenting on a University of Chicago test he'd happened upon.

"Since you asked about seeing sound waves, I thought you might like to see this, he wrote:

"'The University of Chicago had conducted experiments on sound waves illustrating that they tend to behave like a gas in which photons become traveling compressions and hit our eardrums to transfer the sound. The same photons also move as gravity waves and when they hit pressure resistance the gas becomes hotter, making them somewhat visible as either hot or cold spots in the sky. But the article does say they are just barely visible."

The response from Cabe was like an exploding bomb. He called McKay and verily screamed, "Oh yeah, Jens, that's what I saw—waves in the air for an instant! Like what you might see in the distance on hot blacktop but much less obvious. It was my training and experience that gave me the ability to I recognized them.

"Jens, after you and LeAnne get the blanket made, can you do some testing on the modeling of waves. Focus on that portion of the protons that make sound waves visible in response to hot and cold. I'd like to know if we can isolate that phenomenon and if it can be incorporated it into some future research. That testing, by the way, isn't a priority at the moment but an idea to put on your calendar."

"Will do," he said "But, again, I need you to tell me what this is all about soon?"

"As soon as I can," Cabe said.

McKay, who was not privy to the goings on, was nonplussed. "What waves are you talking about? What did you see?"

"Have to tell you later Jens, my boy, but suffice it to say, you have made my day, big time!" Cabe said. "Keep up the good work and, as always, we need everything last week!"

"Whatda ya' mean last week?" McKay said. "Let me rephrase that. What are you actually saying you want?"

"A blanket at least seven-foot by seven-foot just as LeAnne's computer modeled it! Make it," was Cabe's abrupt response. "Call Drobick if you have any questions. Spare neither time nor money. Get 'er done."

McKay, caught the sudden infectious enthusiasm in his boss's voice, and immediately began pondering how they could get it done quickly, but also began considering its new product's potential.

Cabe called Drobick immediately. "Hey Mike, guess what? I'm not crazy after all. I just talked to Jens and he said that under certain circumstances sound waves can be seen briefly. It has to do with hot and cold, or in my case, the cool of the shade and the heat of the sun did the trick."

"If I were Palumbo, I'd probably say something like, 'You still mining that old gold spur!'" Drobick said, meaning by talking about seeing sound waves which isn't supposed to be possible.

"Don't tell me you've been infected with Palumboisms," Cabe said with a smile in his voice. "When it comes to the visible sound waves, I think that I had to have it reconfirmed to myself as much as anyone."

"I can understand that one," Drobick said. "Speaking of Palumboisms, he called and thinks he's located a medical clinic we could rent that was closed down a while back. He read an ad that said it has a brain scanner that's up for sale too. Owner's willing to sell or lease."

"Sounds like a good possibility," Cabe said, "let me know."

47

Levi Warns His Son

The family conference was over. Nathan was buoyed by his father and mother's understanding. With reluctant acquiescence, he agreed not to try another "Reuben-type" stunt. "With your gifts, Nathan," his mother said, "you must have great compassion and no vengeance in your heart. If you do, it could easily destroy you and that would destroy us."

Nathan thought about what his mother said. He had to admit that part of his attack on Reuben was vengeance driven. He also realized that vengeance can be hard to control in the heat of the moment.

Ally then asked, "Can't you test on animals instead of people?"

Levi stepped in and explained that animals don't experience emotions the way people do. Animals seem to act viciously because of their innate need for food or on instinct. There is no vengeance for animals. They also fight for mating dominance to protect their territory and self-preservation. Unfortunately, intentional bullying is strictly a human/primate trait and, for the most part, that is what Nathan is reacting to.

Levi asked Nathan about the extent of what he thought he could do. "That's what I'm testing," Nathan said. "At first I thought it was just a natural response to fear and stopping things I didn't like, but I'm realizing that there's more to it than that. I wonder if I can refine the individual elements. I'm thinking that the athlete test is telling me that it's possible to do some good and fight bullies too."

"That's something we can't do for you," Levi said, "meaning we can't tell you to stifle your abilities. But we can tell you that to act for the greater good enlarges your soul and to act contrary to the end diminishes you. Defining what is good and what is not may be your most difficult choice. Remember, allowing anyone to face their worst and most challenging events in a person's life can provide them with their greatest rewards and progress and potentially make a person stronger."

Nathan left for school the next day with thoughts of his new challenges. What is good? When is it good to stop an act that may strengthen a person in ways not obvious at the time? He walked to school with Buddy but on this particular morning was very quiet, which Buddy noted.

"Anything wrong?" Buddy asked.

"I had one of 'those' talks with my mom and dad Sunday, Nathan said."

Buddy smiled and said "Oh, one of 'those' talks!"

Of course, Nathan purposefully didn't correct what Buddy thought "those" meant and fortunately Buddy didn't pursue the question. The two friends continued walking along silently for a while, lost in their own thoughts. Nathan's mind was racing ahead to find and define the right circumstances of another test.

Buddy's thoughts drifted to the concept of having a good friend who you trusted and enjoyed. He decided it was one of the things he enjoyed most. Nathan was a good friend. Having a great friend is the frosting on the cake of life, Buddy concluded.

Some of Nathan's questions had been answered. During the fight when Buddy was attacked, he directed his response at all the attackers. Maybe it would have been sufficient to just aim his power at the leader, get him running and then the others would have taken off too. But it would not have answered the question of whether he could aim at more than one person at a time. At least that question was answered.

Motivation, he thought, had to be considered, especially when he reflected on what his parents had told him, especially his mother. Nathan's maturity continued to undergo a transformation. He loved his Mother and thought about the power of mothering, not just what mothers physically do for children, which, he knew was infinite, but his Mother imparted to Nathan a new understanding of compassion. She had taught it to him by example with all the work she had done for the less fortunate.

He realized that carefully considered compassion had to be his motivation. By extension, he also realized that ill-considered compassion can be detrimental to those in need. Strength comes through trials and even bullying can come in many forms, not all physical.

His next test, he decided would be defined by an effort to specifically help someone. Nathan had tutored many students, particularly in math and science. In understanding and working with those students with challenges, he'd been putting his Mother's teachings into practice. The funny thing was that it was his unique difference that always seemed to get things started.

Once the tutored student got over Nathan's eye color and saw how much he could help them him, his notice of the eye color quickly disappeared. His students quickly learned to dwell on their positive progress, not what he looked like. It was a hidden side benefit of his tutoring that neither he nor the students were directly aware.

Nathan conducted three very low key tests. In all three cases, he projected the feelings of one student's learning to the feelings of another student. He was in particularly tight control of himself maintaining his motivation for good. In two of the cases, he felt they were positive; the third may not have been. It was his revenge on Reuben and it would have to be the subject of intense introspection. It reinforced his question about what was good for a specific person. Is it better to allow difficulties that may make a person stronger by allowing them to fight their own battles?

When he got home that evening he made some decisions. He needed to know more about his genetic makeup. While his mind was contemplating the next test, he was oblivious to powerful forces continuing to develop around him and he soon would be tested by trials he could not have anticipated. They would be trials that would test him to muster all his strength within and his internal conflict between vengeance and making amends.

48

More Tests Create More Questions

After talking with his Dad, the two decided to try and pick specific issues to test Levi's suppositions about Nathan at New Tech.

A meeting with Phipps was scheduled so Nathan could feel comfortable in his surroundings. Phipps asked if Jerry Seperman could sit in.

"Sure," Nathan said. "We had a great time with him."

The first meeting and group of tests were scheduled. They were a series of definitive blood tests and brain scans using a Connectome Scanner, one of the most advanced brain imaging technologies in the world.

A Connectome Scanner was designed to do a network map of the brain and define anatomical and functional component connections for a vigorously functioning brain. By evaluating a stimulated brain it revealed brain disorders. What was also true was that even this amazing machine's designers could not have anticipated a brain and network like Nathan's.

The meeting went well. Nathan felt comfortable enough to tell them that he was as interested in the whole process as they were. Phipps sensed a change in Nathan from a boy, somewhat unsure of himself, to a more self-confident young man.

For Phipps, Nathan's sudden increased maturity wasn't expected, at least not in that short a time. Phipps wasn't exactly sure how to explain it after his first rather clumsy effort to conduct a low level examination of Nathan.

Of course, Phipps was not privy to the discussions in the Farnsworth household just a day or two before, discussions that released the unspoken restriction on both Nathan and his parents about his abilities. That release brought a renewed focus for the three Fransworths who were trying to answer questions that lingered like a dense fog on the floor of a frosty valley.

Rather surprisingly, Nathan was looking forward to the battery of tests. Maybe, he thought, "I'll get more answers too."

49

Cabe Accelerates Abduction

Just two weeks after getting the instructions from Cabe, Jens and LeAnne were able to model netting that would keep 97.3 percent of the requisite sound wave protons in check. It was a small improvement from the initial calculations, and as close as reasonably possible toward the desirable one-hundred percent goal.

Even though the necessary materials were expensive, they were, with some persuasion, available. Using his experience creating the dome technology, McKay gave the specs to a hi-tech fabric manufacturer for NASA. The blanket with silver and copper infused carbon threads and the comprehensive modeling LeAnne had done, along with McKay's newly designed weaving techniques, allowed development and completion in just a matter of days. Of course, a boat load of pressure from McKay and Cabe's involvement didn't hurt either.

The testing they expected to do should only take a few days once they had the materials in hand and were ready to deliver. Ready to deliver for what, McKay wasn't sure, but Cabe said he'd tell him sometime down the road. McKay hoped it was a short road.

"Remarkable," Cabe said when McKay called him.

"Not so much," McKay said "A lot of the fundamental work was done when we did the dome but Leanne's input was vital."

"Appreciate, the extra effort," Cabe said.

With what Cabe considered the primary obstacle mostly overcome, he began pushing the preparations in earnest to take and test Nathan.

His first call was to Palumbo. "Blanket's design ready for production," he said with no preamble. "Mike told me a little, about shifting from the cabin to a building. What's the latest with that and the testing equipment?"

Palumbo had been tasked with finding a place to house and provide for the equipment to test Nathan along with housing extra people for a short time. His first choice has been the Fallen Leaf Lake cabin. It would have been deserted for the late fall except for a few noisy hikers, who loved to wander around gawking at the palatial estates of the rich. Those gawkers made it a risk too big, plus moving the necessary equipment just forced a reassessment.

His work to protect creative copyrights and navigating the intricacies of those turbulent seas was good training to pull off this wild escapade. What was not obvious in intellectual property wars was that the pirates were vicious. The Nathan Venture wasn't much different than his IP wars.

Palumbo saw a potential building on Craig's list and Google-earthed the whole area around San Pedro Harbor and found a building that met the needs he determined were necessary in the old section of the San Pedro commercial district.

The San Pedro site seemed an apt place and had tons of benefits. There would be immediate transportation of every kind and quick access to all kinds of equipment in a super busy environment with all sorts of activities going on. Since comings and goings were so routine, any trucking activities or shipping relating to their vehicles would be more than common.

After a quick trip and drive round, he leased the facility on a burn phone. It was on the border between the mostly commercial warehouse space near Pacific Avenue and West 13th Street and the residential areas to the East. The building was older but was in generally good shape. It has been adapted into a neighborhood medical clinic, now closed, because of a move to a newer facility.

The front portion was a typical waiting room with an office alcove. Examining rooms were nearby, empty of people now, but with a few leftover office desks and chairs. The back area had some small operating rooms for minor outpatient procedures and an apartment for a twenty-four hour nurse. Some critical factors for Palumbo were two large roll-up docking doors and perhaps the defining bonus: both of the building's loading docks were inside the building and out of sight of prying eyes.

The building was located not more than several blocks from Ports O' Call Restaurants and tourist traps near the slip spaces for private boats, fleets, for-hire fishing trawlers and to the north stood the Vincent Thomas Bridge. Container loading docks were also scattered along the fingers of the harbor.

The port area could be defined as busy, busy, busy. Ships were, of course, constantly docking and embarking. The building was in a vacant block and thus almost no traffic, either vehicle or foot.

The area's local newspaper, San Pedro Daily Pilot, reported the continuous docking dates and times for ships from all over the world. It was a never ending flow of economic energy and a major artery of daily commerce. Eighteen wheelers carried the products of the world to and from the Los Angeles and surrounding areas.

The 110 Harbor Freeway was a few blocks also to the north. Palumbo mapped out a dozen ways to enter and exit the area. He arranged to lease a fifty-two-foot motor launch for a week and moored it less than a half mile from the clinic. The more escape routes the better, he concluded.

Local gendarmes were amazingly observant of anything that seemed out of place. With their years of experience of patrolling their town, there was an almost instant recognition if something looked out of place. As patrolmen they'd developed an instinctive capacity of how to read the local topography and how to use that knowledge in any chase or search that might occur and of course had contingency plans of possible scenarios.

Palumbo took Cabe's call who rattled off in a staccato style of why he'd made the change. "I leased it under a Panamanian company for three months with a two-year extension option. Mike probably told you it's in the San Pedro area, with lots of shipping and trucks around so it won't be unusual if things are moving in and out of the building. Itold them it would be converted to an import scheduling company that specializes in planning for commercial shipping using the Panama Canal. Also, we bought all of the equipment outright, told them we'd later donate the stuff to a clinic in Panama.

"It's in immediate move-in condition. I already have Wolfe sending the blood testing equipment which should be arriving by Wednesday. Once that's there and equipment plugged in, we're good to go.

"I sure as hell hope this is all worth it, Max," Palumbo said. "We're out on a limb, on a tree with branches in the far reaches of the cosmos. If the one we're on breaks, we'll never stop falling."

"Big rewards, big risks," Cabe said. "And if I can tap into the potential here, you, Drobick and several other people will be independently wealthy."

"Can you put the next step on my desk ASAP," Cabe asked, "the instant all the pieces are in place?"

The blood testing equipment and related lab materials had been packed and were scheduled to be shipped from Wolfe's facility directly to the clinic upon Palumbo's call. The bill of lading would list excess duplicate medical equipment to be donated to the Central American country. He made the call and arrangements were made to have a cleaning crew thoroughly scrub the existing equipment in the building and the specific area where testing would take place.

A one-week stock of food for four was brought in and stored ready for any potential eventualities. Hopefully, Palumbo thought, it would never be used.

The post-testing routine was going to be essentially backwards with a couple of exceptions. The cleaning crew would be recalled and the equipment again scrubbed. A packing crew would come in, pack all the equipment and have it delivered to the Bethany Christian Fellowship Charities who were making arrangements to deliver the equipment and related materials.

With the clinic situation awaiting the arrival of the equipment, Palumbo turned his attention to the actual capture of Nathan. He once again scouted the areas where he knew Nathan would be and where and how he could be picked up for his transport to San Pedro. Deflecting his ability to transfer emotions, he had to assume, would be mitigated by Cabe's blanket. Unfortunately, there was no time or way to test it.

Palumbo outlined several elements of his plan including creating a diversion on the opposite end of town when the caper went down. Secondly, he knew Buddy would be otherwise occupied with band on the day of the big event. There would be the grab between two vehicles. When the driving vehicle would drive up as Nathan reached the vehicle in the lot, he would be trapped against the SUV in the parking space parallel to the street and close to the sidewalk and the drive vehicle. It was also under a tree near where the pickup vehicle on the street would stop. The two vehicles formed a sort of passage along the sidewalk Nathan would have to walk through.

The small van would have magnetically attached signs with a party balloon company logo and very small company name in a hard-to-read font. It would look authentic but be hard to identify by name. At the first opportunity, the signs would be ripped off leaving the van signless, in case there were witnesses. About all anyone witnessing the abduction might remember of the signs would be a colorful bunch of balloons that would be gone in mere seconds after the kidnapping, and the vehicle would become a nondescript copy of the unnumbered thousands of vans in the Los Angeles basin.

The small van would then be driven to a semi trailer and driven in with Nathan inside. Nathan and Palumbo, who would be charged with keeping him under control, would ride in the closed semi trailer while Jeeves would drive the truck to San Pedro.

By the time the first transport vehicle was within a mile of the chosen site, all of the vehicles involved would be removed from the area. The van with Nathan would have disappeared into the semi-trailer. Palumbo made a last minute change in his proposal since he realized that he could get the vacated vehicles far away from the site. He arranged one to be delivered to a parking lot where a couple of college students, hired by a transfer company, would drive it to Pennsylvania. The second vehicle was left at another site in Long Beach to be driven to Georgia.

Palumbo calculated that the vehicles, being very generic looking, wouldn't have a detailed description, except maybe for the signs and those would be gone too. The two vehicles would be well into Nevada by the time they might be searched for, and even then the descriptions would be very sketchy. A couple of days later they'd be well beyond the Mississippi. There wouldn't be any specifically identifiable vehicles to be found in the area.

Finally, Palumbo's plan included a fake 911 call of a kidnapping, triggering an "amber alert warning" in South Pasadena, a town contiguous to San Marino. The report would be of a boy similar looking to Nathan and it would be just prior to Nathan's abduction.

A second report a couple of minutes later would be called in of a man shooting from a house not far from the falsely reported abduction. The usual cooperation agreements between towns tended to draw away patrolmen from Nathan's target location.

Timing was critical.

50

Blanket is Snagged

With Cabe pushing hard to get the blanket done, McKay and Allred worked over time. The carbon fiber material was ordered but failed to be delivered and suppliers were less than forthcoming about when it would be available. The delay was, most probably an overly optimistic sales department's estimate of delivery time.

There was only one supplier in the world that could produce the specially ordered material based on McKay's specifications. His particular interest in the carbon was that it provided almost no interference in the netting's function. Adding the silver and copper polymers didn't make it exactly a product right off the shelf. Reluctantly, McKay called Cabe immediately but found him unavailable, so he sent a text and then waited for the sound of an explosion from the fortieth floor of Century City towers.

The explosion would have to wait along with the order. Cabe was going over the plan with Palumbo and had left instructions not to be disturbed. The clinic preparations sounded good to Cabe. Wolfe would be in charge. He wanted to conduct at least two full blood workups so comparisons could be made. They would also have to run at least three brain scans for as many comparisons as could be done in the short time they had. He'd use three different stimuli for each.

Palumbo told Cabe about the boat and a couple of other escape possibilities in San Pedro, including a freighter they could board in a worst case escape scenario, no questions asked.

"How about the timing?" Cabe asked, "Do we have the adequate time lines calculated? There are a ton of variables."

"I think we have those down to a minimum. I've picked a good location; it's a day that Nathan usually walks home alone because Bass, his chum, has band practice. There's a large parking lot that's not busy where he walks home. There are some huge trees planted in parking strip openings but the rest of the sidewalk goes right to the curb on most parts so we can get close. The trees give us a little shade making the area darker and protected from eyes in the sky. If we time it right we can grab him in seconds," Palumbo said.

"I've got a suggestion on the pickup. Have a vehicle in the parking lot close to the sidewalk and grab site. Have a guy in it making an obvious display of eating lunch. Have his door open and when Nathan walks by have a second vehicle drive up putting him between them. Open the front door of both vehicles to cut visibility in the event of witnesses. This is something that has to be right the first time. The distractions you've mentioned are good and should divert attention."

Vickie buzzed Cabe. "Boss, you've got an urgent call from McKay, sorry he's called five times, I think it's important and I think it may be involved in your planning from the sound of it."

"Thanks Vic," he said "I'll take it."

Cabe picked up the phone and looking directly at Palumbo rolled his eyes. There was no doubt that there was a problem that affected the plan.

"When?" is all Cabe asked.

"Three to five weeks," McKay said.

"Get on their case and stay on it," Cabe came down hard. "Push 'em every day if you have to. It can't be five weeks. It's got to be well under four. Late October, no later!"

"Yeah, Jens, I know," Cabe spoke into the phone. "I appreciate the extra effort. What's the time after receipt of the material? Construction, testing, right, two, three days. Got it,"

This was the first real hang up in Cabe's plan so far. Nearly everything had gotten done and configured into his thinking without a hitch. The problem was that without the blanket the plan would be impossible. Even the blanket idea was sketchy.

Cabe had already calculated for some delay but his "type-A mentality" never liked delays. Life always seemed to be a battle between the want and the wait.

"Well, the 'Best laid schemes,'" he said. "Are we mice or men?!"

Cabe and Palumbo continued to detail their plan. Cabe blurted out, "I knew things were going too good. But we've been through it before. We'll handle it!"

Little did he know that his and Nathan's future would hit many more not-so-small snags and not in the too distant future.

"'Let's set the plan for October twenty-seventh. If we don't make the date we'll retool," Cabe said.

Cabe, deep in thought, turned and looked out his massive office windows. Out of the blue he asked, "What's the time frame for the clinic set up? How's Wolfe doing on the equipment? You got Jeeves on board? I think he's perfect for this."

"Recruited and on board," Palumbo came back and with his famous wry grin said. "Couldn't do it without 'em. I think we should keep this as close to the vest as possible. Gotta say boss, you sure do make my life interesting, even if I get twenty to life in Folsom on bread and water."

"I've made an executive decision about the plan. Since we're already walking on fracturing ice here, I think we may as well go full bore in assuming that all the dates will be met. Hang on a sec," Cabe said. He then texted a message to McKay asking what the last possible date was that he could expect the blanket to be delivered. That way he would at least have a concrete goal in mind."

When Drobick postulated that a drone was frequently surveilling Nathan, the whole tenor of the discussion changed to: "lets get his info, while keeping him safely from someone else kidnapping him."

"Will do," Palumbo acknowledged and went to brief Drobick on the situation. Cabe nodded his agreement and turned back to his window as Palumbo walked out of Cabe's office and directly into Drobick's. Palumbo filled him in on the general highlights of the plan and added that he hoped that the wait was not more than a couple of weeks.

"I'm in, so let me know what you want me to do." Drobick said.

"I'm pretty sure we'll have adjustments as we go along, but I'll let you know as everything gets refined. I'm assuming that our final set up should be no more than two days max," Palumbo said.

In roughly a couple of weeks, the decision to abduct an eleven-year-old boy would be implemented. It seemed like both an instant in time and an eternity to Palumbo.

"Time," Palumbo pondered, "what a contradiction in reality. Does it exist or not? Who knows?!"

51

Tests Set at New Tech

Phipps decided to have Levi and Nathan meet him in the cafeteria to reduce anxiety for the boy. It was a fascinating place. The discussions between students, professors and administrators, along with friends and visitors were often highly animated and participants were the very definition of concentrated cerebral energy. The "food fights" took place intellectually. After watching something that seemed so familiar and friendly to him, Phipps suddenly worried that Nathan would be cowed by the lively gesticulating brainiacs around him.

He shouldn't have worried since lack of brain power was not one of Nathan's weaknesses.

When the pair arrived, Nathan was not only unafraid; he assimilated the energy as if downing a massive shot of Red Bull. Once again, Phipps noted the expanding maturity the boy exhibited and thought to himself, "Nathan will soon outgrow both junior and senior high school. Where he might go from there may not allow rational conjecture. I guess we'll see soon enough."

"Nathan, Levi, welcome to New Tech's real gene pool. Kind of wild, don't you think?" Phipps said. This was Levi's first venture into this setting. He preferred a quiet brown bag lunch packed by Ally to the noisy din of the cafeteria. His love of the Idaho quiet didn't mix too well with the boisterous lunch court but the intellectual banter fascinated him.

"Doesn't seem to be a shortage of academic stimulation, hot topics and interesting people," he said. "Whadda ya think? Nathan."

Nathan surveyed the milieu of mind melds and slyly said, "Sort of reminds me of the bar scene in Star Wars. A kind of Mind Mastication Emporium" he added.

"That's about right," Phipps chuckled.

The three got into the cafeteria line, selected their choices and sat down at an empty table. Between bites, Phipps outlined what they had planned for Nathan. "What we're going to try to do, Nathan, is examine your brain so we can begin to understand your abilities. As far as I can tell, you may have the most interesting brain in this room. That is saying something and it could be far greater than this small sample.

"I think I told you last time that Jerry Seperman is going to work with us on this. Since you know him, I figured you might be more at ease. He has an assistant, Joan Fonda, who'll be helping too. We'll want to do some comparative blood tests, a physical and psychological exam and three brain scans.

"The most important thing I want you to know is that you can stop at any time if you are uncomfortable with any procedure, I mean anything, a nod or blink, and I can stop it," Phipps said. "Or if you want, we can spread the tests over more days."

After providing other details, Phipps asked if Nathan had any questions.

"I'd like to see the blood slides and scans, with explanations," Nathan said. "I figure that's fair. I also want my dad there to explain what's happening and telling me what things mean. And I want to know your read on the results, once we're done."

"Fair enough" Phipps said to Nathan. "We can do that. As a matter of fact, I'd like to personally invite you to some discussions with our researchers so you can participate when we collate the data. I believe that would help both you and us sort out the results. "

Levi, who'd been listening, asked Phipps if they could put a timeframe for the tests and results to make Nathan feel less anxious. It was a question that may have been more for Levi than Nathan.

"I'm thinking of Saturday, October twenty-fifth." Phipps said. "It'll keep the foot traffic in the department down and out of the way with fewer interruptions. What we want to do shouldn't take more than about five to six hours. If we start at eight we can be done not long after lunch. That sound OK?"

Levi turned to Nathan and despite the conversational ruckus that was going on around them, asked his son if he was ready. "You know you don't have to do it," Levi said.

"I'm down with it dad," Nathan said, sounding not only confident but looking forward to it.

"OK Bernie. Seems like we'll be here on the twenty-fifth, at eight," Levi said. "Just a week and a half."

52

Disturbing News

Jeeves and Palumbo began rehearsing the abduction, the details were crucial. Van signs were put on and ripped off as part of the practice. One of the elements that came up in the process was neutralizing Nathan physically. Even though he was only eleven, Palumbo wanted to make it appear that he had collapsed and his solution of choice was a taser. Anyone briefly witnessing the situation could easily mistake a taser shot knockdown for a fall if the taser was discretely held and the two vehicles on either side with one door open obscured the scene.

That would give Palumbo time to throw the blanket over Nathan. Hopefully this would help control his switching powers while he was pulled into the van. It could even appear that he was assisting Nathan.

The exact street and site selected were driven many times around that area with escape routes and locations also planned and rehearsed.

Cabe, in the meantime, was suffering almost continuous meltdowns as the hours ticked off with no word on the "blanket." To escape the frustrating uncertainty, he threw himself into getting his Cable News Media duties brought up to date in preparation for freeing his time for the week of October twenty-seventh.

Generally, Cabe had a TV monitor going in his office usually with the sound low. But as a diversion, he walked over, turned up the sound and as fate sometimes intercedes, it would have been better for the talk show host Fred Schultz, had the sound not been turned up at that moment. Cabe heard Schultz let out a string of profane invectives aimed at commentators from another network.

Cabe was continuing to wonder seriously about Schultz and his increasingly bizarre sphere of leftist politics and anyone who deigned to disagree with the host's assessment of anything and everything.

Given Cabe's current state of mind, it was unfortunate for Schultz. The Cable News Media owner had had enough of the talk show host's filthy mouth and lack of coherent thought. He walked to the door, opened it, and said with extra enthusiasm, "Hey, Vic, could you get me Jamal on the phone before you leave please?"

Although she was picking up her purse she said, "Sure thing Boss," and called him on speed dial.

"Jamal," was all Cabe said to the president of his news network.

"I already don't like the sound of that," Jamal said. "How bad is this going to be?"

"Depends whether your last name is Schultz," Cabe said. "That pathetic turkey is finito! His contract is up in November. It will not be renewed. Tell him as of the end of his show today that his new shift is at midnight on every other holiday. I warned that SOB and he ignored me. Also tell him that any public explanation about the lineup change had better be a description of how to kiss my tush with gratefulness in his heart. Otherwise, it'll be a court fight and he'll be buried in paper and lawsuits that will focus on his description of women. I'll skin him alive."

"Whoa," Jamal said. "That's a specific order? Do I have any leeway to modify it or should it be verbatim?"

"Don't miss a tittle!" Cabe announced. "I am fed up with hosts on my cable news shows using profanity which wastes precious air time, produces shallow thinking and clouds clarity of thought. Worse, it shows a terribly lazy vocabulary."

"No problem, Max. I'm on the way there now. You providing flak jackets?" Davenport asked.

"Not even safety glasses," Cabe said. "Tell him to tread very carefully. I'm beyond out of patience with his foul mouth and non-existent brain. You and I can schedule a lunch to talk about a replacement. I'll call you later."

Believe it or not, letting that steam off about Schultz was something he'd wanted to do for eons. It was like pulling out a festering sliver and putting Neosporin on it. The healing started immediately and his Schultz explosion also, somehow, made him feel better and more confident that the details of the Nathan Venture would work themselves out. Cabe's moment of satisfaction didn't last long. Drobick was on the phone when he returned his attention to his desk work, and the report was disturbing.

"What's up, Mike?" Cabe asked.

"I just got a call from Sanjy and Billy," Mike said. "They found some irregular code in some of the information they sent to us. Fortunately it was all hardcopy stuff for us so it did not appear to be digitally traceable. It appeared to be some mundane random code, but when they couldn't locate its origin or specific need they became suspicious.

"Turns out that the computer material we got from the school had already been accessed by someone else and I'd bet it was New Tech again. Whoever did this had to have been working on Rock Creek for longer than we have. They think the code apparently notifies someone when any other inquiries are generated that could be even remotely related to Nathan. Nathan's name, of course, came up on our search and someone has been surreptitiously notified.

"One of the questions is: Do they know it's us or did Sanjy and Billy hide it well enough that it doesn't trace back? Still can't determine that, but I think we have to assume the worst. And worse than that, although Billie said he and Sanjy can't trace any specific recipients of the earlier info, but they think there are linkages to New Tech. Sound familiar?" Whoever is doing this is as good as hackers get.

There is a glimmer of hope and another worry. The fact that we haven't been visited by authorities has to mean this isn't official, but that makes the threat to Nathan that much worse."

"Things can get complicated," Cabe said. "Even with your effort to keep some space between computer data and the hardcopies, we have to assume that we could be compromised. Did either say if they could see what specific info could lead them to us?"

"Not really," Drobick said, "but it could possibly have alerted someone that inquiries were made, even if our searches were not specifically directed at Nathan. We already know from the recording of the street camera test that there may be a connection between New Tech and Nathan, way beyond the fact that his dad works there. The drone thing is another level of danger and there was that little piece of intel that someone in the genetics department wanted to be sure Nathan was adapting well to Rocky Creek, with an offer of help if necessary, as you probably remember from Sanjy and Billie's report."

"I'm going to make some assumptions," Cabe began, "First we would have seen more suspicious information coming our way if they knew what was happening. Second, there would be some direct action to confront us if they knew who we were and Third, since we've seen neither, I'm assuming we can move forward.

"My question is what happens when the balloon officially leave's earth. If anything is going to happen I think it will likely be then. Even if they don't know us now, once we grab Nathan their flood gates to find any original hacker source will be opened big time and possibly, even if I think it's remote, we could be caught in that net."

"Brings up a question we should have been more focused on," Drobick said. "Once we have the information from Nathan, how do we return him with the least amount of hoopla? If the roofies work the way we hope, we could walk him into an ice cream store, buy him a sundae and no one would know the difference. Surveillance cameras could be a problem, but I think we could get over that with simple disguises. Nathan wouldn't remember anything but would be conversant with us the whole time. We could tell him that his Dad is coming to pick him up and make a call to notify him saying, "Nathan was spotted at Baskin & Robbins or the like.""

"How're the other preparations coming?" Cabe asked.

"Palumbo says they're going fine," Drobick said. "Jeeves and Dick will be fully ready by the time the blanket gets here. Which, by the way, McKay asked me to pass along some good news for once. He's been pushing the fabric guys and working with them and getting a new weaving concept going. October eighteenth is the new expected delivery date. That gives more than enough time to do some in-shop testing. He said you were allegedly having a 'Schultz eruption' that he didn't want to get in the middle of and thus the call to me."

"Shultz eruption? That's an accurate description. That's some good news, by the way!" Cabe said. "At least that won't hold us up. Now if it just works the way we are hoping."

53

Consequences Still Trouble Cabe

The intense preparations for what was going to be a fast two-day event struck Cabe as interesting. In all his corporate activities and particularly his big successes, whether events or money deals, the culmination was a signature that would frequently last for mere moments. The reality was, those moments had hour upon hour and days and months of preparation. Some projects extended over years.

The extraction and categorization of the information gleaned from Nathan would undoubtedly take months if not years to analyze, but one of Cabe's regrets was he would only have one chance.

Once again Cabe's skills, his capacity to recognize and adopt new technology or ideas, would be tested. In addition, he had to project them into the future and anticipate most of their ramifications and potential commercial applications. For him it was an extension of self-awareness. Like nearly all great innovators and visionaries, he was self-aware at a very early age.

Filling his work schedule was easy. Filling his imagination with the possibilities of projecting emotional feelings was exhilarating. His motives understanding how to extract and use Nathan's innate gifts didn't conflict him much because his altruistic internal compass told him he was doing the right thing. He had also projected that in the process there was money to be made, a huge amount of money, but the power was at higher level. As smart and visionary as he was, he failed, or perhaps more accurately didn't want to recognize and include what a malevolent weapon this power might become. Cabe wanted to think of it only in expanding his communications empire. That was merely a self-justification.

Adapting Nathan's waves seemed obvious and easy to Cabe. He'd worked with visual and sound broadcasting waves from his childhood. He just had to find their frequency, create and adapt them to broadcasting and create the machines to mimic Nathan's abilities. But Cabe's wants were an overriding reality. He didn't want to really face the concept that emotional elements in the human mind are not always easily predicted.

Cabe had not been around Nathan to see what Phipps was seeing. Nathan was becoming self-aware at a rate and depth no one could have foreseen. Adults always think they're fully in charge until they run into their own two-year old tyrant. Cabe and Phipps though separate individuals were after a similar goal. Both assumed authority and believed they were fully in charge. They would soon find that prickly lessons for assumptive adults are frequently more traumatic than for children.

54

Searching for Answers at New Tech

Saturday rolled around much faster than Nathan thought it would. His tutoring and the committee to distribute their benefactor's funds to a school in need had kept him busy and engaged. Unlike his experience in his Idaho school, when he was too young and without much understanding of what made him exceptional, his participation and growing self-awareness was beginning to mark him as a leader among his peers. It was a position he hadn't experienced before but was growing to enjoy.

Ally, insisted on going to the tests with Levi and Nathan. She was a momma Grizzly, Levi thought. These guys don't know what's coming if they do anything to Nathan she didn't like.

Fall was relentlessly giving way to cooler temperatures. Most of the deciduous trees had dropped at least half of their leaves. The green grass of Huntington Drive had lost its bright-spring green color, although for Southern California, it was still beautiful. Levi and Ally had fought this lab rat day, for Nathan. They hoped it would provide some answers but feared that it would raise harder questions.

Ally rolled down her window and gulped in the luscious, crisp fall air. She wondered what she could do to help Nathan as he grew. How does a mom teach her son, who had the kind of power that she had no clue how to address? Like moms everywhere, her response was unconditional love, but in Nathan's case, that wasn't going to be enough. He needed guidance for which she had no instruction manual.

Phipp's plan started with a full brain scan using a Siemens 3 Tesla 32 channel Tim Trio with an AC88 gradient insert. A second scan was scheduled for the middle of the test period at about eleven-thirty, with the last scan following the blood tests at the end. Dividing up the scans should give some potential atypical results to compare.

Second on the agenda was a full physical. A campus doctor, Dr. Jaret Chandler, was invited in to do the examination. Dr. Chandler took about forty-five minutes to do a battery of tests on every sense, organ and skin. He also did a series of muscle testing and body fat percentage. Ally got a little defensive about that one.

"He's a kid for heaven's sake," she said. "Why the heck do you need a body-fat test? In sixty day it will be out of date anyway."

"It's OK Ally," Levi calmed. "They're not going to do you or me," he added with a smile. He introduced her to the rest of the people participating in the tests, Dr. Phipps, Dr. Seperman, Dr. Chandler, et cetera.

Ally's response was, "Is everybody a doctor around here?" she said, not really expecting an answer.

"Pretty much," Levi said, "except for Dr. Seperman, who is a post doctoral scholar, and his assistant is also a PDS."

Following that, Dr. Ava Gage gave Nathan a series of psychological tests, hand dexterity, puzzle solving and some intellectual problem cracking. She also conducted a forty-five minutes interview with Nathan. When her tests and interview were over, Dr. Gage began walking out. She deliberately glanced directly at Phipps, raising her eyebrows twice and subtly whipping her hand like she was shaking water off of it. "Talk to you later Dr. Phipps," she said with some ominous overtones.

Next the second brain scan was conducted. This time Nathan answered several questions and was asked to do some mental gymnastics during the scan to engage his brain in various ways. Ally's fears were allayed by Dr. Phipps who explained. "We can determine what portions of the brain are responding which tells us that each part is functioning properly."

By the time this scan was done, it was noon. "How about some lunch?" Phipps suggested. "Want to head back to the, what did you call it, 'The Mind Mastication Emporium? Somebody learn a new word this week?"

"Sure," Nathan said. "You coming Jerry?" he added.

"Can't Nathan. Got to do some more set up for the blood tests. That's my bailiwick. Joan, why don't you go with them? I can finish getting things ready here," Seperman said.

"I'll bring you a sandwich," she said. "Pepsi?"

"How about regular lemonade and if you can bring it back a little earlier than the rest of the guys I'll munch while we work," he said.

"Your wish is my command," she smiled. "Back in a bit."

Seperman went about his protocol alignments. He had determined to do several typical tests: a complete panel and count, A1c, fibrinogen, a series of others, and one he was particularly interested in: a C-reactive protein blood test that measures the level of inflammation in the body.

Seperman had only gotten a glimpse of the first slide test he looked at when Nathan and his friends had come to the lab a few weeks before. The first look at the computer file on Nathan's blood seemed to indicate that there was absolutely no inflammation anywhere in his body. The CRP test, he surmised, would confirm more accurately whether there was some element in Nathan's blood which was able to suppress any random inflammation that could occur.

Another element he wanted to focus on was the potential C-reactive protein risk factor for the progression of macular degenerative disease. This might be extremely important, especially in light of Nathan's highly oxygenated blood at birth which could have affected his eyesight. The contradiction, as Seperman saw it, was that instead of reduced eyesight or blindness, Nathan's eyes were substantially enhanced and seemed to be the focusing lenses that directed his projecting capabilities.

Fonda got back to the lab with his sandwich and lemonade shortly before the group got back. "Here's the beef," she said.

"Ha! Ha!" Seperman said, "It's a turkey sandwich," which he wolfed down as he worked. "I've got everything ready including a series of comparative samples."

"I'll prepare some slides and dishes," Fonda said, "and get them ready to store for further checks."

"Sure," Seperman agreed.

In the cafeteria, the four were just finishing their lunch during a much subdued Saturday.

"You doing OK, Nathan?" Phipps said. "There's only some blood drawing we have to do and the final scan and you're outta here by half past one, at the latest!"

Ally piped up and said, "I'm ready for that." Levi smiled and simply nodded in agreement.

As they walked back to the lab, Phipps pointed to the pictures of scientists lining the walls of the corridor. It was an impressive list, particularly to Levi. He recognized many of the names that formed the basis of his studies. A singular thought crossed his mind, would Nathan's picture be here someday recognizing him for scientific excellence? Then another thought crept in…hopefully it wouldn't be as an anomaly of nature. That thought was painful.

Nathan climbed onto an examining table. Fonda put a wrist cuff on him to check his blood pressure. It was perfect for a boy his age. Perfect, she thought. What other perfections might I find in this amazing boy?

As the final blood collection began it was separated into a group of vials to be catalogued. It appeared to Levi that the subtle boss-assistant relationship between Seperman and Fonda waned. Fonda didn't have the expected deference to Seperman at times. Odd he thought. Fonda made some personal notes she didn't share. She ignored Seperman, when it seemed to suit her, and to Levi, she appeared to have an agenda of her own and a semi-hidden haughty attitude Levi didn't like.

Phipps walked Nathan over to the scanner. "One last thing," he said and we're done. Still OK?"

Nathan shook his head, "yes."

The final scan took about 15 minutes and the test collecting was finally done. It was time to head home.

Levi said he'd be out in a couple of minutes after briefly talking to Phipps. Ally and Nathan walked around the beautiful grounds for a few minutes in what seemed like an incredible oasis of peace and then headed to the car. Ally seemed more relieved than Nathan to have the tests over.

Levi asked Phipps about the timing of the analysis.

"I'm expecting about three or four days for the preliminaries," he said. "We know most of the normal basic info now. It's the more complex elements that we have to check and double check. We need to fit Nathan in among a myriad of other projects, but he promised Levi that it would be ASAP. 'Oh,' and we'll be shut down tomorrow so we'll start first thing Monday on the mundane stuff. The psych evaluations and brain scans may take more time. Blood work, as you know, we'll be able to do much more quickly."

"See ya Monday, Bernie, I appreciate your help. If this can help Nathan and us to guide him, I think it will be well worth the effort. And please tell everybody thanks. I appreciate their kindness to him and to us."

55

Blanket Delivered, Abduction Set

While Levi and Ally returned home cautiously optimistic, Cabe's world was in full swing that same Saturday.

Instead of waiting for McKay to deliver the blanket to him, Cabe went to his lab. To most, the lab looked like a massive jumble of wires, boxes, screens, speakers, monitors and a bunch of stuff that even Nicolas Tesla might have paused at. The layout looked like a jumble but it was a "well-oiled machine" or maybe a well wired insulated conglomeration. The smell of electricity seemed to float above the oscillating screens like the persistent layer of smog that hovers over the Los Angeles basin on inversion days.

"I think I know why you're here," McKay said. "I've got it over there. You asked about the specific sound wave protons that could be seen. Let me show you something interesting."

McKay went through the explanations and his and LeAnne's modeled projections. Cabe listened intently, seemingly satisfied with the results. There wouldn't be, nor could there be, any real-life human test of the wave inhibitor blanket. McKay handed Cabe the material configured in the size requested. It was smooth and highly flexible and had a slightly metallic coolness to it. Cabe was expecting the silver and copper threads to be more pronounced.

"Where are the metallic fibers?" Cabe asked. "I would have thought we could feel them more."

"That's one of the beauties of this material and the nature of how I arranged the weaving pattern," McKay said. "It works in a way that maximizes the reflective properties for waves, but is essentially invisible to the eye, and even somewhat pleasant to the touch."

"By the way boss, I filed a patent through the company. I think there are applications on this material that could be beneficial," McKay said.

It was another one of those parts of Cabe's management style that seemed to contrast with other corporate structures in the industry. Cabe encouraged research using company facilities, with a generous sharing of the royalties if the products were successful including patent sharing. Many companies would have claimed all the rewards, but for Cabe, he found this profoundly motivating for his creative employees. He further allowed the use of equipment during off hours, providing everything was approved and catalogued, including the nature of the projects and their ultimate goals. Any project could be worked on when it didn't interfere with the normal activities of the department. Many of his employees took advantage of the policy and it paid handsome dividends for all involved.

The blanket material met all the needed specifications. It had what looked like a slight checker board pattern, a consequence of the weaving concept McKay developed.

Cabe thanked McKay and Allred for working quickly and efficiently under intense pressure, and hurried to link up with Drobick, Palumbo and Jeeves.

"Here's the necessary jewel for this operation," Cabe said. "How's everything else?"

"Good to go!" Palumbo said.

Drobick and Jeeves nodded their agreement.

"It will be close to three on Monday as possible," Palumbo said. "The actual abduction shouldn't take more than five to ten seconds. I know I've told you all of this before but just to refresh everybody's memory, here it is again. About ten minutes before we get Nathan, a couple of anonymous calls about a forced abduction of a ten year old boy will be called in to The South Pasadena Police Department. The call will give a location that will be right along the San Marino and

South Pasadena border. The phone call should trigger an Amber Alert and pull San Marino police to the east.

"Several minutes later, the San Marino police department will also receive an anonymous tip about a man with a gun barricaded in a vacant house on the east side of the Ritz Carlton. We expect a convergence far away from The Nathan Venture with the expectation that both departments will correlate their responses. With all that, we'll be underway. Any second guesses boss?"

"No, but remember, I don't want even a scratch on Nathan or any of you. Abort immediately if things go badly!" Cabe said. "You've got tomorrow to get everything refined down to a gnat's eyelash. Be ready, get it done and San Pedro is ready, right?"

"All set," Drobick said. "Last warning on that abyss Max. Are you ready if this goes south?"

Cabe nodded his head slowly up and down and then asked, "You ready, Jeeves?"

"Have you ever known me not to be ready?" Jeeves shot back.

"Never," Cabe said."

"Text me, 'Nothing ventured' if everything is successful and 'punt' if not."

With that, Cabe simply said "GO!" and walked out.

56

Who's Evaluating Whom

Phipps called everybody into the conference room. He was exceptionally stern as he faced the powerful group of intellectual talent he had in front of him. He had told everyone not to bring electronic devices of any kind. Pencils and pads were all that was allowed.

"I would like to remind you that these tests and the materials collected are to be kept separately in my safe. We are dealing with a colleague and friend and his son. Anything we do that could subject them to harassment or other ordeals can't be allowed. We have to be particularly careful. If Nathan were one of your children or other member of your family, you'd want to protect him and his parents. I also realized that you probably don't need reminding, but I'm reminding you anyway." Phipps said.

"I'd like you each to do a "couple-minute" first impressions bit of what you think. Make any possible suggestions we may not have thought of regarding either these tests or future tests that might help. Dr. Chandler, would you start, please?" Phipps nodded his head in Chandler's direction.

Chandler said, "The kid's in great shape. There was nothing that even came close to a physical problem. Every response was off the charts. Acuity, hand/eye, nerve response, appearance, internals, literally everything was maxed out or beyond. My initial reaction personally is that I don't think I've ever seen a kid in as great a shape as Nathan overall. Maybe it was those Idaho spuds, who knows?

"From what I see, he's even sharper than most of the exceptionally bright kids I see here who are older and he's only eleven. And physically, I'd say he's as perfect a specimen as you get in a young man, although as a scientist, I think I'd make a few reservations until after the other tests we're doing are thoroughly evaluated."

"Anything else?" Phipps asked.

"Not for now, but on some levels, Nathan scored so high I may have to raise the top test projections." Chandler said.

"Jerry, Joan, anything you want to share? I'm assuming you've done a few quick preliminaries," Phipps said.

"Jaret is right on with his 'just about perfect' comments," Jerry said. "His blood work seems to be great with regard to his health. However, there are some potential abnormalities that are going to require closer inspection. They're definitely not negatives—they appear to be extra positives. Just can't put numbers on them at the moment."

"Joan?" Phipps asked. "How about you?"

"Hate to be the rain cloud in this parade," she said, "but I feel we're setting a tone that we don't want to begin with. I'm with Jerry that the blood work findings don't just appear excellent there are potentials that seem unlimited. I just want to be a little more reserved. I've seen too many questions in other preliminary exams that pop up after the first look. Those are my only reservations."

Phipps echoed Joan's take. "The brain scans are, as far as I can tell, highly significant. Problem is, I'm not too sure if they're telling me something I believe. I hate to leave us all with that, but I think Joan's right with including some judicious reservations. I'll be back on Monday to start a more realistic examination of the test results. Hope everybody does the same."

"Ava, you seemed quite taken by Nathan?" Phipps probed.

"May I break protocol here?" She said. "If everybody doesn't mind, I'm extremely nervous talking about a psych evaluation in a committee rather than in consultation with other psychologists. That's just a professional no-no, in my opinion. If you don't mind Bernie, sorry everybody, I'd rather talk to you alone. If that turns out OK, then I'd be happy to discuss Nathan further. I'm worried that there may be some interpretations of things I can't confirm.

As everybody knows, head cases need more than one interview if possible. I know we're all going to keep this quiet, but I guess I'm a little paranoid; does that make sense for a psychologist? Everybody knows we shrinks are all a little paranoid! Insert smiling emoticon here!" she added.

"Oh, and Bernie, I'd like to talk after this meeting for a sec," she said, "if that's OK?"

"No problemo, to quote Aaaahnuld," Phipps said. "We have a boy's life and family in our hands. Caution is prudent."

"Let's all remember that Nathan is a young man no matter how advanced he appears," Phipps said. "Why don't we take tomorrow off, do some thinking about our individual areas of expertise and the directions we want to consider. I'd like to let my brain juggle the conclusions for a while."

The meeting broke up and Phipps and Gage went to his office. Phipps grabbed a couple of cups of green tea from his percolator and sat down, handing one to Dr. Gage.

"So what's on your mind? Dr. Gage?" Phipps asked.

"I'll make this relatively short." She said. "I didn't really want to be speculating in front of everybody.

"I realize that I'm kind of new to this game, unlike everybody else. But here goes. Nathan is nothing short of amazing. I'd say his intellect is off the charts but you'd be right if you concluded he hides it. I'm not sure why, but maybe because of previous incidents in his life. I see this sometimes when people are interrogated under difficult or threatening circumstances. In our short time, I didn't get into the why and I'm not sure he would have answered. He showed me only what he wanted me to see. He was literally too smart to get trapped by any of my psychological snares.

"At times, I wasn't sure who was interviewing whom. If it were up to me, I'd have a battery of psychologists doing extensive testing and consultations. Since that's not an option, and you wanted a quick report on my interview, you've got yourself an eleven-year-old mountain of a problem. He is so capable, and has a potential I'm not even sure I can measure. I can't even be sure which mountain I'm climbing. That's going to take some time."

"I know it doesn't seem like I should be able to reach these conclusions this fast but I'm fairly sure they're accurate. I just don't have corroboration and the final problem to this puzzle is that Nathan harbors a fairly deep, though tightly controlled, sense of vengeance and at the same time, he also has a deep empathy. It seems like such a contradictory mix. And the "why" is the mystery that could take years to decipher.

Oh, and you should try to interview someone with those eyes. They weren't eyes; they were penetrating lavender lasers, if there's such a thing. "I had to finally pull out the Dr. Freud "no eye contact card." I asked him to lie down on the couch and close his eyes and relax as much as possible. Most of my insights came after that. He was so friendly, relaxed and cooperative. I feel like 'I was the one psyched out, not Nathan.'"

Phipps sat back for a while not responding immediately. Finally he said, "What bothers me, Ava, is that you've put this together in such a short amount of time. Do you really think it was long enough to get it right? With your preliminary thoughts, I can understand your reluctance to share. I'm sure any hearsay analysis would be all over the board and if leaked could be exceptionally damaging to Nathan and his family.

"Sorry, I'm just kind of thinking out loud here. I'm beginning to feel even more personally responsible in Nathan's case. If you would please; do some chewing on it over the weekend and then let's get together next week. Knowing you, I expect that your evaluation won't change much but I think it will be critical in how we help Nathan and his family." Phipps said.

"I feel the same," she said. "It's the reason I'm trying to be extra careful. But, Bernie, you realize, even in this short first session, this kid is a massive career maker!" she said. "Appreciate your time. I'll call next week. Any time better than another?"

"Try Thursday. I've pretty much got the morning free," he said.

"Thursday then," she said as she left.

Phipps collapsed into his chair, leaned back, plunked his feet on the desk, closed his eyes and tried to diminish the Everest she just dumped on him. "I'm going to enjoy tomorrow and try to free my mind for Monday," for now, he let his mind wander. "We can start in earnest after some rest."

57

Homeless Take Over Clinic

Dr. Wolfe flew down to the Long Beach Airport where Palumbo and Jeeves picked him up. The drive to San Pedro was a short distance but time was protracted. "Compared to Spokane this LA traffic is almost incomprehensible," Wolfe said.

"Well, it's Friday and everybody is getting fired up for the weekend," Jeeves said. You're lucky you got here now instead of waiting till it heats up around three-thirty and you're zipping along at a mind-boggling two and a half miles an hour.

"Thanks, but I prefer the living in the metropolis of downtown Spokane!" Wolfe said. "I'll get my work done and high tail it outta here."

Setting up the equipment wasn't that difficult or time consuming. A generator was used so no hookup was required. Since the entire clinic area was thoroughly scrubbed, it amounted to plugging in three blood testing machines and calibrating them. A technician had been hired by the landlord at the request of Palumbo to make sure the scanner was working properly so the scanner was ready several days before Wolfe arrived. Most of Wolfe's time was consumed by triple testing results against standards to make sure they were reporting accurately.

Wolfe chose to stay at the clinic building. Free Wifi was available from somewhere nearby so he didn't even have to have a special connection for his lap top. He kept in touch with everyone via text and Palumbo had everything stocked so no one had to go out unnecessarily, even for food.

Palumbo and Jeeves returned to LA and began final preparations for Monday at three o'clock. By late Saturday afternoon, Wolfe was also satisfied with his preparations. He'd set things up pretty much the same as his labs in Spokane, but ever the worrywart, everything had to be perfect.

With Cabe on the verge of getting the results he'd spent a lot of money and time chasing, his anticipation level was sky high, tempered by pangs of conscience, stoked by potential benefits but heavily leavened by his fear that his plan would go awry and his life would be shattered. As the events from that first day unfolded, the events had grown in his mind and he had to follow where they led. He was ready to pay the price if the venture failed, but potential unimaginable rewards superseded fear.

58

Backfire

Monday morning was grey and somewhat dismal in contrast to Saturday's beautifully clear fall morning. Everything seemed to be unfolding in slow motion. Palumbo and Jeeves ran the route twice to the 210 freeway in the morning. All the necessary equipment was double checked: especially the operational lights on the truck, balloon signs checked, all vehicles gassed, in place and running smoothly.

Drobick drove the vehicle that would be stationed along the sidewalk and in the parking lot. Timing was critical. Jeeves and Palumbo timed the walking speeds to mark the precise point at which Drobick would open his front door, blocking much of the view from any incidental witnesses from the east.

The extra touch Drobick had suggested was a wallet lying on the ground outside his SUV. Drobick would be in the SUV eating a sandwich and give the impression that he was oblivious to the wallet. He anticipated that Nathan would pause and bend over to pick it up, thus diverting his attention away from the road to his left. The assumption was the diversion would make Nathan a little more physically manageable and easier to throw the blanket over him.

At that exact moment, Palumbo's plan was to drive a van with a non-descript sign on the side saying Kmetzsch's Spring Green Lawncare. He planned to open the sliding side door precisely across from the vehicle in the parking lot. Nathan would be sandwiched between the two vehicles with doors open and with trees overhead, no easy visual access from any direction, including above.

Jeeves would then taser Nathan, knocking him out while Drobick threw the blanket over his head, hopefully blocking Nathan's chance to use his switching powers. He'd be whisked into the van and injected with a roofie while his eyes and whole upper body were covered. Palumbo would then smoothly drive away while Drobick did the same in the opposite direction.

Planted trace evidence, an empty Coke can with forged finger prints and a few misleading items were placed by Palumbo in the area, along with some dirt traces before be grabbed Nathan who would be tie strapped on a pad in the van. The whole kidnapping would be a matter of seconds, or so they expected. The pieces were in place and ready at two-forty five. Nathan could be seen walking his route along with a few others but they were quite a ways behind him walking with their faces in their phones.

At two-forty eight p.m. the South Pasadena Police Department received two anonymous phone calls reporting that an eleven year boy was being forcibly kidnapped on a street on its western border that was contiguous to San Marino. An immediate Amber Alert was issued. Virtually every police car on patrol in both city police departments headed towards the area.

Since the reports police received sounded completely credible, dispatchers sent patrolman to the east side of San Marino. The west side was left void of patrol vehicles. A few minutes later another call was made claiming shots were fired from a vacant house on the west side of the Ritz-Carlton between the alleged abduction site in South Pasadena and several blocks into San Marino.

Any patrolman not necessary at the reported kidnapping site headed to the shots fired location.

On the west side of San Marino everything was in place. Nathan reached the designated pickup site exactly on time. And as predicted he bent over to pick up the wallet to return it to the man eating his lunch in the truck. A second later, Palumbo screeched to a stop sandwiching Nathan between the two vehicles. Jeeves, jumping out of the van, fired the taser hitting Nathan in his lower back while, at the same time, Drobick came out of his vehicle with the blanket.

The war plan axiom proved true immediately. (The first causality of every war is the battle plan) How could anyone have anticipated that when the electricity of the taser hit Nathan, it would explode like a Tesla coil with bolts going in every direction and backfire on the kidnappers? Jeeves jumped out expecting to retrieve Nathan's limp body, but Jeeves and Drobick were zapped with what could be described as emotional lightening.

While Nathan was incapacitated, Drobick had just enough time to put the blanket over his head and tie straps around his feet, knees and wrists, Jeeves laid prostrate on the sidewalk, awake but not knowing what had happened.

The taser affect wouldn't last too long but the roofie would keep the boy quiet for long enough.

Adrenaline flowed into Palumbo. He unceremoniously lifted Jeeves off the sidewalk and heaved him into the van. In an instant Palumbo was behind the wheel and smoothly but quickly heading down the road. Drobick too, was hit, but not as severely as Jeeves. He jumped back into his SUV, slammed the door and also drove off at the upper end of the speed but under control so as not to draw attention.

It took all of about seventeen seconds, more than the length they'd planned for. Drobick removed the signs, drove the untraceable vehicle to an unattended lot where vehicles were placed for pickup and notified the transfer company. An ignition key was put in a Hide-a-key and affixed to the top of the passenger side wheel well. A short time later a student walked into the lot, grabbed the keys, and headed to Pennsylvania. It took no more than twenty minutes, before the vehicle was headed east. Drobick's part was complete.

Jeeves, initially dazed by the impact of the emotional storm, recovered quickly, at least enough to keep things quiet in the back. That storm was utterly disorienting but now gave a third member of Cabe's entourage a good inkling what Nathan could do. Although Nathan hadn't consciously aimed his power at the men, he had become a kind of unintended and unconscious conduit. The emotional purple lightening or Tesla coil-like strike was scattered and unfocused but still a powerful charge.

Palumbo drove under tight control to avoid looking stressed, to an area about two blocks away. He ripped the brightly colored *Sofia's Balloons* signs off the van. To see the two vans side by side they would have appeared to be the same vehicle, but Palumbo wasn't through. Since the van was small he drove it up a ramp and into a semi-trailer and closed the back door. He casually walked to the semi's cab, got in and drove off. Changing the driver of the truck would have to wait a while longer.

Jeeves continued to be slightly dazed, but as time went on, began to return to his normal self. Palumbo asked how he and Nathan were doing.

"You mean other than having my head explode?" he said. "If this is what Cabe was talking about, I can tell you it's not something you'd want to experience. I'm wondering if the taser was just an unexpected channel or if this was directed by Nathan. I'm betting that this was more random, but if this kid can deliver a straight on full blow of these emotional outbursts, this is way beyond what I would even have dreamed could be possible.

"Ya wanna know something crazy?" Jeeves asked.

"Absolutely!" Palumbo said.

"I assumed I was somewhat aware of what the boss went through, but I've realized, I didn't have a clue about the massive emotional explosion that was flung in all directions. I'm just guessing what happened in this case, but it was a powerful jolt." Jeeves said. "I wonder if maybe the taser just screwed up his aim or if it was just an unintended consequence of the taser's mode. Apparently the adrenaline and emotional feelings that both you and Drobick were feeling, along with my own emotional feelings being amplified a hundred fold came smashing into my brain like an anvil. It's just hard to know what happened exactly.

"I'll have to think about it some more. I'm finally getting why Cabe's been so insistent. Nathan used somebody's emotions against us. Think about that, he was handling three grown men while being kidnapped and still almost got away. I'm sure as hell hoping that the blanket works because if it doesn't we might as well climb into the broiler now," Jeeves said.

Palumbo had enough paranoia to check every light on the truck, the plates and tires. It could be a long drive to San Pedro especially with busy traffic and ever-vigilant highway patrolmen. The back windows of the truck had been blacked out. This was permissible under state law, as long as the driver's side and the front passenger window was clear.

There was still a question of whether the blanket was preventing Nathan from coming down hard with his power. When he came out of the medication which quieted him, he'd be aware but still wouldn't remember anything. It did, though, intensify the need to have the blanket work. The only way that could happen would be allowing him to wake up.

That happened much faster than expected. Nathan's ankles were strapped together as were his hands. The blanket went over him and he was unable to see anything and began to struggle against his restraints. Jeeves knew exactly when the Rohyphenol would wear off and Nathan would need another injection if he continued to fight the ties.

They'd apparently gotten away smoothly, but because of nearly tripling the ground time with the taser problem, a couple of Nathan's young classmates of had seen a little of the scuffle, although most of what happened was obscured. Alicia Ashton wasn't sure what she'd seen exactly but she was concerned enough to call 911.

"911, how may I help you?" the police dispatcher said.

"My name is Alicia Ashton and I think my girlfriend and I just saw a boy get kidnapped," she said.

"What's your girlfriend's name?" the dispatcher asked.

"Eliza Braxton," Alicia said.

"Are you talking about the boy in South Pasadena?" the dispatcher asked.

Alicia was a little confused. "What boy?" she asked, "we're in San Marino."

"Tell me exactly what you saw and what time did it happen?"

"A few minutes ago," she answered.

"What is your exact location?" the dispatcher asked.

"We're on Roanoke Road, behind the Green Tree Mall in one of the parking lots," Alicia said.

"Alicia, how old are you?" the dispatcher asked.

"Twelve," she said.

The dispatcher heard the fear in the young girl's voice and knew it was serious. A young person's phone would receive the Amber alerts and she was wary that this might be a prank, but this was not a prank.

"Alicia, I'm Officer Gabrielle Bennett, but you can call me Gabby. I've already dispatched a patrol car to your location. However, we've had a situation happen that seems to be similar to what you're reporting, so it may take a little while for the patrolman to get there. Are you safe?"

"Yes," said Alicia.

"Did you get pictures? How far are you from your home?" Gabby asked.

"About two blocks and no we didn't get pictures" Alicia said.

"Are there any neighborhood safe houses nearby?" Gabby questioned.

"Not too close, we're on the sidewalk at the mall's back parking lot," Alicia said. "I think there is one about a block from here."

The dispatcher was getting nervous for the girls safety. Two potential abductions and another couple of kids alone who may have been witnesses demanded that she help them find safety as soon as possible.

"Is the mall closer to you than the neighborhood safe house?" the dispatcher asked.

"Yes," Alicia said.

"OK, Alicia, I want you to start now and go directly to the Mall as fast as you can, but do not get near any cars or people. Go into the mall and find the security guards and ask them to stay with you until the officer arrives. I will redirect the officer to the mall. You stay on the phone with me until you get into the mall and find guards. I'll let your Mom know where you're going. Please stay there even if either of your parents gets there first. Can you do that?" the dispatcher asked.

"Yes, we can do that quickly," Alicia said.

"Who is your closest parent to location that I can phone, Alicia," the officer asked.

Alicia gave the officer her mother's phone number and she passed it to a second dispatcher who was now involved in the call. The dispatcher's office went into even higher mode with calls coming in from all over the area on the other amber alerts. But, Alicia's call was so unusual it was given their primary attention with diversion tactics by the kidnappers crossing the mind of both dispatchers.

With that thought now in the air, all evidence would become suspect.

The second dispatcher called Alicia's Mom, Rosie, and explained the situation and then immediately notified mall security to find the girls. Alicia's mother said she'd be there and was just a few minutes away. "Please Rosie, be careful driving. We want you to get there safely. We're pretty confident that any problems have passed."

Within a couple of minutes the girls were in the mall with the security guards. Alicia's mother arrived just minutes later.

It was at least another few minutes before the patrol officer got there.

Gabby was still on the phone with Alicia. Her mother thanked Gabby profusely. Savannah said she'd stay and talk to the officer and left her address with the dispatcher.

"Badge 437, on location with the girls in site," Gordon said into her shoulder mic as she walked up to them.

The officer, Gordon, asked the girls to sit down on the mall benches with Alicia, her Mom and Eliza. Eliza had called her parents too and they were on their way.

Officer Gordon asked the pair what they'd seen. She explained to Alicia's mother what had happened with the other reports and explained that there was some confusion. She wanted to be sure the girls were safe, but also needed to get as many details as possible.

They told their story. They hadn't seen a lot, but did see one man on the ground and Nathan, a boy they knew from school had been walking on the sidewalk. He had walked between two vehicles and then was gone. They'd been looking into their IPods and only noticed a man being lifted from the ground and Nathan not there anymore.

"Do you know Nathan's last name?" Officer Gordon asked.

"No," Eliza said, "but we both go to Rock Creek School where he goes."

Officer Gordon spoke into her shoulder mic telling the dispatcher to check on Nathan's last name. She then turned to the girls again,

"Alicia, you start. Please try to remember exactly what you saw with as many details as you can remember.

"We were walking down the sidewalk behind the mall here. We were talking and texting. I noticed a car parked in the lot along the sidewalk. The front door toward the sidewalk was open and a man was sitting in the front seat maybe eating lunch. Nathan was walking not too far from him. I was looking down at my phone most of the time. A few seconds later when Nathan was near the car in the lot, we saw a second vehicle drive right up to the sidewalk beside the parked car and screech to a stop.

That's when we both looked up and froze. A guy jumped out. Then a second later he was on the ground and the guy from the car under the tree jumped out with some kind of sheet or blanket. It looked like they kinda threw it over Nathan and that's the last I saw of him. Then both cars took off."

"Did either of you see a license plate? Did you take any phone video? Gordon asked.

Both of the girls shook their heads no.

"What color were the cars?" the officer asked. Do you remember what they looked like? You know what trucks, vans and SUVs look like, right?"

"Yes, I think they were a smaller van and SUV, they were both kind of dark, maybe blue or black, I think," Alicia said. "One, the SUV was kind of bigger than the other."

Eliza said she thought one was maybe black and the other dark blue.

"Eliza, please tell me what you saw," Gordon said.

"Like Alicia said, we were looking up and down at our phones. She kind of screamed and I looked up just in time to see the car on the street drive right up to the sidewalk. I think I saw some signs on the side of the van. The only thing I remember was that there were balloons on the side. A sign or something," Eliza said.

Gordon immediately called in information about the balloons

sign and the potential colors mentioned by the girls. "Last seen heading east on Roanoke she said. "Please go ahead Eliza."

"I saw a guy throw the other guy lying on the ground into the car in the road. I didn't see Nathan at all. It was like he was walking along and then he wasn't. That's about it," Eliza said. "I think maybe the one was a van."

"Any faces?" Gordon asked. "Race, ethnicity?"

Maybe white, both girls said, but they described big dark glasses on them and maybe mustaches, or something on their faces. Alicia added she thought she noticed a scooter about a block away and that was it.

The officer said, "Let's walk out to the area where you were and where you saw Nathan." They showed the officer where they were but were a little reluctant to go to where they saw Nathan grabbed. It was in the farthest parking lot from the mall building. Gordon thought, "Away from the building and most cars, under trees, two cars to block visibility. That definitely sounds like it was carefully planned."

Gordon took the girl's phone numbers and addresses and by that time Eliza's parents were there. Gabby suggested that the girls go home and asked that they write down anything they thought of that they might remember later. Leave a message with the officer at the desk or with the detective department at the station," she said and gave each her card.

The girls and their parents left for home and Gordon made some more notes and forwarded the info to Detective Sanchez's email and returned to patrolling. This time she stayed on the west side looking for vehicles matching the description reported by the girls.

Gordon got on her radio to dispatch and said "Badge 437 reporting: Appears credible. But the girls are eleven and twelve and were looking at their phones just prior to the abduction. Suggest we get a team over here to check out the site. Maybe some possible clues that I can see. There could be a possible additional witness who may have been driving a scooter, according to one of the girls. But he could have been past the incident."

59
Kidnapping Surprise

Phipps suggested that those involved with Nathan's examinations spend the morning putting together their information and that they meet again at 2:30 p.m. It took some time getting everybody on the project to be ready for the meeting because of other responsibilities.

In analyzing the brain scan data, Phipps found information which was beyond his experience reading any other person's scan, much less his full comprehension. Levi had intimated some of the things he had suspected regarding Nathan's brain development. But Phipps didn't want to accept them and frankly didn't believe them. To accept them would have meant everything he'd studied up to this time in his life would necessarily be subject to possible reinterpretation. He didn't want to deal with that.

Nathan's scans, he realized, would challenge everything in Phipps scanning experience. Levi's theories were proving true. Nathan's brain had triple the normal number of sucli on the surface of his brain. It made room for more neuron clusters that could connect and reconnect essentially compounding themselves. The scan Phipps was seeing confirmed the "tension-based theory" of the brain folding in on itself to overcome the effects of the human skull's size limitations. Nearly all of these signs were visible in Nathan's scans.

Einstein's slides showed the asymmetrical shapes and sizes of anatomical quirks on his cerebral cortex. But Einstein was dead, and Nathan was very much alive. Phipps ached to do more comprehensive testing. He would particularly like to be much more tailored and nuanced with future tests now that he had a better starting place. To introduce stimuli while scanning Nathan's brain, and recording the outcomes he knew would be Nobel Prize material. He also realized, sadly, that it probably would never happen.

Phipps was surprised that pretty much everything that Levi had speculated was accurate and now apparent. What Levi was unable to see was the influence of the nature of Nathan's birth on the development of his corpus callosum. The connection between the left and right sides of his brain was not just a flimsy connection but in Nathan's case, a hyper-connection capable of sending cascading input and information between the two sides of the brain in ways Phipps could not explain. He'd seen nothing like this in all his experience.

Then, there was something strange. It appeared to be a kind of network that Levi had also predicted. It was barely visible, almost as though the scans merely suggested the network rather than showed it. Phipps was at a loss to infer what it did. Again he reminded himself that this was the brain of an eleven-year-old boy that had not reached mental maturity. Puberty was around the corner. What would that mean?

Just as he was finishing his findings, he realized he was scheduled to meet with his group of academics and he was already about twenty-five minutes late. He put his speculations on hold and went to the meeting. Everyone was there and ready. He suggested Gage start the meeting since she hadn't reported originally.

She made some typically academic equivocations and provisos before she started but essentially, in less grandiose terms, explained her first interview with Nathan that she discussed with Phipps. Next, Seperman began to reconfirm his findings when his assistant asked to leave and take what she described as a critical phone call. Phipps, of course, granted her request. Seperman confirmed some Phipps scan findings that Nathan's mental maturity and capacity was not at an end but just beginning.

Phipps was mere minutes into his reports when Fonda returned to the room with the blood drained from her face.

"Nathan's been kidnapped!" she announced.

She was hit with questions from everybody in the room.

"I don't know anything else. I only know he's gone," Fonda said.

Everyone opened their smart phones to news apps while Phipps turned on the television and all eyes refocused on the big screen.

60

Farnsworths Agony Over Son's Kidnapping

Phipps called Levi about Nathan's kidnapping but said he'd called the police, who told him that they hadn't released the boy's name pending the notification of the parents. He also told Levi that this could become a media circus, especially if it was discovered New Tech had been doing special testing of Nathan.

Then Phipps added, "I'm coming to get you and Ally right now."

Levi immediately called Ally to tell her the horrible news, which put Ally on the verge of hysteria when she learned of Nathan's abduction. "We have to hold ourselves together," he said. "Pack at least a week's worth of clothing changes and tooth brushes and that kind of stuff. "It'll take me 15 to 20 to get home, he said. Don't answer the phone unless it shows it's me or the San Marino Police Department. Talk to no one else. The police will most likely be there before I will, but we'll be moving to a safe house and I don't know how long we'll be there."

"This is a confirmed forced stranger abduction now and we'll become the focus of attention. Better we go undercover. Phipps says New Tech has graciously offered us the use of one of their secure houses here on campus for protecting us from what is sure to be a media onslaught," Levi said.

"Why do we have to hide?" Ally asked. "Do we know if he's alright? What do the police know? Why did they take Nathan? We don't have any money and how big a ransom would it have to be?"

"I don't know any answers at all, Ally. We just have to be strong," Levi said. "But the media is going to jump on this because of my connection to New Tech and if the fact leaks that Nathan has been undergoing tests here, which it most likely, it will stoke a media frenzy of chaos and we'll become the biggest targets. Bernard understands that and that's why he's trying to protect us. We'll have a much better chance dealing with the kidnappers if we don't have to fight media too. Remember Ally, we've got to be tough for Nathan. I'm on my way."

The officer and Levi got to the Farnsworth home at about the same time. The officer confirmed officially that Nathan had been abducted, but that they had not identified Nathan to the media as yet but would after this meeting with Levi and Ally.

Phipps, to his everlasting credit, was a rock for the Farnsworths. He immediately began to sooth, support and protect them from the pending media onslaught and vowed to help get Nathan back. It was a promise that might be impossible to keep and the cost to him professionally and could be enormous.

With Phipps efforts to get Ally and Levi into a safer situation, he began to brood over a looming question that bothered him greatly. How did Fonda know Nathan was kidnapped if his name hadn't been released yet? He didn't like what the answer might be as to why Fonda seemed to know before the police announcement.

61

The Case Goes National

From the screen a Warning Alert flashed, cutting off the regularly scheduled programming.

"On air in five, four, three!" Stage manager Noah Albert went to silent counting out the last two seconds with his fingers and pointed at the anchor.

Carolanne Cassity watched the count and heard it in her ear bud then began the Amber Alert:

"We have just received a report from the San Marino Police Department that an eleven-year-old, boy has been forcibly abducted from a sidewalk near the Green Tree Mall. Police have not yet identified the child.

"According to the police report, two vehicles, one believed to be a small van type and a larger unidentified vehicle were involved. Witnesses told police the vehicles were dark colored, possibly black or dark blue. The abduction was apparently well planned and occurred at about three p.m. No other sightings have been reported in the area. We will continue our alerts as more information becomes available."

Cassity tossed to her co-anchor, Jameson Olsen who was headed to the scene of the abduction.

"Apparently, Carolanne," Olson reported from his cell phone, "There was a lot of orchestrated confusion surrounding the situation. Separate phone calls to authorities just minutes before this abduction were received in what seemed to be a highly coordinated kidnapping.

"There were two calls reporting what police now believe were fake reports of an abduction in South Pasadena right across the boundary from San Marino. A third call was made about alleged gun shots fired at a San Marino home just blocks from the fake abduction.

"I'll be on the scene in moments," Olson said, "and report back."

Cassity asked, "Do we know if there's a connection between either the first reported abduction or the reported gunshots, or a connection to the second reported abduction?

"I can't confirm either at this point, Cassity," he said, "but I'll check in as soon as we get on scene. Current speculation is that the calls were distractions to draw police away from the intended target."

"Thanks Jameson," Cassity said.

Cassity paused, saying: "One moment please, we're getting new information," obviously listening to someone speaking to her through her ear bud. A crew member handed her a sheet which she read. "I've just been given a press release from the San Marino Police that the name of the boy abducted is Nathan Farnsworth, a student at Rock Creek Middle School in San Marino. He is four-feet eleven inches with light brown hair. Anyone who may have any information relating to this abduction, please notify the FBI or the San Marino Police Department immediately.

"We'll update this report as we get new information. Once again, there has been a forced abduction Amber Alert issued for an eleven-year old boy by the name of Nathan Farnsworth. This is Carolanne Cassity for KIVI-TV."

62

Surprise, Surprise

Jeeves had some military experience driving big vehicles so he changed places with Palumbo and drove the semi toward San Pedro while Palumbo watched over Nathan. It became obvious to Palumbo that once the trauma of the event was over that either the wave-blocking blanket was working or Nathan had chosen not to attack.

Palumbo stayed skeptical and kept a close eye on the boy because he now knew the chaos the young man could cause.

Palumbo was very thorough. He'd rented a Volvo City tractor with a standard 53-footer and had magnetic signs for the doors on either side calling it TNV trucking. The sign included the phony name and address but more critically the USDOT number. He'd bought a packet of bills of lading at a truck stop that was near a plant that made Top Ramen. He also bought a package of wire seals to crimp onto the locked trailer latch. He filled out the bill of lading with the cargo listed as Top Ramen. It was a light load that would not give away the fact that the trailer only held one relatively light vehicle.

He also a fake commercial license for Jeeves, the best money could buy. It was worn just enough around the edges to give the appearance that he'd been driving for a while.

There were no check points between the two towns so the idea was to drive exceptionally carefully to their destination and because of their cargo. Traffic at about 3:30 in the afternoon was almost bearable as the typical afternoon commute in Los Angeles began to slow substantially after that.

Despite the traffic the trip was uneventful. Jeeves had taken a somewhat circuitous route and within an hour and a half was driving over the Vincent Thomas Bridge and was within sight of their destination. Jeeves called Palumbo and reported their pending arrival saying he was just pulling off the freeway with relief in his voice. Within a blink of hearing Jeeves express relief he heard him shouting a highly disquieting "Oh great!" after which the phone disconnected.

Palumbo just about went into full panic mode. He felt the truck slow and knew something was up. He had no idea what the "Oh Great" meant. He had to assume that they'd been pulled over by a California Highway Patrol cruiser. The sound in the van was muffled and outside ambient noise didn't help either. It couldn't be heard outside the trailer, unless it was practically a scream. He moved closer to Nathan, ready to stifle any noise he might make. He told Nathan he had a bottle of water for him if he kept quiet. The boy said "OK," and received a bottle with the cap off. Palumbo sat him up against the side of the van then put the bottle to his lips and Nathan took a big gulp.

The outside noise, especially from the freeway made it necessary to ramp up normal conversation just to be heard. In a way, Jeeves appreciated any noise that could cover sound from inside the trailer.

Jeeves' had driven straight into a random truck inspection by the San Pedro Police Department. With two mammoth harbors next to each other and ships picking up cargo constantly, trucks were ubiquitous and a standard mode of shipping. He just happened to be one of the "lucky" drivers who had been motioned by officers to drive into one of the designated lanes.

Jeeves had been in many dangerous situations with his life in jeopardy during his Army deployments. But this was a strange type of fear. If he were caught with a kidnapped boy, his life would be ruined, not to mention his reputation, which he guarded jealously. It was a reality he'd thought about in the abstract, but now that he faced it in the real world, it was a whole different kind of dread.

He eased the Volvo into the level one inspection lane and stopped as the inspector's open hand closed into a fist.

"You know the drill," the inspector said, sticking out his hand for the driver's CDL, driving logs and bill of lading. "Turn all your lights on in a minute and I'll have you pump the brake lights."

Jeeves heart was pounding, he began to sweat even in the much cooler fall ocean weather, and his speech was labored, "Got it," Jeeves said, trying to control his response to make it sound as conversational as possible. "Sorry if I'm sounding a little gruff. I'm just getting over the flu. What's the occasion? Officer," looking at his name tag, "Ward?"

"Standard procedure," the inspector said as he pulled on a pair of rubber gloves, adding "How else can I make my pay and our esteemed councilmen get the opportunity to spend other people's money. You're a lucky one. You landed in the level one lane. That means I get to check under your truck with my little creepy crawler, check the air brakes and everything else that crosses my mind. Let's take a little walk."

The officer took off heading for the back of the truck with Jeeves in tow. As they reached the rear doors, the inspector said, "Oh my, what have we here? A seal that is not fully snapped shut. What's in the truck, Mr. Ellington?" as he looked at the license and bill of lading in his hand?

Jeeves said, "Sorry about that," reached over and finished snapping the seal shut.

"Says here that you're full of, aaahhh--Top Ramen!" he said, looking at Jeeves.

"Yeah," Jeeves said. "Every college student's wet dream--a life time supply."

The inspector, chuckled, "Can't I tell you how much of that crap I've eaten over the years. And do you know that, believe it or not, I still like the stuff? How's that for a little crazy."

Jeeves breathing slowed down some and he began to relax. "Down right insane if you ask me," Jeeves said. "It's sort of like hauling a truck load of ping pong balls."

Officer Ward continued walking around the truck thumping tires the outside tires and using an iron rod for the inside tires before checking off boxes on his electronic pad that resembled a Kindle.

Just as quickly as Jeeves relaxed he found himself in panic mode again. The officer laid down on a mechanics crawler and zipped under his truck checking out, as he said, everything that crossed his mind. Then another "What have we here?"

"Now what?" Jeeves thought.

"Says right here on my little measuring device that your inside tire tread on the back tandem is at 3/32s. Better keep a close eye on that," he said. "I'd just love to collect a couple of hundred on that one. It'd just about make my afternoon. You've passed the inspection but keep an eye on that lousy tire on the trailer."

Jeeves exhaled slowly and mustered a grin mixed with a "flu" cough, "Thanks, I'll keep an eye on it."

By now, Palumbo was envisioning prison bars. Why and what is taking so long? Inside the trailer and van he couldn't hear anything but a word or two over the constant roar of cars from the freeway. Jeeves had just said something, one word that Palumbo had heard and thought sounded stressed. Inside the truck Palumbo knew whatever was going on outside, Jeeves prided himself on not getting flustered so "How bad was it?" crossed Palumbo's mind every several seconds.

He heard Jeeves getting back into the cab. "Finally," Palumbo said. Then nothing. No start up! No good-bye that he could hear. And then he heard Jeeves slamming the door after getting out of the truck again. What's going on? There was simply nothing he could do but sweat.

At last he heard Jeeves slam the door getting back into the truck. The engine started and he felt the trailer jerk slightly and begin to pull out, than jerk to a sudden stop. Again, Palumbo could hear Jeeves getting out of the truck answering,' yes sir,' to the officer. "Now what?" he thought. Within seconds he heard bangs on the doors on the back of the trailer. "We're screwed," was all he could think.

Then, as if nothing had happened, he heard the padlock on the door handles click, and actually heard Jeeves say, "Sorry about that officer." After a couple of minutes he was climbing back into the cab and heading out of the inspection lane.

Palumbo called Jeeve's cell within 10 seconds. Jeeves didn't pick up. "What the hell is going on," he thought. He tried again about two minutes later. This time Jeeves answered and said quickly, "I'll tell you when I pull into the building. It's just a few blocks. Don't want to get a ticket talking on a cell," and just as quickly hung up.

To Palumbo, it was an eternity. In reality it was about fifteen more minutes before Jeeves was backing into the building's enclosed interior loading dock.

Jeeves jumped out of the truck and clipped the seal, raising the door of the trailer and installing a couple unloading ramps for the van. Palumbo drove the vehicle out of the back. Within minutes, Jeeves and Palumbo took Nathan into a holding room.

Finally Palumbo asked "Jeeves what happened back there?"

"It's called 'induced cardiac arrest,'" Jeeves said, like he was getting back at Palumbo for his unrelenting smart-mouth jokes. "No big problem as it turned out, thankfully. It was a random truck inspection by the San Pedro Police."

"What about getting in and out of the truck," Palumbo pried.

"Had to get in and out to test the lights," Jeeves said.

"What about the last bit. I thought you were leaving, then you get out of the truck again and it sounded like you were fooling with the doors to come into the trailer. Well, in our haste we forgot to click the pad lock. Luckily the tab was still intact, so he let me just lock it.

"How was it back there?" Jeeves asked.

"OK, that's enough. I get it. We we're both rather stressed." Palumbo dropped his interrogation relieved it was over.

Palumbo texted Cabe: "Nothing ventured."

63

Doctors Shocked

Despite Phipps' apparent ambiguities about Fonda announcing Nathan's kidnapping and his name she shouldn't have known, Phipps said, "I think we need to get a preliminary report prepared on Nathan as soon as possible. Jerry, can you and Joan finish a prelim with what you have?"

He asked everyone to get their reports ready as soon as possible. Chandler said that he was satisfied and that his report should be fairly complete as it was. "I'd have to do a much more thorough exam to change anything from my comments in our original meeting," he said, "so I'll print that up and have it to you shortly. If you'd like me to do more I'd be happy to do that, Bernie, just let me know."

Dr. Gage was circumspect as usual. "Do my best," she said, "but you know….without several sessions, it's difficult to separate speculation from more established norms."

Phipps thanked everyone and asked for their reports the next morning.

He returned to the home where Levi and Ally were staying. As Phipps had predicted, the street and front yard where the Farnsworth home was would be swarming with cameras, and TV taping equipment, including news trailers with the reporters who gave their update reports. The reporters could smell a long-term story like sharks and blood. The fake abduction and shots-fired near Nathan's kidnapping had everybody reading between the lines of the San Marino Police Department report. Speculation was rampant and the twenty-four hour cable networks continued to survive on speculation and gossip.

When Phipps arrived he found Ally was nearly inconsolable and Levi not much better. They asked if there'd be ransom demands. Why would anyone want to kidnap Nathan? The three tried to sort out any reason why Nathan would be taken. It was obviously highly planned operations with major costs. It simply didn't compute.

Police detectives soon knocked on their door and Sergeant Brian Mendoza introduced himself along with two other detectives, Paul Jackson and Linda Shumway.

Mendoza spoke first, calling Levi and Ally by their first names. "Levi and Ally, there is no way for us to fully understand your pain over this, but we want you to know that we're going to do everything we can to find Nathan. The FBI is already involved and we're working closely with their people. We're here to find out how we can help and install a phone recording system," he said, "but before we start, do you have any questions?"

Nathan's parents had a million questions. "How do we know Nathan will be OK? Was he taken for ransom? How do we get him back safely? Mendoza was as kind as he could be in answering everything he could but, as he explained, "we can't know if this is a ransom situation, but I hope you'll allow us to work with you in getting Nathan back."

Levi and Ally looked at each other. Levi, as a state officer with the Idaho Fish and Game Department, was used to working with credentialed agents. He looked at Ally and said, "Any help you can provide."

"Have you received any phone calls?" the detective asked gently, "and may we start the phone set up?"

"No and sure," Ally said, and then added, "Please," pointing at a nearby table.

"We have a device that can record either of your cell phones and anywhere a call originates including most VPNs," the detective said. "All you have to do is plug your phones in like you're charging them. It's an automatic system and any call you get will be instantly traced and saved. Do you have a land line in your home?"

"This isn't our home," They both looked at Phipps, as did Mendoza.

"I believe there is a land line here, but it's a school line. No connection to Levi and Ally," Phipps said. "It may be convenient for them to use this line to go directly to the detective department at the station. You can call them without tying up their cell phones or your home line."

"We'll immediately transfer your home landline to the landline here" Mendoza said. "The equipment can handle that too. Please answer the phone on two rings or less. We don't want kidnappers thinking you're recording this. Our equipment will capture the signal even before it rings.

"Mr. and Mrs. Farnsworth, I've worked a number of kidnapping cases both with San Marino and other jurisdictions. What we try to do is anticipate any move a kidnapper might make and record any communications which he, she or they make. I want to be frank. Most kidnappings are by family members, moms or dads usually. That's obviously not the case with Nathan. It's currently classified as a stranger abduction and that puts it in a different category. All jurisdictions will be used to their fullest."

"Is there anything you can think of that would have made Nathan a target? I don't mean to be rude but do you have money disputes with anyone or family arguments? Is there anything that could be a motivation for kidnapping him?"

"No, none of that," Ally said with a pained grimace on her face, "do you think this could be sexual?"

"As much as I'd like to say no, it's impossible to know," he said, "But let me say that from the initial reports of the witnesses, there were at least two vehicles involved and at least three men. That, to me, suggests a well-orchestrated plan. The fact that those vehicles seemed to have disappeared suggests even more planning. This is pure speculation but I think it could be something else entirely.

"There's another possibility. Are you doing any research at New Tech, Levi that he could be considered a 'target?' It may be that Nathan could be used as ransom for that. It's a little out there but we have to stretch now and look at any possible option."

Levi told Mendoza, "Not unless they're interested in fish guts."

"I'd like to be reassuring, and promise to get your son back, but until we get more information we just don't know," he said. "I know I may sound a little harsh but please understand that the lack of communication from the kidnappers and the obvious organization it took to pull this off could mean many things. I know that this is an impossible situation to go through, but truth is more important than speculation about what could happen. As you know, the FBI has been notified and they're already cranking up. We just have to gather as many details as possible and figure out the nature of the abduction. The truth is, all we can do is wait."

Levi looked the officer in the eyes and asked, "How do we know if this is a ransom case?" Levi was already beginning to realize that ransom was not the motivating factor.

Mendoza explained that until a ransom demand is made, it's not considered that kind of abduction. He added, "Every phone call will be heart pounding as, I'm sure, you're already finding out. Officer Jackson will stay with you and monitor phone calls. With his equipment he will be able to filter out most crank calls and media calls. The media outlets have already been told not to call your home phone. If you have questions, Jackson's trained to give you the best information we have. We won't sugar coat things. As a parent myself, I'd want the info we give to you to be as accurate and complete as possible.

The television was on, but the sound was turned low. Ally, her eyes red from crying, was glued to the screen ready to turn up the sound the instant another update came on.

64

Potential Threats Turn Ugly

Jeeves, Palumbo and Wolfe took Nathan into the clinic area and placed him on a bed prepared for him, still covered with the blanket.

Wolfe told Nathan to remain calm. "You're not going to be hurt," he said. "Do you understand, Nathan?"

Nathan, still a little groggy from the ruffies, said "yes."

The three men finished the final preparations for the pending tests. They then wrapped Nathan's ankles and wrists in soft material and put tie straps around both before the original straps were removed. Wolfe asked them to leave the clinic area until the tests were completed.

"I'll handle everything from here and I want to be sure Nathan has the fewest possible targets to aim at."

Palumbo and Jeeves were only too happy to let the stress of the San Pedro trip fade away.

"Holler," if you need anything," Jeeves said, and they left.

Nathan had been quiet. Wolfe turned to him and said, "Nathan I'm going to draw some blood, do a physical examination and some brain scans, do you understand?"

"I have already had the blood tests and scans," Nathan said, failing to realize fully that he'd been kidnapped.

"Where were those tests," Wolfe asked.

"With Dr. Phipps at New Tech," Nathan said.

"When," Wolfe asked not expecting the answer. "And what were the tests for?"

"Last Saturday," Nathan said. "They wanted to understand why I'm different and how they can help me."

"Well Nathan, we're going to do some more testing," Wolfe said. "I would hope that you'll be cooperative. I recognize that you have certain abilities that I must avoid. The thin blanket that is covering you will prevent you from projecting emotions into me or anyone else. I'm the only one in this part of the clinic and I will have the shield between us at all times. The more cooperative you are, the quicker this will go, and the sooner we can take you home." Wolfe said.

"I understand," Nathan said.

For the next few hours, Wolfe conducted and cataloged blood tests, carefully storing samples and slides while always keeping the blanket between them and contemplating the statistics and potential this chance offered. Under the influence of the drug, Nathan was quite cooperative. It took a while for the doctor to do comparative scans with adjustments over time and make sure he had what he wanted.

Between the first tests Wolfe put Nathan into the scanner and monitored his brain under a few stimuli prompts. The preliminary results for Wolfe were as astounding to him as they had been for Phipps. But Wolfe, even though he was not a psychologist, had had extensive experience in his statistical abstraction studies evaluating variations and potentials. His findings were similar to both Phipps' and Gage's preliminary conclusions.

Periodic injections kept Nathan calm.

Wolfe texted Jeeves telling him the tests were done except for the last scan that he'd conduct tomorrow morning. It was 9:47p.m. Jeeves put together a sandwich and drink in the room and a bed prepared for Nathan.

Nathan went into the room exhausted at the events of the day totally drained of energy. He ate about half of his sandwich and after a couple of swigs of milk, collapsed on the bed and fell into a deep sleep.

A camera kept an eye on him as he slept.

65

Take 'Em Down

Drobick was nursing a cup of coffee and mentally still trying to accept his part in this kidnapping, when he got a second frantic call from Sanjy on a burner phone about what he described as a full frontal cyber assault on his systems.

"I know two things," Sanjy said. "This is not the police or FBI but it's as powerful a cyber attack as I've ever seen. With all the firewalls and safety blocks we have, I don't know if we'll be able to do anything but shut down."

Drobick immediately went to Cabe to tell him the story. "Max, this is spinning out of control I thought Sanjy and Billy had taken all the precautions possible. Add to that all of our own precautions and it's getting uncomfortably 'iffy.' The only good thing (or maybe it's a bad thing) is that the search to find out who's hacking the school proves in reverse that it was not the cops but then you can only assume it has to be unknown bad guys.

Cabe said. "We've got to move your guys for their safety! You do that because my mind is totally on Nathan."

"Would you please ask Wolfe to call me when he's finished with the tests," Cabe said, "and let me know how things went. By the way, how are you doing?"

Drobick called Palumbo. "Anything new, Dick?"

"You mean after my three heart attacks? Don't mind me; I'm still trying to get over the surprise inspection that Jeeves drove into. But everything is OK, at the moment. Wolfe is done with most of his testing and has one more scan tomorrow morning," Palumbo said.

"Got a freaky call from Sanjy and Billy and they're telling me that they had a big cyber attack on their system. In the middle of their call, someone blew in their door, destroyed most of their equipment and beat 'em up. Told 'em to stay out of San Marino, which they took to mean: "stay out of the school's computer and don't hack into any info on any kids there." They specifically didn't mention Nathan by name, but one of the people made it clear it was the boy they were watching. Drobick said the reference to San Marino made it obvious. It's apparent these are some people we'd call hazardous who want Nathan left alone.

"Remember the random code the guys ran across during their hack of the school? Sanjy and Billie think the attack came from whoever entered that random code. They say it wasn't the FBI or Police, but we don't know what it means for us. All I can say is to be super aware. The cyber and physical attacks have to be connected. What's still not clear is whether the attackers realized that we had hacked the school information. I don't think so at this point, but they might if they pursue it further.

"Just remember, there's an unknown faction out there that is vicious and aggressive. I guess our suspicions weren't merely paranoia after all. The videos showing the New Tech car and scooter suggest there must be a connection, and with New Tech's computing power, who knows what could happen. Just watch out." Drobick said. "Oh, and would you ask Dr. Wolfe to call Cabe as soon as he finishes?"

Because Drobick's concerns put Palumbo on edge, he went ahead and texted Wolfe to update Cabe, and also asked how Nathan was doing. Wolfe said "He's done for today--worn out and in bed. I doubt he will have a refreshing sleep under the circumstances. "I think he's doing well considering the tension but it will be a major relief to get him back home."

With Nathan in bed for the night, Wolfe called Cabe.

"What's your assessment?" Cabe asked.

"Look Max," Wolfe said, "This was an absolutely crazy thing to do, but that having been said, he is a one-of-a-kind kid. There really are no comparisons that I can find or have ever heard of. I suppose that it's possible, and perhaps even probable, that a child would eventually be born with these kind of gifts, but even so, the test results are astonishing. So far the blanket is blocking his 'waves' but I don't know if that will continue or if he'll be able to find a way around its dampening effects.

"I took the liberty of bringing an oscilloscope after you described the waves. The fact is you're right. The waves are apparently gathered from all parts of the brain, with the callosum lighting up both sides and kind of condensing or funneling the waves to the target.

"As of now, based on what you told me, he's directing the waves through his hands. I don't expect that to last because I think he'll outgrow the need to use his fingers. It's probably just a way for him to focus at this point, but he's changing all the time. The last scan tomorrow morning will give us a way to compare differences in him. They may be miniscule but measurable. That'll be our last test and then Palumbo's plan is to return him to the mall near where he was taken."

"It's going to take some time getting this into a plausible report. With the oscilloscope reading, I think it may be possible to recreate the waves and broadcast them as we discussed, but it might take a whole lot more testing and measurements with Nathan to get the right amplitude, frequency, rise time, and a host of other refinements. I could be working on this for years if I'm not in jail, that is."

"Palumbo said Nathan was doing fine, asleep, he told me," Cabe said. "What's your assessment?"

"He's fine but as you might expect, he was exhausted after the ordeal of the kidnapping, drugs and testing. "We'll have breakfast tomorrow, complete the test and get him back home. He won't remember anybody or anything about what happened or anywhere he was after the Rohypnol. But I don't think there is any question that, in the long run, there will be side effects. I just can't say what they might be. I'll get the data together and we can sit down and go over it. And I may have said this before, but he's a young boy and he's just beginning to learn what kind of power he has. Experiences like this could wind up helping him refine them under duress for his own protection."

"Amazing," Cabe said. "I may be crazy but I still feel like the possibilities of these waves doing what they do would be an historic broadcasting breakthrough. Call the next chance you get if you would." Cabe said thanks, and hung up.

Sixty seconds later Cabe got a call back from Wolfe. "Max, I didn't get a psychological evaluation from Nathan because that's not my field of expertise but my opinion from my short time working and talking to him is that he is exceptionally empathetic with a streak of vengefulness. But I also think there may be no limit to how far his power could go.

"As a child he might want some payback after this and he very well may seek to get it. And one final thing, he's capable of retaining powerful emotions of those he's taken from people. That means that every time he uses his power, the greater his arsenal grows, so to speak. That's it, call tomorrow," and Wolfe hung up.

Cabe went into his dome and sat down. It was completely silent which is exactly what he wanted. A lot of thinking and a truckload of regrets entered his mind. Compassion and empathy, revenge and payback, he pondered. Yes, tomorrow is another day, but what kind of day will it be?

66

Triple Kidnapping

Seperman and Fonda turned in their report to Phipps and said they were headed out to see what they could do. The pair left the school and met with the team they'd hired to track Nathan. Fonda had recommended the trackers and vouched for their professionalism and Seperman didn't question why someone like Fonda would know people with these skill sets. The pair's plans for examining Nathan included close monitoring. They utilized the facilities and vehicles of New Tech, assuming they'd blend in and not raise suspicion in the community. Cabe's people became aware of the surveillance but couldn't make a definitive connection that was useful.

"What can you tell us?" Seperman asked.

The two men and a woman team were paid mercenaries who had kept a surveillance watch on Nathan since before he and his family had come to San Marino. Seperman had seen the papers on Phipps' desk revealing Nathan and instantly determined what he wanted to do.

"We got a glimpse of the abduction, but using the drone we couldn't get too close with the trees, so we didn't see that much except that it was obvious that he was taken. Nothing we could do so we followed the van. They ripped off their signs and eventually drove it into a semi-trailer and closed the door," Royker, the leader of the three, said.

"Were you seen?" Fonda asked.

"Definitely not!" Royker said. "We scrapped ground surveillance and went to drones when we discovered somebody else was watching him."

"So where is Nathan?" Seperman said. "Is he OK?"

"That's a little harder to say," Royker said. "Witnesses said, as you probably heard, there was some problem. We could tell one man went down and had to be thrown into the van by another guy. The trees again, but as far as we can tell there wasn't a problem for Nathan but just the stress of this kind of a situation can take its toll. Oh, I think they threw a kind of metallic looking blanket over the kid but that's a guess since our visibility was sketchy."

"Anything else?" Seperman asked. "Was it difficult to track them?"

"Not at all. We pulled in the drone and followed in a car. The truck was maxed out at sixty-two so it was a breeze to keep up. I'm pretty sure they didn't want to attract any attention. The biggest problem was negotiating the traffic and keeping them in sight," Royker said. "Would have been better to have had a tracker on 'em!"

"They took a roundabout trip with no problems but I thought they were going to bite it big time when they took the off ramp and ran right into the waiting arms of a San Pedro Temporary Truck Inspection Station. They wound up in the level-one lane. I could tell the driver was sweatin' bullets," he said. "He must have been carrying a false CDL, bill of lading and seal."

"And the location?" Seperman said.

"It's a recently vacated clinic building in the older industrial part of the city," Royker said. The area is full of vacant commercial buildings. The building's got two enclosed loading docks and roll up rear doors for trucks. You can't see anything when the doors are down, so we don't know what's in there but it used to be a medical clinic or something, according to the old sign on the front. There's no telling what they're doing to him."

"I know exactly what they're doing," Fonda practically yelled, "They're testing the hell out of him just like we did Saturday. They won't hold him there long.

"We'll set up there and move as soon as the door goes up in the back. Seperman said, "I'll be in front with another guy."

"Get the team ready now, Fonda ordered. We've got to get him tomorrow morning! "No excuses, tasers only, super low key but we must get Nathan, period. I haven't come this far to lose him now. Jerry and one other guy will handle the front. We'll go in the back, you put their guys on the ground. No screw ups. Anybody who hurts Nathan had better have a casket ordered!," Fonda said. "Surprise is on our side, but time is critical because I don't believe they'll hold him long."

"We're heading down there now. Give me the address and we'll look around while you guys get there by midnight and we'll put a plan together, she said. "There's no telling if or when

they'll move him but I'm assuming the tests should be done by tomorrow. I'm counting on them taking off immediately. Get ready tonight, move tomorrow morning,"

Seperman told his team, "Text one of us that your "flat's fixed" when you've picked your locations for tomorrow. Oh, and come looking a little touristy."

Seperman and Fonda headed onto the Harbor Freeway. As they drove they wondered how Nathan was prevented from using his power. "They've got to have some way to divert or disperse the waves he sends out. I think that's what may have happened to the guy on the ground when they grabbed him. There's also the problem of controlling him during the testing," Seperman said. "An issue we'll have to face."

"Our blood testing at New Tech suggests some drugs will affect him, but I'm just not sure how long they'll last. They will need to have him pretty compliant for the tests," I'm hoping that if Nathan sees us, he'll remember us." Fonda said.

Monday afternoon rush hour traffic was horrendous as usual, but by 9 p.m. that evening they were pulling into San Pedro when it was 62 and evening traffic had thinned out. Seperman drove immediately by the building where Royker said the boy was being held. The Green Medical Clinic sign was faded and peeling. The back side of the building and parking lot was on the alley between vacant structures. The area was deserted and empty of vehicles and the truck bay doors were closed.

"It may not be easy to surprise anybody," Seperman said. "The front door looks chained shut with a plywood cover. The front window near the door could be a possibility, though. Chances are that it's tempered glass. Since it's near a sidewalk it could be a quick way in. I think we should plan on waiting until the back door starts to roll up and go in from there. I'm expecting that they'll come out that way. Get our guys ready. You cover the back and I'll be in the front with one guy. If anybody comes out the front we'll be ready. The sides are closed off all together against other buildings so it's front or back only."

Fonda felt her phone vibrate and read the" flat tire" text and she glanced at Seperman and told him, "the rest of the crew's here." She sent a message back to meet in the parking lot west of The Ports O' Call Pagoda entrance.

"Traffic's light. It's cool down on the water front so, be prepared, "she wrote informing Seperman. Restaurants were frequently open to fit the 24-hour-a-day traffic of the port.

After the crew texted their arrival, the seven filed into a convenient restaurant open all night and found a quiet table near the water and went over the operation ahead. Seperman sketched the building lot layout and marked point of attack. They had a house fruit drink specialty with sandwiches at about 11 pm left the area to set up.

Royker sent two of his people, a man and woman, to the neighborhood near the building and said, "Jog around the area keep an eye on the building and particularly back door. Any problems, let me know," he said.

The "joggers" took Seperman's car and Seperman and Fonda got into the crew's van. They drove around the area getting familiar with the back of the building and with the attack points at the roll up doors. Two other team members kept watch on the building front and back with no movement of any kind. Seperman got a text reading "quiet at the church." By 6 a.m., everybody was deployed. Seperman took the front with one team member and the pair of watchers in the front moved to the back along with Fonda and the rest of the crew.

67

False Freedom

Wolfe took Nathan from his room. Instead of covering Nathan he kept the blanket between himself and the boy. They had breakfast with Palumbo and Jeeves. Fortunately, Nathan didn't give them a problem. It was pretty obvious that Nathan had a fitful night's sleep and the continuing drug injections seemed to make things worse.

Wolfe told Nathan that he would remove his leg ties if he kept calm.

"We have only one more test Nathan and if you're quiet and don't try to run we can finish and get you back home. If you're not quiet I'll leave your ankle tie strap on. Wolfe said.

Nathan agreed to behave and Wolfe loosened the leg strap but left his hands tied. After breakfast at 7 a.m., Wolfe walked Nathan into the scanning room near the front window. The outside of the glass was about as grubby as old unwashed windows can get. Much to Nathan's surprise he could see out and saw Jerry Seperman leaning against a car across the street while another guy was looking under the hood of a car and talking on his phone. To anyone watching, it looked like the vehicle had broken down and the driver was calling for help.

Although shocked, Nathan was calm and passive but his mind was at full speed. He was relieved and knew he had to let Jerry know somehow that he was just inside. He wondered how and why Seperman was there and how he found him. Those questions would have to wait.

As Wolfe fired up the scanner array to check Nathan's brain, he realized something was very different from the last two sets. Nathan's waves seemed to be emanating more powerfully, although not directed at anything. The doctor assumed he had started thinking hard about something which was a worrisome change because the boy's neurons were firing off in a tightly controlled pattern.

During his first scan Nathan noticed that Wolfe couldn't see into the cylinder of the scanner. A piece of the metal trim on the scanner had come loose and was sticking out in the tube directly above his hands. It hadn't meant much when he first saw it, but he decided he had to get away because he wasn't too sure if these people meant to dump his body somewhere. Maybe they were just pretending to return him to have his cooperation for the tests. In any case he became more aware and began to focus his mind on escape. The drug had not fully worn off, but perhaps Nathan was just beginning to overcome its effect.

Brain scans usually are divided into three five minute segments. As scanners arch across a subject's head it gets very noisy. That was perfect for Nathan as the machine slid him deep into the cylinder's depths.

He quietly laid on the carriage while Wolfe started the scan and focused intensely on the readings. "Won't be long now," Wolfe shouted from the other room looking through the glass partition that separated the doctor from the machine and boy.

Nathan's chances for escape were growing slim. He knew he had to get his tie straps off as quickly and quietly as possible but the nylon straps were hard to cut with about anything other than a pair of dykes. His other problem was that he had to control his brain function to mask as much tension as possible. The instant he was in the cylinder, he tested the metal trim to see if he could cut his restraints. Even though the metal was pretty dull it had possibilities. He soon realized it would take some time, but vowed to get loose. He started rubbing the straps on the broken metal and then heard Wolfe tell him to lay still.

"If you're not still, Nathan, we'll have to do this again!" Wolfe said. "I don't want that and I know you don't either."

With every ounce of control that Nathan could muster he quieted his brain and strained to be still, while working at cutting his restraints. He could tell that the rubbing created some noise which was only masked by the noise of the scanner. He had three five-minute windows to get free and then what would he do? He didn't know but with his hands free, there would be a much better chance with his legs already free.

The three scans seemed like seconds to Nathan since he hadn't cut all the way through his wrist tie straps enough to break free, but he got a good start. He was dejected when the last segment was completed. He thought about a thousand ways to try to use his power on Wolfe, but between the machine disrupting his waves and the blanket that was shielding Wolfe, his chance at escape looked grim.

"Sorry Nathan, that last segment was no good, we'll have to do one more," Wolfe said.

Nathan almost shouted "great!" He was confident that he could cut through enough of the nylon to break the tie. I may not get all the way through, he thought, but it will be close enough to work the straps back and forth to break once I'm out of the cylinder. Then came another setback, but also one more chance. Before Wolfe pushed the eject button he heard Jeeves enter the observation room. Nathan knew he might overcome Wolfe but not both Wolfe and Jeeves with one of them using the blanket, especially if his straps didn't break immediately. His heart dropped off a cliff.

"How's the progress?" Jeeves asked.

"Just finished! We can be out of here in minutes," Wolfe said.

"We'll have the van ready to go in five. Palumbo has arranged for the cleaning crew to be here tomorrow morning at five. They'll re-clean everything, load all machines and drop them off at a charity a few blocks from here. Everything in the building will be on the way to Panama by tomorrow afternoon. No one will know we were here," Jeeves said.

"If Nathan's memory is as clean with the roofies as this place will be tomorrow, there'll be no record of anything." Jeeves said. "Can't tell you how glad I'll be to be out of here. I'll go get the van warmed up. It's loaded except for you and Nathan and I'll check one more time and pack up anything that's even half traceable. The cleaners will do the rest, so holler if you need help."

"Here," Wolfe said, "These are all the blood tests we've done including the results of all the brain scans. There'll be no evidence left of the machines either."

Jeeves left for the building's loading dock with the precious readings. Nathan realized his only chance to break free was to incapacitate Wolfe and break the front window. He could faintly hear Palumbo and Jeeves working in the back. Nathan started wiggling his wrists as hard as he could without causing notice. Wolfe pushed the button and Nathan began to feel his dream of escape slipping away again.

Wolfe walked into the scanner room with the wave blocker blanket in front of him. Nathan began to violently jerk his wrists back and forth.

"What the hell are you doing Nathan?" Wolfe screamed. "Jeeves, get in here!"

But Jeeves couldn't hear as he had just started rolling up the back door to drive the van out. In an instant four figures burst through the door and tasered Palumbo and Jeeves. They were quickly hooded and tied with duct tape. It was over in seconds. There would be no help for Wolfe.

Wolfe's time was up too. Just as Nathan saw the blanket in front of Wolfe, he broke his ties, pulled the blanket from Wolfe hands, and sent an unimaginable tsunami of emotions, pent up from his two days of captivity that drove Wolfe slumping to the ground in misery. Nathan grabbed a marble paper weight from a nearby desk and threw it with all his might like skipping rocks on an Idaho lake surface as hard as he could. Success, this time, meant breaking the window and providing access to the outside and freedom. He thought he'd rather be cut climbing through shards of glass to freedom than on a slab in the morgue.

The tempered glass explosion surprised Nathan and had him ducking for cover. This time he used the carbon blanket to protect himself from flying chunks of glass. He had no time to think about what had happened nor did he know what made the glass shatter into thousands of tiny roundish type pieces making a floor of glass that could cut. Since he was barefooted he threw the blanket over the sill and glass covering some ground, all the time yelling Jerry, Jerry!

Seperman heard the explosion and dove to the ground to avoid the glass and paper weight which narrowly missed his head. His cohort who also ducked, dropped his phone while the car hood dropped on the man's head, and he yelped in pain. When Seperman's partner regained a semblance of composure, he picked up his phone simultaneously hearing Nathan's yells. He ran toward Nathan reaching him at the curb, grabbed around the waist, and carried him over the rest of the glass.

"Come on, Nathan," Seperman yelled, "get in the car." Before leaving, Seperman made sure to hold onto the blanket and both jumped in the back seat.

Seperman's compatriot, now with a bloody bump on his head, slammed the hood down, and jumped behind the wheel. Seperman and Nathan, holding the strange material, jumped into the back seat yelling, "Go! Go! Go!" The car sped away, Nathan in the back seat with Seperman feeling much safer than in the hands of his former kidnappers."

The slightly metallic looking material Nathan had used to get across the glass was incredibly odd, Seperman thought. It must have been the material he was told about when his spies had witnessed the abduction. "What is this material Nathan?" he asked.

"It was something they used to separate me from them," Nathan said.

By that time the driver had texted "out" to Fonda as he saw Nathan coming through the window. It was the signal to break off the attack at the back of the building. Since everything in the back had occurred within the covered loading dock area, not even a curious passerby would have seen anything.

For the first time since 3 o'clock the previous afternoon, Nathan felt free and safe but then collapsed. He cried on Seperman's lap under the strain of his drug-induced ordeal and fell asleep under the protection of the man who'd shown friendliness and some fun at New Tech.

On receiving the "out" code word, Fonda broke off the attack at the back of the building. With Palumbo and Jeeves on the ground Fonda's crew walked out quietly. Seperman and Fonda were gone with Nathan in less than 30 seconds.

Thirty second after that, Palumbo and Jeeves began shaking off the effects of the taser and freed themselves of the tape restraints. When they did, they rushed into the clinic area and found Wolfe still suffering the effects of Nathan's power. Wolfe got the worst of the three by far. With the loss of Nathan in the attack, it was imperative that they finish clearing the building of potential evidence and get out.

Despite a lot of action in the back of the building, only the exploding window was visible to the outside world, and even that wasn't seen amid the vacant buildings.

Using a burner phone, Palumbo called the cleaning service and told them to start their sanitizing immediately and earlier He also explained that he'd left an extra thousand dollars on

the seat of the cab to have them arrange to have the broken window covered with plywood. He had told them to clean and deliver the equipment and return the truck to the renting agent on Mormon Island.

Yeah right, the cleaner thought to himself. I'll do the cleaning, deliver the equipment and truck and pocket the ten large and let the bums have the building. Palumbo had assumed that possibility and realized that if the homeless did move into the building through the broken window it would help mask any evidence. If the crew did get the plywood up that was okay too. He'd spread stage makeup and fake blood in various places to raise even more questions about what had happened in the building. They'd also left a crunched klieg light in the back of the building long enough for potential neighbors to see it and assume somebody was shooting a movie.

As bad as the abduction of Nathan was to Palumbo, they did have the full tests results. Even with that success he dreaded his call to Cabe.

68

News Circus Hits San Marino

The New Tech campus home protected the Farnsworths from the circus that was going on in front of their own house. Even though it was only hours into the kidnapping the media was in a frenzy as rumors swirled around the New Tech campus and the yet unverified guesses about Nathan's uniqueness. Rumors about a learning disability, physical malady, or some other problem made the kidnapping story far beyond that of a typical Amber Alert story the media couldn't ignore. The fact that there was no obvious physical evidence other than the disappearance seemed to feed the insatiable appetite of the public. In the news business such unanswered questions could fuel near riots.

Updates were broadcast on the half hour. Researchers found bits and pieces of the incidents about Nathan in elementary school in Idaho. Their tenuous nature fostered intriguing possibilities of Nathan's extraordinary differences or lack thereof, and stoked the media fires even further.

Even Blaine County, Idaho, Sheriff Jim Close was interviewed. A TV reporter from Coast to Coast-Live asked the sheriff about a log entry that had Nathan's name on it. Close's response was a terse, "No comment!"

Ally and Levi, were nearly frantic trying to think of ways to find Nathan. Their desire to help him prompted their move to California. Now they were under constant stress as they followed the news reports which included a couple of facts believed to have come from two young witnesses. They apparently told police they thought there had been three adult males and two cars. Police refused to verify either the number of men or vehicles. The scant facts were like throwing gas on the fire. The less the media were told, the more intense became their demands and speculation.

By Tuesday morning, the story went national, albeit only a fifteen or twenty second Reuter's rip-and-read with a New Tech graphic on one cable news show. Although Amber Alerts are not necessarily national news, with New Tech attached, along with a potentially special needs child, the story was starting to explode. By noon that day, it was a forty-five second on-location stand up.

"There is a new development in the Nathan Farnsworth kidnapping," reported Noelle Otley of Coast to Coast Live. "We have learned that police reports from Blaine County include a reference to a Nathan Farnsworth, but the reason for the reference was not available. Local residents here in Idaho have confirmed that a Nathan Farnsworth lived in Carey, Idaho, until about a year ago, before, they said, the family moved to California. Levi Farnsworth took a position with the Newton Institute of Technology in the Genetics Department. Local birth announcements in Twin Falls from eleven years ago also confirm that the boy was born in a Twin Falls, Idaho, hospital.

"Apparently, Carey residents were aware of the Sheriff's log reports about Nathan but have been exceptionally tight-lipped about the reasons. We will continue our updates as we learn more. Noelle Otley reporting from Carey, Idaho, for Coast to Coast Live."

News anchor Brent Kelly said, "Thanks Noelle. "The parents of Nathan have not been available for comment and at this time, their whereabouts are unknown, raising more speculation about the story behind this kidnapping. An update on the 'Abduction of Nathan Farnsworth' is scheduled on the hour."

After watching the news report, Phipps told the Farnsworths that he was going to send an assistant to retrieve more of their clothes and personal items because there was no way to know how long this would last. He sent two people to pick up the things on their list they needed from their home. Reporters engulfed the two assistants as they pulled into the driveway. Reporters yelled at them demanding answers for questions they couldn't know.

A driver in one of the press vehicles followed the pair as they left the Farnsworth residence and stayed right on their bumper. Within a block a San Marino Police vehicle pulled the press car over.

It was no surprise that it was Detective Paul Jackson, who had been helping protect Nathan's parents during the frenzy of the abduction coverage. It wasn't a surprise that it was Jackson, who radioed for a code ten-oh-one, and punched in the license number into his computer. It was obviously a Los Angeles Times vehicle since the Times logo was on the door. The reporters were not pleased to lose their stop. Jackson asked for license and registration.

"Any reason you were tailgating that vehicle?" he asked, with an amused smirk.

The reporters accused the officer of interfering with their responsibilities. Jackson went back to his unmarked car detective car and ran a wants and warrants with no negative returns. After a few seconds the car the press was following were following disappeared down the road, Officer Jackson, said, "I'll let you off with just a warning this time. Have a nice day," he said with a smirk.

The clothing and other items needed for a longer stay at their temporary home arrived. The return of the two helpers also made the prospect that this would be an indefinite and excruciatingly painful experience sunk in even more deeply.

69

Schultz In Trouble Again

Tuesday morning was agony for Cabe. He cleared his calendar of anything that was not critical. He had anticipated the test would go well and Nathan would be returned to somewhere near his home by now with no ill effects. He'd then be let off with his memory of the kidnapping and kidnappers totally forgotten.

Halfway between this agony and torment of not knowing what was happening, he got a frantic intercom warning from Vickie. "Trouble on the way," is all she said.

Two seconds after that, Harry Schultz stormed past Vickie's desk and into Cabe's office.

Without waiting to be acknowledged, he started in on Cabe. "That SOB Jamal put my show on holidays at midnight; I want my time slot back! I have a contract that goes through November. And I demand that you give me the lead cover on the "Abduction of Nathan Farnsworth."

Cabe remained silent.

"Did you hear me? I demand that you tell that a-hole Davenport to give me my effing slot back." This is pure b.s.!" Schultz screamed.

Cabe had looked up when Schultz stormed in but purposefully looked back down at his desk and kept writing and even failed to acknowledge that Shultz had entered the room. "What do they say?" Cabe thought, "The opposite of love isn't hate, it's indifference," and he was antagonistically indifferent to Schultz. That made Schultz even more belligerent and obnoxious.

Of all the things Cabe didn't need now was a profanity-laced rant from someone he considered an intellectual termite. After a time, Cabe leaned back in his chair, looked at Schultz but still didn't react to him. He let Schultz prove the truth of the complete vacuum that inhabited the man's skull. Schultz continued to oblige with another string of expletives while Cabe continued his silence, staring right at him.

"Well? Are you just going to sit there?" Schultz continued.

"You're right, Mr. Schultz," Cabe said softly. "I'm going to tell you what I think about you. You haven't got the intelligence of a Blob fish. On second thought, that's a slur against any self-respecting Blob fish. Although you could be his twin.

"You just don't understand do you, Mr. Schultz? If you'd quit drinking from the septic tank maybe your language skills could increase the number of terms you actually understand. You can't grow beyond that miniscule group of trash words you tend to think are explanatory but which really are an illustration of your profoundly lazy thinking and vocabulary".

"You…….." Schultz started again but froze when he looked into Cabe's eyes.

"Just a moment, Mr. Schultz," Cabe said, and speed dialed Jamal Davenport. "Hello, Jamal. Mr. Schultz has barged into my office unannounced and demanded that he be given some things. Would you please have all Mr. Schultz's belongings collected, put in a box and left at the front registration counter? Also, please inform security that all of Mr. Schultz's building passes have been revoked and that if he enters the building that he get no farther than the location of his box of stuff at the counter. Oh, and one other thing, make sure he is escorted out by armed security; I think a four guard surround will be sufficient! Thanks! Get with you on this Shultz issue ASAP."

"Oh, and Jamal, one last thing, please retain Joseph and Thornton and sue Mr. Schultz for breach of contract, spare no expense!" Cabe returned his phone to its cradle.

"Mr. Schultz, you have given your last profane diatribe in my office and on my air. You have exactly five minutes to exit this building and…"

Vickie interrupted Cabe on the intercom. "Palumbo is on the line sir."

"Thanks," Cabe said. "Please have security get up here to escort Mr. Bad Breath out of my office. Five minutes," he said, looking directly at Schultz.

With Schultz hightailing it out of his office, Cabe picked up the phone. "Go!" he said.

70

Taken—Again

"Not good," Palumbo said.

For the next fifteen minutes, Palumbo described the terrible events of the morning, ending with the loss of Nathan, and adding that Wolfe, Jeeves and himself were unhurt.

"They were professional," Palumbo said. "Very professional! I'd say maybe standard black helicopter stuff. What I can't figure out is how they found us so quickly? They had to know that we were in that building within minutes of our arrival for them to set up a takedown like this.

"Is Nathan back?" Palumbo asked. "Back home I mean?"

"No," Cabe said. "Not a word. Not even a hint. All of the reports from TV updates indicate that there is nothing new at the moment. Even law enforcement isn't even hinting anything new. How long has it been since Nathan's been gone."

Palumbo said, "I'd say fifteen to twenty minutes since we got ourselves untied, got Wolfe and got out in the van. It could be as many as thirty minutes. I can't believe they wouldn't have reported him found already. It would have been impossible for this not to leak."

Palumbo and Cabe came to the same conclusion at almost the exact time. It was unfortunately obvious. There was another set of kidnappers who apparently had been preparing to take Nathan too. The fact that Cabe had moved, maybe just days before the second kidnappers were prepared to act, caught them off guard. That could be considered good or bad depending on how you looked at it. But the "professional" part, as Palumbo described those who had broken into the clinic building to take Nathan, was fraught with questions they didn't even want to ask.

"Tell me more about what happened to Wolfe and the blanket," Cabe said. "It's traceable. So if Fonda's got the blanket it's more evidence against her. If someone else has it, it could be linked back to us."

"Jeeves went to tell Wolfe we were ready to go. Wolfe said he would be finished in five. Then Nathan got free somehow and apparently threw something through the window, and hit Wolfe with a jolt and he was put out of action. Wolfe didn't see anything but the floor. It was pretty obvious that Nathan got out. At the same time they hit us from the back and I can only surmise that they had people in the front too. I'm certain that Nathan would have jumped into anything available to get away from us. But I'm not sure about what happened then."

"What about the blanket?" Cabe asked.

"No clue," Palumbo said. "It wasn't in the room or on the sidewalk. He might have used it to put down on the glass because he didn't have shoes on. Or, maybe a vagrant could have taken it. I just don't know. You've got to assume that he or, more than likely, they, have it and Nathan may remember what it does."

"That's very discouraging. I'm sure it won't take them long to figure it out and then he'll have almost no protection for himself," Cabe said. "I just spent my whole life's ration of righteous indignation on Harry Schultz a few minutes ago and he's looking a lot smarter than me right now. At least, I don't have to deal with him anymore."

Cabe and Palumbo went over the situation with the clinic building and any connection that could lead back to them, but Palumbo explained he didn't think there were any. "The cleaning company guy who drove the equipment over to the charity probably took the cash for the window and didn't fix it. I'm pretty sure they're going to deny anything that might connect them to the building for self protection. They're certainly not going to want to be tied to taking cash money or be connected with a possible kidnapping. They'll super glue their lips shut or say we just cleaned the building took cash and never met their clients.

They'd cleaned up the building and wouldn't want any connection to any kidnapping. The black helicopter guys certainly weren't going to say anything either, whoever they were.

"We've got to clean up our own mess and more importantly get Nathan back safe and sound. Nothing else matters at this point including my empire--least of all my empire," Cabe said thinking, "why did it all seem so simple at first?"

71

Which Kidnappers

As Nathan lay sleeping, Seperman began looking at the blanket he had taken from the sidewalk. It was nothing like anything he'd ever seen but he could tell it was infused carbon fibers. The material was incredibly strong and amazingly light. He guessed it was similar to carbon materials used in stealth bombers.

With a little assumptive reasoning, it became apparent to him that it was some kind of blocking device. Seperman was more than a little excited. This material might help him test Nathan much more extensively. Ever since he had become aware of Nathan, quite by accident a few years before, he was mesmerized by him. He'd inadvertently seen some papers and calculations on Phipps desk about Nathan.

The scholar in him became obsessed thinking about the puzzle that was this boy. He began dreaming of a Nobel Prize with break through research on the nature of projecting or really taking emotions out of one person and putting them into another. Deeply studying the convergence of genetics and circumstances that created Nathan and his power was frosting on the New Tech scholar's dream research prize. It was just too much for him not to think about, to not be involved in. He began collecting data, but his dream totally distorting his moral compass.

Seperman established a group to observe Nathan when he discovered that Levi was coming to New Tech. It became, essentially, a constant surveillance from the time Nathan arrived. Seperman also mentioned his fascination to his lab assistant, Joan. She had immediately become absorbed and on board. But over time, as they worked together and planned their research into Nathan, Seperman came to realize she had known about Nathan much sooner than when he first told her about the boy's existence.

Despite his reticence, Seperman aggressively ignored the question of Fonda's prior knowledge. His "Nathan obsession" overruled his natural discretion. The potential money didn't hurt either. Fonda said she was going to school with the help of an international syndicate interested in creating genetic products. She told him she was sure they'd fund practically a carte blanche check book with no questions as long as she was involved. The prospect for Seperman of nearly unlimited funding was irresistible since he wouldn't have to continue begging for government grants. For what he had in mind, there was no category in any grant book that he knew of.

None of that mattered now. His phone vibrated. It was Fonda. "How's Nathan?" she asked.

"Sound asleep," he said. "Doesn't seem to be too worse for wear although that's an early assessment. But, what I have here is a whole different kettle of cod."

"What's that," she asked.

"Remember the waves that Phipps talked about in his brain scans?" Seperman said.

"OK," she said, "what else?"

"I think the blanket is a kind of shielding against the waves emanating from Nathan. It could render his ability to direct emotional projections null. I think it's what they used to control him. There could also have been some drugs involved because I see several needle marks. Ruffies, I'd bet. What worries me are potential emotional injuries not just physical," he said.

Fonda suggested to Seperman that "Since this all happened so abruptly and with no anticipation, why don't we meet at the end of Pier F Avenue. GPS it and you'll see how to get there. It's only about ten miles and we'll have total privacy. There's a warehouse at the end of the dock, and I'm told there's a ship moored there. We can decide our next steps. You also might want to check in with Phipps and tamp down his questions."

"Got it." Seperman said. "Is there a bed there?" Seperman asked."

"I'm sure there is. They've got temp sleeping quarters for crewmen and officers in the building and secure rooms for special cargo."

"I think this boy is going to have some more rest but the longer we don't return him the more restless he'll become. The pier looks to be about fifteen minutes away. Be there shortly," Seperman said and hung up.

As he looked down at Nathan, he couldn't help but feel protective. Even if he did have plans to do just about the same thing as the original kidnappers. It didn't change his growing connection to the boy, especially after Nathan had run to him so trustingly. Seperman's own boyhood was not all that different from Nathan's. Nathan was different and so was Seperman. A studious, completely science focused kid with the IQ to get him into New Tech at eighteen, and one who didn't have too much in common with his peers. He faced the same typical brainiac jokes and alienation from the so-called popular kids in high school an experience which ended early, he recalled thankfully. College was a whole new world for Seperman with what seemed like an unlimited vista of opportunities.

Seperman had always been the smartest kid at every school he'd attended but at New Tech it was a different story, he was truly among intellectual peers and the academic competition couldn't have been more cutthroat than for any pro football game. For academics, it's publish or perish which becomes more important the higher one climbed the academic ladder. Nobel

Prize opportunities weren't easy to find, but Nathan, Seperman believed, would change that for him. In this case Seperman's intellect didn't fail him but his judgment did. He saw the Nobel stage, but was so blinded by it that he didn't, or perhaps refused to see that faulty means could have greater destructive consequences than the rewards of lofty dreams.

What he didn't face was innate fear that some people might develop toward Nathan. Seperman's own experiences with bullies was exactly what Nathan capabilities would have fought against. Seperman may have been harassed for his uniqueness, but he was not feared. Fear of someone's power alone was a factor that would be hard to evaluate.

Seperman arrived at the warehouse and took Nathan in. He met Fonda and asked, "Where's his bed? I'll take him there and be there when he wakes up. He asked Fonda to get things set up for a more permanent situation for the boy. Fonda left to continue directing her preparations but what Fonda prepared was not at all what Seperman expected.

Seperman watched Nathan sleep for about an hour and a half. Nathan began to wake up, and then the boy realized that he was in a room he didn't recognize and bolted to his feet.

"Where am I?" he asked. What's going on?"

"We rescued you from your kidnappers and brought you here for safety," Seperman said. "Joan is getting us some lunch. We'll get you home soon."

"Kidnappers? I wasn't kidnapped," Nathan said. "I was walking home from school. That was the last thing I remember. I want to go home. Why are you keeping me here?"

Seperman realized that Nathan had no memory of his ordeal. Roofies! The needle marks! Seperman was suddenly stunned to realize that he was now the kidnapper Nathan would remember. The previous kidnappers were thorough and had planned well. Scrambling to come up with a plan Seperman determined that he would anonymously tip off police to the location of the building where Nathan was originally kept.

While Seperman's distorted desire for academic stardom continued to cloud his reasoning, it was also dawning on him that he was in way over his head. This was deception on a monumental scale. Nathan was now under threat, Fonda was starting to exert some independence that he didn't like, and he was now seeing quickly that the only way to salvage his life was to take Nathan home safely. But it also appeared that that couldn't happen and a deep resentment and anger was consuming him along with the bitter realization that Fonda had used him from her first day at New Tech.

72

Fonda Takes Over

Fonda now set about putting the final touches on a plan that she'd started since she genetically postulated and then discovered Nathan's birth. That plan would take Nathan out of the US to a temporary location before he'd be moved again. Of course, she had a host of possibilities for where the first landing location should be and she had been preparing a final destination for him for a long while. Because of Nathan's unexpected kidnapping she had been forced to put her plan into action ahead of schedule but since she'd been preparing for years it only took a couple of adjustments to be ready to go.

She stationed a specially outfitted ship at a pier beside a warehouse in Long Beach. The warehouse was owned and operated by the same syndicate she had told Seperman was financing her post doctoral work. Although Seperman wasn't there to watch Fonda bark orders, it was obvious that she was much more than a student financed by a worldwide entity. She was, in fact as Seperman would soon learn, the powerful founder of that syndicate, Universal Macro Genetics.

Fonda ordered the ship's crew to prepare for Nathan's arrival. Her next call was to her company research and development department to discuss the blanket used to control the boy, but an in-depth understanding of its makeup would have to wait. She also forwarded as much information from the New Tech testing meetings as she could.

A university setting with its protective protocols was way too limiting for her. There would be no limitations when she had Nathan in her own testing laboratory. The possibilities she anticipated, were endless.

The ship, which she stood watching while crewmen began preparing for an extended stay for herself and Nathan, was not what it seemed. It appeared to be an old vessel with peeling paint and lots of rust. Beneath that rusty façade however was an ultra powerful modern vessel that could outpace the fastest American Naval ships. It included Radar jamming capabilities and a surprise that would eventually astound Cabe and his team.

The engine room was equipped with a Northrop Grumman-type high temperature superconductor propulsion motor that was more than double previous naval power tests ratings and had three million Newton-meters of torque and producing 50,000 horsepower. The engine was also less than half the weight of conventional motors but could power the ship at top speed of 66 knots on a calm sea with a hull that was equally high tech.

The not yet visible inner hull was essentially a type of large catamaran but high enough off the water to include a whole second hull. Syndicate engineers built a retractable false bow and stern so when moving into port the ship appeared to be a rusted old cargo ship. Fonda had had her scientists hack into computers and steal the construction designs, including the ultra sophisticated modified catamaran. Even the U.S. government had not yet chosen to spend the money on a quarter-sized proto type design.

A super sophisticated ship wasn't the only weapon in Fonda's empire. She controlled business and semi-criminal interests all over the world and was worth many billions. It put her well into the multi-billionaires club along with Cabe.

She anticipated that it would have normally taken three to five days to resupply the ship and prepare it for its mission timeline but under the circumstances, the three to five days, had to be cut to one day and no longer.

She'd told her research department about the blanket and what Seperman had said about it. Her scientists had called back excited to confirm that it was a kind of projected wave disrupter. "How did they determine that the waves were similar to sound waves and a disrupter would work," she asked. "It could not have been just dumb luck!" "No!" she had been told.

Someone figured out projected wave powers were related to sound waves, although who and how was undetermined. Sound waves are invisible and without an oscillator of some kind.

When Nathan had used his powers they would have been invisible, so it was a counter-intuitive mystery that sound waves would not only be invisible to the eye and at the same time soundless.

While Fonda continued her preparations, Seperman continued to placate Nathan, but it was getting harder. "We don't know who kidnapped you and until we do, we have to be careful."

"How did you find out I'd been kidnapped," Nathan asked. "Why don't you call the police or at least let me call my mom and dad? This isn't sounding right, Jerry.

"Let me see what we've learned," Seperman said. "Let's go see if Joan has learned anything."

The pair walked out into the warehouse and wandered around as Seperman called to Fonda. For a moment she was stunned to see Nathan out of the room walking free. She stifled her surprise so as not to startle Nathan but flashed a disapproving look at Seperman.

As long as Nathan didn't feel threatened, the chances of him using his powers was not a problem. But for Fonda, it demonstrated that she needed to see what protection the blanket could actually provide. She assumed there might come a time that it would be needed, perhaps much sooner than expected. It was becoming apparent to her that Seperman seemed to be rethinking his commitment to studying Nathan. His connection to the boy, both his natural protective instincts and his internal connection, was growing through their shared experiences as youngsters. She recognized that it was a major problem that would have to be addressed soon.

Fonda needed more time and wanted to encourage Nathan's acquiescence so she suggested that he could go out onto the dock and look at the ship. She then immediately contacted her research department. A way to control Nathan was getting more critical and time sensitive every minute. Since she had the blanket she could use that, but her problem required a long term solution, a solution that was pure Fonda and wasn't at all nice.

Sheldon Kris, her chief of research, answered the phone. "How goes the battle?" he asked Fonda.

"Things are getting unpredictable," she said. "I need to have some confirmation on using the blanket. The only thing I can do now is assume that it worked sufficiently for the other group."

"Nothing is for sure," Kris said, "But I'd say it's at least a fifty-fifty chance. In addition to that, as with any preliminary report, there are issues that we may not have measured properly and won't be able to without having it in hand. The data from the New Tech tests suggests that it should work but the same tests also suggest that there is a good chance that Nathan may eventually be able to overcome it. For now I'd say it's our only option.

"When we get him on board the ship and do some direct testing, then we'll know," Kris said.

73

The Big Switch

The group met in the dome. Cabe allowed himself 30-seconds of lamenting before he began barking orders. "Drobick, get a secure line into the Police department and the New Tech genetics department and see what comes in."

"Also, since the only clue we have of this whole venture seems to be coming from someone at New Tech and their surveillance of Nathan, I want to know about every call to every person in Levi Farnsworth's department. I'd bet a gold coin the size of Schultz's mouth that there's someone there who has the answers or knows somebody who does, and maybe we can find that connection. Check emails, texts, phone calls, social media and anything else you can tap into for everybody that has anything to do with Nathan or Levi.

Cabe asked Jeeves what he thought about talking with Rocky Creek Principal Reese.

"Could be useful," Jeeves said.

"Let's see if Reese can tell you anything, check Nathan's friends, that sort of thing," Cabe said. "I'm hoping our involvement in the sister school project will encourage him to help us. I think he'll understand that we feel a connection to Nathan because he's been part of that project, besides being a boy from San Marino."

"I'm on my way boss," Jeeves said, sensing Cabe's escalating commitment. It's a way to redeem himself, Jeeves concluded. After all, it was a less than stellar idea to take Nathan in the first place.

"Palumbo, we need to put together the best possible team of eight operatives of former seals, rangers, or delta force or whatever and have them ready to go within minutes. Spare no expense, only the best and with training that they know how to protect Nathan. You said you thought there were four on the back door that hit you. I think we have to assume that there were at least two or three more on the front door. I want one guy with a dart gun or taser to take down the guys who did this."

"And Mike, once we've pinned down the situation, I want to set up a full-time top flight group to do some serious hacking since I'm assuming this might be a long term search. Just to emphasize it, I want to know anything and everything especially about the connection to New Tech.

"I think we should go over that video of the original test. As I recall there were some New Tech vehicles around. That's the only lead we have as far as I can see and it keeps eating at me. There were two references to New Tech…and I don't believe in coincidences," Cabe said.

After the conversation, Jeeves left immediately for San Marino. He called Reese and explained the situation. Reese said he thought that Nathan had some buddies and would confirm who the boys were by the time Jeeves got there.

"How's everybody holding up?" Jeeves asked. "I've got a confession to make Fred. The guy I introduced as my assistant was actually my boss and even though he didn't get too involved, seeing the kids--now especially Nathan--he was hit hard by this, and he's taking it personally. He wants to help in any way possible. We're already working to find Nathan. He made a contribution to the Police Department to help in the investigation but wants to do more. Anything you might tell us would be appreciated."

"Needless to say it's the talk of the whole school. You're, out about, what, 25 minutes?" Reese asked?

"Yeah, maybe 20 minutes," Jeeves said.

"I think I can locate Nathan's friends and have them here by the time you get here. We'll see what they can tell you. I'll sit in to represent the school. His two best friends are good kids. With their concern for Nathan, I'm sure they'll help." Reese said.

"Be there soon," Jeeves said.

A lead foot put Jeeves at Rock Creek even sooner than he expected. He went into Reese's office. They talked a bit and Reese said that he'd found two kids who were Nathan's close friends. He called them into his office and introduced Buddy and Miguel to Jeeves.

"Buddy and Miguel, thanks for talking to me. You know the situation. I'm trying to find out anything that may tell us what happened to Nathan. I know you may not think you know anything but any piece of information could be helpful. Can you tell me what you were doing on the day and time of the kidnapping?" Jeeves said.

Buddy said he was at band practice and Miguel said he was doing some work for the Sister School project. They also said they'd talked to the police, along with lots of other kids.

"Have you and Nathan done anything out of the ordinary lately?" Jeeves continued.

"Tell Mr. Bills about your trip to New Tech," Reese suggested, encouraging them to relax and start talking more easily.

Miguel volunteered, "We saw some cool blood samples of tigers and stuff on Saturday and then got our hair electrified. That was real cool. And we even have pictures of our hair all sticking out."

Buddy pulled out his picture of his hair standing on end. "Here's another one with us using the slides and electron microscope," Buddy said.

"Who's the guy standing by you?" Jeeves asked.

"That's Dr. Seperman. He was helping us with the slides and some other stuff," Buddy said. "He was really fun."

"Was anybody else there?" Jeeves said.

"Dr. Phipps, and Dr. Seperman's assistant Ms. Fonda," Miguel said. "Our moms were there too."

"Do you remember their first names?" Jeeves asked.

"Jerry was Dr. Seperman's first name," Buddy said. "I remember that, but I don't know the others."

Miguel didn't remember names either. "Seemed like everybody around there was 'Dr.' somebody," he said.

"Have you seen anybody around the school or walking home that may have followed you," Reese asked.

"No," the two boys responded, and then they asked if Nathan was going to be found safe.

"We're going to do our best," Jeeves said. "The police and FBI have committed massive resources, and we're trying to do everything we can to help them find Nathan. And even if it doesn't seem like it right now, you're helping too. If you think of anything else that you want to tell us, please talk to Mr. Reese and he can call me."

The boys left and Jeeves thanked the principal for the help.

"It doesn't seem like they knew too much," Reese said.

"I'd agree," Jeeves said, "but you never know. In cases like this the smallest detail can help get things started."

"Speaking of names," Reese said. "Is Jeeves your real name?"

Jeeves smiled and told him no. "It started as a joke with my boss and me. We were boyhood friends and when I came to work for him to manage his residential properties he called me Jeeves once and it just stuck. You know how that goes. Really appreciate your help and if there is anything we can do to help here at the school let us know."

"By the way, I think your Sister school project has been great. Lots of other kids in the school are starting to help. It's been a good project because it gets the kids to think about helping others. I'll call if we get anything else, but remember rumors fly at schools," Reese said.

"Thanks again," Jeeves said.

Jeeves called Cabe and gave him the report. "Doesn't seem like much," he said, "but there is the New Tech connection again. They even ran their own tests on him so somebody there is intensely interested."

He gave the pertinent names to Cabe and said he was returning to the house to get some of his normal work done early to free himself up for whatever came up later.

Cabe didn't recognize Phipps or Seperman's name but Fonda might be a different matter if it was the Fonda he knew of. Other than a couple of movie people, Cabe knew of one prominent name in genetics—Joan Fonda. She was involved in genetics research in Switzerland, although Fonda was a relatively common name in nearby Italy, the Fonda name in Switzerland was a big name with big money attached to it. If there was a connection, she would have the where-with-all to mount a significant attack. From what he'd heard, the group had some significant big criminal involvements. Probably a long shot he thought, but coincidences are like root canals, you don't really want to think about them, but when they are real, they get your attention.

74
Getting Violent

Billie was standing at the kitchen counter starting a sandwich, he was also talking to Drobick on his phone about getting a group of hackers together as Cabe had ordered to fight previous hacks. As they talked, Billie's smartphone, went off with a warning ring Billie hoped he'd never hear. In a matter of ten or fifteen seconds there were five intruder alerts booming from every device in the room. It was another full-frontal cyber attack on every firewall and obstruction he'd set up on every device he owned. The warning ring tone was a blasting Jaws theme: Dah-duh, Dah-duh, Dah-duh, Dah-duh, the devices blared over and over again.

Sanjy, who was at work, heard the attack warning on his phone too. He texted Billy immediately and told him he was on his way home. He was there in less than ten minutes, only to see Billy frantically trying to squelch the attack. "Any luck?" he shouted as he rushed through the door.

"Some," Billy answered. "I don't think they got much more than a chunk, but the scope of it was amazing." Sanjy sat down and began working on saving their system's data from their many years of work.

While Billy worked on stopping the attack, Sanjy began double checking the pair's backup system and trying to determine if the hackers were attacking their off-site server as well. Most of the material they had collected for Cabe was saved but some of their proprietary programs were mangled. It would take a major effort to reestablish them in a workable form.

While the two were engaged in an all-consuming effort, the front door exploded into the room in splinters, driven by a directional blast. Right behind that was a team of four men who proceeded to demolish the computers, servers and everything else in sight, including pounding on the two men who were trying to prevent the demolition of every system in the room. What the cyber attack didn't destroy, namely the hardware, the attackers' acid and hammers did.

Drobick heard the entire attack on the open phone on the counter. Apparently the phone was spotted because right in the middle of this mayhem Drobick heard an unidentified man speak into the phone. The noise subsided except some groans from Sanjy and Billie.

Drobick heard the phone being picked up and a man say, "Who is this?"

Drobick said quietly but with authority, "You first!"

The man replied,"stay out of San Marino." and hung up. He didn't even know if there was any connection to the issue at hand but apparently, that didn't matter.

Billie and Sanjy were left with lots of bumps and bruises, but alive and furious. Even with backups, it wouldn't be easy to recreate their systems. An even bigger question was, what do they do now?

75

War Room Goes Operational

"Mike, get your computer guys on these names at New Tech," Cabe said. "It may be nothing but who knows? See if they can find out full names and connections, if any. Oh, and see if they can find out about any phone calls that might give us some leads. Please call me back immediately on the Fonda employee and everything they can find out about her."

Drobick reminded Cabe about the attack on his computer guys and how they were beat up. "It's bad stuff and there's not much they can do immediately, but this is a major threat to us."

Cabe sighed. "I've started something that I must finish. We need to set up a war room. Get Sanjy and Billy a new place to live for their protection and put security there. Check with Jamal and see if he can arrange some high security space here in the tower that we can use, even if it's another floor. Get them every system and component they need. They have to be moved to safety. See if they want to do that, if they do, get that started. If not, find somebody else because I'm seeing a long hard battle and we need to be prepared with totally committed people."

"I don't think committed is a strong enough word for their attitude right now," Drobick said. "They are steaming. Not only will they come on board fulltime, they're going to want some revenge. They'll want to go after these people in ways I don't want to think about."

Cabe threw his head back, "They're not the only ones."

Drobick realized that the size of what was about to happen was going to expand in a big way. He could see Cabe was setting up 24/7 for the long term. "If we set up a war room, Max, we have to bring in a lot of other people. They have to know what our goal is."

Cabe took his head out of his hands looked directly at Drobick and said, "Our goal is to get Nathan back safely. For now, the fact that he's a San Marino kid and we were working with him on a project is going to have to be enough. If anyone wants more information, tell them I feel like I have an obligation, and that it's a personal responsibility because I've met the boy and consider him a friend. I have worldwide assets to apply to this. If they don't like it, tough. But I believe that when they hear it's a worldwide hunt for Nathan with our resources to back it up, they'll want to be a part of it. It's just got to be quiet because we don't want to interfere with the police investigation and maybe we'll be able to help."

Drobick called Jamal and arranged a meeting to explain what Cabe wanted to do. Drobick found the response to Cabe's concern for Nathan intriguing. To most people, the ultra-rich have a kind of aura about them, because they have means to get pretty much anything they want that is usually purchased in some way. But in this case to return Nathan safely was a goal that even billionaire money couldn't guarantee. All it could do was provide a means to that end.

It didn't take much for others to simply accept Cabe's premise that his connection to Nathan had become a personal project. In fact, that personal attachment became their attachment too. They wanted to help because they all knew about Nathan's abduction. No one could have known how long that might take.

CEO Jamal was recognized as the resident organizational wizard at Cable New Media and Drobick appreciated his talent. He set up a high-tech communications office and laid it out so the people in the room could easily access worldwide input, and each other's data. Jamal found the best techs to wire it for every kind of electronic search device known. He arranged to have the company's best computer guys work with Sanjy and Billy to find new equipment and making it operational post haste.

Drobick tasked Billie and Sanjy to get the war room up and running by first finding the records for staff at New Tech which didn't involve too much hacking. The faculty and staff lists at New Tech included the names Gerald Seperman, Bernard Phipps and Joan Fonda were listed as post doctoral graduate assistants. All were top notch people, according to the blurbs. Then came the kicker! In the donor section of the school's general information, Universal Macro Genetics, a company that they discovered after some digging, was owned by a cover corporation in which Fonda was the major share holder. UNG was also identified as having donated two million dollars to the school's genetics department about a year or so previously.

Drobick called Cabe immediately and gave him the news.

"That's a very ripe pile of manure," Cabe said. "I hate coincidences! What's Fonda's connection with the other names?"

"She's Seperman's top assistant," Drobick said. "What is nuts about this is that I also saw her New Tech picture, and guess what?" The UMG's corporate picture of Joan Fonda and the New Tech picture nearly an exactly match; you can see a tiny difference, although they're very similar. This gives me pause about just how long this has been going on. They must have been using a kind of corporate doppelganger to keep Joan free to roam, so to speak. But she's using the same name. Sounds screwy to me."

"This is worst case," Cabe told Drobick. "It's just too strange to consider anything but a connection to Nathan. It suggests that there was involvement long before we were even aware of Nathan. Fonda doesn't do things without extensive planning, maybe years of it. If she's in, she's all in. She's also international and if she's involved it's likely she will move Nathan out of country, meaning we may never see him again.

"What I'm not understanding is why she is playing second fiddle to Seperman. He may be the top geneticist at New Tech and as good as she is, but, she spends more on her lipstick than he makes in a year. What is their connection? I'm wondering if they don't really know who she is. It just seems screwed up with Fonda as the assistant? That's just not going to happen, at least not for long. She'll take over, you can make bank on it.

"Mike, this is critical," Cabe said, "because she has the resources and the amoral character to do just about anything, I suggest you keep your guys on the phone calls, especially hers. Have them find those correlations. Oh, and see what facilities Universal Macro Genetics has in the Los Angeles region. Since she does business all over the world, I'd be surprised if she doesn't have something nearby and you know, I don't have to stress the urgent time constraints we're under. I'd guess that she won't hold him here for more than a few days at most, maybe just hours!"

"I think we might discover what's happening when we find out who's calling who boss!" Cabe said.

Back in his office, Drobick called Billy and told him to focus on Phipps, Seperman and Fonda, and particularly on the phone calls between the three. Cutting into the phone call connections were more complex and time consuming than most hacking processes. There wasn't anything for the rest of the day on the calls, although Billy called Drobick to tell him that there were some serious firewalls erected, particularly around Fonda.

"We'll be on it all night," Billy said.

"Call me the second you find anything. Any hour!" Drobick said "OK?"

"Got it," Billy said.

76

Fonda Takes Over

Seperman and Nathan walked around the dock looking at the ship and watching the delivery truck loading food and other necessities into the ship, The Universal Star, under Panamanian registry. The salt air made Nathan feel much better but it did not quell his growing feeling of helplessness. The two days of captivity so far had made Nathan hypersensitive. However, ironically, he felt his capacity to use his power had increased, although he didn't know why; worse, he didn't see a way to use it in this situation.

If Nathan had maintained any memory at all about his captivity or escaping his first captors, he would have understood that his ability to appropriate emotions had grown because of the stress of his experiences. It was something he had anticipated from his self tests and in his act of escape in which he had drawn upon all of his collected experiences to incapacitate Wolfe. Had it not been for the drugs, it would have been more evident to him. His ability to focus was increasing even in the midst of the chaos that surrounded him, perhaps because of the chaos.

They walked back into the building and Nathan again asked when he could go home. Seperman said the cook would be bringing them dinner shortly and he and Fonda would talk. Seperman tried to reassure him by saying that all was safe, they'd be heading home soon. It was something that had been coming to a firm realization in Seperman's mind. Nathan had to be returned safe and sound. It became obvious to Seperman as events coalesced, that Fonda had other, more sinister intentions. His own limitations were becoming obvious too. His thoughts of a Nobel were being overcome by his quickly growing personal connection to Nathan and his culpability in the abduction.

The ship's cook came in a short time later with dinner for Nathan, Seperman and Fonda. As they ate, Fonda quizzed Nathan about anything he might have remembered from his first abduction. "All I can tell you," Nathan said, "is I'm not sure about anything. I'd say that at least one of the guys might have was a black guy 'cause I saw a wrist flash, but the guys I saw all wore plastic gloves before the taser fired. That's about all."

By the time he'd nearly finished eating, Nathan was beginning to sense Fonda's malevolence coming at him. His recognition of Fonda's intentions triggered a violent response in him. Fonda, too, realized Nathan was reading her malice and she signaled to the cook who'd been standing nearby who pulled out the disrupter blanket hidden under his apron and threw it over Nathan's head pulling it down on the sides and holding him around his waist tightly.

Seperman was stunned by the sudden attack on Nathan and screamed, "What are you doing?"

Fonda yelled back, "Shut up you spineless idiot!"

Seperman went beet red! He grabbed her shirt with his left hand and with all the power he possessed in his fist, smashed her in the face, a payback for all the bullies he had faced in his school career. She went down with a broken tooth and nose but also kicked him in the thigh, knocking him off balance. As he fell he clipped his head on the corner of a table and rolled to his back with a thud. His head hit the concrete floor, stunning him. She was back up as fast as she fell and with his stomach exposed she dropped onto his solar plexus with both knees and all her weight, violently forcing all the air out of his lungs. Everything he'd eaten for dinner came up and out like "Old Faithful." He laid there gasping and helpless.

Bloodied but without any hesitation, she kneed him in the ribs breaking or cracking at least one. Fortunately for Seperman there was no punctured lung, but his gasping for air continued. The cook could only watch as he had been harshly warned to not let Nathan go under any circumstances. "Let the boy go," she warned, "and we'll become quivering masses of instant tapioca."

She grabbed Nathan from the cook and told him to get Seperman and throw him into the makeshift prison room while she carried Nathan there with him struggling and kicking. By the time the battle with Seperman was over, the cook had strapped bands around the boy's ankles and body. Once again the boy could do little but chafe against the restraints. The strength of the carbon fiber material was incredible and added to his imprisonment.

Nathan was thrown in first followed by the cook dragging Seperman into the room that was normally used for high-value cargo. It was, in effect, a huge safe with ventilation. Fonda yelled at Seperman to remove the rope, take the blanket and throw it to her. She pointed a gun the cook had given her straight at Seperman's face and warned Nathan, "You even blink and I'll put a bullet in Jerry's throat," which she said with venom Seperman could scarcely fathom.

Nathan complied, but was now fully engaged with applying any power he could use searching his mind for any hint of a way to extend his control, first beyond the blanket, and secondly into areas where he had never been. The blood was beginning to dry on Fonda's face as she grabbed the blanket and slammed the heavy door shut.

"That genetic slime broke my tooth and nose. I'm gonna genetically alter his brain," she said.

Seperman had not fully recovered from the slam to his midsection. Nathan tried to comfort him but Seperman said, "This is my fault Nathan, you should be kicking me too, but please understand, I was blinded by the power of your genetics. I saw a Nobel Prize, not the evil nature of Joan or the extent of her plans. It's become obvious to me that she's been planning this for a long time."

Nathan soothed the gasping geneticist, thanking him for trying to save him. "I'm sorry she did this to you."

The doctor, who'd been brought aboard the ship for Nathan's care, would now have to treat Fonda's injuries. Now his arrival had to be moved up too to treat Fonda's injuries, but she also knew in reality it might delay their departure if she needed any extensive care. Given the need for immediate departure, that was unlikely.

77

New Reports Hurt Farnsworths

News updates continued dominating every news cycle. Sighting tips poured in but none were confirmed. Late Wednesday evening the police received an anonymous call claiming that Nathan was being held in a vacant building in San Pedro. The caller didn't identify himself, and although it seemed a fool's errand, police followed up anyway.

San Marino Detective Paul Jackson took the call and immediately called the San Pedro Police Department and asked them to button up the building and area. He told San Pedro this may be the best lead we've gleaned from a host of useless calls. San Pedro detectives sealed off the building and as soon as he could get there, Jackson went in with the San Pedro swat team.

As expected, it appeared to be an unleased building. The broken front glass still lay on the sidewalk and inside floor of the front room, but that could have been done by the half dozen or so homeless vagrants and junkies who now inhabited the place. Police rounded the people up and moved them out while they searched. Evidence contamination was the biggest problem and interviews with the various inhabitants produced nothing because the transients were more interested in a financial reward than helping police. One woman said she'd picked up a stage make up container in the storage area but said it was empty.

There were only two possible clues the police could determine from the preliminary once over was a broken window and a makeup container. The squatters were questioned about how the front window had been broken out and the significance of the stage makeup container. But it was apparent the glass had been broken out from the inside but it would be hard to confirm absolutely because the nature of tempered glass is that it can explode in all directions. Plus, with the squatters using the window as their entrance, proving anything or even making links to someone would be difficult, if not impossible.

Everything was contaminated. Additionally, the squatters had seen to it that the building became an instant trash heap with rusty shopping carts filled with trash treasures, and junk distributed throughout the rooms that the new residents claimed as their territory. The homeless had created an almost instant dump.

The container of makeup was seen by police as a positive and a negative. The makeup was evidence, but evidence of what? If it had been used in the building, it would be possible that the previous renters were just making a movie and the call was merely another false lead along with the broken window that could have been a movie scene gone awry.

Police noticed that several machines appeared to have been taken out of the building which wasn't a surprise. They contacted the owner who explained the short-time lease which was paid in cash. The owner said the buildings in the area were mostly vacant and he had been desperate to get anything he could. Everything was done by phone and payment was sent by courier and there was no receipt and the envelope was tossed. It was a dead-end for police.

News of the building investigation leaked to the media. News crews flooded into San Pedro only to be quarantined to a block away from the building. Rumors were rampant. There was a body. Then there was no body. Then there was evidence of a movie being made and speculation that Nathan may have been executed in a snuff film. Reporters continued their outlandish parade of rumors among news people. Nothing was confirmed, but the fodder of ratings is that the more bizarre the speculation, the higher the viewer count.

Each report contained a smidgeon of truth for credibility! It was just enough to make it useable on the air, but not enough to satiate the appetite of the teeming masses.

Levi and Ally quit watching nearly all the updates. Most were rehashed speculation that only added emotional pain for the distraught couple. Detective Linda Shumway gave them the news about the building tip, but it was just too tenuous to confirm or deny anything.

Phipps could not have been more kind or generous. School officials were equally solicitous in helping the grieving parents. But there was only one way for them to get through the pain--by forcing themselves to breathe one interminable minute after another.

While Phipps had been more than helpful to the Farnsworths, he began to worry about what was going on with Seperman and Fonda. They'd called but had not reported in since Monday. Whatever they were doing, he hoped it was helping find Nathan. With his unease fomenting like an infection, he realized he trusted Seperman, but Fonda had been around for less than a year and he didn't have any long term history with her. Phipps hoped he was just being paranoid, but deep in his mind, the disquiet wouldn't go away.

The news media promised updates but scant substance was reported.

78

No Question Now

Drobick's hackers were able to locate some phone calls going in and out of New Tech's Genetics Department, but there didn't seem to be a problem with any of them, until the last call Seperman made to Phipps popped up. The call seemed to have an odd origin.

Sanjy called Drobick who asked Cabe to get on the line. "Go ahead, Sanjy," Drobick said.

Sanjy started by saying, "Nothing looked out of the ordinary until we noticed a call yesterday from Gerald Seperman to Bernard Phipps. What was strange was that it bounced off a phone tower at Long Beach Harbor. In fact after triangulating, it could only have come from a warehouse at the end of Pier F Avenue. I had my guys check the San Pedro Pilot and it's saying a cargo ship docked there two days ago," he said.

"Registry?" Cabe asked.

"Panamanian," Sanjy said.

"Owner?" Cabe asked anticipating the answer.

"Universal Macro Genetics, Inc." Sanjy read from the paper.

"Why am I not surprised," Cabe said. "That's a critical piece of info Sanjy, good sleuthing. Dick, take the chopper and a drone. Get as much intel as you can on that location and keep us informed. Tell your guys to get aboard ASAP. I can tell you, you're dealing with a ruthless individual and situation. We've got to protect Nathan but I know Fonda's people will be armed to the teeth. We'll have to be armed as well but I want taser options too.

"We'll have to assume they're either in the building or on the ship. Depending on what Dick finds, I'd prefer to go in tonight. Harbor and warehouse lights will probably make night goggles unnecessary!" Cabe said.

Cabe pushed Sanjy to drop the phone call search and get all the information he could on Seperman and Phipps. "Call Mike. Remember, details, details. They'll be the key. Call me back two hours ago!" Cabe said. "Now Go!"

79

Drone Chase

Palumbo was already on the way to start his surveillance on the area. He met the chopper on the top of the building, grabbed a drone and operator from Cabe's news department and took off. He briefed the drone operator, Tory Deveraux, saying they were observing a ship and a warehouse building on the F Avenue finger. He swore both Deveraux and pilot Matt Weller to secrecy, saying that a boy's life was at stake.

Weller said there was a perfect landing area on the point on the Nimitz pier finger. The drone could be operated from there.

"Do it," Palumbo said.

Within twenty-five minutes the chopper was settling onto an open area near a grove of trees just past several nearby warehouses. The trees helped cut prying eyes from their operations on the pier. Pier F was directly across a harbor, more than a mile from the ship and warehouse they wanted to watch. Weller immediately established a fixed GPS location to begin a surveillance flight to the tip of the pier F warehouse. Palumbo focused high powered binoculars on the building and cargo ship.

Palumbo warned Deveraux to keep the drone as obscure as possible but as close too.

"I'll keep it at five hundred feet to start. At that height with the noise of the harbor it'll be almost impossible to hear and have a very small visual presence. We can go in closer if necessary," Deveraux said.

Palumbo continued looking at the facility and saw nothing out of the ordinary. A delivery truck with a sign reading ShipFast Supply Services was parked beside the ship, while a crane was lifting full pallets into the hold.

A few minutes into his surveillance of the pier Nathan and Seperman came out of the warehouse for a walk. Palumbo saw the young boy and man watch the loading for a few minutes and return into the building. Nathan's gait and general body language told him everything he needed to know, Nathan wasn't happy. He speed dialed Drobick while keeping his binoculars on the ship and building.

"We got em in sight," Palumbo told Drobick.

It appeared to be just a resupply delivery that had maybe fifteen or twenty minutes to finish loading its cargo. A forklift took the last pallets off the truck and placed them on the dock. The ship's crane operator immediately began picking up and stowing the pallets below deck while the truck driver stood around until his bill of lading was signed.

Without ending his call to Drobick, Palumbo asked Jeeves to flag down the truck and get what he could out of the driver and any information, before it got off the finger. Jeeves took off. In the meantime, Drobick said Cabe wanted a night raid to rescue Nathan. Palumbo acknowledged and there were a few hours to dusk so they could prepare their equipment and plan.

"You got guys to help?" Palumbo asked.

"They're on their way--only five guys though; they'll be there any minute. Any estimate of when Fonda might take off?"

Palumbo said. "My guess is on the early morning tide which would be a logical time and not draw any undue attention estimating maybe five or six."

"Five or six!" Drobick said. "I'll tell Cabe."

Time dragged waiting for darkness to fall. Well before dark, Deveraux frantically called Palumbo. "Something's going on," he reported. I'm seeing some action and bubbles near the stern, too much for divers. I think the ship is beginning to warm up its engines and there's another strange thing! There's a fuel tanker truck with what appears to be aviation markings. It just unloaded its whole tank into the hold. What do they need plane fuel for?"

Palumbo had a suspicion about the aviation fuel, but at the moment was much more worried about the ship warming up its engines. He called Jeeves again, "Hey, you've had some Navy experience, what's with bubbles at the stern?"

Jeeves said, "Oh, crap," they're warming the engine. We may have no more than an hour or so to be in place. That's not an absolute but if we are going to save Nathan from being taken out of America, we bet rolling ."

"They also just loaded a tank of aviation fuel aboard. Aviation fuel?" Palumbo pondered what that could mean. "I didn't see a heliport on deck, and I don't see any deck opening for anything like a helicopter or anything that could come out of it. I can't understand why anyone would load plane fuel with nothing to use it in. It doesn't compute."

"It's definitely an anomaly. I just don't like putting plane fuel and size together. And, we've got a question I don't even want to think about." Jeeves pondered. "Rocket launcher, big gun, who knows. But that's not the problem now. That ship could be under way within an hour so we can't wait! How big would an opening have to be for a copter?" Jeeves asked with the aviation fuel question plaguing his thoughts.

"Something like 30 to 50 feet" Palumbo guessed.

"We can't worry about that now. Don't move, we're on our way," Palumbo yelled into the phone. He continued his commands. "Pack up, now! We're going."

"Hey Dick, how we gonna' get there? Jeeves took the van and all I've got is the helicopter?" Weller said.

"NO! NO! NO!" Palumbo screamed. "This is NOT going to happen. I will not let Nathan be taken! On second thought, don't pack, get me a set of ear phones and have Deveraux stay on the ground!

Keep the drone going no matter what. Record everything and stream a copy to Cabe's computer. Keep me posted on every change!"

80

Into the Air

Like a cavalry charge to save the day, a second black van with five heavily armed and highly trained mercenaries arrived at the drone site. Johnny Rex got out of the front seat and shook Palumbo's hand. Rhodes Strategies at your service he said. Palumbo, under totally self-imposed and monumental control said, "Sorry, no time for introductions Rex. It's a go now situation."On the way he filled the men in on what he knew. They got to Jeeves location on the pier in less than seventeen minutes, out of sight of the warehouse and ship.

They split into two groups when they got to Jeeves. Rex, who knew Jeeves and his experience and training, said, "Suggest Jeeves and I take the tasers and focus totally on getting Nathan. Since we don't know the layout of the ship, we've got to make some assumptions. Below-deck living quarters are most likely in the bow if not on the deck. I'd guess that they're holding Nathan in one of those areas. Since it's a person, I suspect that the holding tank is probably below deck and at this point, I'm assuming that the cargo is pretty much stowed by now. I'm one guy who can at least keep them ducking for cover and seal them off which will reduce negative encounters from there.

"At this point, I'm assuming that the officer will be planning in the Captain's quarters and not paying much attention outside the ship. We should be able to take them by surprise."

Palumbo warned Rex about tasing Nathan. "Don't do it under any circumstances. Just take my word for it." He also realized Fonda knew nothing about the reactions hitting Nathan with a taser could have. He wondered if she would learn the lesson he had learned and more important, if Nathan had learned ways to amplify and direct the power of a taser.

"OK! No problem." Rex said.

"Getting Fonda and Seperman unharmed is also a priority," Palumbo said, "but remember getting Nathan safe and secure is the reason for our mission." Palumbo pulled up pictures of Seperman, Fonda and Nathan on his phone and passed it around to the operative's cells.

Palumbo weighed another vexing question. How is Nathan going to react to yet another "rescue?" He might turn against anyone and everyone with the experiences he's been through. Palumbo explained to his crew that it was critical to get Nathan, but that there could be confusion. "Most likely he'll be covered in a metallic type blanket. Just assume that it's him and grab him and go! For you own safety don't remove the blanket for any reason!" It was an absolute command.

Roads ran on both sides of the finger and went directly to the warehouse next to the ship which was at the tip of the finger. Getting to this point had taken at least thirty minutes. Deveraux phoned Palumbo and simply said, "Saw two people moving into the ship's rear deck! Don't see anybody covered in a blanket yet. Engines are idling but the ship could get moving any time."

"They gonna' need a tug?" Palumbo asked.

Jeeves and Rex said "no" simultaneously. Rex added they've got lots of room to get from the dock, and ship traffic is light at the moment. A tug would just slow them down so I figure they can just cast off and run. Because they're at one of the closer docks to open water we're not going to have much time.

Weller called with another report. "Something's goofy," he said, narrating into the phone in real time as he saw it. "A woman is coming on board followed by another guy, can't see them too well. It looks like she might have bandages on her face. But she's headed to the ship and another guy is coming out of the warehouse and he's got a kid. Two other guys are preparing to cast off. No time left."

The preparations the crew would like to have made were down the tubes and Palumbo yelled. "Can't wait, GO!"

The two vans headed down the west side of the dock and got to the warehouse just as the cook was carrying the blanket-covered boy up the forward gangplank. Fonda's men heard the roar of the vans coming full-throttle toward the ship and grabbed their rifles and made it to the ship's deck.

Rex, hanging out the lead van's side door, shouldered his weapon aiming at the first threat he saw.

The final man from the warehouse carried last minute items in a couple of bags, but he also had an AR15 slung over his shoulder. He heard the vehicles coming and dropped his bags. Before they hit the ground he turned his rifle into a firing position. But, amazingly before he could fire, Rex put a round in the guy's upper thigh from a vehicle skidding to a stop. It sent the crewman to the ground onto his bags just feet from the gang plank. Somehow, Fonda's wounded henchman made it up the plank and behind the railing wall.

Jeeves dispatched one of the team to check the warehouse for anyone else, while the rest headed toward the ship taking cover wherever possible. After a quick scan inside the building, it was apparent that it was empty except for a banging coming from the locked storage quarters. There he found a heavy iron door and a pounding coming from inside. "Lay face down feet to the door," Seperman was ordered. "You move, I shoot, got it?"

"Yes!" Seperman yelled through the door, "but please hurry, they've already taken Nathan to the ship."

Seperman heard the door unlock and saw it swing open. He pled, "We can't let them take Nathan!"

"Chill," we're here to rescue Nathan," Seperman heard Rex's team member say.

Seperman came out very meekly but yelled, "We've got to get Nathan now because they're going to take him out on that ship. I'll help anyway I can." The two headed to the dock where the ship was tied up. By this time, shots rang out from the railing, but Palumbo's men held their fire.

81
Making it Personal

Cabe was frantic. He ordered his helicopter pilot to fly him directly to the pier. He came in very low and landed before Palumbo's crew was in place or even aware he was there. He ran to the end of the finger's east side road and to the warehouse just in time to see Nathan following a woman going into the ship's rear-deck room. Cabe and Nathan's eyes locked for an instant unleashing the same all consuming feelings that flooded his mind, as they had the first time. Nathan's penetrating eyes went rummaging through his emotional soul in that instant.

He couldn't believe that Nathan was to be cooperating with Fonda without any resistance at all. "Why," raged in Cabe's mind. Nathan could have taken Fonda and her crew right to the ground without much effort. Nathan had to know be was being kidnapped again and would remember everything since the roofie injections had stopped.

Nathan remembered the incident with Cabe, but only had enough time to grasp the foremost thought in Cabe's emotional essence: "Save Nathan!" He didn't remember the first kidnapping for which Cabe was responsible, the roofies had taken care of that, but this time Nathan's last thought of Cabe was that he wanted to rescue him.

Now, things had changed. When Nathan was forcibly taken from his men, Cabe's commitment to recover him became his all consuming obsession. It was now all-out war for a boy of unparalleled capabilities and ultimately it become a war with almost no limits except one: Nathan's safety!

Neither Palumbo nor his men had seen what Cabe had seen. They were focused on the young man whose head was covered. Before Palumbo and Rex and his men realized, Seperman rushed from the building and ran straight through the flying bullets onto the ship yelling Nathan, Nathan. Miraculously, he wasn't hit by a bullet but when he got inside the railing, he was hit with a flying fist. He was then, unceremoniously picked up and thrown overboard.

Rex screamed instructions at his crew as he led the charge onto the ship. Palumbo was only a step behind him running through the smell of cordite and rushing onto the deck. Fonda's people quit firing and disappeared below.

Palumbo yelled at one of his crew to help Seperman up the peer ladder. By that time, Rex had reached the door through which the blanket-covered Nathan had been taken and charged through it without hesitation fearing Nathan could be quickly hidden in the bowels of the ship. As the door swung open it hit the man holding the boy. Palumbo was through the door just in time to see both the man and boy hit the floor.

"Don't remove that blanket," Palumbo reminded from behind while Rex tasered the man on the ground to prevent him from coming after the now retreating rescuers.

Rex grabbed the child and ran for the gangplank. Jeeves and his crew saw what Rex had done and ran for the van. As they did, the ship pulled away from the dock full throttle like a Chris Craft Runabout on Tahoe Lake. It was, by all appearances, a cargo ship but the depth of its earth shaking vibrations and staggering power could be felt even through the dock deck.

Palumbo, Rex, and the still covered Nathan along with the crew, got back to the relative safely of the lead van. With help Seperman got up the ladder onto the dock while rubbing his bruised ribs. The stench of the harbor water clung to Seperman like a leech. He wasn't perceived as a threat so they let him go into the warehouse to try and find dry clothing.

Palumbo was euphoric! "Everybody OK? That was much quicker and easier than I expected." When everybody loaded into the two vans, the driver stomped on the gas and streaked up the dock's eastside road. Much to their shock, they nearly ran over Cabe who was standing in the middle of the road.

Palumbo let out a startled yell with a couple of questions, "Max" What are you doing here? How did you get here? You look like you just ate a box of cat litter. Don't worry, we have Nathan, and he's safe!"

Cabe's face dropped into a black plague mask of despair.

Palumbo was dumbfounded. "I thought you'd be ecstatic. What's going on?"

"The bad news is that's not Nathan. He's a decoy." he said. "The worse news is that they have Nathan and I don't know what's next."

"We've got 'em, right here," Palumbo said, pointing to the boy.

Cabe's voice dropped to a whisper, "That's not Nathan."

"We've got him!" Palumbo insisted. "We grabbed him right off the ship."

"First, look at the blanket." Cabe said. "It's not ours. Take it off and see."

Palumbo grabbed the blanket and jerked it off the boy's head. It was not Nathan and not the right blanket either. A small face with dark eyes stared back at Palumbo. His heart sunk. Now there two more problems, who was this boy and where was the special blanket? "I knew it was too easy. It was just too easy and I should have known. I should have looked, damn, I should have checked for "proof-of-life confirmation" no matter what."

The boy interjected himself into the conversation in an understandable but thick North Korean accent, "My name Kim Ye-Jun. Who you want? I live on the street. I was in old San Pedro and these guys promise money if I did what they say. They said it would be easy and all I had to do was put this blanket over my head. It sounded strange but it not sex thing, I could tell. I want to go back to street--I not here legally. I don't want to go back. Let me go and I find my way. America is easy."

Cabe paused, turned his head and looked directly into the eyes of the boy. "I'm glad you're safe. Will you let me help you?"

Ye-Jun looked at him with street-wise reticence. "Like what," he asked.

"If I help you get to be an American," Cabe said softly, "would that be good?"

"And what would I have to do?" Ye-Jun asked with infinite suspicion.

82

Implementing the Plan

Cabe turned to Jeeves and said, "She's still got the blanket, but that means the cop's won't get it. "My helicopter is just down the block. Take me there." Jeeves drove noticing Cabe's obvious pique and indeed, behind a stack of containers was his copter. "How far can the drone fly?" he wondered .

"About a couple hundred miles at 50 knots, kind of depends on speed and wind resistance," he was told.

"Can it go faster?" Cabe asked.

Devereaux response was "Yeah a little, but the range would be much shorter. Racing drones can hit more than 85 mph but this is our station drone, we don't usually need that speed."

"Get the drone in the air and chase that ship down and don't stop until your drone is out of fuel," Cabe said. Get every shot you can until it dies! Record everything! Get as close as you can! Text or call as often as you need to!"

Deveraux didn't hesitate. He inserted his fully-charged most powerful drone battery, and it was in the air moments later. Fonda's ship was almost two miles away getting up to nearly 20 knots by this time and the chase was on. Little did Cabe know just how long that chase would last.

Cabe turned back to Ye-Jun. "Let me get some things set up. Are you up for a helicopter ride?"

With the typical directness of a street-wise child, Ye-Jun said, "Yeah, but I'm hungry. You got food?"

Jeeves pulled out a packet of jerky and handed it to the boy.

Palumbo shook his head. "Is there ever a time you don't have the right thing, Jeeves?"

Jeeves smiled, "Of course not, what would ever make you think that?"

Cabe called Drobick, "Mike, I've got a project for you that's critically important to me. I have a young man here who needs our help." He explained that he would bring Ye-Jun with him back to the office and gave instructions to start procedures to get him on his way to citizenship. "Shelter, food, clothing and safety to start with and we need to start with a school and a sponsor."

Drobick knew Cabe's tone of voice and so knew not to ask too many questions. Cabe told him the boy was about twelve, just under five feet and very slender.

Jeeves took a side glance at Cabe and said. "I think I know a school that just might be the answer," He said. "You know any English writing or anything Ye-Jun?"

"I good student." Ye-Jun said. "But in North Korea. I learned English myself, can spell words too."

Jeeves said, "Well you had to be pretty darn smart to escape from North Korea. I'll bet you'll do well in school here."

Cabe ended the conversation abruptly. "I'll take Ye-Jun with me. Can you get everything cleaned up around here Dick?"

"Done," Palumbo said. "See you at the office."

83

Fonda Shows True Colors

The ship reached full speed quickly. Fonda was being treated by a medical technician who also attended to the crewman who'd taken a bullet to his thigh. Fonda's wound was painful, but with her capture of Nathan, the pain seemed dulled. Her mind was racing with her assumptions of unlimited options. She thought about the potential possibilities Nathan represented and the stunning reality that he was in her possession.

"Bring Nathan in!" she said." Nathan appeared in a short time. "Remember that video I showed you of your parents Nathan? They'll continue to be under surveillance 24-hours a day. Don't forget it."

He shook his head "yes." He was shaken to the core feeling hopeless and livid at the same time.

"We'll talk some more. But remember, you screw around and they're the ones who'll get punished, not you. I'll kidnap one and then the other. It'll be hell for them and you'll never see them again and they'll never know what happened to you," she hissed. "Anything less than full compliance and you'll be back under the blanket in a concrete cell."

Just before he left, Fonda revealed her true evil nature telling Nathan, "Let me explain how this works. If you think you can catch me off guard and disable me so your parents won't be killed, I must notify my people by a specific method not to kill them. If it's not the right kind of call or right message Levi and Ally will be dead in a matter of days. Just keep that in mind."

Nathan staggered and was half dragged to his cell by the two guards controlling his every move. He collapsed on his bed and needed and wanted quiet and thinking time. But, as sometimes happens to people under unrelenting stress, his mind shifted into hyper drive. He could not stomach the standing threat against his parents and he chaffed at the need to vigilantly wait, but his resolve hardened while his mind plotted. He was young, but his vengeance would be apocalyptic. He would remember every threat to his Mom and Dad but this time the fear and emotional state would be his own.

He hated the very thought of Fonda using his parents as targets to control him. His mind raced back and forth questioning his gifts, glad he had them, but knowing that they were the cause of what was happening. Fonda, he concluded, was a black widow. He said out loud. "I don't like black widows."

Nathan's compulsion to keep a list of revenge targets rose to a new level. In this case, the payback was laser focused on Fonda. Nathan thought, "She will pay." Then another thought came into his mind. "Maybe, if I can switch emotions into someone else's mind, and twist those emotions for my benefit, there would come a day in which he would test her in ways she wouldn't be able to comprehend." There were now three uncompromising reasons to live and expand his power to save his Mom and Dad and get Fonda.

As quickly as his mind became a hornet's nest of thought it shut down and forced him into a deep sleep, with his promise to himself burning into his memory. What was to come out of that promise would have to develop in an unknown future, but knowing that it would eventually happen was a certainty to Nathan. The honing of his powers was only beginning.

Fonda went to the ship's bridge even with her painful injuries. She didn't slow down at all since they would be fixed and heal shortly, she reasoned, but for now she just had to escape. This was a part of her plan for which she had prepared for a long time and had looked forward to since she first theorized the genetic birth of a child like Nathan. Everything she'd planned had happened except the glitch in Nathan's kidnapping. But now she had Nathan, and her anticipated genetics research would be taken into a genetics realm never before even contemplated.

"Prep the bang," she yelled into the com. "Notify me immediately when ready."

"Aye! Aye!" came the reply. The crew had been drilling for this event for months. It took them about forty minutes out of port before they signaled readiness. The original plan had been a more deliberate exit, but their race out to sea was forced 'on a moment's notice because of the attack of Nathan's kidnappers. Since the system had never been tested, they were more than anxious to see everything actually happen.

A second reply came back from the chief engineer: "Professor Aronnax says Ned is ready."

The third and final reply came confirming: "Mosquito ready."

"Reverse engine, come to a full stop," the captain ordered. When it came to a dead stop, Fonda ordered the bang in thirty seconds. By this time they were about thirty miles out to sea and had been doing about thirty-five knots. For a ship of that configuration and size, the wake was huge and the massive pounding engine filled their ears and its smell filled the air.

84

Report from Deveraux

Deveraux was ecstatic when his drone caught up with Fonda's *Eiger Express*. "A pretentious name," the drone operator thought, "for a cargo ship." But following it with a drone had been easy. As it moved west the daylight stayed a little longer and the wake was like a huge series of beacon lights guiding the way. It reached the ship at about eighteen miles out. By twenty miles he'd connected his video feed to Cabe. What came next had the drone pilot yelling "Holy crap! I can't believe what I'm seeing."

It took a few minutes to notify Cabe his feed was running, but what he'd witnessed in the process would be just the first of three events that would signal what seemed to be impossible news in Cabe's effort to save Nathan.

"I've caught up with them," Deveraux reported. "It appears that they're headed toward the Cortes Bank. I don't know if they know I'm here, they might have equipment signaling they're being followed but it may not matter." In the middle of his report Deveraux he interrupted himself. "Those idiots are crossing the separation zone"

"Separation zone?" Cabe questioned.

"The zone is the area between shipping lanes for ships going in and out of port. Ships going out stay to the right. It's the same for ships coming in; they stay to the helmsman's right, just like driving on a street and keeping space between inbound and outbound.

"I would suspect with the dodgy way they left port that the Coast Guard might be getting calls from other ships because it wasn't standard departure protocols. I figure I've got a max of about a hundred miles on the drone fuel—hey it's coming to a stop. "Holy Crap," the drone pilot thundered into Cabe's ear.

"What did you say?" Cabe said."

"You will not believe what I'm seeing. Take a gander at your monitor, sir." There was an explosion aboard ship and it went all around the deck. The rusty old hull was blown off the sides and the pieces are now sinking. What's left is a huge silverish, I don't know… some kind of ship."

Cabe broke in. The video is coming in. "What's that on the sides?"

"Wait," Deveraux continued, "this is crazy. There are two pontoons or outriggers beginning to extend out from the primary hull. Pontoons!" he mused. "They're swinging out from the center. A suspended center hull is emerging. That thing will go fast."

"Can you stay in the air and keep up? This is not good. "Cabe said.

"Not sure at this point. At the rate of fuel use for top speed with the wind out there, I've probably got forty to fifty miles left, max," he said. "If that thing can hit fifty knots or more, it's going to be questionable. Either way we'll lose the drone."

Cabe directed Deveraux to keep going and let him know if anything changed. He watched the monitor as the huge catamaran began to pick up speed. Within a short distance it reached forty knots. He had no question that it would easily hit fifty-plus knots on smoother seas. He counted his luck when it slowed by three knots so he could follow a little further back.

Cabe left the video on and asked Drobick if Palumbo and Jeeves had returned?

"They're still about thirty minutes from the office," Drobick said.

"That was amazing display Mike," Cabe said. "It proves, without question that Fonda has been planning this for a long time. I wonder how Nathan and the crew on that ship felt when the explosions went off. We saw what went off, how would it feel to be in the middle of the explosion."

85

Going Nemo

Fonda's ship's captain received a security alert of a potential drone in their area. The captain told Fonda of a possible drone following them. "Can't provide details or who might be piloting it because it's too small to get much of a reading or shoot it down. "Doesn't really matter," he said. "The Coast Guard has probably gotten a couple dozen messages about our rather unorthodox departure by now and is likely on the way to cite us.

"We didn't exactly follow protocol as we left," he said. "The Coast Guard cutter is a pretty far piece back but they'll put a copter in the air in a few minutes when they discover they can't keep up with us. We're about sixty-six miles off shore and thirty-five to Cortes Bank. They should be reaching this location about the time we go Nemo but all they will see is bubbles."

The same explosion that Cabe watched his monitor wasn't just a visual experience for the ship's crew, it was physical. The Eiger Captain warned everybody on board, batten down the hatches, she's gonna blow. Fonda, the crew and Nathan took refuge.

The whole ship shook following the countdown which screeched live on the com, "5, 4, 3, 2, 1." The Captain, his crewmates and Fonda and Nathan felt the vibration to their bones. After the first major blast, there was an immediate series of smaller controlled explosions around the entire cargo ship's railing. It all felt like one detonation. Within seconds the entire old outer hull was on its way to the ocean floor

Although the new hull had a darkish chromish surface, it was actually a carbon metal composite. The next surprise was even more startling because the hull and outriggers of ship's surface reflected the water from all sides. It's surface acted like a giant mirror, making it much harder to distinguish with the naked eye, It blended almost perfectly. The hull surface intermingle the blue water and white caps of the sea, while the top of the ship reflected the blue sky and white clouds.

The composite, while amazing itself, was no more impressive than the exterior design. Stealth showed from every angle. Both the human visual version and the radar systems had difficulties seeing the sleek torpedo of a ship.

As the opposing pontoons swung out, the center hull was raised out of the water. When the outriggers were fully extended, the captain ordered quarter speed ahead but soon was at full speed.

With the ship riding on the pontoons above the water, drag was significantly reduced. Within minutes the vessel was cutting through the water somewhere under fifty knots and even though the Coast Guard was catching up while the ship sat idle, when the silver catamaran took off, it wasn't long before the Coast Guard cutter was falling well behind.

The Coast Guard Captain Gage Apgar delayed deploying his helicopter when he saw that the ship had come to a halt, a decision he'd come to regret. When it was apparent that the ship was moving again, it was so fast he had a hard time believing the speed of what he'd assumed was a rusty cargo ship.

Captain Apgar had seen the explosion on radar from quite a distance. Soon thereafter his radar images became unreliable, popping in and out and finally disappearing altogether. He had expected the ship to stay dead in the water and thought he'd reach it soon but he now had no clue what he might find.

Fonda ordered her crew to secure Nathan on the Mosquito and prepare to launch it into the air. "We'll go as soon as we reach the designated point east of Cortes Bank." she said. The Captain cut in and announced that the Cortez arrival time was expected to be about seventeen minutes.

"The Coast Guard has launched a helicopter," The Eiger's captain said to Fonda. "Should be to our current location in about twenty."

"We'll be long gone by then," Fonda said.

86

Beneath the Waves

"Checking in," the pilot said.

Cabe turned back to his computer to see the progress of the ship. He'd been distracted with other issues and anticipating Palumbo's arrival. He hadn't checked the monitor for a while. "That thing is hauling tukus," he said in awe.

"I'm estimating about fifteen minutes or less to Cortes Bank at the speed they're going. From there they could go in any direction without impediment," Deveraux reported. "I heard on my radio that the Coast Guard has launched their helicopter, but it's the only thing now that could catch them. It'll take the Guard at least twenty minutes to get there. Even if they do, the Coast Guard copter wouldn't be able do much but report and threaten. They'll be in International waters very soon, and at this rate they'll be beyond the Coast Guard's jurisdiction.

"I can't' figure out what Fonda thinks she can do. She can't outrun planes if the helicopter can't do anything and I suspect planes have already been scrambled. They simply can't get away so it just doesn't make sense! Even if they reach International Waters, their course can be tracked," Cabe said. "Let me know if anything changes."

Deveraux's drone could barely keep up, and he knew it was close to running out of power. The gleaming vessel was less than a minute from the banks and he had no idea what would happen then, and figured he had five minutes of battery left.

Palumbo got back to the office just as Cabe ended his report.

"Mr. Cabe," Vickie said. "Mr. Palumbo is back. He's parking now and will be up in a couple."

"Thanks, Vickie," Cabe answered. "We'll be using the dome, could you please check and see if it's stocked?"

"Sure," she said, dispatching one of her assistants to do the job.

Within minutes Palumbo came into Cabe's office. They hadn't said more than hello when Deveraux buzzed Cabe again.

"Check the monitor, boss." Cabe turned the monitor so he, Palumbo, Jeeves and Drobick could watch but quickly switched to the big screen.

The vessel was coming to a stop again. "This is just insane, there's hardly any deck on that thing." Cabe said as though he was trying to understand the ship for himself. It looks like, like what?--more of a submarine almost. I've never heard of a submarine with pontoons though."

All four men watch transfixed on the large screen. Right before their eyes, they could see what appeared to be a crack about fifty feet long in the center of the surface of the deck open up and immediately a pair of doors folded back from the top side center line.

Jeeves was first to grasp the meaning of the crack. "Geeze, that's amazing. Those are like upside down Mercedes gull wing doors. They're following the contour of the hull of a submarine. They're folding back from each side. That's got to be a twenty-foot hole dropping into the hold and a space big enough for a--what? There's a plane elevating out of that hold."

Drobick spotted what Jeeves saw. "You're right, it's a stinking plane!"

The men stood watching through the drone camera directly northwest of the ship. The shadows fell just right and they could see nearly every detail. Within three minutes the plane was at the top of the deck. It was obvious that the aircraft was a close replica of an F-22 Raptor naval version with vertical takeoff and stealth. It was also an obvious knock-off of an American military aircraft, probably Chinese.

The plane's wings had been folded up to accommodate its storage in the ship. As two crew members folded the wings out and locked them into place, the rising platform locked itself into place too. The powerful engines on the sleek aircraft started to warm up to prepare for its assent on lift off. By the time it was in place on the launching pad, the engines were warmed up and the wings were locked and ready to go.

Deveraux took the drone to within three-hundred feet of the deck because he realized the importance of getting a close shot of what was happening. In not more than a few seconds, they watched as a woman came running out of the wheel house and under the belly of the plane. She climbed in through the bomb bay door. Minutes later the plane fired up and rose slowly and smoothly off the deck. When it reached the suitable altitude and there was enough power, the huge engines pivoted, sending the plane into a rocket-like trajectory into the atmosphere.

Seconds later, the plane was out of site of the drone. The pilot asked Cabe what he should do. "I've got a couple of minutes left."

"Keep on the ship as long as possible" Cabe said.

Deveraux said, "The drone could be going down anytime. I suspect the Coast Guard Copter isn't far off but I can't see it yet" and he noticed that other things on the ship began to change.

Cabe turned to his men and said, "We've got to go to the dome and make some decis...."

The drone pilot cut in on his phone link without hesitation and spoke again is disbelief. "What is going on now?" He said, forgetting there were others watching. "Take a look at the pontoons. They're being sucked back tightly under the ship. They seem to be fitting into cut outs right into the hull. It looks like water is being pumped into the pontoons like ballast tanks. All eyes were again glued to the wall mounted TV.

The monitor showed a huge mist that was beginning to come out of the top and sides of the ship. Soon the entire ship was covered. The drone camera could see nothing but the misty fog and the surrounding water. A series of waves began spreading out from under the mist like a giant washing machine. The ripples suggested that the ship was sinking.

"I've got just seconds left in the air," the pilot said.

Almost as abruptly as the mist appeared, it began to dissipate. The drone started losing its fixed stability. The final shot was of an empty sea where the ship and mist had been. Only a shrinking wake and bubbles from under the surface were left. For a few seconds after the last drone shot, the wake bubbles came popping up in a southerly direction.

The screen went blank..."she's gone," Deveraux said.

The silence in the room was palpable. What could they say?

Cabe broke the quiet. "That was stunning. There's just one explanation. This was a plan that has been in operation for a long time. Excellent job Tory! Come on back and please write up a report with your impressions since you watched the whole thing. I'm more interested in your questions of what was happening so please get it to me ASAP. Don't leave anything out."

Again the silence in the room dominated.

After they sipped their beers for a moment Cabe spoke.

"If anybody says 'this is another fine mess you've gotten us into,' I'll fire him for five minutes, without pay!"

A couple of snickers and the response that everyone knew was coming, "Is that a promise?" Jeeves said. The tension relieved slightly.

The four men were bound by the intensity of their shared experience that was now a full commitment against two enemies: Fonda and time. They'd done an utterly stupid thing in kidnapping Nathan in the first place and blamed themselves fully for Nathan's second kidnapping. Redemption was all that mattered now.

The next period of silence was broken by a phone call from Sanjy. "Mr. Cabe, something big is happening at the San Marino Police Department and the FBI. As far as I can tell, Seperman made a call from somewhere in San Pedro or Long Beach and they've been putting two and two together and have concluded that Seperman and Fonda were involved. At the moment it appears they're the target.

Phipps seems to also be pushing the authorities in that direction since he'd become suspicious of Fonda and the 'convenient' big grant to the department. Then there was what she and Seperman seemed to know even before the tests with Nathan. The kidnapping was just another straw that made it obvious as to who was responsible. It also sounds like they're discounting the importance of the old town San Pedro building, assuming they were already planning to move Nathan to the Pier warehouse. The FBI and San Marino now believe Seperman and Fonda held Nathan temporarily in the building, but moved him so it's not a primary issue. The pier is the big thing according to what I'm hearing.

"They appear to be mounting a search on an area around a pier and building. 'It's Pier F' or something like that. I'll get back if I find out more specifics."

"Thanks, Sanjy," Cabe said. "I totally forgot about Seperman. What happened to him?"

Palumbo lowered his head and mumbled. "We policed our brass, loaded up and left when Seperman went into the room to get some clothes to change into after being thrown into the drink. I suspect they'll find him shortly. He's going to stink like a garbage scow covered by that old port water. And I don't think he'll find too much to change into."

"Geez, Dick." Drobick said. "Did you think about this? There's a connection there to us."

"As a matter of fact, I haven't been thinking of much else, with the exception of Nathan." Palumbo said. "But let me suggest some things that in the long run may be beneficial. When he's questioned in detail, he's going to have to lawyer up immediately. If he admits he kidnapped Nathan from us he's admitting to the crime.

"I don't think the cops are going to believe a wild tale of kidnapping from kidnappers, in either case. Anything he says is suspect, so he's got to keep his mouth shut about that. He's one smart dude and I'm pretty sure that he will implicate Fonda and throw her overboard in every way possible. With his story of being thrown overboard himself, he's going to be a more sympathetic witness. He might even get a medal 'cause he can expose Fonda as the mastermind she is and claim he was duped along with New Tech. His lawyer will negotiate a deal with the FBI, and he'll be smelling like a rose not stinky harbor water.

They'll take anything in return for his information and his lawyer won't let him say anything without full immunity. Even with immunity, I expect he'll keep everything he can quiet, especially about us. There'll be nobody to refute what he says. No use for him to get in any deeper than he already is at this point. I'm thinking he'll consider us on his side now."

"I calculate that Seperman thought this was his Nobel Prize gig from the beginning, and Fonda came on board at a critical juncture. He thought he was using her and he'll tell them he was manipulated by her and her offer of funding the project that might get him a Nobel Prize.

"I figure this could be beneficial because he's just as enraged at Fonda as we are. He didn't know squat about the ship and the rest of it, but he can provide enough to police to send them after her. He could easily be more than ready to cooperate not just for the sake of his own hide. Besides, he can argue that he was called to the site by Fonda and may even get some sympathy. I would guess that we won't have any problems from his story to the cops."

Drobick weighed in. "I can guarantee that the authorities are focused on Fonda. With her extremely loud escape, I think most of the police power is going to be directed at her because she's got the motivation and money to pull off what she did. It's also obvious that she'd been planning this for a long time, while Seperman was duped by a promise."

Cabe said. "Hang on for a sec." Cabe dialed Jackson. "Jamal, how's the war room going?"

"Up and running." Jamal said. "Sanjy and Billy are well under way and there is plenty of room for expansion. Anything else?"

"Remember that satellite mapping company we were looking to buy a while back?" Cabe asked.

Jackson said, "Yeah, I remember. The Sat Map Mining and Survey Company, they're the highest quality satellite image maker in the market, a mile better than Google!"

"Buy it. Don't let it get away. What was our top dollar?" Cabe asked.

"They were asking 3.2 billion." Jackson said. "I thought that was too high since Google already has a general satellite monopoly."

"Go to 3.5 if necessary. Don't lose it," Cabe's tone was nothing short of a command.

Jackson, realized the company had Cabe's offer go south the first time, he might offer under 3 billion. "Let me see what I can do and I'll get back," Jackson said. "I'll give em a last chance and see what happens.

The other men under the dome, had frequently heard that tone in Cabe's voice, but this time is was even more intense. All three of them were wondering how he could be thinking about purchasing a business at this point in time. Little did they realize that in Cabe's mind, he had no good leads and it would be one of the tools that just might eventually provide some possibilities in finding Nathan, or at the very least, track Fonda's moves. Cabe would spare no expense.

Life is the first and foremost right, the real concept for all of human liberty, especially for Nathan. Nathan's freedom was now Cabe's consuming inferno. He knew this was going to be a war of the billionaires but he had to justify his stupid plan and save Nathan in seeking his repentance.

SWITCHER END
VOLUME ONE